ANGEL DOWN

MICKY O'BRADY

Angel Down
Copyright © 2021 Micky O'Brady
Cover Design: www.KimG-Design.com
Interior Format: Dorothy Dreyer

Published by Snowy Wings Publishing
PO Box 1035, Turner, OR 97392

ISBN eBook: 978-1-952667-23-7
ISBN Paperback: 978-1-952667-24-4

Table of Contents

Prologue... 1

Chapter One - Fame-Shmame-Lame 11

Chapter Two - Angel Down 19

Chapter Three - Can You Hear Me Running.................... 38

Chapter Four - Busted 46

Chapter Five - Fragile Tendrils 55

Chapter Six - Opposite Day 70

Chapter Seven - Old Zoo 85

Chapter Eight - Practice Makes Perfect 100

Chapter Nine - Carousel 109

Chapter Ten - Forum 122

Chapter Eleven - Stigmatized............................... 140

Chapter Twelve - Concert................................... 159

Chapter Thirteen - Turbine 173

Chapter Fourteen - Aftermath............................... 189

Chapter Fifteen - Carousel, Reprise........................ 206

Chapter Sixteen - Hive..................................... 217

Chapter Seventeen - Overload............................... 231

Chapter Eighteen - Intercepted............................. 245

Chapter Nineteen - Boundaries, Lost 265

Chapter Twenty - Planning.................................. 273

Chapter Twenty-One - Lair, Repeat.................................. 290

Chapter Twenty-Two - Closer 307

Chapter Twenty-Three - New Developments.................. 317

Chapter Twenty-Four - Assembly 329

Chapter Twenty-Five - Dark Place, Bright Light............. 350

Chapter Twenty-Six - Balance of Power.......................... 359

Chapter Twenty-Seven - Till Death Do Us Part 371

Chapter Twenty-Eight - Landing Bay 379

PROLOGUE

The day that revoked all scientific theories of evolution and rewrote physics down to the smallest particle happened to be a Monday.

A quite ordinary Monday, to be precise—a Monday in late October, beautiful on all accounts, sunny and warm, a rare treat at that time of the year in Washington DC.

In front of the White House, a rather large crowd of tourists gathered. Next to them, a TV crew did their best to ready themselves for taping a report about the president's latest bill to pass the Senate, although they kept getting distracted by two children running back and forth between them and their parents. One could almost hear the news crew's sigh of relief when the two kids were called over by one of their mothers.

"Lea! Jeremy! Seriously, come over here, group picture!" A blonde woman in her thirties waved to catch their attention, and after the third try, it worked.

The boy, Jeremy, maybe six or seven, stopped the younger girl by her sleeve. "Coming!" He took Lea by the hand and together, they skipped over to their respective parents. She was a tad smaller than him, maybe a first grader, if that. From the ease they had with each other they could've been siblings, but one look at the adults waiting for their offspring to arrive changed that assumption: Besties, yes—brother and sister, no. The girl had her father's almond eyes and dark hair, and her mom's open smile and slender face. The boy on the other hand was a miniature version of his dad: sturdy build, tousled brown hair and a chin that gave him a stubborn look. Granted, his dad's face showed no smear of chocolate on the cheek, but other than that they came from the same mold.

"Hey, sweetie." The girl's mom gave Lea a quick hug. "Remember to be good once we're inside, okay?"

Lea frowned. "Mo-om. I'm always good."

"I know, honey. But I also know who's a bit more *active*. Right, Jeremy?" She gave the boy a loving light smack on the head.

He rubbed the spot, protesting. "Aunt Sarah! When you call me Jeremy, it sounds so serious."

Sarah laughed. "That's because I am, *Jezza*. I'd like you two to not take the White House apart, so try to keep it down once we get inside."

Jezza folded his hands in front of his chest and gave his best impression of an innocent look. "No worries. I'm an angel."

Sarah rolled her eyes but couldn't hide her smile. "Right. Angel of Destruction. But joking aside, you're in second grade already. Can I trust you to watch over Lea? You know, you being older than her?" She winked at him, and Jezza stood straighter.

"Of course. I always do."

"I know you do. Thanks, bud." Sarah tousled his hair once more. "But now, selfie time. First visit to the White House at age six."

"Seven." Jezza held up seven fingers.

Lea stuck out her tongue at him with a frown.

Sarah gathered both kids at her sides, one on her left, one on her right. Then, she waved to her husband Hisashi and Jezza's parents, Sienna and Matthew. "Guys! We have like two minutes left, let's make it count."

Everybody gathered around the three of them. Matt took the phone from Sarah and lined himself up with the group. "I'll shoot the pic. Longer arms. Say cheese!" He clicked the button about twenty times. "There. That should be—"

A shadow fell over the area—and not the kind a cloud would cause, no... a shadow as dark as the night, as if somebody had switched off the sun. Sounds of surprise burst out of people's throats as they looked up to the sky.

The sounds of surprise turned into screams.

"Oh, my God!"

"What is that?"

"We're going to die!"

"Shit! Somebody notify the police! The president! *Shit!*"

Cars honked, tires squealed, sirens went off somewhere as darkness spread, and with it came panic. The shouts grew louder, more urgent as everybody's gaze clung to the gigantic grey structure hovering in the sky above the White House. No, above *the whole city.* Nothing but a grey wall going on forever with integrated lights shining or blinking here and there and strange, foreign markings covering most of the surface.

"Is that... military?" Sienna held on to Matt with one hand, the other gripping Jezza so tight, his fingers turned blue.

"No way. That's... a spaceship," Sash murmured.

Sarah reached for his hand, never taking her eyes off the structure high above them.

"Mom?" Lea wrapped her arms around her mother's hips, as high as she could reach. "What's that thing? I'm scared."

Sienna drew Jezza closer to her body. "Guys. Do we run?" She nodded to the people all around them, some of them standing frozen, staring, some of them running, screaming, panicking.

"Where to? This thing is never-ending." Matt shook his head. "Whatever it is. I mean—"

An opening appeared. Several blinding white lights turned on, illuminating the retreating hatch and the ground beneath it right in front of the White House and less than ten meters away from Lea and her parents. Everybody on the surface sucked in a collective harsh breath.

"Whoa."

"Is that—"

"Are there—"

"Wait, somebody is coming out—"

Sarah's fingers dug deeper into Lea's shoulder as her eyes grew wider. "Oh my God, unbelievable. Guys, see that? It's—"

All around people froze.

"Is that—"

"No, it can't be."

"Lord, have mercy."

"Angels! Are they angels—?"

They were. Down from at least a hundred meters above the surface floated five winged creatures. The closer they came, the clearer it became they indeed looked like angels. Wide, feathered wings sprouted from their backs, their controlled beats keeping the beings upright on their descent to Earth.

"Holy mother of God." Sarah made the sign of the cross. "Angels."

"Mom? Mom?" Lea hugged her mom closer. "Who are they? What do they want? Why is it so dark?"

Sarah and Sash exchanged a glance.

"I don't know, sweetie," Sarah answered. "They look like angels, and… well, I'd say if they would have wanted to harm us, they could've already."

Lea yowled into her mother's hip.

"No worries, honey. Mommy and Daddy are here."

"Let's hope to God you're right. Pun intended." Sash held on tighter to his wife's hand. "This thing is too big to run from, too big to hide from. And judging by its size, it wouldn't have a problem taking everybody here out. The fact that we're still alive… Positive, all things considered. Right?" He squeezed her fingers twice, the apple in his throat bobbing up and down with a hard swallow.

The winged beings glided toward the surface. The closer they came, the more details became visible. Four were dressed in black outfits, some kind of uniform with thick belts, pockets, and markings. Their white wings stood in stark contrast to their outfits and gave them an eerie beauty.

Still, their radiance paled in comparison to the fifth angels' true magnificence. Dressed all in white and in the center of the group, the other beings focused their attention on him, the one with the all-black wings on his back. He seemed even larger than his companions, a good foot taller and more muscular than any of the human males down on the surface.

And all five of them looked strikingly beautiful.

"Unbelievable," Sarah whispered. Her eyes filled with tears. "And we're witnessing it."

The beings swept down and landed in front of the White House. Like a switch flipped, the chaos of the surrounding area turned into dead silence the moment they touched down. Everything stood still. Every person. Every car. Even the air had stopped moving. The only activity came from the news crew struggling to get it all in—including spaceship, aliens and the reactions of the people on the ground.

"Of course, the first aliens to land on Earth land at the White House. How cliché," Sienna mumbled under her breath.

"Not aliens. *Angels.* It's fascinating, isn't it?" Sarah took a couple of steps toward the group of angels, Lea clinging to her like a baby monkey.

White House security stormed through the gates, weapons at the ready. "Freeze! You're—"

The black-winged angel raised his hands. "We come in—"

Already on the edge by the events of the last minutes the security guard's reflexes took over.

He fired—

BangBangBang!

—but his shots never reached their target. With a slight pinging sound, they hit *something,* like an invisible barrier, about a foot in front of the aliens and clattered to the ground.

Scared cries broke from dozens of human throats, only to turn into surprised murmuring the moment people realized guns would lead them nowhere here.

One of the angels with white wings laid a hand on a small, rectangular device attached to the belt at his right hip. Without even glancing at it, he drew a pattern on its surface with his index finger. He looked at the black-winged alien. "Shields holding. Full strength, sir."

The black-winged angel turned around, taking in the scene in front of him. "Thank you." He stepped forward, closer to the area where Lea, her family and others gathered. "Children of the Lord, we mean you no harm. We come in peace." Although he didn't raise his voice by much, it seemed to roll over the entire town. The surface of the ship sprang to life and turned into a huge screen, every section bigger than a football field, and all showing the same feed: the five angels surrounded by humans, standing in front of the White House. However far this ship stretched, everybody near it would be able to see and hear the broadcast. Startled, the news crews took in the competition in the sky, but nonetheless continued to record their own material.

The angel carried on. "Too long has it been since the Holy Father has sent word to Earth, but now His patience is wearing thin. War has turned His beautiful creations to dust and dirt. Hate has poisoned your minds and taken hold inside your hearts. His soul is bleeding for you, His children."

He took another step forward, palms raised. Any closer and people could touch him. The alien retracted his wings tighter as more and more curious humans gathered in front of the group, many with their cellphones out and recording, many more with open mouths and wide eyes.

One of the angels clad in black raised his voice. "Step back. Give room to Luke, our leader!"

The black-winged alien lowered his head in thanks before he continued. "People of Earth, we come in peace. We come to help the Lord's children develop their full potential. We come to serve the Lord, and help humanity live by His rules. From today on, my brothers and I will watch over you, and you will find the right way to serve the Lord once more. His love for you is great, but fear His wrath shall you not live by the words he gave you."

Lea's mom wiped away a tear falling from her eyes. "I can't believe it. First contact."

Sash raised an eyebrow. "Sounds more like contact, reinstated.

The sequel," he whispered under his breath.

"It's still beautiful." Sarah inched forward toward the angels.

"Mom, no," Lea whined and let go of her mom's hip. She dug her heels in, the fear on her face real.

"Sarah," Sash hissed, but Sarah was focused on the angels in front of her.

"A new age for mankind. Truly amazing." She reached out a hand and brushed it over the tip of the angel's black wing.

"Sarah, no!" Sash's shout came too late. With lightning speed, the angel whirled around, eyes hard, his previously soft features distorted in anger.

"You," he growled, for all D.C. to hear. "You have dared to touch *me*, the Lord's creature?" He closed his hands into fists, and when he opened them, a blue light shined from them.

Gasps of surprise erupted from everybody. Some people staggered back, creating distance between themselves and the angry being with blue, glowing palms.

The Angel raised his voice. "So let this be known as the Eleventh Commandment. *Thou Shalt Not Touch Those Descended From The Heavens.* To touch us equals blasphemy, and it will be punished by death."

As the Angel raised his hands and aimed at Sarah, Sash jumped forward at his wife and daughter. "No!" he yelled, shoving Lea to the side and knocking Sarah out of the Angel's way in one fluid movement. Lea staggered, and only because of Jezza's quick reaction and catch did she not fall.

The Angel raised his voice. "Let it be known as the Twelfth Commandment. *Nobody is to keep another one from deserved punishment.*" He aimed both hands at Lea's parents, and—ZOOM!—the bright, blue light erupted from his palms, hitting

Lea's parents square in their chests.

For one hundredth of a second, Sarah and Sash looked exactly the same—frozen in time, a surprised expression on their faces—and then they were gone, without a trace left of them.

Lea's jaw dropped in shock, her gaze frantic, terrified. "Mom! Dad!" She screamed, she struggled against Jezza's hold, she kicked and thrashed. "Mom! Dad!" Tears streamed down her face as she bruised herself working against Jezza's strength.

"Lea, no! No! Hold still, please, I can't hold you like this, please! *Please*!" Jezza held her strong like a bench vise, the only thing keeping her from pummeling the angel and being incinerated like her parents.

But she wasn't alone with her screams. The entire crowd erupted in a flurry of shrieking and shoving. Two humans had just been incinerated in front of their very eyes by Angels. *Aliens*. Panic came easy. The news crew tried their best to keep their wits and record the situation, but two of the camera assistants had run already, leaving one operator alone with the news anchor.

The leader raised his voice. "Silence! As of this day, His creation will be under supervision by us. The Lord calls us His Founders. Together, you and us will serve His will. I do not foresee any punishment to be necessary again. Peace and prosperity will be brought to all of you."

Lea clung to Jezza, her knees shaking, her jaw quivering. "Mom! Dad!" Lea's cries came out as sobs, the desperation in them piercing the commotion around the White House.

The black-winged angel looked down at her, one brow raised. For a moment his features hardened, but then relaxed as he kneeled down in front of her. "Child, what is your name?"

Lea's breath came out heavy, irregular, harsh as she backed

harder into Jezza, trying to keep her distance.

"What is your name?" His black wings folded closer to his shoulder blades.

"Talk to him," Jezza hissed into her ear, never relaxing his hold on her. "Come on, talk to him!"

Lea's chest heaved up and down with frantic little breaths. "Lea." Her voice cracked with that single syllable.

The angel smiled, and when he did, he looked so beautiful it was hard to believe what had happened a mere minute ago. "Lea. What a heavenly name." He stood and looked down at her. "From now on you shall be known as the Protégée. The Founders will make sure your life will miss nothing."

The news camera zoomed away from the Angel for a wide-shot including the news anchor. Her face was ashen, hair a mess, the hand holding the microphone shaking. But she still did her job, because this was the story of her lifetime.

"… more about their motives is unknown, but what started as a peaceful encounter has turned into death of two American citizens. Right in front of our very eyes, a woman touched the… the lead angel, and was…" She swallowed hard, eyes drifting over to a bawling Lea held by Jezza. "She was killed on the spot, *without a warning*, and so was her husband." Another hard swallow. "Although these beings look like angels, they have killed mercilessly, and… and I cannot tell you how this is going play out, but I do know that whichever way this goes, this child here is the first victim of what is to come."

Her voice dropped down to a whisper as the camera moved to show Lea. "She's the First."

CHAPTER ONE

Fame-Shmame-Lame

" . . . **a**nd may the Lord and the Founders watch over us today. Amen." Sister Mariana circles the left side of her chest with her right index finger and places a palm across her heart. "Remember, your homework is due tomorrow. Three pages on your favorite way of serving the Founders. Single-spaced, one-inch margins. No cheating."

The class groans, but quietly. Groaning louder means disrespecting the Founders, and that in return means detention. I gather my books and pens. Guess there goes my afternoon—

"Lea?"

I whip my head up. "Yes, Sister?" I swear, I didn't do anything. Behaved all class. All week, as it is.

Jezza brushes past me, bumping his hip into my shoulder. "I'll wait outside," he murmurs under his breath. Because he knows from experience this might take a while. Dang it.

Sister Mariana straightens her black tunic. I'll never get it why nuns wear these things, service to the Founders or not. It must be uncomfortable, especially the scapular and cowl. She winks at me. "You're exempt from homework, *if* you're willing to present your article in class. What a great opportunity to talk about serving the Founders, especially when it comes from you. The class would truly appreciate it."

I doubt that. The class would probably rather sit through

Scripture interpretation for a whole day than hear more about—
or from—the famous Protégée, but as always, the Sisters don't get
it. And how could they? They devoted their lives to the Founders.
I had mine ruined by them.

On the other hand, screw the rest of the class. Three pages.
Single spaced. I force my face into the crude resemblance of a
smile. "I'd be honored, Sister. Shall I bring the article tomorrow
then?" Sorry, guys. Gotta do what'cha gotta do.

Sister Mariana claps her hands like an excited toddler.
"Wonderful. Yes, please. Sister Mary has given you enough money
for two copies, I presume? Bring one for the orphanage to keep,
and the other one we'll frame and hang it up in the classroom."

Frame. Really. I cringe. "Of course, Sister. Then if you don't
mind, I'd rather get going to make sure they're not sold out..."
Fat chance, but she buys it.

"Hurry up, my dear. That indeed would be a pity." She waves
dismissively, and off I go. *That would be a pity.* Yeah, mainly
because I haven't even started the three pages yet, and I don't
intend to. Maybe she knew chances of getting that homework
from me were slim anyway and that's why she threw me that
bone… or not.

Whatever.

The moment the warm Los Angeles air hits me in the face
when I step out if school is pure heaven. Ah, freedom. I suck in a
big breath. And another one.

"That was fast. Dodged that bullet for a change?" Jezza rolls
his dark brown eyes and slides off the little brick wall next to the
school's entrance. He knows how it is with me and the Sisters—
of course *he* is done with his homework already, knowing him. If
I were half as good as Jezza, I'd have no problems in school or in

the orphanage. In fact, it's only because of him I haven't gotten into more trouble. He's good at walking the line between obedience and freedom. I, on the other hand, tend to overshoot in one or the other direction.

Jezza takes me by the sleeve and turns me away from the entrance where Sister Eva is locking up the school behind us. It doesn't take long for a hundred and fifty students to leave the building once the bell rings. "No detention, right? You didn't do anything?" He gives me a worried glance and I shake my head.

"Nope and nope. Surprisingly, on both accounts. She offered me an exchange. No homework, but I present my *super-famous* article tomorrow."

"Have you bought the magazines already?" He leads me toward the school yard's exit.

I give him a nasty glance. "You know me better than that. Of course not."

He grins. "Hoping they're sold out?"

"How'd you know?" If only I was so lucky. "I really don't want to present my *super-famous* article tomorrow." Who cares if the class doesn't want to hear it? I don't want to hear me droning on about life as the Protégée either.

Jezza's smile turns into a frown. "Uhh, does Sister Mariana know you didn't…" He lowers his voice. "That you didn't quite elaborate on *that* topic during the interview?"

I chuckle. "Nicely phrased, and no, she doesn't, or she wouldn't have made the offer." I'm positively sure many of the Sisters are going to be disappointed. *Founders' Servant* interviews the Protégée, and she can't even come up with anything good.

And it's true. I can't.

Jezza sighs but keeps it down. "You know, at one point, you'll have to make up your mind. It's either or." He throws a quick glance over my shoulder at Sister Eva walking toward the staff parking lot. "Decide in which direction you want to go." He gives the side of my left breast a quick and subtle brush. Nobody would pick up on it even if they were watching us, but—

"Are you freakin' crazy?" I hiss at him. "Want to make it even more obvious?" With a quick turn, I bring some distance between us and cross my arms in front of my chest. Seriously. There's a reason I never change in front of the girls in the orphanage, and it's not because I'm a prude. Plus, if the Sisters saw Jezza's small caress, we'd both be in detention. Community work. Hugging, holding hands—heck, any kind of touching—is bad enough, which is why we're so careful. As it is, we're walking a fine line, one that my questionable fame bought us. After all, I'm the Protégée, the Founder's little pet project, and Jezza is the boy who was right there, next to me, eyes as wide as mine, but arms strong as steel for a seven-year-old as he was holding me back.

Jezza rolls his eyes. "Just sayin', Lea. Another six months and we're done with school, and then you can't hide behind that anymore. Then you'll have to choose, and I just want to make sure you're choosing something that'll work for you. Hint-hint." He points to my left side, and I tighten my arms in front of my chest. Should've never let him see the tiny tattoo I dared to get when I turned fourteen, but when for a short delusional while Jezza and I became more than friends… couldn't really hide it. He loves the little x with that inconspicuous dot on top of it etched into my skin where nobody should see it—where nobody will hold me accountable for it.

Without me noticing, my fingers caress the spot on the side of my boob underneath my left arm. I sigh. "You're right, but can I take it one step at a time, please? For now, I've gotta buy two magazines to keep the Sisters happy, and then… well, I still have six months." I hold my chin up high and Jezza shakes his head in mock despair.

"Okay, but then don't complain if they recruit you into soldier duty. Or…" He pauses for effect. "Servant duty." All that's missing is a warning finger held up.

"I know!" I hiss at him. "I'll figure it, out, okay? Servitude ain't gonna happen, even if I end up scrubbing toilets." Anything is better than serving *them.* The sheer thought of trailing behind a Founder, head lowered in submission, catering to their every need, brings the acid in my stomach to a roil. No matter what I end up doing, it won't be that. I wouldn't even make it through training, because, secluded with my Founder for days on end, until I was deemed sufficiently prepped? I'd probably either end up killing myself or the Founder, which would equal killing myself. So yeah, no Servitude for me. Plus, a big, fat, one-third of each year is recruited to serving the Founders in one way or another anyway. They don't need me.

I hope.

Deep down, I know the chances of them not recruiting the famous Protégée for some kind of publicity stunt is slim, but I might jump off a bridge before I ever open a door for a Founder, there's always that.

Jezza is unimpressed by my little fit. "You know, sometimes I don't get you. You can choose your destiny, Lea. You can choose what impact you can have, and maybe you should do that before destiny chooses you."

Whoa. "Really, Jezza? A speech about destiny? As it happens to be, destiny and me are old acquaintances, if you don't remember. And because of that, I'll be fine not meddling with her for the next century!" Been there, done that. Thank you very much.

Jezza ignores me. "I'd say you'd fit right in. L.A.'s mayor pledged to be a New Servant last month. The Secretary of State. CEO of the *L.A. Times*. All New Servants. It's the in-thing to do, apparently." He wraps his right thumb and index finger around his other wrist, like the bracelet that seals the deal when pledging Servitude.

I place a hand across my heart in mock reverence and use the same sarcastic tone he did. "I'd so love that company, really. We could all drink cocktails together in-between catering to our Founders. Lovely idea." We both know those people pledging *New Servitude* and keeping their jobs *at the Founders' discretion and because of their high regard for human customs* means nothing else but that we can't trust them anymore. Obviously, they're playing for the other team now.

Bye-bye neutrality, and hello, biased *L.A. Times* articles.

It's nothing but another trick by the Founders to take more control over us while letting us think the opposite. They must have a really good marketing team.

I kick a pebble across the pavement. "C'mon. Let's go." Spending even a second longer on school premises than strictly necessary is just sad. After a couple steps, I realize Jezza isn't coming. I turn toward him. "What? Old age? Let's go." I wave him over.

With four long strides, Jezza catches up with me, a slight flush on his cheeks. "Uhh, not today. I've got... I'm busy." He lowers his gaze. "I think you're old enough to make it home yourself at this point."

Huh? "Are you working?" Jezza has been jobbing as a waiter at the Hollywood Bowl. Whenever there's an event, he gets to put on a penguin-style waiter's outfit and serve the attending crowd.

"N-no. Just… busy." He looks at a spot right above my head.

"Oh." My mouth drops open. "Uhh, sure." That's a first. This is our daily habit we kept up since first grade, no matter what. After school, Jezza walks me home to the orphanage and then goes quote-unquote home to his foster family, i.e., his ninety-year-old neighbors he lives with. When both his parents got a job in NYC, and Jezza neither wanted to leave L.A. nor me during the last year of school, they were so nice to offer a room for him. Needless to say, *his* freedom is limitless, while *mine* is the tightest corset one can wear. But speaking of, walking home alone, I'll take it. At seventeen, that shouldn't be a challenge. "I'll see you tomorrow, okay?"

"'Course. See you then." Jezza grabs his backpack and is gone around the corner in less than ten seconds—ten seconds that I stare after him, flabbergasted. Had he given me this kind of freedom a couple of months ago, we might still be a couple. A secret couple, obviously, *for the Lord will judge the sexually immoral or adulterous* but still a couple.

Oh, well. There's a reason why Jezza and I didn't work out. Actually, many reasons, the most obvious being his protective behavior around me. I'm not his little sister, and even if I was, he's barely a year older. Doesn't buy him much in terms of life experience, especially not after repeating a grade and joining my level. Still, I can't deny there was something between us, something more than growing up together, more than supporting each other through the Transition when the Founders took over, more than knowing every detail of the other one's life. Jezza is a good-looking guy. Always was. Tall, wide-shouldered, with a hint of rugged masculinity that popped up overnight when he hit puberty. Over the last two years, he has grown from a lanky teen to a self-assured young man, and I'd lie if I said I wasn't attracted to him. Add his obvious flirting, and there went my virginity.

My cheeks heat up. Point proven that my vows to the Founders don't mean anything.

But then, I never said they did.

CHAPTER TWO

Angel Down

It doesn't take me long to make it to the magazine store up on Vine. Their selection is limited, but they always carry the newest Founder-approved newspapers and magazines, which is why I'm never here. The only good thing about the Founder overload is that there are no pictures of *them* assaulting me from all angles. It's forbidden. *Thou shall not take the image of those worshipped by humanity.* Fine with me. Worshiping ain't happening either way, but whatever.

When I enter the store, the scanners installed on either side of the door blink green once. "Cleared. No Founder contact detected." *Ugh.* As if I'd ever touch one and get away with it. Scanners are idiotic, but mandatory in almost all public settings. What do they even measure? DNA-traces? Some kind of radiation? Who knows—and who cares?

"Thanks, bro." I give the scanner a thumbs up. Not that it cared.

I let my gaze drift over the shelves. The most-read magazine, *Luke's Gospel,* takes up all of the top row. It's like that in every store, because it's mandatory, since good ol' parent-killer Luke's the Founders' leader and head of their Council of Elders. Every new decree comes from Luke, every new rule is his doing, every Founder and human officially responds to him. Fine. He's the boss. The part I don't get though is the fan-girling—see exhibit A,

Luke's Gospel from last week: *Meeting Luke: A Day at the Court of the Lord's Messenger.* The cover shows a photoshopped picture of a very, very excited woman in her late twenties on her knees in front of a being made from pure light, with only the outline of his black wings visible.

Yeah. I can guarantee that's not what he looked like when he killed my parents, but I guess people forget easily.

I don't, which is why I'm thankful they're forbidden to take pictures of Founders and decorate all their precious magazines with them. I'd be getting an allergic reaction every time I came in here, and that would be plain annoying.

Anyway.

I scan through the editions of *Founders' Servant.* Astonishing how frequently they publish. How much is there to write about the Founders? It's not as if they liked being all close and personal with us. All they do is feed us enough crumbs to keep the crowds happy and controlled, while they stay in their forums on Earth or up in their hives, their ships. But hey, it seems to work. Only a couple of the older editions from last month are still available. Hot commodity, right there.

October 1st: *Bible, Torah, Quran—Pillars of the Founders' Legacy*

October 15th: *The Moment that Changed it All—One Man's Journey to the Founders*

November 1st: *Three Moving Stories about People Making a Difference in the Name of the Founders.*

And last, but not least, November 15th: *Interview with the Protégée: Choosing My Way.*

Whoa, wait, is that me on the front cover? What the hell did they do to my picture? With a flick of my wrist, I open the magazine to page ten, my interview. "Holy mother of God, how dare you—" I whisper. Anger rises up my throat, bringing the taste of bile with it. Every single picture of me is photoshopped.

Every. Single. One.

Oh, and I'm not talking about removing a zit. I'm talking about major photoshopping. "They gave me freakin' long hair! What. The. Hell." I know why they did it. Because short hair can be seen as vain. Long hair is elegant and can easily be tied up into a knot or a ponytail. Short hair needs maintenance, and maintenance equals vanity. *Of course,* we can't have the Protégée be shown with short hair. What would people think?

I snap the magazine shut. Whatever. Who cares? Still, my jaw clenches as I get in line at the register behind the only two other customers. Without thinking, I stop at least two meters behind them, a safety-feature ingrained by years of PTSD: the male is a Founder. That alone would be reason enough to stop and stare—after all, they rarely leave their hive or the forums—but this one is even more special. This Founder brought his very own servant—his very own *virginal* servant, a requirement, just like the complete devotion and will to serve. Funny enough, that detail counts for both male and female servants. Pretty quaint and idiotic, but that's the Founders in a nutshell. Even if it wasn't obvious, she was his servant by the fact that no Founder would spend any time with a human unless they served him, the bracelets around their wrists would give it away. Vinculums. Servitude-bracelets. Hers small, with intricate decorations engraved into it, his wider and simple. Both glow in an iridescent dark red. Those two must've been assigned to each other for a while. They say the better the human connects to her Founder and the better she serves him, the deeper the glow.

This one must be perfect then.

I chew the inside of my cheek as my gaze glides over the two. She's in her early twenties, a beautiful blonde girl with curly hair and a contagious smile, no matter how grumpy the magazine guy is while ringing up their purchase. She looks at her Founder like he was all she needed for life, always keeping at least the required foot of distance between them. Like a lap dog, she's waiting for his attention, and it makes me sick to my stomach. She must know they mean death, every single one of them. One touch, blue Caerulean shooting from their palms, gone. I might be a loser in school and, well, life, but I know that commandment by heart. In my sleep. *Thou Shalt Not Touch Those Descended From The Heavens.*

How she can live with one of *them*, I don't get it. All day long nothing but a Founder? Most humans even sever the contact to their families completely once they're pledged, because they're called to a *higher purpose.*

Right. Higher purpose—no way I'm buying that BS, but then, I've never been very religious. My mom was, and look what it got her. After I was *turned into an orphan*, I stayed away from religion as much as I could in an orphanage founded in the name of the Lord, which means that apart from my parent's death, I had an easier time than others during the transition.

Coming to terms that God, Buddha, Allah, or whatever name we called the divine leader of the world by, was an actual person, and to top it off, the same one no matter the monotheistic religion… That took some getting used to.

Some people coped better than others, but in the end, the Founders got them all under one umbrella. We all obey the one Lord, the Founders' leader. You're welcome to pray, but please, pray to the one Lord and His Founders.

Clearly, the Bible, Torah, Quran and whatnot also have all had a renaissance and update. Add the polytheistic religions—who were in for quite the shock, I may add—and we got ourselves a brand-new and shiny world religion. Awesome.

The Founders took whatever humanity had to offer in terms of religions and beliefs and morphed it into the New Scripture. Gone are the Bible and Torah, gone is the Quran. What stayed is a mix of all their sacred texts, the ones they say actually happened. Jesus' resurrection? Happened. Not tough when you're a Founder with almost unlimited healing abilities. Moses parting the sea? Happened. Also not too difficult if you have support from a technologically advanced race. Wine from water? Yup. Founder-technology. Noah's Ark, on the other hand? Nope, didn't happen. Fairytale. A tad of this, a tad of that, a dash of exclusiveness by adding the *New Book of Luke*—voilà, a Founder-centric pseudo-religion. The Psalms and proverbs the Founders intended for humanity to live by stayed as well, and now we're living with *a united religion founded in reality*. And people eat it up. Some, at least. The ones who always felt a higher power guided humanity, who craved an omnipotent being in control.

Well, that's what they got—them, and everybody else with them.

Thanks, guys.

The Founder shakes out his wings the slightest bit, careful to not extend them all the way, or he'd bring down the store. He's dressed in the traditional black outfit of a Watcher, complete with tight tactical pants, a fitted black vest cut off at the shoulders, and all the bells and whistles that come with that job, i.e., Black Box and Raptum, attached to his belt.

Like all Founders, he looks like he stepped out of some kind of fashion or modeling magazine. Their race might be mixed—skin tones ranging from almost-translucent white to the darkest black, with all types of shades in-between—but no matter their skin color, they're all beautiful. Lord forbid a Founder was less than perfect.

The one in front of me is no different. With his flawless skin, muscular body and his long, wavy brown hair, he could be part of a rock band if not for the wings.

Yeah. That totally destroys the look for me.

The Founder holds out a hand and the girl presents him his wallet with a little bow of her head and a blissful smile on her face.

Gag.

The clerk lays the Founder's purchase onto the counter next to a big display of letter openers. "May your day be blessed, Founder." He delivers the mandatory traditional greeting with a nice bow. Good boy.

"And yours as well." The angel doesn't spare another look at the man when he takes the bag and gives it to his servant.

Her bracelet reflects the sun as she takes the bag and wallet. "Thank you, Master." Another bow.

Thank you, Master. Bow, bow, bow. I might just find a corner and puke.

Without another look back, the Founder leads the way, his servant trailing two steps behind him after she opens the door for him, the scanner giving them a farewell with a friendly "Good-bye, Founder and servant."

Yeah. No way in hell I'm going to become a servant, even if I have to scrub toilets for the rest of my life. I mean it. Not. Going. To. Happen.

The clerk doesn't seem to be the biggest fan either, that's at least what I read in his expression when his eyes follow the Founder—like he wanted to throw one of those $12.99 letter openers right after him, pointy end first. Yeah, good luck with that: the little Black Box on the Founder's belt doesn't let anything through it perceives as dangerous, be that a mosquito or bullets courtesy of White House security. *Zap*—and that's it. All Watchers carry this perfect shield, and together with the Raptum, the extendable claw fitting perfectly around a person's neck, they carry all their little hearts desire for taming humanity. Not that they needed it. Besides the occasional pitiful uproar of the Resistance, humanity has submitted quite nicely. We're well-behaved prisoners on our own planet.

Once the door has closed behind the Founder, I step forward and lay the two magazines down at the register. The clerk sighs, as if scanning another purchase was too much to handle. Or maybe it's relief the Founder is gone, but hey, at least he paid. He has the right to every item he desires, without pay. Must be nice being a Founder.

"That's three ninety—" The clerk cocks his head to the left, recognition flaring in his dull eyes.

Yep. That would be the moment he adds one and one together.

"You're…" A quick glance left and right. "You're the First." The apple in his throat moves up and down.

The First. Not *the Protégée.* The *first victim*, not the *girl protected by the Founders.* It's the small but crucial matter of point of view. I like that guy much more all of a sudden, especially because he made the connection despite the awful picture on the title page. Ugh, on the other hand, that also means a new hairdo is in order. I like my privacy, or what's left of it.

"Yeah. I am." I give him a small smile and weave my fingers through my short hair. Can't really go much shorter than this, or I'll look like a boy. Huh. Come to think about it, that would be the ultimate way of hiding from the press. The Protégée here, the Protégée there, who the hell wants to read that crap? Should be clear by now I'm not role model material, no matter how much the Sisters pressure me into all things Founder-related.

Clerk pushes the magazines over to me. "No charge for you. May peace be victorious." His index and middle finger form a V as he taps them twice over his heart.

Holy freakin' moly.

My eyes pop open wide, and only because I'm moderately level-headed do I not jump back in panic.

I take it back, he's crazy. I don't like him at all. Using the sign of the Resistance right out in the open? In front of the Protégée, who, for all he knows, might be the Founders' pet? Death sentence right there.

I rip the magazines off the counter. "I'd keep that to myself if I were you," I hiss and turn on my heels. Note to self: avoid magazine-guy. Not even my pseudo-fame could get me out of that pitfall. If that Watcher from a minute ago had seen us, we'd both be dead.

And really, crap like this is not worth dying for.

Needless to say, I make sure I get out of that store real fast.

People like that clerk, they don't get it. Resistance. Resisting. Right. We're alive, the Founders are uniting humanity for the greater good, and there hasn't been war since they arrived over a decade ago. Win. That's gotta count for something. Am I a fan of this Founder-centric lifestyle? Maybe not the greatest. Do I feel like I need to fight them?

Hell, no.

My life has been *touched* by the Founders enough, I'd say.

I walk so fast others would call it a jog, but for me as a runner it doesn't count. Not out of breath? Then it's not a jog or a run. Plus, it's not far from here to the orphanage, and luckily, the streets are not too busy. This being L.A., one can get completely screwed by traffic, although nothing beats the chaos from that one day a few months ago where the Founders held a Tribunal up at the Hollywood Bowl. That sucked big time, mainly because they filled the Bowl with Council members from all hives across the world, and safety was a big concern of theirs. Hence, they had LAPD close down all roads in Hollywood, bringing Los Angeles close to a traffic collapse that day, especially in my neck of the woods. Good thing Tribunals don't happen that often, or I'd have another reason to hate the Founders.

Huh. On the other hand, let them have Tribunals and punish their own. Usually the Founders' justice comes swift and hard— for humans. We get incinerated, they get nothing but a lousy Stigma burned between their shoulder blades. It's the Founders' way of punishing and marking their own as lawbreakers. One Stigma acts as punishment and a reminder. A second will cost a Founder his wings and be his *Fall from Grace*. Stigmas are given by dear Luke, the clan leader, only, and it has happened what— four or five times in the last decade? Meaning, I'm sure more Founders than that have messed up over the last decade and gotten away with it.

Screw them.

I wish Jezza had worked at the Bowl already then. Would've liked to know what they finally got one of those bastards for. Although does it matter? It's one single Founder. Humans take more punishment in higher numbers on a daily basis.

I speed up since the sun is almost gone. Should be okay though. Regulations state that if I started a task during daylight, I may complete it even though it's after nightfall. I know my loopholes, or else I'd never be out after dark, Founder-decreed curfew and all.

As I make my way home through the almost-dark and foggy streets of Los Angeles in November, the soldiers assigned to watch over the burned-down former Resistance hideout on Gregory step aside to let me pass, their faces blank, their posture perfect. Still haven't figured out why we need armies of soldiers when the Founders came in peace and our wars are gone, but I let them be, they let me be. Good deal.

The sun sinks behind the grey houses on my right as I cross Melrose and head toward Larchmont Village. My parents took me here a lot when I was younger. Farmer's market on Sundays and the best pizza in town. Not that I remember much of it, but Jezza does, and he likes to tell those stories of the good old times.

The memory plays out in front of my inner eye, bringing a peaceful serenity I'm missing most of these days.

No thinking.

No planning.

No responsibility.

Me likey.

That is until I pass by the old church on Melrose and Vine. Yelling. Shouts. Screams.

"Get him! More! Harder!"

A heavy thud followed by a pained grunt pierces the relative silence.

"Again! Give me the damn bat—" The dull sound of an impact, followed by another grunt and cough.

"Talk, demon! Talk or you'll pay—"

I stop dead in my tracks.

Serenity?

Gone.

Adrenaline?

Pumping.

Another sound of something hitting a soft body, another suppressed pained grunt and yowl, both shooting straight through my heart and into my soul.

Now, I should probably keep on walking. I *should.* It's dark, not the best neighborhood, and I'm a girl. They tell us we're the weaker sex.

I should *so* ignore the shouts.

But I don't.

Nope. I sprint into the parking area in front of the church, right to where the fog is the thickest and the street lights don't do much to penetrate it.

"Hey!" I yell as soon as I can make out the silhouette of three people—no, four. Three standing, lined up in front of a fourth on his knees, his chest heaving heavily up and down, breath coming out in chokes. His arms are spread away from his body, his face turned up to his attackers, and this pose, it's giving me chills.

With the three guys around him ready to strike, it looks like an execution—an execution where the guy on the ground has already accepted his fate. Where he is *welcoming* it.

One of the three guys standing holds a baseball bat high over his shoulder, ready to strike, and the outlines of the other two look no less hostile in their fighting stances, fists up.

What. The. Hell.

I drop my backpack and storm forward, hands balled into fists. "Hey! Three against one is unfair. Piss off!"

Two of them throw a quick glance over at me, their faces hidden beneath hoods, but the third one, the only one who visibly jerked when I yelled, stays focused on the guy on the ground. He raises the baseball bat as high as he can and delivers one hell of a blow to the other guy's head. I scream out at the same time as the bat connects with that poor guy's skull. His head whips around and blood splatters from his mouth onto his thick jacket.

Holy crap—that can't be happening.

The third guy lifts the bat again, ready to do more damage.

Shoot.

Arms spread out wide, I jump right in front of the bleeding guy on the ground, legs shoulder width apart. "Stop! Are you guys crazy?" It's not as if I was in a fighting stance, but my hands are up and ready to defend myself and the guy on the ground. Seriously, I'll scratch their eyes out or whatever. Three against one is not going to happen on my watch, no matter what the other guy did.

Hooded guy number one, the one in the red shirt, shoves the guy with the bat into the shoulder from behind. "Shit, one more, J. Don't stop, he's almost softened up. Make him talk. *Now!*"

"Oh, hell no, you won't!" My heart hammers like crazy as I put my hands on my hips and stare at the three guys. Tall. Wide. Definitely stronger than me—okay, that was lame. Everybody is taller and stronger than me.

I hold my chin up high. "I give you one chance to run away.

One chance. You don't take it, I'll scream, and I'm good at that. Or if you come closer, I'll kick your balls all the way up your throat. Bon appétit." I glare at them, and the guy with the bat and his face hidden underneath a black hoodie takes a stumble step back. That's right, buddy. We don't go around and beat people up.

"Fuck off, bitch." Red-Hoodie steps closer to the one with the bat lifted above his shoulder and hisses, "Finish him."

"No, you won't," I say with the conviction of a prize fighter. As if I could do anything if they decided to hurt me too. But *fake it until you make it* has been my unofficial motto for forever, and it works.

Also, *never show fear.*

Which is why I turn around as if the three stooges didn't bother me at all. Never mind my heart hammering against my chest as if itself carried a baseball bat.

"Hey." I bend down to the bleeding guy. "Are you okay?" Well, duh, stupid question. After the last blow, he's on all fours, head lowered, blood caking his short, black hair and dripping from his face onto the dirty asphalt. I saw the hit he took, and it wasn't his first. So no, he's not okay.

Obviously, Sherlock.

Two steps and some shuffling, hissing and whispering behind me. Then, "Step away from that thing."

Thing. Assholes. "Nope."

Instead I reach for the boy's upper arms and help him up from all fours to a kneeling position. His black down jacket is thick and moist. Fog or blood. Fog, I hope. "Come on. Ignore the idiots."

"Holy fuck," somebody hisses and another one sounds like he was choking, but so far, I haven't been hit by a baseball bat. *Yet.* I consider that a good sign.

Someone grabs my shoulder and yanks me away. "Are you crazy, Lea? Get away from him!"

Lea?

Lea?

In my mind, the connection is made before I have time to understand it.

I know that voice.

But there's no way he would—

I let momentum carry me to a half-turn. For the first time, I really get to look at the black-hooded guy with the baseball bat, and I wonder how I could not have known it the second I joined this little get-together, semi-darkness and hood or not.

"Jezza?"

I could swear he flinches, while Blue-Hoodie curses. "Fuck, man. Run. If she can ID you..." He has a phone aimed at the scene in front of him, since when, I can't say.

Red-Hoodie shoves Jezza in the shoulder. "You're not running. You finish them off both now, the animal and—"

Jezza lifts his head, lips pressed into a thin line. He holds the bat higher. "Out of the way, Lea. Get away from him. Now!" He barks at me, and it's the last straw.

"What the hell, Jezza? You're beating up people now? What's wrong with you?" I stomp my foot.

"You don't understand—"

"No, I understand just fine!" I spin around and try to take the black-haired guy's hands. He yanks them away from me, but come on. Accept help when you need it. This time I'm faster, grab his hands and pull him up to standing. Something warm and sticky squishes between our palms. Ugh, blood.

"Shit, is she—"

"Will you finally finish him off? Hell, do I have to do everything my—"

"Lea, no! Don't touch him! Don't—" Jezza voice is filled with panic, but I don't hear it.

I hear nothing but the soft gasp coming from the boy in front of me when our hands connect. One more attempt to pull free, but when I hold on, his fingers curl around mine as if I was a lifeline. His next breath comes out choked. "You know, the oaf is right. I'll get you in trouble."

That's the moment he looks up at me for the first time, and that's the moment my heart stops.

Blue eyes.

Clear, light, crystal blue eyes, like the sky on an early spring morning, so bright they shine from the inside and light me up to the depth of my soul—and yet they look beaten. Resigned. Sad. He's young, maybe a year or two older than me. Angular jaw, some stubble, straight nose and high cheek bones. Tousled black hair. Despite the blood splattered across his face, he is beautiful somehow. Almost perfect.

Beautiful. Perfect.

Beautiful, perfect—an *animal*. A *thing*.

Click.

The pieces fall into place with an audible sound effect.

Beautiful and perfect.

Because Lord forbid a Founder was anything less than perfect.

The next breath hitches in my throat.

I'm touching a Founder.

I'm touching a freaking Founder.

A wheezy breath leaves my throat. "You're—"

"Guilty as charged." He gives me a crooked smile. "You probably should let go." He throws a pointed glance down at our hands.

Shit!

Instinct takes over, rips my hand out of the boy's—*the Founder's*—and sends me two steps stumbling back.

A Founder.

Founder. Founder. Founder. That one word plays on repeat and it won't stop.

Founder. Founder. FOUNDER.

I touched a Founder.

Like mother, like daughter.

Every new breath comes harsher than the last, every heartbeat pumps less and less blood to my brain. My body has realized what my mind is still processing. I'm as good as dead.

"J! Here!" The sound of a gun being racked pierces the night and my mental fog.

"What? No! We never said—"

"Fuck you, do it! He's wide open! If he won't talk, it's our only cha—"

"I can't kill him. It's a sin—"

"Yes, you can!" Red-Hoodie shoves the gun at Jezza, then picks up two large rocks from the ground.

Across from them, the Founder takes a step forward, chest out, shoulders back. "Yes, you can. Or try, at least." It comes out with a sigh. He takes another step forward.

"Fuck!" Jezza racks the gun and aims at his chest.

I stare at the scene in front of me openmouthed. This isn't happening.

Not.

Happening.

Jezza is pointing a gun at a Founder.

A gun.

At a Founder—a Founder who is waiting for that bullet. Resigned. Submissive. Surrendering.

He's going to let himself get shot.

What the hell is wrong with everybody here?

Bile rises up my throat.

No, no, no, no.

Jezza shooting a Founder is committing the ultimate sin. He's throwing his life away, and I'm ninety-nine percent sure it's not even going to kill the Founder. Hurt and incapacitate him for a while? Sure. But kill? Nope. Takes more than that, as in *cutting off his head.*

Like in slow motion, I watch his chest rise and fall with puffy breaths, his trigger finger curl…

…and curl…

…and—

Things happen too fast to process. One moment I'm a bystander, the next I've thrown myself in front of the boy. *The Founder.* "Stop!"

As if tasered, Jezza's finger flies off the trigger. "Jesus Christ, Lea! Are you crazy? You—"

Behind me, the boy draws in a hoarse breath. "What—"

"Fuck it, J! Shoot! Shoot!"

"But Lea—"

"Obviously, she's on *their* side! Screw her!" Red-Hoodie throws one of the rocks at me and rips the gun out of Jezza's hands. The stupid rock hits the side of my face, and while it hurts, the pain dulls the moment I see him point the gun straight at me. He snarls. "Shouldn't have protected the demon, girl."

Life slows down to a crawl. Look at that, death by gun. Not what I expected. Not ever, and especially not after touching a Founder.

Red-Hoodie doesn't take his time like Jezza did. His finger curls and—

BANG!

A draft of air, a movement too fast for the naked eye to see, a ripping sound—and the boy is in front of me, jacket torn at the seams and two white wings sprouting from his back, spread wide and extending at least two meters in each direction.

Not even a millisecond later, the bullet hits its target.

The boy grunts once, but doesn't stumble. Doesn't fall. Doesn't die.

Oh no, quite the opposite. He opens his fists, both palms glowing blue. "Not. A. Good. Idea." He lifts his hands.

Jezza and his buddies finally realize what they've done: that they shot a Founder. They're as good as dead. Blue-Hoodie is the first to turn on his heels as he pockets his phone. With a strangled squeak, he stumbles and barely catches himself, doing his best to scramble away from the Founder and the blue light that will end his life within a nanosecond.

Red-Hoodie grabs Jezza by the shirt and yanks him around with him. "Move!"

"Wait! Lea—" But Red-Hoodie drags him away with such a force, he'd fall if he fought him. Fall, and stay to be killed. For a moment, Jezza's wide eyes meet mine—and then he's gone.

Which leaves me alone with the Founder. Whom I touched. Who's obligated to end me for that. Who's charged to kill. His whole body is coiled and tight, ready to strike. Not even the extended wings can hide the irregular up and down of his shoulders. No matter it won't kill him, this wound must hurt like hell. He balls his fingers to a fist only to stretch and curl them again, the change of the caerulean blue intensity throwing weird shadows into the fog. Any moment now, he's going to throw up his hands and eliminate all three of his attackers in one single sweep of blue light. Kill them. Vaporize them.

"You've had your chance. Didn't take it. My turn." He raises his hands, and I'm back where I was ten years ago.

A blast so bright it hurt my eyes.

A sound of complete and utter surprise.

The smell of ozone so bad it made me nauseous.

"Stop!" The word is out before I know it was me saying it. Croaking it.

Another second passes before the boy—*the Founder*—whirls around, wings up for the duration of the movement to not knock me over. Blood seeps through his jacket below his right clavicle. The little bit of light from the street lamp behind him throws a halo into the fog above his head, and as the wings lower, he truly looks like an angel.

An angel of death.

It's all the incentive I need. Self-preservation kicks in, at its finest.

I whirl around on my heels and run.

CHAPTER THREE

Can You Hear Me Running

I run.

I run into the fog as fast as I can, so fast, my legs hurt after a mere thirty seconds, so fast, my lungs are threatening to explode, so fast, I don't know where I'm going.

I run.

Run, run, run.

There is nothing else but running. Running, running, running. If I didn't, he'd kill me, and I really, really don't want to be dead.

I don't want to end up like my parents.

My feet pound against the asphalt so fast it's a wonder I don't fall, my heart pumps at a speed it almost outruns me, and my mind is stuck on two sentences, repeating them over and over and over:

Jezza tried to kill a Founder.

I touched a Founder.

Jezza tried to kill a Founder.

I touched a Founder.

Jezza—

I barely cross the street before a car speeds through the crosswalk. Shoot, close call. If I don't watch it I'm gonna be—

Dead.

Yeah. I'm dead anyway.

Correction, it's *three* sentences my mind is stuck on: Jezza tried to kill a Founder. I touched a Founder. I'm as good as dead.

Don't know how long recovery is going to take him, but it's gonna happen fast, and then I'm done for.

I sprint around a corner and barely avoid some guy hurrying home from a walk with his dog. "Watch it," he hisses, but I'm gone already. Run, run, run. Faster, faster, faster. No time to think, no time to stop. No time to be caught, because it doesn't matter if it's the hooded guys or the Founder, I'm still dead.

It takes more than willpower to not let that thought consume me, because if it did, I might as well jump in front of a car right now and get it over with.

Wheezy, short breaths leave my lungs, breaths cut short by panic.

Another corner. Must not run straight. Must keep them guessing. Must stay hidden from aerial view. I let the fog swallow me, plunging into the darkness and soft noise that is L.A. after curfew, and run, run, run for minutes that could be hours, hours that could be days.

At one point, I stumble over exposed roots in the uneven sidewalk and take a tumbling fall into some kind of bushes in an un-fenced front yard. Thorns, twigs and whatnot poke and slice me, but who cares? I scramble back up and ignore the pain.

Can't go back to the orphanage. Can't go anywhere public. As soon as I enter any of those buildings, it won't be *Welcome back, Lea Akiyama*, but *You have violated the Eleventh Commandment* together with sirens and an automatic call to the Watchers.

Crap, crap, crap.

My breath comes out wheezy and hoarse. What am I supposed to do now? I have his freakin' blood all over me, every scanner I walk through, hell, every scanner I even walk by will light up like a Christmas tree because I *touched a freakin' Founder.*

I dart past parked cars and trash containers, cross another small street and stay away from any light as much as possible. Okay. Okay. Think, idiot! Can't go to the orphanage. Not until his Mark has worn off. How long does it take? Well, how should I know, it's not as if I ever planned to touch one of them! Gah!

Another corner, and this time I catch myself when I stumble over protruding roots. Watch out, dammit! Last thing I need is a real fall or accident. Hello, ambulance crew and mandatory scanners. Good bye, life.

I struggle on and keep on running. Never have I been happier to be in shape. Never.

An opossum crosses the street in front of me and runs toward a tree in a front yard farther up ahead. With two quick jumps it vanishes in a hole between two branches.

I skid to a stop, panting.

Idea.

Okay. Good. Why not? Resting my hands on my knees I bend over, gasping for air. Shouldn't be that much out of breath, but the fear of the Founder's wrath has me on edge. Surprise, an angel out to kill you does that. Anyway—the opossum is right. Hide in plain sight. Not too plain, obviously, or there are going to be scanners, but still.

After giving my lungs a couple more seconds of a break, I straighten up and start jogging as my idea begins to take shape.

The Santa Monica Pier has been abandoned for a good decade. It's a sad place, but maybe that's why I like it. It suits me. Nobody ever comes here, and that suits me even more. Plus, it brought back memories when I discovered it about two years ago on one of my longer runs. I mean, not that it was that hard to find—the broken down Ferris wheel is still impressive, and so are the other rides, kaput and rotten as they are, but still. Nobody goes here, thanks to the high, wooden fence, barbed wire, and one or the other Psalm or Proverb, or whatever. *Keep your lives free of sin and waste, and be content with what the Lord and Founders provide to you, for they are all you need.*

It still strikes me as odd that denying humanity play and fun is what the Lord wants, but it's what the Founders claimed when they closed down almost all entertainment besides the occasional classic concert all those years ago, and nobody was going to fight them on it.

Not when the descent of the angels signified the Lord's love for us.

Not when their ships hovered above sixty major cities across Earth with enough firepower to destroy us all.

Not when people eagerly waited for a leader to unite Earth, and when for the majority of hardliners from almost every monotheistic religion their prayers were answered.

Nope.

Living a life serving the Founders became such a big deal either way—whether people liked it or not—stuff like the Santa Monica Pier didn't rank high enough to even be an issue.

To me it did, but then to me, most things Founder-related are an issue.

At this point, I've slowed to a leisurely pace. I stay close to the pier and cross the beach, then stroll into the water, as if doing nothing more than taking a moonlight walk. During curfew.

Ahem. Still, this place isn't very frequented anymore for obvious reasons, but running into the water, splashing and making a scene would be the fastest way to call attention to myself, no matter if I'm at least somewhat hidden under the pier or not.

I hiss as the water rises first to my knees, then to my hips, then to my belly button. Cold. On better days, it's not quite as freezing, but today isn't one of them. Within a couple of minutes, I've made my way to the end of the pier, at least a hundred fifty yards out from the shoreline and more swimming than walking. Doesn't matter.

I find the wooden pillar that must've been somebody else's friend once, like it became mine. "There you are, buddy," I whisper and pat the mossy and slimy surface of the single pillar that has metal rungs embedded in its body. Right now, I might be the only one crazy enough to visit this place, but at one point I wasn't. And while I could've scaled the fence, barbed wire and me don't get along. Granted, I'd take the sting of barbed wire any time of the day if it meant not getting roasted by a Founder, but this way to my little hiding place, it has proven its worth.

I pull myself up and roll under the railing and onto the pier.

Made it.

My lungs feel like they're on fire, and my body shivers. Shakes. Rattles. With an effort equaling moving a mountain, I work myself up to standing. Must find a hiding spot. Like, now.

The wooden planks under my feet are soft, weakened by years of harsh sunlight eroding them. Good for me, it muffles my steps—not that I expected anybody out here, but still.

I sneak through the darkness past abandoned stores and restaurants on my right. To the left, the sea and night sky are doing their best to impress me, but it's hard to appreciate beauty when it feels life is teetering on the edge.

I've been at the pier plenty since I discovered it. A good spot for thinking—during the day. At night?

Eerie.

Creepy.

Cold.

Those ten years after the Founders put out their decree to close most entertainment-related businesses have pulled a number on this place. The Ferris Wheel at the end of the pier lost a couple of cabins. The roller coaster further to the center collapsed into a heap of tracks. The tents and umbrellas decayed to torn rags while many of the kiosks and stores have broken, shattered windows or roofs missing shingles.

To be honest, it looks like a scene from a horror movie.

"How fitting," I whisper into the night. Since it turns out this is kind of my personal horror movie.

The deepest and richest joy comes from fellowship with the Lord, they said.

A day in his court is better than a thousand elsewhere, they said.

For those who love the Lord all things shall work together for good, according to His purpose, they said.

Yeah, and how did that work out for me so far?

The only light guiding me out here, away from the coast, is the Moon's. While the street lamps are still there, I doubt they'd work even if they chose to keep them on. They didn't, so it's pretty much the Moon, stars, and my imagination.

As careful as possible, I sneak forward to the one fallen-off cabin perfect for me. Who knows when it detached from the Ferris wheel, or whether it came to rest upright against a former waffle shop on its own, or because somebody put it up, but none of it matters. All that does is that nobody is in it, and that it's covered by a canopy, with a bench I can lie down on, and far away from any light source or scanner. Perfect for me.

I curl up on the bench as tight as I can. November weather and nighttime swims don't go well together, no matter this is California. I'm freezing, and the plastic bench doesn't make it any better. Neither does the adrenaline wearing off.

Deep breath. Deep breath, Lea.

After a minute or so, I feel a tad less anxious, because whenever I'm here, the past embraces and comforts me. It's closer, more real. I can almost hear kids squeal and laugh, can almost smell the cotton candy, can almost feel the touch of my dad's arm around my shoulders. Almost.

Another series of shivers wrack my body, and only half of them are from the combination of wet, thin school clothes and freezing pacific water cooling me down. The other half comes from the fact that if I don't play this right, I'm dead.

Ten years.

It's been ten years last month, and at this point, remembering is becoming difficult, and I don't mean *that* day. I didn't need David's cruel reminder to keep it prominently featured in my nightmares. No, I mean *life*. Regular life. Nothing is left of those six years with my parents. Not a photo, not a note, not a single thing. With every day that passes, I fear a little bit more that one day I'm going to forget what they looked like. What they sounded like. What it felt like to be loved.

Whenever I'm here, though, I'm a bit closer to them. Not that it would help me today. Oh, I'm going to be closer to them all right in no time, as in reunited in death.

Because at this point, I'm as good as dead.

ANGEL DOWN

Dead if the Angel finds me.
Dead if I get found by a Watcher.
Dead if I go near a scanner.
I work on a dry swallow.
Looks like no matter what I do, chances are I'll end up dead.

CHAPTER FOUR

Busted

The morning comes too soon.

Would've loved to stay asleep and tightly wrapped in a delusional blanket of blissful ignorance for a while longer, but neither the rising sun nor the annoying seagulls have mercy on me.

After a few hours of tossing and turning, last night feels even more like a bad dream. My gaze drops to my arms, covered in scratches from my wild dash through back alleys, bushes, and whatnot. "Not a dream, sweetie pie," I whisper. Plus, my hands are still covered in blood. *His* blood. So much for my trip through the Pacific up to the pier taking care of that. "Gah!" I try wiping my palms on my thighs but stop after one wipe. Not smart. The Mark will fade off my skin eventually, but as long as blood sticks to my clothing, I'm screwed.

Fifteen minutes later, I've used the one working restroom to scrub my hands, arms, and face. Every little cut stings, and I have way more than I thought I did. And bruises. Tripping over roots in my mindless escape didn't help. The stupid rock Red-Hoodie threw at my face didn't help either. My temple feels puffy on that side. Ow.

In lieu of a mirror, I wash as much of my exposed skin as I can. Better safe than sorry. The question now is, how long does it take for the Mark to fade? And once it does—what do I do then?

Or until then? No matter what, I'm screwed times two. Even if I hadn't committed a sin by touching the Founder, there's still Jezza and his two hooded buddies.

If I'm honest to myself, I might have to stay here for a while. A long while. A very long while. Which, yay for me, makes this the ideal hiding spot. At least I have a functioning restroom with running water. I have shelter—kind of, at least. And, last but not least, I have my emergency stash.

Having come here every couple of weeks has its advantages. Over time, I brought a few luxury items to make my stay more fun, like potato chips, canned fruit, power bars. Nothing is worse than sitting here hungry, and yes, I have checked the old retail area already. Nothing's left, and even if it was, I doubt it'd be edible after all this time.

I retrieve my stash from an old, broken freezer in the waffle store. Not that it kept the stuff cold, but it kept the birds off it. I carry the bag over to the edge of the pier where the roller coaster's broken tracks and wagons keep me hidden from view from either side.

Amazing how much this morning feels like any normal day, and yet it's far from it. It seems like my best friend found wrong friends and then beat up a Founder, but I can't make sense of it. Since when—I mean, how… No, why…

Ugh.

I sit on the ledge, feet dangling off the pier, and open a bag of chips. Maybe that's why he couldn't walk me home today. Yesterday, I mean. *Hanging* with his new buddies. I lower my head onto my forearms and groan. What a mess. Even if I return to the orphanage—

The seagulls around me break out in alarmed shrieks.

My gaze flicks up and—

"Shit."

There, about a hundred meters out in the sea, flies a founder. Brilliant white wings, black clothing—and he's flying right at the pier. At me. I drop the chips and jump up and back like tasered.

"Shit, shit, shit!" I run to hide—but whom am I kidding. Even if he's not a Watcher who found me by scanning the area, I don't stand a chance: better vision. Better senses, period. He'll see me, sniff me, feel me, or whatever. He knows already I'm here, Watcher or not.

I skid to a halt.

Okay then.

Showtime.

If he's a Watcher, he'll check his Scanner and see I'm marked. If he's not… I may stand a chance. Either way, I won't go down being killed from behind.

I turn and look up.

There he is, a mere twenty meters in front of me, descending slowly, wide wings keeping him afloat like a bird sailing down from the skies.

With an ease I don't have in any movement he lands a couple of steps in front of me.

No uniform.

Vibrant blue eyes.

Black hair.

Perfect, heavenly features.

Him.

The boy from last night. The Founder. Minus any signs of the gunshot wound, or the beating he received. Guess that answers my question how fast that stuff would heal. Too fast for my taste.

My stomach cramps, and all of a sudden, I'm ice cold. He found me. Not good. So not good.

But I don't fall to my knees. I don't offer any respects. Least of all I bow. I think we're kind of past that at this point. It is his obligation to kill me, and I'm going down with my head high and seeing eye. Not cowering. Not groveling.

The Angel comes closer, wings three-quarters extended, and stops a mere meter in front of me, head tilted to the side, a curious expression on his face. Well, I'll give him something to satisfy his curiosity.

I pull my shoulders straight. "You're the one they beat up." Not the traditional greeting. Reason for punishment right there, but it's not as if it mattered. Dead is dead.

His left eyebrow raises. He nods once, slowly. "You're the one who kept them from shooting me."

My glance drops to his chest. "Didn't work out so well then, did it?" I jumped in front of a gun for him, call it reflex, call it compassion, call it anything else than me being on the Founders' side, but I did.

And then he did the same for me.

That, right there, is something I never expected. A Founder protecting a human. *After* said human touched him.

His expression darkens. "Worked out fine until those idiots lost all sense of reality."

What an odd bird, no pun intended. Besides my life taking a turn for the worse last night, it wasn't the typical encounter with a Founder. No Founder lets himself get beaten up—but he did. At any time, he could've summoned his blue Caeruleum and obliterated Jezza and the others in a flash of light, and yet when I found him, he was taking the beating as if he deserved it.

And he was about to let Jezza shoot him.

Probably wouldn't have killed him no matter what, but something's seriously wrong with that guy.

And it doesn't matter. I touched him, had his blood on my hands, and he found me. One plus one equals two, and two in this case equals… yeah. Bad for me.

I clasp my hands together behind my back. For one, it makes me stand straighter and look more unaffected, for another it hides the shaking of my hands. "So, you're going to kill me." Not a question. A fact.

The guy jerks. "What? No!" He brings both hands up, palms open, like he was calming a rabid dog. No blue light. Just two regular, harmless palms. His eyes are large as he shakes his head. "Why would you think that?"

"Why would I think that?" I was so right. Something's wrong with him. "Because, if you don't remember, I touched you. I still have your blood all over me. So, excuse me for assuming you're here to finish me off, like any Founder would!" I glare at him. Stop playing with me, idiot!

He runs a hand through his short hair, tousling it up even more. It makes him look more boyish instead of uber-perfect. He huffs once. "Yeah, of course. And that's the problem, don't you think?" His gaze meets mine and pins me to the spot. Something in their blue invites me to come closer, to let down my guard, but I ain't stupid, because, is that a trick question?

"What do you want me to say? I've committed an Unforgivable Sin already. What more do you need?"

He sighs. "I don't need anything. In fact, I could care less that you touched me." His cheeks redden. "I mean, it was nice for you to stick up for me, even after you knew I was a Founder. Not many humans would do that, I've come to find out."

I open my mouth, then close it. There's something so sad in his voice, it makes me feel for him. Time to change the topic. I'm not developing pity for a Founder. Please. "So, why'd you come back then?"

He shrugs, and it comes with a shy, crooked smile. "Curiosity, maybe? And it's kind of my duty to track you down." The Founder points at the blood stains on my shirt. "By the way, that's going to cause you some problems." His gaze roams over me head to toe, and it's really nothing more than an evaluating glance over my body, but hell if it didn't make me feel self-conscious on a whole new level. Self-conscious and confused.

He cocks his head. "You need to get rid of those stains."

Duh. "Well, thank you for that thorough advice." Not that I didn't know that myself.

The Founder sighs again. He has that sound down like a pro. Makes him sound older, although like I said, he can't be that much older than me: well-built and more mature than any humans the same age, but he's still no older than eighteen. Not a Watcher. Not trained in the art of fast and merciful killing. Just a fledgling, not initiated yet, not accepted into the circle of adult Founders and trusted with their secrets.

A cute little fledgling, although a very well developed one.

So, I decide to push my luck. "If you don't have anything else, I've got stuff to do." I turn on my heels and walk past him toward the spot where I dropped my chips. Keeping my back to the Founder goes against everything I've taught myself over the last years, but I do it. I keep my head high and posture straight, as if I wasn't worried about him at all. Even when I sit down, the railing keeping me from falling forward into the water, I refuse to look back.

My hands shake, so I pick up the chips and shove a couple into my mouth.

Still shaking.

Still no sound from the Founder.

After two more bites, he sighs again, then his steps come closer and—

And he takes a seat to my left, keeping a good arm's length distance between us that I appreciate.

The last bite of chips turns stale in my mouth. Why is he—?

"Look, I'm sorry I got you into trouble."

I choke on my next breath. "What?" I wheeze. Did he say he was *sorry*—

"You heard me," he grumbles. "Didn't quite plan for that to happen."

"Sure hope so, man. It would make you one heck of an asshole."

The Founder laughs out once, a sound so warm and full, it chases away some of the anxiety of sitting next to him. "You're right. I guess it would." He grins at me and then swallows hard when his eyes fall onto my bag of chips.

I could swear I hear his mouth watering the way he looks at it.

Odd. Nobody is as spoiled and as catered to as a Founder. But then... I tilt my head. "Hungry?"

His lips tighten and he picks at a larger splinter of wood that came loose from the wooden planks. "Nope."

"Okay then." I shove another handful of chips into my mouth. Pause.

The boy—the Founder—picks at another splinter. "Maybe. A little. Been... a couple of days."

"A couple of days? Dude, why didn't you get food? Don't know how to shop?" Wouldn't rule that out. Founders live protected in their forums, their exclusive suburbs away from our human cities. This one is obviously far from home. Our closest forum is in the desert two hours east from here. So, who knows if the little protected baby boy had to shop on his own ever before.

"No, I do know how to shop. I just haven't figured out how to do it without money."

My jaw drops. "S'cuse me?" Without money? Who the heck cares? "Uh, newsflash. You're a Founder. You don't need money to get anything." *Ask and you shall receive,* at least if you're a Founder. It's nice if you pay, but you certainly don't have to.

He harrumphs and tucks his wings in, so only the outline of feathers peeks past his back, a white halo around his body. "Maybe. Didn't feel right though." He uses a finger to draw a pattern into the dirt on his right that I destroy when I turn toward him and pull up my leg. What the heck is wrong with him?

"Are you sure you're a Founder? Just asking, because—" Because so far I haven't met a Founder who didn't kill the human who touched him, or who wasn't all about being superior to us. Oh, excuse me, *of course* they're superior to us. Of course. Heavenly beings. Powerful heavenly beings. Created by the Lord. Here to reunite humanity. Well, that part at least is working well, because what other option did we have?

In the beginning, we tried. I mean, you can't swoop down from the skies in front of the center of western democracy and start killing American citizens without expecting a backlash. Yeah. Said backlash lasted exactly twelve hours. Half a day until the whole planet knew the balance of power had shifted away from us and toward the beings in their fancy, tear-shaped spaceships.

America sent missiles. It cost us the White House and thousands of lives. Israel attacked their hive with all they had. I'd say they can be considered lucky they survived, because Russia didn't fare quite so well. Moscow still isn't inhabitable. And just like that, Earth wasn't ours anymore, or maybe it never was, if we're to believe *them*, since after all, they seeded life on Earth millennia ago.

Took us humans a while to switch gears. It's one thing believing or not there is a God, but a completely other thing to know the Lord was—is—a Founder, and that humanity was made in their image. Minus the wings and a couple of other crucial features, but hey, they gave us the gift of life. Gotta say though, somehow it rather feels like it was a deal and they're back to cash in our debt.

The Founder chuckles. "Yeah, last time I checked… pretty sure I'm a Founder." He curls his hand and opens it, blue light dancing across his palm. He sighs and shakes out his hand, the Caeruleum gone within a second. "All I am. A Founder."

I should get up and walk away. I should stop talking to him as if he were a normal person and not one who could end me within a second. I should. But somehow, I can't. Something about him has me on edge, but not in a scary way.

For a moment, I hesitate, but then I turn the bag of chips and lay it in the middle between us. "Chips?"

CHAPTER FIVE

Fragile Tendrils

If somebody told me I was dreaming, I'd believe them.

No way I'm sitting next to a freakin' Founder, sharing my food.

Nope. Not happening. Maybe I got hit in the head and this is all made-up by a concussed mind. Although, if it was, I surely wouldn't see him in that much detail, wouldn't see how his feathers move with every soft blow of wind passing over us. Wouldn't catch his scent, something fresh with a hint of vanilla. Wouldn't see him trying to hold back from shoveling food into his mouth, and failing miserably.

But then, it must be a dream, because I'm sitting here with a Founder, and I'm very much alive.

I swallow a mouthful of chips. "Okay. Spill it. Why are you doing this?"

"What?"

"Not killing me." I hesitate. "*Being nice.*"

He avoids my eyes and looks up in the sky. "Kind of my fault you're marked, right? It's my blood after all. And that only happened because you helped me, remember?"

"Yes, but given that you're a Founder you didn't need my help—"

"Looked like I did."

"Even then helping you doesn't make up for the fact that I

touched you. Twice." Once on top of his clothing which could—*could*—be forgivable, once on his hands, skin-on-skin. So not forgivable, no matter the circumstances. Just one more way in which the Founders are lacking reason and common sense, but nobody's asking me, I guess.

The Founder shrugs. "It doesn't. Not if we go by the law. Not if we ask a Watcher." He pauses, eyes boring into mine. "But if you ask me, the rules don't apply."

I wipe my hands on my thighs. "They don't?" Sister Mary would have a heart attack. Belief system? Shattered.

His cheeks take on a pinkish hue. "Rules and me don't get along so well."

A laugh bursts free before I can stop it. "You are the weirdest Founder I've ever met." Granted, I've been trying to avoid them, but still.

"I'll take it as a compliment, Lea." He takes a handful of chips.

A spike of something shoots through my veins. "You know my name?"

"'Course I do." He hands the bag to me. "I'm a good listener."

"Ah. Jezza mentioned my name."

He shoots me a glance. "The guy with the bat."

Now, my cheeks warm up. Well, I said Jezza's name yesterday like he said mine, and it's not as if the Founder would find my good old friend Jeremy by his nickname… "Yeah. About that, listen. He—"

"I get it."

"You do?"

"Yeah. I've done my research. Seventy-eight percent of humanity are not happy with us. Fifteen percent love us, and the rest don't care either way."

I pop open a bag of gummy bears. "And why would that bother you?"

He stops chewing. "Wouldn't it bother you if the planet you lived on rejected you?"

"Well, yeah, but I doubt any Founder besides you thinks like that."

A muscle in his jaw twitches. "You're right with that one. They don't." His wings pull closer together on his back, so much that all that's visible is a small frame of feathers behind him. "But anyway. What's your plan?"

"My plan?" I mumble through the food. "I don't have one. Wait for the mark to wear off, go back to the orphanage." He cocks his head, and I explain. "My parents died when I was six." Killed. By a Founder, to be specific. Somehow, those words don't come out though. It's a fragile peace we have here, and I'm not going to be the one to ruin it.

He flinches. "Sorry. That must've been rough."

"Yeah. But I'm okay." And even if I wasn't, I'm not going to bare my soul to one of *them*, nice or not.

He helps himself to another bite of food. "You might want to get a bit more specific in your planning. It will take the Mark a while to wear off..."

None of his business. I dig into the gummy bears. Good stuff. "I'll stay hidden." Not that I had much of a choice.

"That might not be an option."

What the what? Is that a threat? I stop chewing and give him a cool glance down my nose. "Oh, yes. It is."

He tries again. Clearly, he can't take a hint. "The Mark is strong in you—"

"Who are you? Yoda? Never mind the Mark, I'll handle it." I

shove the gummy bears over in his direction, and this time he grabs some more and sits up. Good. I don't need to hear how screwed I am, and there's only so much leveling I can do with a Founder.

We eat in silence, and for the first time, I have the chance to really look at him. Careful, from beneath my lashes, but still. And obviously, I was right with my first assessment. He's definitely cute, but then, all Founders are easy on the eyes. So yeah, sure, he has those cover-of-a-magazine-features: an angular chin like chiseled from marble. Deep-set eyes that shine so bright, I wouldn't put it beneath them to have some kind of power source lighting them up. A lean and powerful body. Wide wings, and his have the most interesting shade. They're not *just* white. They're blindingly white and so bright in the sun, they leave an afterimage burned into my retina when the sun hits them at the right angle. Hey, I'll take it over black wings, because the last time I saw black wings—

Yeah. Not going there, because against all odds and expectations I don't mind his company. Much. I can ignore the wings and pretend this is a regular guy, which, besides the fact that I'm still alive, might be the most astonishing development of the last fifteen hours. What has me intrigued more is… well, he's here. With me—a human—and he's… caring.

Despite all their reassurances to the contrary it's not something the Founders are known for.

The guy crumbles some chips between his fingers and throws them out for the birds, who go at them like crazy. He gives me a careful glance from under his lashes accompanied by a sigh. "Here's the problem. This Mark—"

I groan. Seriously, take a hint! "I don't want to talk about the

Mark."

He nods at my blood-stained clothing. "Well, you'll have to. This Mark will take a while to fade. Not days. Probably weeks, but can't say exactly."

What? "Weeks?" I squeak. Weeks? That's not good. Not good at all!

His brows pull down into a V. "Yeah, Weeks. And FYI, to rain on your parade some more, you aren't safe here. You need to hide better."

I lean forward onto the lowest rung of the railing and let my gaze drift over the Pacific. Okay, that changes things. Weeks. Weeks away from the orphanage and hidden. Maybe I shouldn't have shared my chips but kept them for the bad times looming on the horizon. *Weeks.*

On the other hand, who is he? Why should I believe him? For all I know, he wants to scare me out of hiding to—well, I don't know for what, he could kill me here as well as anywhere else, so not that it mattered. But then, I have yet to meet a Founder without an ulterior motive, so my trust in his advice is limited at this point. "Thanks for your input." I give him a sloppy salute.

He flinches. "No, really. You need to hide better. I mean, I found you."

True. I cast an eye at him. "Yeah, how'd you do that, by the way?" And how is that supposed to make me believe—or trust—him more?

He shrugs. "A hunch. But my point is, if I can find you, so can they, and whenever they do, you'll only have one option, which I doubt you'd like. Unless you always planned on becoming a serv—"

I wave my hand to shut him up. "Never mind. Yeah. Sure. I'll hide better." Or not. Or if I did, I'd probably not tell him, current truce yes or no. Plus, I'd rather not give him any information that can lead to another *hunch*, finding a new spot is risky enough. Running. Passing by public buildings with scanners. Searching for a new hideout as Watchers are circling the skies, checking the population through their scanners.

I can feel his gaze on me, but I refuse to look at him, although I gotta say, it makes me nervous. Not in the I-should-really-run kinda way, no. It's more like an awareness spreading. A warmth that rises from my toes up my body until I'm sure my cheeks are red. I flick a left-over piece of precious chips into the sea below me.

After a couple of seconds, the angel sighs and rubs his hands together, clearing them from crumbs and salt. "Would it help if we had a scanner, so you can see why I'm asking you to do that? I might be able to get us one."

Now my heads flies to the left. "*Us?* When did we become an us?"

He stretches his wings a little bit farther and angles them, so the wind catches the feathers, ruffling them. "Probably when you knew I was a Founder and you didn't run." His blue eyes slice into mine, and it brings another rush of warmth, headier and stronger.

"Oh well," I grumble, "Knew I should've run."

"That's what common sense would've told you, yes." He chuckles and winks. "But speaking of running. What about your buddy? And his violent friends?"

Jezza.

Appetite? Gone.

"Dang it." I drop the gummy bears onto the pier. With this ginormous mess going on it's easy to forget about Jezza.

"What if he tries to finish the job the other guy gave him?"

My jaw drops. "You mean, to kill me?"

The Founder nods.

I shake my head so fast, it hurts. "Nu-uh. Not going to happen. He was trying to defend me, if you noticed."

"Fine job he did." The Founder growls and rubs his chest where a mere twelve hours ago blood was seeping through his jacket.

Well, granted. The Founder was the one who took the bullet for me, not Jezza.

Huh. Oxymoron right there, but… "Speaking of. I don't think I've thanked you for taking that bullet for me." I blush. "So, uhh, thank you. I hope it… I mean, it didn't…"

"Hurt too much?" His lips curl up. "It did. Like a mother—Well, you know. Still pretty sore. But one good thing about our genes is the healing." True dat. They can heal themselves and help others heal. Pity they never do it to help humans. Cancer could be eradicated. People could survive all kinds of accidents. But nope. It's against their laws, and no Founder would ever heal a human. So much for compassion.

He still rubs that spot, and the next sentence comes out much softer. "It would take more than that to kill me. Way more."

And yet he was waiting for it.

I drop my gaze to the food between us and play with the packaging. "If… if you don't mind me asking… why did you let them beat you up anyway? You could've ended them at any time. They targeted you because you're a Founder, and you—"

"Let yourself get beaten to a pulp?"

"Yeah." I look up and our eyes connect. He holds my gaze, defiance and something softer, more vulnerable, in his eyes. That look, it sneaks out and anchors itself to my soul, Founder or not. It speaks of a sadness rooted so deep it must've been there for years.

The apple in his throat moves up and down once. "Let's just say I was in the mood for punishment, and those guys were willing to deliver." His tone is neutral, with a slight hint of bitterness, and that bitterness, it finishes the job, cracks my heart open and makes me feel for him. Nobody deserves to be beaten half to death. Nobody. No human, no Founder, and nobody should feel they deserve it, no matter what they did.

I swallow hard. "Why?" It's a mere whisper, because suddenly this got way more personal than I intended it to be.

He crumbles another chip between his fingers, gaze never leaving mine. The longer he looks at me like that, the more the world around us shrinks to only him and me. The blue of his eyes captivates me and locks me in, even though the boy stays silent and almost completely still; so still, that if it wasn't for his thumb and index finger destroying the chips, I could swear time had frozen around us.

Five seconds.

Ten.

Fifteen.

The Founder sucks in his lower lip, closes his eyes for another second, and then stands up in one fast, fluid movement. "Anyway. I… have to go. Don't go anywhere, and please stay out of sight at least. I'll be back soon, with a scanner." He takes three wide steps away from me and spreads his wings, shaking them out once.

And dammit if I don't want him to go.

"Hey, wait!" I call after him and scramble out from behind the railing.

He stops and turns, wings tucked in closer to not brush into me. "What?"

I skid to a halt. "You… you haven't even told me your name."

He cocks his head and gives me that crooked smile. "You didn't ask." He lifts one hand in greeting. "Jamin. Jamie. Nice to meet you, Lea." One wink that shoots right to my core, and he lifts off with one big push, wings spread wide, the breeze catching under them and lifting him up and higher.

"Nice to meet you too, Jamie," I whisper.

Jamie.

The next hours, I'm either not sure meeting Jamie really happened or cursing myself for letting it happen. More than once, I consider running, but it's not a good idea in broad daylight. Scanners everywhere. Witnesses too numerous to count.

If I wanted to run, I needed to do so at night, and maybe he's right and I should. The less people know where I am, the better, Founders included. *Jamie* included, because I'm not sure I should trust him. Yes, I'm still alive, and that's a major bonus point right there, but I'm still at his mercy. He could change his mind at any given time and then I'm screwed. My parents may have been the first to fall victim to the Founders, but by no means were they the last. Punishment comes swiftly and isn't postponed. Every Founder can kill an unlimited number of humans without breaking a sweat. To them, we come a dime a dozen, and we pay dearly for our mistakes. Only once, but dearly.

As the sun rises and the day warms up I hide in the same Ferris wheel cabin I slept in last night. Not because Jamie asked me to, but because even though this area is deserted, Santa Monica and the PCH are not, and I could easily be spotted.

After a while, I fall asleep only to jerk awake when somebody touches my knee. "Shh. Lea. *Lea!* Wake up!"

"Hell!" I scramble up, heart hammering like somebody put a defibrillator to it. "What the—?"

Jezza.

"You?" I scoot back to create distance between him and me. "How'd you find—?"

Hurt lights up in his eyes when he sees me move away from him. "How I found you? I know you, Lea. This is a place you came to with your parents, so of course I'd be looking here. Figured you wouldn't take a hotel while you're marked with Founder blood on you." He scans over my body, eyes narrowed. "And seriously, what were you thinking? You touched a Founder, Lea! You of all people should know how badly that can end!"

Whoa. Low-blow.

I jump to my feet, fingers curled to fists. "Thanks for that reminder, Jezza! No, really, I needed that, because I was this close to not give a dime and walk out there like that!" I jab a finger in the general direction of Santa Monica.

Anger tightens his features. "You're welcome for the reminder. And just so that you know, I've been searching for you all night, and the only reason why I haven't given up yet is because no infraction was reported, and if that fuckin' Founder would've found you, you'd be zapped out of existence already." A muscle throbs along his temple. "And when he finds you—and let me just say that this here is not the smartest hideout you could come up with—then it won't matter what you did last night, it won't matter he didn't finish you off last night. This time he will kill you. No doubt about it."

No, he won't.

My mouth opens and closes, yet I don't tell him. What am I supposed to say? *Oh, sorry, he found me already, but he's kinda… different? Nice? For a Founder, at least?*

Yeah.

No.

Jezza curses under his breath. "You have a Founder gunning for your head, and here you are, out in the open…"

Okay, granted, maybe picking this spot was not my smartest move given that Jamie also found me already, but the way Jezza's standing there, judging me, preaching to me as if it wasn't his fault that I'm in this mess, rubs me the wrong way.

My skin pricks with anger. I cross my arms in front of my chest. "Oh, but please don't forget whose fault that is. Wait—who was *beating up a Founder* last night? What the hell, Jezza?" Might as well get that talk out of the way. I shake my head left to right. "Where are the hooded guys, and what is going on with you?"

He sighs and opens the little door supposed to keep passengers from falling out of the cabin. "No hooded guys. Listen, Lea. I… we need to talk." He steps aside to make room for me as I move out of the cabin. "You know how the Sisters got me to enlist as a soldier to support the Founders?"

I nod. Of course I do. It's something I didn't—and still don't—know how to handle. He was there. With me. He saw what they can do. How Jezza could enlist… I don't get it. Just because the Sisters convinced him to give it a shot and got him a job interview? Once there, he aced all entrance exams. Best in all physical tests. Second-best in all written exams. From there on, his career path was clear and Jezza seemed all excited. With him, the Founders will gain not just a soldier, but a leader, but I'm going to lose a friend. My best friend.

Jezza sighs again and scratches his head. "So, I'm not really enlisting because I want to serve the Founders." He moves into the shade of an old awning.

"You're not." I take position across from him, back toward the sea, facing him and keeping an eye on the pier. He had two buddies with him yesterday. I trust him. I don't trust them.

"No, I'm not. I…" He pinches the bridge of his nose with two fingers and releases it together with a big breath. "Lea… okay, this is kinda hard, but… I've joined the Resistance. I'm going to be perfect for them once I'm high up in the food chain with the Founders. Their inside mole. I'm—"

No freakin' way. "What?" My jaw drops open. "Are you crazy, Jezza? That's a death sentence right there! You know what'll happen if—no, *when* they find you out, because they will! You—"

"It's what I want to do, Lea!" He mimics me and jabs a finger in the general direction of Santa Monica. "I'm tired of this! Tired of living the life they choose for me, of watching my every word, of serving the Lord I've never seen nor care about, and all that crap! I'm tired of it! And if I can make the smallest bit of a difference, or heck, maybe even more than that, then I'm going to take that chance!"

A rush of hot betrayal shoots through my veins. "And you didn't even think to tell me? Nothing? Not a word? If I hadn't stumbled across you beating up that Founder last night, when would I have found out? At your funeral?"

Seagulls flutter up and shriek. For a second, a large shadow crosses over us, the short drop in temperature bringing goosebumps to my arms. Or maybe it's Jezza's idiotic and risky behavior. The way he deflates is all the answer I need. "You wouldn't have told me. Ever." I shake my head. "Wow. Just… wow, Jezza."

He chews on his lower lip. "If I had told you, you'd be at risk, and I'm doing this to help people, not to endanger them. Especially you." He looks at me like a puppy dog kicked to the curb.

So what was last night then? Jezza's initiation? Or has he been with them for a while, and if so, how the heck could I not have known? Jezza is my best friend—my only friend—and we're family.

I *should* have known.

I groan. "You suck, Jezza. You really do." But I get it. Well, part of me gets it. The other part will hold this betrayal against him until we die—which, in Jezza's case, might be sooner than I expected. "Why can't you just find something else to do? Look at me, I'm blissfully floating around in a bubble of cluelessness."

Jezza cocks an eyebrow. "Right now, I'd say that bubble burst when you got that Founder's blood on you." His expression hardens. "Speaking of. That Mark changed things."

"Ya think?"

"Obviously." He ignores my sarcasm. "Passed by the orphanage this morning. They're in panic mode, because their precious Protégée didn't come home last night. You don't have much longer, and it will be all over the news, plus search parties. Police. Church volunteers. You know how that goes."

Crap. Yeah, I know. Sister Bethanie, bless her ninety-year-old soul, fainted once on a walk. Low blood sugar or something. Once they realized she was missing, it took the Sisters less than fifteen minutes to get a hundred-people search party together and less than two hours to find her. But what saved Sister Bethanie's life could end mine. Maybe I underestimated the chaos my disappearance would cause. No, obviously I did. "So, what do I do? Besides hide and wait, I mean?" Wait for either the Mark to wear off or my execution commando to arrive? Thrilling choice, really.

Jezza lifts and drops his shoulders. "Well, your options are kind of limited—" He stops in mid-sentence and squints down the Pier. "Shit!" His hands ball to fists. "Get behind me and let me do the talking."

One look down the same direction and my blood pressure spikes into stroke-territory courtesy of the two wide-shouldered guys who must've scaled the fence and are jogging our way: Red-Hoodie and Blue-Hoodie. Just awesome, really, because I'm on a pier! At the freakin' end of it! Outrunning the guys is not an option, and out-swimming them is out of the question.

I grab his sleeve. "What are they going to do? Kill me?" Because that's what Red-Hoodie wanted yesterday, and his reasons haven't changed. I can still ID Jezza.

He flinches. "I don't know. Hud won't, but with Ice I never know. I don't think so, or they would have their guns out already."

Not the rousing endorsement I was hoping for, but I guess I'll have to take it.

The two guys, still wearing their hoodies from last night, only with the hood down on their shoulders today, slow down to a fast walk once they realize I'm not running. They stop a meter or two in front of us. Birds around and above us break out in alarmed shrieks and fly off one of the old store's roof.

"You found her." Red Hoodie nods at me behind Jezza's back. "Good job."

"Thanks, Ice, but you better keep your hands off her."

Ice grins. "I don't think that's your decision to make."

"It's not yours either."

"Oh, but I think it is." Red-Hoodie reaches into his waistband and draws his gun.

I suck in a sharp breath, and so does Jezza, but before I can do as much as get my hands up to defend myself, a shadow falls over us accompanied by a brush of air—and with a thump, Jamie lands in a crouch behind the two hooded guys, wings extended wide, shoulders stiff. He jumps to his feet and raises his palms, blue light glowing from them. "The oaf was right. Again. Not your decision to make."

CHAPTER SIX

Opposite Day

As if slapped, Ice and his buddy whirl around. While Blue-Hoodie looks like he wants to run, Ice raises his gun. "You," he hisses, recognition flaring in his eyes. "In the mood for some more punishment?"

Jamie keeps his palms aimed at them and growls. "More for payback today."

No trace is left of the boy who gave himself over to the beating, or the boy who sat next to me a couple of hours ago and talked to me like equals. This is a full-blown Founder, head to toe and in-between. His wide frame looks even more impressive with his wings extended, their feathers thick and full. Despite wearing some kind of tactical pants and shirt it's clear the body beneath that doesn't carry a gram of unnecessary fat. Nope. He's muscle, through and through. Dangerous.

What would have made me run in the opposite direction a mere twelve hours ago now makes me understand the fascination people have with Founders. They're powerful. Powerful, beautiful, and about a dozen other words that end on *-ful*. Revengeful probably too. Or graceful, like Jamie, despite the sheer aggression radiating off him. "Lea, get away from them."

Jezza chokes on his next breath. "Wait, how does he know y—" I can all but hear the *click* as the gears fall into place and he realizes that *the Founder I touched* found me already. The one *gunning for my head,* as he put so nicely.

I shrug. "We've met a couple of hours ago." And it was surprisingly… normal.

Jezza shakes his head, disbelieving. "You met *after* you touched him?"

I nod.

Jezza unfreezes with a strangulated grunt, takes another step back and pulls a gun from his waistband. "Power down, Founder! You're not going to finish what you started, no matter what you're playing at!"

He carries a *gun*? What the—

Jamie doesn't flinch. Keeping both arms extended, it takes no more than a slight adjustment to aim one at Ice plus Hud, and the other one at Jezza. On his left wrist a small, round device is attached to a leather sleeve I could swear wasn't there earlier today. "How dramatic. You're only making me more angry, human. I'm going to let Lea live, but I'm considering revoking that privilege for the three of you." He wiggles his fingers, the blue light dancing across his skin.

The threat isn't lost on Ice. "You try, and we'll fight you every step of the way, Demon. We've got enough bullets between us that we can bring you to your knees, and then…" His free thumb makes a slicing gesture across his throat.

Jamie's Caeruleum cranks up in intensity. "You won't even get to fire the first one, human. Not today. Last chance. One, two—"

Oh, holy cow. "Stop it! Both of you! Everybody! Can we maybe get through this without any killing?" I throw my hands up in exasperation. "Yes, you're all dangerous and bad, but Ice—" That was Ice, right? "—your chances are minimal. You know that. Your bullet didn't kill him yesterday and most likely even several won't. They might do nothing to slow him down, and then *poof*." He'll be dust before he can make true of his threat and cut Jamie's head off—so far, the only proven way to kill a Founder. I turn to Jamie. "And you didn't kill me, so please, don't start with these knuckleheads. They're annoying, but not worth it."

Jamie raises an amused eyebrow at me.

Jezza whisper-hisses in my direction. "Yeah, speaking of. He found you—why are you still alive?" His gaze darts back from Jamie to me. "What did you do? Where's the catch?"

I put my hands on my hips. "Geez, Jezza, thanks for the empathy." Doesn't mean I hadn't wondered the same thing, but still.

Ice's grip around the gun tightens to the point of his knuckles turning white. "But a very good question. Why would a demon not fulfill his duty and kill—" He tilts his head to the left. "Wait a second. I know you. I've seen you before. Before last night." He laughs out once. "No way. No freakin' way." Another laugh, this one condescending.

The muscles in Jamie's jaw work overtime. "You don't know me. There are lots of us."

Ice's grin turns smug. "Let's just say you're memorable." He takes one step closer to Jamie, closer to the palm that could kill him in an instant. "I'd like to offer you a deal, Demon."

Jamie huffs, unimpressed. "Right. A deal. You're not exactly in the right position—"

"Oh, but I am." Ice looks pointedly first at me, then to Jamie's sides. "Beautiful wings you have, mate."

Pause.

Pause.

Pause.

Both guys stare at each other, Ice's face controlled, cool, superior, and Jamie's chest rising and falling out of rhythm, expression on his face unreadable. His hands ball into fists, capturing the Caeruleum's blue light for a second before it's back aimed at Ice.

A growl leaves his throat. "What do you want?"

Boom.

With this one sentence, the power balance has shifted. Whatever passed between those two, it gave Ice the upper hand. And he knows it.

Ice tilts his head. "Glad you're a reasonable chap. Here's the deal. My proposition is easy. Actually, you both might like it." He gives me a fake happy thumbs up. "I have need for people, especially on the inside, and guess what, Demon—you fit the bill. And you, little miss, you're manpower we need. You two have just joined the Resistance. Congratulations."

For one unbelievable second, silence hovers. I didn't hear that right, did I? Then, Jamie laughs out once. "Funny idea. But not going to happen."

Right he is. "I second that. Not going to happen." Joining the Resistance? Excuse me? I don't know what's more laughable, the thought of me joining, or of Jamie. No, easy. A Founder working for the Resistance is about as impossible as unicorns and dancing fairies. Not going to happen.

Ice doesn't mind the difference in opinion. "Oh yes. It is going to happen. In fact, it has just happened. Membership cards will follow, stat."

Jamie regards Ice down his nose, a scowl on his face that could kill on sight. "I'd dial it down a touch, if I were you. You're an easy kill, human—"

Ice's smile turns over-confident. "Yeah? Then why don't you show me how easy it is to kill me? All I hear is talk, talk, talk." He holds up his gun, lets it dangle from his fingers—and shoves it under his waistband, taking a step closer to Jamie. "Show me," he whispers. "Be brave."

"What the hell, Ice?" Hud pulls on the other man's shirt. "You crazy? Keep your gun out."

Oh, crap.

Is he suicidal? Whatever Jamie's deal is, he must have a limit. Taunting him is so not the right way to go. Anytime now he'll—

Ice shakes Hud off and inches closer to Jamie, a challenging gleam in his eyes. "No, I'm not crazy. Just well informed. You, my dear Founder, will join the Resistance and pledge your allegiance. You know why. And as an additional incentive, there is a video of last night, ya know?" One raised eyebrow addresses me. "I assume you know that is a death sentence for you, my dear? Touching a Founder? If it should ever leak, I mean…"

An abyss opens beneath my feet. "You'd sell me out?" He'd throw a fellow human under the bus, just like that?

"Can't have you run around identifying my men. So, you better reevaluate your priorities. You cooperate, or else your video goes viral, and then bye-bye." He wiggles his fingers, then focuses back on Jamie. "So yeah. As I was saying. Video. Of you getting touched by a human. And not killing her." He pointedly looks at his cuticles and blows on them. "Just saying. Somebody might be interested in that."

The tension between those two is so loaded, all the tiny hairs on my body rise in response. Never mind joining the Resistance or not, if this blows up—if Jamie blows up—I have a different problem. "Guys, maybe we should—"

Jamie prowls closer to Ice. Instinctively, Jezza and Hud take a step back for every one he moves forward—not me though. Not Ice. He holds his ground, only the fast beat of the pulse in his neck suggesting he isn't quite as comfortable as he wants Jamie to believe.

I twist my body so I'm in-between Jamie and Ice, arms outstretched, a referee in this potential death match. "Seriously, guys—"

Jamie stops before my outstretched hand would've touched him. He curls his fingers into a fist, capturing the blue light on their insides. "A video," he growls, eyes shooting daggers at Ice. "You don't know a thing, human, and whatever you think you know will bite you in the butt. I am a Founder. Not a human. Neither a resistance fighter, nor a traitor to my people, and I don't care about yours."

I gotta say, he has a point, to a point, at least. "Us joining is not going to happen, so back off." Us—there is this stupid us again. When did that become a thing?

Ice remains unimpressed. "It isn't? You like to reconsider?" He steps back from my hand, and, in one smooth motion, draws his gun—and aims it straight at me. "Because if you're not on my good side, you're definitely on my bad one. I don't have a problem finishing what I started yesterday. You're a risk factor."

A wave of cold rolls over me, numbing every cell down to its core. "You're kidding me." I was trying to keep them from hurting each other and now—

"Sorry, hon." Ice doesn't sound sorry at all. "Nothing personal."

The lump in my throat is hard to talk around. "Feels like it though, asshole." I stare into the nozzle as if I could see the bullet waiting for me.

Ice's smile turns sugary sweet. "And, Demon, you can thank me after I kill her. She's only a human, as you so nicely phrased it. I'm sure you won't mind if I take care of your and my problem. Our problem."

Click.

Safety is off, and time slows to a crawl. My next breath comes out in a wheeze.

Jezza: "Fuck, Ice—"

Jamie *growls,* the blue light picking up in intensity.

Hud whispers, "Shit."

Ice: "One. Two. Thr—"

"Fuck it, Ice! She's the Protégée!" Jezza stomps his foot and punches a fist into his palm.

With a screeching sound, life goes back to full speed.

Jezza is panting, eyes wide, hands up and extended toward Ice, as if he could calm him down like that.

Everybody's eyes are on me, wide, disbelieving, including Jamie's.

Ice's almost pop out of their sockets. "She is—you are the First?"

And there we go again. My only life-defining attribute, and apparently also my only life-saving attribute. "Uhh, yeah. That's me. The First."

The apple in Jamie's throat bobs up and down as confusion flickers over his face. Ice on the other hand chuckles. No, snickers. Actually, laughs full out, clapping his thigh with the hand that doesn't hold the gun.

"Oh my God. This is hilarious. Fate delivers me the one

demon with a conscience and tops it off with the Protégée. Hilarious." He snickers some more and wipes a tear from his eye. "But fun aside. Here's the deal. The new and improved deal. Demon, little Protégée, you two are still becoming valuable members of our little society. If you want to live, that is. But we're going to spice it up. Maybe peace will indeed be victorious." His index and middle finger form a V as he taps them twice over his heart. "Because you, my dear Protégée, will become the Demon's servant."

Silence.

For a moment—a blissful, peaceful, way-too-short moment—I'm a hundred percent sure I misheard what he said. Because it can't have been real.

"I'm not becoming a servant," I say at the same time Jamie says, "I'm not taking her as a servant."

Glad we agree on that.

Ice hands his gun to Hud and crosses his arms in front of his chest. One foot taps a fast rhythm onto the wooden planks. "Too bad, so sad. But really guys, you have no choice. You know *you* don't." He nods at Jamie, whose wings arch higher. The briefest emotion flickers in his eyes, gone too fast to identify before he has it back under control.

I get Ice's next nod. "Neither do you, hon. The Watchers will eventually find you, and once they do, they'll scan you and this one's Mark is all over you. *Boom,* you're gone."

"You have little faith in my abilities to hide." I cross my arms in front of my chest. Granted, at this point, I don't have much faith in said abilities either, but I'll take it over slavery. If I can make it off this pier, I can make it, period. It's going to be tough for weeks, but I can hide. I can get through this.

Ice rubs his chin. "Okay, let's say you're awesome at hiding and got lucky… I mentioned I have a video, right? Of you touching a Founder? Twice? I'm sure the Watchers would love to get their hands on it."

And there's that. "Oh, come on! You're such an ass." I stomp my foot. "Seriously?" It's me signing up for slavery or death?

Ice winks at me. "Aww, hon. I'm fine with New Servitude—"

"Well, I'm not." Traditional Servitude, New Servitude—same difference. Only distinction is that New Servitude gives the human a tad more leeway. Not freedom: leeway.

"Plus, I got you a good one for Servitude. He's cute—"

"Now, hold on a second." Jezza holds up one finger. "I'm all for Lea joining the Resistance—"

Excuse me, what? *Now* he starts talking? And this crap? "Really? What's gotten into you? Are you—?"

He shoots me an angry glance that shuts me up. "As I said, I'm all for it. The Protégée-slash-First is going to be a big help. I told you, you needed to decide what you wanted to do with your life, and forcing the decision in the right direction… I'm fine with that. What I'm not fine with is tying you to *him*."

That's not quite the only thing I'm not fine with, but I'll take it.

Ice sighs like a father annoyed by his children, although he's not that much older than us, late twenties maybe. He'd probably look younger if he hadn't shaved his dirty-blond hair down to a four-millimeter buzz-cut, but oh well. "Summing it up. Girl, you play along or you're dead, by me or a Watcher. Demon, you play along or… the video leaks, and well, you know."

You know what? There's nothing in the world that could bring a Founder to cooperate with a human, no matter he didn't kill me.

For an eternal second, Jamie closes his eyes. Any time now, he's going to come up with an idea how to best kill Ice, or at least how to inflict some serious damage, and then I won't have to worry about this ridiculous idea anymore. Sorry, Ice. Not personal, either.

Jamie's eyes fly open again, a sad, beaten smile pulling the corners of his mouth up. His hands curl into a fist—and the blue light turns off as he lets them sink down.

Uhh… My stomach twists. "You… you're agreeing?" I blink twice. "Why?" Why, why, why? And where does that leave me?

"Good boy," Ice purrs, stuffing his hands down his pockets.

A wary expression flickers across Jamie's face when he directs his next words at me, ignoring Ice. "May… may I suggest we go down this hellhole together? Unfortunately, he has a point. That's why I wanted to get the scanner, to show you." Jamie raises the wrist with the leather sleeve and round scanner-disc attached to it. He tilts it to read the display. "You're not only marked, but knee-deep in the Red Zone, and without proper shelter, you're an easy find. The only reason why no Watcher has come to investigate at this point is because you did choose your hiding spot well off the beaten path. But with a Mark of this magnitude, it's only a matter of time."

My blood pressure drops through the floor no matter his validation of my hiding abilities. What kind of parallel universe am I in where a Founder tries to convince me to join the Resistance? Together with him?

He watches me with a serious intensity. "Red Zone," he

repeats for emphasis, tapping the scanner once.

Red Zone. "I got it," I grumble. Okay, he's right. They are all right. This Mark is a biggie. But then— "I'm of no use to you when I'm marked. How can I *work for the Resistance* when I'm lighting up on every scanner I walk past?" I push my chin forward. Got you there.

Ice seems less than impressed. "Actually, not a problem. Honey, please realize, I'm giving you your only way out, and just for emphasis, playing along is your only chance. What do you think will happen when you don't return home? Will they just write off their precious Protégée? No. They'll look for you. Hard. And when they find you…" He makes an explosion motion with his hands. "*Boom.* Good-bye, Protégée. Becoming a servant is the only way to explain why you're not coming home, because—"

"Because I'm in training," I whisper. Oh, holy crap. He might… he might have a point. Judging by what Jezza told me about the panic in the orphanage over my skipping curfew… But if I was in training, secluded from society until my training was complete, it would be different. One notice by Jamie to the orphanage and nobody'd be looking for me. After all, it would make sense for the Protégée to answer the call and become a servant to the Founders. To cater to their every need. To serve and make a contribution, so that her life is spent best for Him, the Lord, in return for sparing it all those years ago.

Oh, the irony. The only option to save my life is to do the one thing I swore to never do, fake or not.

Jezza stomps over to Ice and yanks the other man around by his shoulder. "You're talking crap. Whatever you're playing at— servants aren't allowed to touch the Founders either." Jezza jerks his chin first at Jamie, then at me. "Stop messing with her.

Nothing will explain a Mark of this magnitude—"

With a quick turn, Ice frees himself from Jezza's grasp. His gaze hardens. "Obviously, you're behind, Jez, so let me break it down and explain the game for you. I'm not messing with her. Ask him. Servants are one of the few groups they do cut some slack. Am I right, Mr. Expert-in-all-things-servant?"

Terse silence hangs between them. Jamie's eyes harden with the scathing look he sends Ice. "During *training*, yes. Mistakes happen. Working closely with a Founder for 24/7 while learning the ropes is bound to leave some kind of Mark. We even expect it to a certain degree, but that only counts for training. Once a servant has pledged their oath, any contamination leads to punishment." He yanks his thumb across his throat in the same slashing gesture Ice used a few minutes ago.

I don't like the sound of that. Fear clamps itself around my heart, strangulating it for all its worth. Nothing about this sounds good. Nothing. I can't run, I can't hide, and I can't join the Resistance—least of all as a servant. This must be a bizarre misunderstanding of ginormous proportions.

As if Jamie could read my mind, his mouth curls into a soft, regretful smile. There's a warm sheen in his crystal blue eyes that tears at my heart and wiggles itself into my soul. "I'd prefer you not getting killed by my people, Lea. Posing as my servant *in training* and staying hidden is your only chance to get away with the Mark on you, as much as we both dislike it. If we work together, we can do this."

My heart dares to stutter at the meaning of his words. He cares. He cares whether I'm dead or alive—but why would he? Why—?

"What. Are. You. Playing. At?" Jezza growls at Jamie, pulling himself up to his full height.

"I'd say the game both of us are trying to play is called survival," Jamie deadpans. "Both our options are limited at this point." He keeps his voice exceptionally level.

No kidding, but why is he on board with that? I shake my head. Never mind this parallel universe where a Founder agrees to join the Resistance rather than destroy the humans in front of him. At the moment, that doesn't even rank close to my top concern.

"But… But I don't want to be a servant." It comes out as a croak.

Anything but a servant. Anything.

Jamie's voice is soft, a warm breeze for my soul. "I know. And I don't want a servant."

And yet here we are.

Ice rolls his eyes. "Oh, for heaven's sake. Listen—"

"No, actually. You listen." Jamie pulls his shoulders straight. It gives his wings a little tilt, the feathers ruffled by the slight breeze. "You may have the upper hand for now, but the only thing I'm agreeing to is training. Nothing more. We're not going through the Pledge-Ceremony. We'll call off Servitude training before that becomes an option. We can cite irreconcilable differences. Neither of us will get a Vinculum." His gaze gives me a lightning-quick scan.

Heck, I hadn't even thought that far. The Vinculum, stupid Bracelet of Servitude. Once a Founder and his servant have gone through training, they take the Pledge in front of Michael, which is nothing else than the human swearing his or her loyalty to the Founder. Then they both get that idiotic bracelet, the Vinculum, around their wrist as the official sign of their *connection*. Vinculum translates to *bond* from Latin—and, ironically, also to *prison* and *captivity*. Fitting, since once it's fastened around somebody's wrist, it can't be removed. It's for life. Needless to say, I don't want it. Ever.

"Exactly," I squeak. Because once they snap a Vinculum onto my wrist, it'll stay there, and then good-bye, freedom. As if on command, the tiny tattoo on the side of my left breast itches, protesting the very thought of that idea.

"My, my. And here I was thinking all girls liked their bling." Ice cocks an eyebrow at me.

I level him with a cold stare. "Oh, no. Not this one."

Jamie takes a threatening step forward, his body coiled, tension in every muscle. "Are we clear on that? Training, yes. Pledge, no. I can pretend to play the game, but I'm not taking an official servant, whether it's traditional or a New Servant."

A dry, amused huff from Ice. "One should think you learned your lesson, Demon."

"And one should think that was my problem. You have others, me being one of them."

Both guys glare at each other until Ice shrugs. "Doesn't matter to me. Do what you want. I couldn't care less if you pledged or not. Or rather, I agree. Let's keep her in training as long as we can. Works better. As long as both of you keep in mind, I'm the one with the video."

"And speaking of. I want a deal for that."

"What? The video?"

"Yes. I expect you to hand over the video—"

Ice laughs out loud. "I'm sorry—what? No, my friend. I'm not giving you the only thing that gives me control over you. I don't have a death wish. That video is mine, because I'm the one in control." The last part is snarled, as he points a finger at his chest.

Control.

The ground opens beneath my feet and swallows me whole.

Yeah, I've lost all control, that much is clear. And not only that. Once more, for emphasis: If I want to survive, my only option is to become the one thing I said I'd never do, become a servant.

To the people who killed my parents.

CHAPTER SEVEN

Old Zoo

If I thought my world had been turned upside down the last twelve hours, the next two bring it to a whole new level.

Everything is bizarre and surreal, almost like an out-of-body-experience.

Ice and Hud eventually leave to get prepped for Jamie's and my arrival, whatever that means, and while the tension in the air decreases to a bearable level once they're gone, it also leaves me alone with Jezza and Jamie.

And that feels weird.

Neither of them speaks.

Jezza glares at Jamie, aggression radiating from every pore. Last time I saw him this mad was… yeah, never. Not even after I broke up with him.

Jamie, with commendable self-restraint, doesn't take the bait though. He keeps his hands stuffed deep into his pockets, maybe to keep his palms from glowing and incinerating Jezza, who knows, but he doesn't say a word.

Neither do I.

I stay silent as we wait for dusk to set in and people to get off the streets, silent as we leave the pier, this time over the fence, and sneak to the dark back alley where the Resistance's car is parked, silent as Jezza slides behind the wheel and Jamie and I get into the back.

Like in a trance, I watch houses rush past us, other cars, a few pedestrians hurrying to get home before curfew hits, soldiers taking position at the biggest intersections, their faces as blank as always. They must get all emotion drilled out of them during recruitment and training.

A couple of women in their fifties stand in front of a church, holding up signs. *We Want Our Daughters. Show Us Mercy.* Right. Another batch of moms who lost their daughters to Servitude. Maybe I should be happy I don't have a family to leave behind. The separation must be hard. It's like losing their daughters.

Dang it. That thought, it gets to me.

A single tear runs down the side of my face.

I feel Jamie's eyes on me, but I don't look, because if I did... I don't know what he'd see. I blame that on him being a Founder. His mere presence is affecting me, only way different than I thought. I don't need to look, I know how he's sitting in the backseat, wings close to his back and wrapped a bit around his shoulders, so they won't peak out under the jacket draped over his shoulders and touch me. I feel when he looks at me, and when he does, tiny knots twist low in my belly, and they pull on some kind of heart string.

It's pathetic. I know.

Worse, it's pathetic and *unacceptable* to be affected by a Founder, but... he cared.

Jamie is the unexpected player out of left field, and no matter he's a Founder, it's his actions that count. As it is, we're both stuck, although I can't say I understand why he is, and it drives me mad. I don't get him. He lets himself get beaten up, and it looked like he welcomed it. Who does that? Now he agrees to work with Ice. What. Am. I. Missing?

Well, obviously it's something. He doesn't seem eager to get a servant, which is a big plus from where I'm coming from. If he was, I'd be fighting this nail and tooth, because I'm not a servant, fake or not. And I'm not a Resistance fighter either. They can name me the First instead of the Protégée all they want, it won't change I was never made for this. It will never be my battle to fight. I have lost too much too soon. Paid my dues. I'm done.

But I've also got to play the game for now. Bide my time, survive, and make sure I get out of this mess as soon as I can. I'd rather be living on the streets somewhere where Founders are not quite so… *prevalent* as here than even pretend for one more day than necessary I was a servant. I'll figure it out. I'll get out of this mess somehow.

Jezza drives us up Vine and over to Franklin, then takes some small, dark street off the main road into Griffith Park. He kills the lights as soon as he is around a tight corner in the street and slows to a crawl. It's that dark already.

The illuminated instrument panel throws eerie blue shadows on his hands cramped around the steering wheel. "Listen. Especially you, Demon. Issaac—Ice—is not the soft and cuddly type. Every threat he brings, he means it. I might be fairly new to this, but I can promise you, if you think you can use Lea, be that as your personal servant—"

"I already said I have no interest in taking her as a servant."

"Said the Founder."

"Said the Founder." Jamie gives me another one of those glances that are getting harder and harder to ignore.

Jezza grabs the wheel tighter. "I don't trust you, Demon. Everything around you reeks of trap. Trojan horse. *Something.*"

Pretty elaborate set up, but I see his point.

Jezza's eyes flick up to the mirror at Jamie in the back. "I'll be watching you, and I won't be the only one. And just as a fair warning, if you misbehave with Lea, I will find you, and then Unforgivable Sin or not…"

"Understood." Jamie's voice is calm. Accepting.

"Wonderful." Jezza pulls into an old, overgrown clearing that probably used to be a parking area once upon a time. He rolls forward, so that most of the car is hidden from aerial view by branches and leaves. "We're here. Move it."

Jamie and I unlock our seat belts and get out of the car, Jamie way faster than me. As soon as he's standing tall, he rips off the jacket Jezza made him drape over his shoulders to hide his wings, and spreads them. A soft groan slips from his lips he covers with a cough.

He points at the trees the car is partially hidden under. "This won't keep Founders from finding you."

"It has so far. Two cars got seen and towed. That's it. They don't have a reason to come looking for us, because for all they know, there's nothing here." And they'd be right with that. Griffith Park used to be one of the most frequented weekend getaway locations, but with the Founders changing things up for us humans, nobody is allowed in it after sundown anyway. Haven't been here in over a decade.

Jamie pulls his wings closer. "So, where are you leading us then?"

"You'll see, Demon. And before you get too excited, this is only our backup location." Translation, should you rat us out, the damage is minimal. Not even Ice is crazy enough to invite a Founder into the Main Evil Lair. Whatever he has on Jamie, it must have a limit. It for sure has for me—namely as long as it takes to get rid of the Mark, and until I get my hands on that stupid video.

"We're usually safe driving to the parking area, and from there, it'll be us on foot. Surveillance up here is sporadic at best, especially at night." Jezza leads the way through the dark. Despite this being a moderately clear night, I still can't see squat, which means I'm the only one stumbling like an idiot. Jezza obviously knows the terrain, and Jamie could see with way less light than now. Great. Feels good being the klutz.

After about five minutes, we pass a structure that looks vaguely familiar, no matter the dark. Round. Pointed roof. A fence around it.

I stop dead in my tracks, yanked to a halt by years of suppressed memories.

No way.

"Is that… is that the old carousel?" Memory brings back the scent of my childhood: popcorn. Fresh waffle cones to hold the ice cream. Warm cheese melting over delicious nachos. Nothing was better than an afternoon spent here. Picnicking, hiking, topping it off with a round or two on the merry-go-around and popcorn to take home. Once in a while, Dad took me here on a Sunday, and more often than not we also brought Jezza.

The pause before he answers is proof enough he remembers it too. "Yeah. Obviously, it's not working anymore." He clears his throat, then keeps on walking uphill. "Glad you're talking again."

"I'm not," I growl.

"Uh-huh."

I throw another glance back at the place of happy childhood memories. Ten years of neglect didn't make it any better, of course. From what I can make out with the little bit of moonlight, the red-and-white roof over the merry-go-round is tattered and torn, and the carousel itself doesn't look much better. But the horses are still there, most even still standing, and if I squint through half-closed eyelids, I can almost pretend it could start at any moment.

Oh, well. Dwelling on it will only add to my misery.

With a sigh, I tear myself from the view and follow Jezza, acutely aware of Jamie's curious eyes on me. Should've known Founders wouldn't get it. After all, they closed down all this in the first place.

We hike in silence. Not even five minutes later, we reach a rock formation and what's left of an old, thick, iron fence, rusted in places, busted and bent out of shape in others.

"Welcome to your new home." Jezza jumps over a row of knee-high boulders and enters a clearing with a rock wall to its three other sides.

Wait, if the carousel was down there, then this is… "The abandoned zoo?" With a *click,* the image in front of me aligns with a decade-old memory of this place. Old, abandoned ruins that used to be animal enclosures. Some large, some small, some designed like an outdoor enclosure with rocks, fake caves, etc., others merely bare cages, but all unused for over fifty years, or since whenever the new zoo opened a couple of miles over. Farther up the hill is—at least was—an old house, graffiti covering every inch of its insides. They might've had reptiles in there when it was still in use, who knows?

Jezza holds out a hand to help me jump the boulders. "Yup. Our backup location."

Huh? I'm not getting it. "How can this be a Resistance hideout?" The enclosures are destroyed, there's absolutely no protection from unwanted view. Nothing but old cages and habitats, all rotting away day after day.

Jezza sighs. "The old tunnels, Lea. Above ground, there's not much left, but below ground, the tunnels are still there. And more. You'll see."

Jamie easily steps over the boulders and groans. "You're down there? There isn't even enough room to spread my wings."

"That's one reason why we chose it, Demon. Another is that Lea is basically glowing in the dark thanks to you, and your scanners won't pick up on it from below the surface." Jezza glowers at the Founder and leads us into the Lion's Den, quite literally. "This used to be the stairs the employees could use to access the cages." He points to a narrow staircase leading up and to an iron-wrought door. "As it is, we'll access the underground through here." He points at the inconspicuous door at the end of the stairs and places his hand on an area next to it.

With a click, the door unlocks. Look at that. I take it the old zoo had some upgrades since the Resistance took over.

Jezza motions for Jamie and me to enter. "After you."

The stairs are old, uneven, and tricky to maneuver. As soon as the last of us—Jezza—has stepped through and closed the door behind us, soft lights turn on. Better. At least there's light, although it still doesn't make any of this inviting.

When the zoo was built, humanity was in a different stage of technological development. They must've been shorter, too, because Jezza and Jamie can barely stand up straight under this low ceiling. For Jezza, that means there's only a couple of inches to the ceiling for him, but Jamie's the one whose hair brushes across it when he's walking tall. Everything is narrow: the hallway, the doors leading to the left and right of it, the few rooms I can throw a glance into. Most of them are empty, and all of them look… old. Rough walls, dirty, with holes and crumbled concrete on the floor beneath them, as if moths or something had had a go at them. The lights dangle off an electric cord that has seen better days. Some of the bulbs are out, and it gives the hallway a creepy, spooky feeling.

After about a hundred feet or so, Jezza stops in front of a door on the right. "This is your room. *Your* as in plural." He hesitates. "Just so that you both know, Ice has made you responsible for the other one. Either of you acts up, the other one pays for it." He faces Jamie. "Which means you act up, I'll hunt your ass down. Got it?"

"Got it." Good for Jamie, Jezza didn't see his fast eye roll, because his attention is on me already. He takes me by the sleeve and leads me a couple of steps away from Jamie. "Lea?" He sucks in his lower lip. "I'm sorry I told him you're the Protégée. I didn't want Ice to… You know, I—" The look he gives me speaks of years of friendship and a time when there was more.

I place a hand on his forearm. "I know, Jezza." He'd never do anything to intentionally hurt me.

He covers my hand with his and squeezes once. "I wish you had listened to me last night. I wish you'd just run, and none of this would've happened." He chews on his cheek. "I'm so mad at you, Lea. I—"

Oh, no, wait a second. "You're not the only one mad, Jezza! You joined the freakin' Resistance!"

"That's different, I—"

"Really? Hypocrite much? You said you were all for me joining the Resistance—"

"Because you wanted to and on your own terms! Not with a

freakin' demon glued to your hip!" He jabs an angry finger at Jamie. "And to me, this is a matter of honor. Of freedom. You and I, we both know firsthand what's at risk when Founders get involved, and I can't let that happen. Humanity has always risen to its challenges, and that's what the Resistance is here for."

I stare at him wide-eyed. "You sound like a recruitment flyer."

His lips press into a thin line. "Whatever. I will spend—and most likely give—my life fighting them. I won't sit by and watch them take Earth from us and turn us into their servants while they're waiting for their Lord to arrive and knuckle us under even more. They will pay for what they did, and I promise you, they won't have much more time." Anger shines from his eyes, and the raw emotion, it scares me. Jezza is gentle. Jezza is good. Yes, Jezza is also impulsive, but he isn't stupid. He'd never sign up if he thought—

I suck in a sharp breath. "You're preparing for battle." If Jezza thinks they don't have much more time...

A quick glance at Jamie waiting in front of the door on the left. "Yes," he hisses, "not much longer. And this battle, it will free Earth."

Oh, hell. I shake my head so fast I turn dizzy. "Jezza, that's suicide. There are way too many Founders. Way too many hives. We don't stand a chance—"

"We do. See, we don't know how many Founders there are, but Ice and the Resistance are thinking—and I agree—they're less than they make us think. No pictures, no videos, no nothing allowed—no way to keep track. They're fooling us, and we let them." His features harden. "But we will win this when the time comes. Until then, I need you to stay alert. I don't trust him. This whole I-don't-take-servants-crap, and then he hears you're the

Protégée and he's all on board? Stinks of deceit, like all of them." His voice turns urgent. "So please, Lea, I need you to watch your back. And in the grand scheme of things, I don't just mean him."

A cold shudder runs down my spine. "Yeah. I get it." Yay for me, because my life rests in the hands of a crazy Resistance fighter—and a Founder.

I've come full circle, it appears.

The room Jamie and I get is small and damp, like everything here. It's pretty obvious Jamie is uncomfortable being underground and in such narrow quarters, and I can't say I like it either, but overall, I still like it a whole lot better than being dead.

Like the hallway, the ceiling is low, even for me. One lonely lightbulb dangles from the center of the ceiling, covered in grime and flickering here and there.

Lovely, really.

The door closes behind us—and the lock clicks once.

Jamie's brows move up to his hairline. "Good to see they trust us."

I huff once. "Don't tell me you expected them to."

"Not at all." His features harden. Guess he's not going to become besties with Ice and Co either.

I cross the room toward the bed on the right side. Neither of them looks any better than the other, but this one is closer to the door in the wall next to it.

I open it. "Bathroom." From the 1950s and cold, with one chipped toilet without a lid and a shower that makes my skin crawl. Somebody has put out towels and clothing on a small, more modern cabinet next to the sink, and I get the hint. Time to get rid of my blood-stained outfit. "I'm calling dibs on this bed." I kick against its frame. "Be back in ten. Need to scrub your blood off me."

Jamie lowers himself onto his bed. "Of course."

I close the door behind me and make sure it can be locked. Wouldn't want Jamie to get a glimpse at my tattoo. I have enough speaking against me already, no need to add that infraction of Founder-laws to the list.

Never has anybody gotten out of their clothing faster than me. I want whatever is left of that blood gone. And if it wasn't so darn cold in here, I'd stay and enjoy the feeling of the water on my skin no matter the burn from all the cuts I received during my headless flight, but as it is, it's freezing in this room.

Everything is cold. The room. The water. The tile under my feet. But hey, at least I'm clean at the end. No more blood. My first step to getting the Mark off me, and it feels heavenly.

Once I'm done and in blissfully clean clothing, I fall back onto the bed I claimed as mine. Exhausted. More mentally than physically, but I feel like my batteries had been running and running and running, and somebody forgot to charge them. I don't know what has me more on the edge, Jezza's declaration war is about to come, or that I'm in the same room as a Founder, although this Founder is not the worst of their bunch, it appears.

With secrets, but not the worst.

Jamie hasn't moved an inch from his position on his bed. His back is turned to the wall, which leaves him facing my side of the room, although he only stares at his wrist and the scanner around it. One finger circles around the reader, almost gentle, his mind far away and lost in thought. His wings are unfurled as far as the room will allow, stretching from wall to wall. Their white tips melt into the corners of the room where the light doesn't reach.

I roll onto my side and look at him. "What do you think they'll do with us? The Resistance." Because I have no doubt in my mind that Ice will find something that will make me wish I hadn't taken this deal. He'd be stupid not to use the famous Protégée. The question is just *how*.

"Don't know. I'm sure they'll come up with something." He turns the scanner off and lays down, wings acting as a pillow under his upper back. Silence spreads, and while it's comfortable, it weighs heavy.

I work on a dry swallow. "Jamie?" I whisper. "Why'd you do this?"

"Do what?" he mumbles.

"Agree to their terms." And so quickly. Without much of a fight. Worse, without conditions.

He keeps his eyes trained to the ceiling. "Reasons."

Reasons. Sure. "I've said it before, you're a weird Founder."

The smallest smile creeps over his face as he closes his eyes. "And I've said it before, I'll take it as a compliment." Within seconds, Jamie's features relax, and it makes him look so much younger, no matter the stubble, or the masculine frame. Why is he out here, alone? Eating my chips like they were the most expensive delicacies? Why does the stupid video of the night he was beaten up scare him so much? Why, why, why?

No matter how hard I try to connect the dots, it doesn't add up. How am I supposed to make sense of a Founder who's unlike any other?

I sit up in bed. "Jamie?"

"Huh?"

"How old are you?"

He keeps his eyes closed. "Does it matter?" It sounds grumpy.

"Just curious. Eighteen? Nineteen?" In a human I'd say rather nineteen, the way he's built.

He stays silent for another couple of seconds. "Probably."

"What do you mean, probably?" Easy question, easy answer.

A muscle in his jaw tightens, the only sign he's not as relaxed as he's pretending to be. "It means I don't know when my birthday is. I'm not initiated yet, that's all that counts. It doesn't matter."

"Of course you have a birthday, you—"

"I don't." His eyes pop open, and the sincerity in his gaze shuts me up.

"Oh." I clear my throat. "Why not?"

His gaze drifts up to the ceiling. "Because it doesn't matter. We live thousands of years. It matters to nobody. Ask my father."

Ouch. I push my upper body up a bit to get a better look at him. "Okay, so your dad seems a bit weird. How can he not—?"

Jamie cuts his eye at me before he focuses on the ceiling again. "Lea, my father is over two thousand years old. We're allowed one child every generation. He skipped a couple of opportunities for lack of appropriate mates, but as it is, I'm child number seventy-six for him. I'm old news." His thick lashes sweep down once.

"I'm sure your mom sees it differently."

"No mom."

"Kinda tough to be born without a mom, unless you're telling me you were some kind of in vitro-baby?" Although I soften my words with a wink, I wouldn't put it past the Founders.

His gaze stays glued to that one spot on the ceiling above him. "Nope. Regular old procreation, but you noticed you haven't seen a female Founder, right? That's because male children stay with their fathers and females are raised with their mothers. None of them are with us on the hives. It's for their own protection."

We know there are no females. Many people waited for the clichéd blonde, curly-haired female angels, and none came. Something Jezza said once comes to mind. From what he told me, the Founders' reproduction is heavily skewed toward the male chromosomes, meaning, four out of five babies born are male. Sister Mary said it was the Lord's way of making the females more appreciated, but Jezza—and other smart people—think it's because the Founders are a warrior race. Ancient, but still. Males died during their wars, so nature favored the development of male embryos to make up for the loss. Now that they're, uhh, *peaceful,* that rift in numbers is way more obvious, especially since genetic manipulation of the embryo is against their belief, for *you shall love the child given to you no matter their sex or gender.*

Founder or not, I feel a tad of pity for him. "So, you never knew your mom?" At least I had six years, little as it was.

"Never. And it doesn't matter. We're raised for independence, not for weakness. And family ties are a weakness, in case you're wondering. That was a quote."

"By whom?"

"My father."

Just what I needed to make me like the Founders even more. I sit up straighter. "You know what? You guys gotta reevaluate your customs. Maybe humanity is inferior to you in most areas, but this one, we're way ahead of you. Family is important, and so is celebrating each and every member, because…" I bite my lower lip. I'm probably projecting, but… "Because of all people in the world, you should mean the most to your family." Oh, and I'm also romanticizing. Happens when your parents are gone. Maybe

I'm emotionally stuck at a six-year-old level, wouldn't be able to deny that completely. Every night, when my mom tucked me in for bed, she told me how much she loved me and how I was the most special person in the world to her. I miss that. Still. And I'm glad I remember her. And Dad. It's tough not to think of the moment Luke killed them, but I try. It doesn't serve their memory well, and Luke doesn't deserve any more of my brain space than he already has.

Jamie regards me with a silent curiosity. Then, like shaking it off, he cracks his neck twice. "Oh, well. I guess I'm special." He turns away from me onto his side, one wing draped over his body like a protective blanket, every feather smooth and radiant.

I swallow dry.

Special.

Yeah.

Maybe.

CHAPTER EIGHT

Practice Makes Perfect

The next three days make me feel like a prisoner, and I hate it. Oh, of course we're being fed, so that's not it.

It's because Ice makes sure Jamie and I know we're his puppets. Every opportunity he gets, he mentions the video, and it drives me mad. Bad enough I'm marked, but having it documented on video means I can never live this down. There's always a way to blackmail me. The sin of touching a Founder doesn't expire. I could be a hundred years old, and if somebody saw the video, they'd still have every right to *bring me to justice in front of the Lord.*

Splendid, really.

As for Jamie, all he gets is loaded glances and even more pregnant comments I cannot make sense of. Yes, the video wouldn't be good for him either, since he's violating Founder law by letting me live, but it's not his life on the line. He'd get a slap on the wrist, maybe a Stigma burned on his back, but that's it. Me? I'd be dead if the footage ever surfaced.

Which is why I do my very best to be a good prisoner.

Doesn't change that I hate it.

Our freakin' room stays locked at all times, unless Ice, Hud, or some other Resistance-jerk picks us up and brings us to the quote-unquote assembly hall, which is nothing more than what used to be the break room for the zoo's employees.

Once a day, we've been allowed topside, and every time someone stood watch while Jamie shook out his wings, or I jumped up and down to get some blood flow going.

I barely got to see Jezza twice in all this time, and the worst part is I can't tell if it's because they won't let him, or because he's staying away from me. He wasn't exactly happy with me over the last couple of days.

Suits me, I'm not happy right now either—with him or the situation.

"Again," Ice calls from across the room, and it's all I can do to keep from punching somebody.

"We've been over it twenty-five million times," I say, my voice mostly a snarl.

"Then you shouldn't have a problem staying *behind* your Founder and anticipating his needs," Ice replies and pops the top of another soda. "Your basic training must be perfect. What happens then is up to your Founder."

"I won't—"

"You will. Basic training, hon. Stay on it. Need I say your life depends on it, or are you smart enough to figure it out yourself? They won't cut you any slack just because the official plan is to turn you into a *New* Servant. You're still a trainee. Your job is to obey."

My lips press into a hard line. Whatever. Screw the Founders and their Servitude, no matter which kind. Traditional Servitude is nothing but slavery, and New Servitude nothing but a hostile take-over of our society disguised as *serving the Lord and his beautiful creatures.* For the last several months, New Servitude pledges have swamped Earth. There's barely a single influential position in the government, in big corporations, in anything, without a Founder tied to the human behind it. We're losing control over our lives, one position at a time, as the balance of power is shifting even more.

Ice swallows the sip of soda. "Again."

Gah!

My Founder. Anticipating his needs. If Jamie didn't look as tortured as me, I'd have stormed back to our room a long time ago. But yeah, Ice has us. I misbehave, Jamie has to pay for it. To my surprise, I would mind that, no matter he's a Founder. Alas, I'm still to find out how Ice intends to punish an angel, but since Jamie hasn't pushed back on anything so far, I bet he won't start then either.

That boy is a mystery to me.

He has this underlying aggression that never breaks through, no matter how frustrated he looks. He keeps it reined in well better than me, and he is the one going against his nature, if we're honest here. Not me. At least the Resistance are my people, my race.

Jamie cooperates, and sometimes, when he thinks I don't see him, when he thinks I'm asleep, I catch him staring at me. It should freak me out—it should totally freak me out—and yet it doesn't.

What freaks me out is that I like it. It brings peace and excites me at the same time, and that's an oxymoron right there.

That alone should be enough to get my brain checked, but it gets even worse. Last night I was about to touch him.

Let's repeat and savor that one. I. Was about. To touch. A Founder.

That's why I should have my head scanned. And to add insult to injury, it felt natural. Just a casual touch of his arm as if he was regular people. And that scares me, because that means it could happen again.

I cannot touch Jamie.

He is not, not, not regular people.

Every touch will fire up the Mark, and while he might not be out to kill me for it, it will prolong our misery. Plus, if it ever happened in public… yeah.

I cannot touch Jamie.

And Jamie cannot touch me.

As it is, he's standing behind me, so close I can feel the warmth radiating from his body. "You almost had it," he murmurs into my ear. "Once more, Lee, and then he'll leave us in peace." I could swear his hand moves to come to lay in the small of my back— but it never makes contact.

Ice claps his hands at the other end of the table. "Hello, Earth to Lea. Again, I said."

Well, at least he knows my name by now.

I take a big breath. "Sure. Of course. Why not." With three quick steps, I pass Jamie and pull the chair from under the table. "Founder." I bow—

"Lower, hon."

I bow lower.

"That's it."

Jamie tugs in his wings and slides past me and onto the chair without a single look, without a thank you. He holds his head high and keeps his features under control. Ice doesn't see the muscle twitching in his temple.

I do.

Clap, clap. "Snap out of it, sweetie. Hush, hush, your master is waiting."

Another deep breath before I take the water bottle and fill Jamie's glass.

And bow.

Lower.

Ice snickers.

For the next fifteen minutes, I become Jamie's servant. I serve him food. I refill his glass. I take care of the dirty dishes. Not once do I speak, not once do I touch him, not once am I visible. I melt into the background of this fake dinner like I'm supposed to.

Gag, *gag, gag.*

Once Jamie has gotten up from the table and I've pushed the chair back under it, Ice slow-claps. "Finally. Wonderful work, honey, really. I knew you had potential."

My hands clench and unclench twice. "You say that one more time and I—"

Ice chuckles. "Easy there. There's actually a method to my madness." He points at the table. "Sit. Both."

Jamie and I exchange a glance. That's new. Usually we'd get escorted back to our room until the next exercise.

"Listen, guys." Ice drums a rhythm onto the table. "You are official." He activates his pad and the title page of the *L.A. Times* pops up. He turns it for us to read.

"THE PROTEGEE ACCEPTED INTO TRAINING," the headline screams, followed by a smaller subtitle reading *"Accepting her destiny, Lea Akiyama has secluded herself from society to begin her life of Servitude."*

Good to see they all gobbled it up, but I can't say it makes me feel all warm and fuzzy. Ice gives the pad a shove and it slides over to us, but Jamie ignores it.

I lean forward and take a look. At least the *Times* used a

normal picture of me. Not photoshopped. Courtesy of the orphanage, I assume. They must be so proud. My eyes brush over the article only to stop at the headline next to it. *Disobedience Equals Death.* A catchy headline with the image of a young female next to it. *Servant Emily Kasczynski has been sentenced to death after breaking the 11th Commandment.* A shudder runs down my spine. Poor girl—

Ice rips the pad away from under my fingers. "Now that that's taken care of, it's time to prove your loyalty."

Jamie cocks his head. "Loyalty."

"Well, yes. Remember? I protect you and keep you safe, and in return you work for the Resistance?"

"I'd phrase it differently but can't say I forgot."

"Super. Anyway, the reason why I had you practice this so much is because tomorrow both of you are going to be attending the Founder Assembly out in the forum."

Jamie stiffens, and a little squeak breaks from my throat, one I couldn't keep in, even if I tried. "But... But I'm still marked." Still in the Red Zone. Waltzing into a forum, the Founders' fenced-off community, is like asking for trouble.

Ice rolls his eyes. "Hint hint, which is why we're doing this whole charade and you're training as his servant. And now that that's taken care of, let's talk business. Tomorrow is the bi-annual assembly of the local Founders' Chapter. I don't need you to attend the speeches, although feel free if you'd like. What I want you to do is participate in a specific dinner. You'll meet a friend of ours, and that person will give you a Masker."

Jamie's head whips over to Ice. "A Masker? You're going to have us transport a Masker?"

Okay, this was crazy before, but now it's suicidal. Maskers are illegal, and I mean illegal-illegal. Only a few underground tech-crazy people have the technology to fabricate those little disks, making them incredibly rare and hard to find. But: maskers can hide a Mark really well from a scanner, which means, they're highly sought after by the Resistance. They give them the freedom to touch a Founder—and by touch, I mean hurt—and get away with it since it covers up the Founder's Mark.

But, hey… "Can I use it?" I'd be free to go topside without Jamie when protected by a Masker. I'd—"

"Please." Ice cocks his head to the right. "No. Of course not. I'm not wasting a Masker on you when you have a reason to be marked."

"Of course not," I snap. Stupid me.

Ice shrugs. "Yup. One of our splinter groups lost it to the Founders a week ago, and we gotta get it back. We have a friend on the inside, but until now, he had no way of getting the Masker out without being noticed. So, yeah, someone's gotta do it, and you, my dear Founder, have way less chance of being searched than one of us humans."

Jamie's wings bristle. "This is insane."

"No. Necessary." Ice presses his lips press into a tight line, while Jamie makes a throat-slashing gesture, glaring at the other man. "You know that's a death sentence if they find out?"

"Then you better make sure you don't get found out. And just to emphasize, I have absolutely no problem throwing both of you to the wolves if you don't return with that Masker."

Holy freakin' cow. Ice is really doing this. *We* are doing this. Tomorrow, around this time, I might be sitting at—oh, error in my logic—I might be *standing behind* Jamie, serving him food in the middle of about a million Founders. While lighting up on every Watcher's scanner. While having no clue if my cover is good enough or not.

"This is bad," I croak.

"I agree." Jamie leans forward, supporting his weight with his arms on the table. "It's too early. If anybody scans Lea, they'll question the Servitude. We expect some degree of contamination, but not this much."

I try really hard to not be offended by the word contamination.

"Then you keep her from getting scanned or you'll think of something. No matter what, you're going. We're testing the waters to implant both of you into society, and tomorrow is perfect. What better way to reintroduce you to the Tribe than have you bring your own personal servant, the Protégée? You two are going to turn a few heads tomorrow, and I'm counting on it."

Jamie's wings angle up, the feathers on end. "I've said it before, whatever you think you know is nothing. You—"

"Enlighten me then. I've wondered that for a while. What do you know about the Council that you're not telling me, Demon?"

Jamie snaps his mouth shut. "Nothing, human."

"Really." Ice crosses his arms in front of his chest looking like he expected this answer, but nonetheless doesn't believe it.

Jamie mimics his stance. "Really."

"Then why do I feel you're keeping me out of the loop?"

"Your regular paranoia? I'm not initiated, not considered an adult in our society. Why would you expect the Council to fill me in on their plans?"

"Call it a hunch."

"Then your hunch was wrong. I'm. Not. Initiated. Yet."

"And you're saying an initiation would make a difference in

that. To you, specifically, I mean."

Jamie gives him a bland look. "To anybody. Thus says the Lord, *"Thou shall teach them my ways and the ways of the Founders. They shall be initiated and welcomed into our society at the brisk of manhood and rejoice in the knowledge they shall gain."*

Ice weighs his head left to right. "Blahblah, spare me those Scripture quotes. All right, maybe my hunch was wrong. Maybe not. We'll see. You bring us the Masker, and maybe I'll be more inclined to believe you."

Jamie clenches his hands into fists as he pushes the chair back and stands up. "This is going to get us killed."

Ice jumps to his feet. "Then play it well, Demon! You better bring me that Masker, or else! Do I need to make it any clearer for you?"

Jamie curses under this breath and swipes his hair out of his eyes. "There are going to be dozens of Watchers! Scanners! And we're going to be the center of attention—"

"Then use it! I want you to use it! We want you in the middle of it, and this is the only—"

I've heard enough. As if in a trance, I stand and walk out of the room. For the first time, none of the Resistance jerks follow me, and I'm grateful for it. A tight band of fear keeps itself wrapped around my chest, and it makes breathing difficult.

Here I might be literally living in a lion's den, but tomorrow, I'm going to walk into the proverbial one.

Survival optional.

CHAPTER NINE

Carousel

My butt is cold.

Actually, everything is cold.

That's what I get for leaving the Evil Lair to catch some fresh air. I wrap my arms around my upper body. Probably should've stayed inside, but I needed to breathe. The last days have shown clearly that whenever I think I can handle what life throws at me, fate one-ups me. Tomorrow is a suicide mission no matter how I try to spin it.

I inhale deeply. The night is cool, foggy, and smells of rain. Good for mental clarity.

I huff. Oh, please. Mental clarity.

With a big sigh, I lean back against the legs of a horse that has seen better times. *Plastic* horse, or whatever they make those carousel figures from. Somehow, I ended up downhill at the merry-go-round, and somehow, I still feel lost. Scared. *Terrified.*

"Hey." Jamie's deep voice coming from behind me makes me jerk.

"Jeez." I cough to overplay the scare he just gave me. "You're sneaky."

He chuckles. "Flew over here. Good to spread my wings."

I glance at him. "They let you fly?"

"Didn't give them much of a choice." He sits next to me, about a meter between us. Jamie has been really good at keeping his distance. Really good. If he were a human, I'd be offended, but as it is, I'm grateful. Like I said, lobster-red-zone…

"How'd you know I'd be here?"

"A hunch."

I give him side eye. "You're good with your hunches."

"Only with you, it appears."

Oh. Well… I cough into my elbow once more. Anyway.

For a while, we look out into the dark in silence. A couple of stars are visible behind the heavy clouds, way more than from my window at the orphanage, but still nothing compared to what the sky maps in school show above our heads. The light contamination makes sure of that.

After a minute or so, Jamie looks left and right. "What is it with you and broken-down entertainment places?" He reaches behind him and wiggles on a horse to test its stability, then spreads his wings a little more and leans against it.

I twirl a strand of my hair. "Reminds me of happier times." A little pang of loss shoots through me. It doesn't grow into the despair I sometimes feel when everything becomes too much, but still it's there.

Jamie stays quiet for a couple of seconds. "Yeah, I can see that. It… must've been nice."

"Yeah. My parents took me here. Before. Before they were killed. Well, obviously." Maybe that's why I ended up here. Find comfort in the past. Maybe that's also why I keep talking. Memory lane has been reopened. "Dad took my mom here on one of their first dates. He told me the story every time we went, and well, being little, I thought that's how things worked and that I'd take my boyfriend here as well." I was a daddy's girl all right. Daddy was perfect to me—my biggest role model.

Jamie fold his hands. "So, you would've taken Jezza?"

Whoa. That came out of nowhere. "Jezza? Is it that obvious?" Ugh. I need to talk to him.

"Kind of. The oaf is very protective of you."

"That he is. We're not together though. Were for like a minute, but he can't quite let go. You know how it is when you've known each other since daycare, it becomes more and then—wait." I narrow my eyes at Jamie, who gives me this blank look. "Do you know what I'm talking about? Do you have a girlfriend?"

An amused gleam lights up in his eyes. "A girlfriend? You coming on to me, Lee?"

My face burns red hot. "What? No, idiot! I was just trying to make it relatable, and—"

He chuckles. "No worries, and no, I never had a *girlfriend*." He pauses, searching for words, then shakes his head to himself with another chuckle. "Not many females on board, as I told you."

Oh. Right. "But anyway. This place reminds me of when I was little, and it's bitter-sweet in more ways than one. I remember so much about my parents, and yet it's all overshadowed by the image of them getting turned to dust." No matter how much I try to keep it out, the images sneak in: how the Caeruleum lit up in Luke's palm, and how *poof*, they were gone. The footage is out there in the Darknet. Illegal and forbidden, but it's there and easy enough to find. Never felt the need though to see my parents obliterated. *Again.* Still see it clear enough in my dreams, thank you very much.

I wrap my arms around my knees and pull them in tight. "I hate Luke for what he did to them. He could've given them a warning. They didn't stand a chance, Jamie. They didn't know. Who kills for the infraction of a rule they couldn't have known about?" My voice cracks. Had they known, they never would've tried to touch him. They'd never have left me alone. "What kind of person does that? Who lets the people shooting at you live and kills the one who brushes over your wings? Who kills without a warning?"

A heartbeat passes as our gazes lock. "A horrible being. I'm truly sorry about what he did to your parents. And to you. I'm sorry."

That one simple statement, those few words, it brings the walls around my heart to a crumble. Not because he said he was sorry, not because that's unheard of from a Founder, but because of the empathy behind them. I blink to keep the tears from falling. "Thank you." It comes out as a croak. "But not your fault."

Jamie picks up a pine cone and turns it in his hands. "Still. My… people."

"But not you." I pause. "Luke is the reason why I thought I could never trust a Founder. And then you came along and didn't care I was human. You could've left me for Ice to shoot."

"Could not. What kind of being would that make me if I had?" He winks, using my words from a moment ago.

A smile tugs on the corners of my lips. "See? That's why you're different. And while I'm not the biggest fan of your race, as you know, you had nothing to do with what Luke did to me and my family. I don't believe the son should pay for the sins of the father." So to speak.

Jamie flinches, then huffs. "Good to know." He plays some more with the pine cone, tension in his shoulders. I don't know where the Resistance got his clothing from, but he is dressed in a new classic Founder outfit. Black tactical pants, some kind of tight shirt, of course also black, because he rocks that color.

The wind picks up and brings a shiver to my spine. *Brr.* Jamie keeps on playing with that mesmerizing pine cone in his hands.

"You're not cold?" He's in a shirt, me in a sweater and jacket. I'd be freezing at this point.

He shakes his head. "Nope. We're doing better with cold temperatures than humans. It's cold up there." He points up, and for a moment I'm confused.

"Oh." I face palm myself. "Flying. Not in the hive."

"Yup." He yanks his right hand back and throws the pine cone into the dark. A human couldn't have pulled that off a few days after a bullet into the shoulder, but obviously, that's not a problem for a Founder.

I look down my arms. The scratches I got from sprinting through the bushes on my wild dash away from the church and the Founder I touched have healed okayishly, meaning, the superficial ones are gone. The deeper ones, from when I fell into somebody's hedge, are still visible. So is the bruise on my temple. Thanks, Ice, for that one. "I'll draw attention tomorrow." I look like somebody beat me up.

"You always draw attention, Lee."

My head whips over—

"I mean, with you being the Protégée, and all."

Oh. Okay. I roll my eyes. "Thanks for the reminder. I meant the injuries though." I must've run through every bush and into every obstacle on the way to the pier.

Jamie tilts his head and gives me the once-over. "It's not so bad."

"And here I thought you had better night vision than us."

He chuckles, and I stick out my tongue at him. "Everybody can't heal as well as you do."

"Oh, please. We don't heal from everything."

"Riiight." Nothing really kills them. If I had Founder genes, my injuries wouldn't be a biggie. *They* heal spectacularly well. And even if not, just lay a hand on the other person, say abracadabra or something, and part of the healthy Founder's life force will transfer into the injured Founder, or something. Another reason why killing them is so tough. It takes a lot to outsmart those healing powers, like incapacitating them and then decapitating them. That'll do it.

Jamie sighs. "It's really overrated. And you know what's the most ironic thing of all times?"

"What?"

He looks down at his palms. "We can kill each other. Caeruleum kills us. No chance to heal it, which is why we are forbidden to even raise it against each other. Funny, huh? We clearly don't mind using it against you."

No, they don't. And I might be at the receiving end of that sooner than I'd like. Especially if I call attention to myself. "Since you mention it, what can we do to keep your buddies' attention off me tomorrow? I know you guys usually don't do that, but could you heal it?" I point one finger at my temple. "Like with other Founders? I can cover the arms, but the temple…" The bruise is too dark to be hidden under makeup.

"Heal you?" A dry laugh breaks free from his throat. "Believe me, you don't want to be healed." He picks up another pine cone.

"Why not?"

Jamie stays silent, then huffs. "Because you humans romanticize it. It works well between Founders, but with humans…" He pulls little twigs and seeds from the next cone.

His dismissal rubs me the wrong way. "Your species has never even tried to help us in that way. We might not have cancer if you guys used your powers on us." But they didn't. *Human, humble thyself in the face of illness and turn from your sins toward the one true, loving Lord.* Right.

His face hardens as he looks at me. "Really, you'd rather have cancer than be healed by a Founder. Wanna know why, Lee? Because healing a human will mark that person. Permanently. That human will carry our mark forever. It won't fade. Never. And you know what happens to people who carry our mark. The Founder might as well have let you die right there and then, because no amount of Servitude will be enough to explain it."

Permanently marked. *Permanently.* Yeah. That's a death sentence all right. I force down on a dry swallow. "Oh."

He huffs and works a hand through his hair. "Yeah, *oh.* And for us, it's the biggest no-no there is. We get away with a slap to the wrist with most things. Unfair, I know, but that's the way it is. The human pays the price for most infractions, not us. But if we heal you, if we break that number one rule…" He sucks in his lower lip and gives me a look I can't quite interpret. "Not even using Caeruleum against a fellow Founder is considered that bad—and that's a sin already. If a Founder dared to heal a human, they'd burn him. *After* they ripped out his wings."

My jaw drops. "They would do what?" I can't have heard that right. Nu-uh.

"They'd burn me if I healed you." Jamie says it like it's no big deal, but it is. It's a freakin' big deal!

"They'd burn you? Alive?"

He gives me a glance down his nose. "Burning me dead wouldn't be a big enough punishment now, would it?"

I'm speechless. I really am. It takes me at least ten second to come up with an answer that doesn't consist of a string of curse words. "That's barbaric."

He focuses on the pine cone. "Never said the Founders weren't. Obviously, you've never read the Scripture. We are capable of incredible destruction. And we don't like disobedience. *For there is eternal fire waiting for those Founders who cannot obey the Lord's command.*"

Touché about reading the Scripture. Am avoiding that as much as possible. Still… "I didn't know they meant it literally." Eternal fire—burning one of their own. A living being. Beyond cruel.

Jamie's eyes squeeze shut briefly. "Everything else we get a slap on the wrist for. This, healing a human? Breaking the taboo? Deal breaker." A heartbeat passes. Right in this moment… he looks young. Vulnerable. A charged silence spreads between us, its tendrils unfurling something in my stomach, something I refuse to name. It's warm. Wholesome. It—

With a loud gust the wind picks up and cold, heavy drops of rain batter down on us.

"Eek," I squeal and cover my head with my hands, but it's no use. Within seconds, the clouds above us unleash their load, and neither the old tent above the merry-go-round nor the carousel's old roof do much to shelter us from the onslaught of rain. It's coming down so hard, we're drenched in no time.

"Don't move." In an instant, Jamie is next to me, only inches separating us. My whole body tenses from the unexpected closeness. He spreads his wings and brings them together above our heads, forming a roof. "Better?"

"Yeah," I croak, "better." In fact, it's a no-contest. The warmth of his body plus the shelter from his wings… my right side tingles from his closeness, and every breath I take, I get a hint of vanilla and something I've come to identify as Jamie over the last couple of days. Happens when you're roomies.

The rain cranks it up a notch, from a soft pitter-patter on the roof and Jamie's wings to more of a staccato beat. Jamie folds his hands in his lap, the pine cone between them. His fingers are long and graceful, like everything on him—and like on every other Founder. But then, he isn't every other Founder. Jamie's different, and I'm not talking about the video hanging like a sword of Damocles above his head. I'm talking different-different. It's the elephant in the room every time Ice gives him a task and he complies instead of killing Ice. Every time he does something against the grain. Every time he falls asleep with this desperate, lost look on his face that only makes room for something more peaceful when he's asleep. Every time—yet I haven't dared to ask him about it again. Maybe I want to keep my illusions he isn't a typical Founder, but something more. My heart does a stupid little jump, and my cheeks warm. I drop my gaze to the ground. Dangerous road, Lea. Dangerous road.

Change of topic, please. "So, uhh, tomorrow." Lame start. "Stuff can go wrong."

"Indeed." He nods slowly. "Loads."

I groan and bury my face in my hands. "That's where you're supposed to say it won't happen, that we've got this."

Another small chuckle. "You've got this, Lee."

Lee. He's been calling me that for the last two days or so, at least when we're alone. It makes my cheeks feel even hotter. "I'm just nervous. A Masker, that's so..." I shake my head. "So out there. If they catch us, we're dead." If we don't get the Masker, we're probably dead too, after we've been hunted down by

Watchers. Seems a lot of things are about to get me killed these days, first and foremost, the Mark on me.

But what if… "What if we took the Masker and ran?" My heart beats faster with that thought, be it from fear of my recklessness or hope.

"Take it?"

"Yeah." Screw Ice and his plans. "We get the Masker, we don't bring it back to the Resistance, but we use it ourselves. Problem solved." My Mark will be covered, and to play it safe, I could hide, and then join civilization once it's gone. No Resistance-crap, no Servitude-crap, no almost-getting-killed-crap. Freedom.

"And they're still going to sell us out. I don't trust Ice. If we turn on him, that video will leak, and then you're dead, no matter if you wear a Masker or if the Mark had worn off on its own already. Video evidence is video evidence."

Ugh, true. "Then our only chance of getting out of this is getting the video."

"I'd say that's a true statement."

Determination takes root inside my heart. "Okay. I'll get the video." Jamie didn't have any success with Ice, but maybe my approach is the better one.

He throws me a sideways glance. "How do you plan to do that?"

"Easy. Jezza can help me." He must help me.

"You're sure he's more loyal to you than the Resistance? Than the cause?"

My mouth opens and closes. I didn't really look at it that way. The old Jezza? Yes. Absolutely. The new Jezza, the one who sounded like a recruitment flyer and kept secrets from me? Not quite so sure. "I guess we'll find out."

"I guess we will. And you're right. A try couldn't hurt, but in case we don't get it… I guess for now, we're playing along. At least until I can figure something out. And I will." He stretches out one foot and taps it into the puddle of rainwater forming on the step below us. "We'll get through tomorrow, and then we'll see."

Compared to me, I'd call Jamie an optimist. "Maybe we can stay under the radar." There will be hundreds of Founders tomorrow. We can play it out low key, meet that guy, get the Masker, and get out.

Jamie spins the pine cone in his hand. "About that… Staying under the radar is probably not going to happen." He turns to face me. "I can promise you I'll do everything I can to keep people away from us, but me showing up with you will be a big deal. A really big deal, believe me."

Oh, heck. "Because I'm the Protégée?"

Pause.

"That would do it."

"What if I get scanned and I'm still in the Red Zone?" The rain drums a nice, soothing rhythm onto his wings.

His lips press into a thin line. "Then they're going to assume I took a servant for a different reason, I guess."

One-Mississippi.

Two-Mississippi.

Three—

"Oh." *Oh.* My face burns red hot. "You're kidding me. They wouldn't. That's illegal."

"There's illegal for you and illegal for us. But punishment only goes in one direction."

Uhh…? "What do you mean?"

"That we perceive ourselves as the superior race, Lee. By the

Lord's law, we can do as we please, and very few things get us punished." His lips press into a hard line. "Not that I could speak from experience, but thanks to my astute observation powers, I'm pretty sure breaking the Eleventh Commandment with our servants is a notch in our belts. Nothing more. You, on the other hand, will get punished at one point. Easily, and without mercy."

I shake my head so fast my vision blurs. "But that's not happening." There are no Founder-Human-couples, as in *couples-couples*.

He gives me a pointed glance. "But then you've heard the same rumors I did, haven't you?"

My stomach cramps up. Yeah, I've heard those rumors—and dismissed them without a second thought because they're crazy: dreamed up by googley-eyed women who've obviously lost all common sense. Nobody in their right mind would risk a relationship with a Founder, even if they were interested. Which they're not.

"Rumors, yes. Nothing more." I can't imagine that poor girl in the L.A. Times risked her life on purpose and started something with her Founder. The epitome of idiocy.

"I'm not saying it's really happening. I'm just saying I've heard those rumors, and I know my people. We have a superiority complex, and the punishment for breaking the Eleventh Commandment is proof of that."

"How so?"

"Again, like I said before. For us, it's a slap on the wrist in comparison. If we touch a human, or if we let a human touch us, we get our wings tied for a month." He pauses. "For the human, it ends differently."

My heart seizes. "I know."

"It's only fair, right? We really like our wings, so getting them tied is a big punishment equal to yours. Because hey, if we scan our servants and they read too high on the scale—or worse, they're not a virgin anymore—they'll be executed. Wham, bam, thank you ma'am." His tone is bitter.

Oh, hell. I blow out a puff of air. "Awesome. So, if they scan me and I light up, they're going to assume…" I let the sentence trail off. The fact that my Mark is sky-high and that… uhh, I did have sex with Jezza… Yeah, I'd be double-screwed, pun intended.

Jamie gives me a small smile. "Don't think so. You're new to Servitude, that'll be it. They won't assume I… well, let's just say I don't have the reputation of targeting human females."

I suck in my lower lip. "Oh. Okay." Pause. But still. "Your people are kind of assholes sometimes, Jamie." I check him from under my lashes for a reaction. He's not like them, but calling Founders names is pretty high up on their list of no-nos.

Jamie rolls his eyes. "No kidding. Never said the Founders were fair. We're way too self-centered for that." It comes out bitter. "But anyway, you're doing better." He turns his wrist over and activates the scanner stuck to the leather brace. "See? Lobster-red is gone, we're down to a nice'n steady fiery orange."

"And how fast. It only took like five days." And will only take like another couple of weeks to be gone completely.

Jamie's lips tilt up, curtesy of my sarcasm. "We'll get there. If they scan you and see this reading, they'd only assume you're slow to pick up on your skills."

He pauses and plays with the pine cone in his hand, keeping his eyes trained on it. "And whatever you see and hear tomorrow, I need you to play it cool. Tomorrow, you are my servant and nothing more." His gaze shifts to me. "Or else we're both history."

CHAPTER TEN

Forum

"Remember to stay silent, okay? Silent. You can't be seen talking to me without me addressing you first. The others will know something is wrong if you talk to me like to a human." Jamie taps a chaotic rhythm onto his leg. "And stay reverent. That's our biggest pet-peeve. Adoration, reverence, devotion. You're going to see Founders with an attitude, and you must under all circumstances—"

"I got it." I grab the steering wheel so tight my knuckles turn white. *Shut up. Adore. Be reverend.* "I—"

"And try to anticipate. A good servant will know her master so well, she's—"

"I said I got it!" I slap the wheel. "I got it, Jamie! I'm going to be as good a servant as I can be, but please can you stop making me nervous? Even more, I mean?" I roll my eyes at him as much as I can without driving us off the road. The moment Ice gave us the keys and let us go, Jamie started reciting every single servant-related fact he's told me a dozen times since the Resistance took us in, and hasn't stopped since. We've left L.A. and driven up the four-oh-five, passed Santa Clarita, and left civilization behind us about thirty minutes ago. This is the Californian desert: wide, beige, and empty.

Jamie deflates. He stills his fingers, and boy, does that silence make me feel better already. I let go of a big breath. "Look. I get it. Believe me, I do. I know what's at stake here. If that video gets out, I have absolutely no shot at survival. For you… I don't know." I throw him a questioning glance. "Since I don't know what your deal is, I assume you're going to get a Stigma, if at all. Big deal, and while I get it's no fun, it won't get you killed. Like you said, slap on the wrist. You'll survive."

His wings do this little jitter-thing when he wants to stretch them out and can't. I hear him swallow. "Yeah. I'll survive," he mutters.

Sigh. "Jamie, listen, I… I'm nervous, okay? Yes, I'm the Protégée, so there was always some kind of Founder involvement when I was growing up, but that was passive. They sent some orders to the Sisters what they were supposed to do with me and that's it. I haven't interacted more with any of your kind than a regular gal. And this today, it freaks me out. So much can go wrong, and then *poof*." I release my right hand from the wheel and stretch my fingers out as if I had Caeruleum radiating from my palm.

Jamie pulls his left knee up and turns toward me. "I get it, Lee. But that's not going to happen. I wouldn't let it happen. Even if you screwed up ginormously—again, not happening—it will be my responsibility to deal with you. And because you're new to Servitude and I'm the forgiving type, I wouldn't punish you too harshly." He winks at me in an attempt to lighten the mood.

"Gee, thanks, man."

"Anytime." He turns serious again. "That being said, I don't want to make you nervous, but we will be under scrutiny. We won't be able to hide. We might get scanned. We will for sure get tested."

"Tested?" That doesn't sound good.

"You'll see." He turns back to face forward. "Point is, take my hints and we'll get through this. As soon as we have the Masker, we're out." He looks out the window, taking in the Wind Farm to our left, where almost five thousand turbines generate enough electricity to power ten percent of California's needs at this point.

"Breathtaking, huh?" I point my chin at the rows and rows of turbines spinning in the wind. Time for a change of topic. I'm on edge as it is.

Jamie nods, his head turning as we drive until whatever he was looking at is out of sight. "Pretty much." He falls silent again and I follow his lead. I need all the peace and quiet I can get, because once we're there, I'm going to have to ace this if I want to stay alive.

The forum looks like the pictures of it in the newspapers.

I've never been there—one, why would I, and two, they are exclusive to Founders. Oh, and servants. S'cuse me.

I'm not quite sure if this village smack in the middle of the desert and at the foot of the mountains was here before the Founders arrived and took over or not. It could've been—it looks like something us humans typically build: dozens and dozens of little box-houses, neatly stacked next to each other, all in the same boring, beige color, all the same design and size. On the other hand, they have been modified for the use by Founders. They added wider doors to accommodate wings not quite retracted, wider sliding windows in every roof for visitors to enter topside after flying over. Plus, everything is way better maintained than many of our residential areas. Thank you, servants assigned to this forum.

Once we have passed the gate that opens automatically for any Founder approaching, Jamie directs me through the village to its center without a single wrong turn. "Been here before?"

He stares out the window. "Grew up here."

"Wait, you did? But then, why—" Why were you so hungry down at the pier? No Founder in the forum—or anywhere, for that matter—would want for anything, which is why I kind of assumed… well, I didn't really think it through.

"Why what?"

My cheeks burn. "Why were you down in Hollywood then? The night we… met." At the church.

A pause before he answers. "Never said I liked it here." And with that, he turns to look out the side, a clear dismissal.

It's not busy at all, and the only other cars on the road sprout the same combo as us: human driving, Founder in the passenger seat. I guess I just met some of my, uhh, colleagues.

"Over there." Jamie points to a wide parking area in front of a large, two-story building. "That's the Central Hall."

And it's lined with soldiers—literally. A seven-year-old couldn't put his tin soldiers in better rows than the Founders have their human toys. The Founders take their safety very seriously.

As I drive onto the parking lot, the soldiers let us pass. A female soldier peers into the car, face a professional impassive mask, her long, curly blond hair pulled into a ponytail. For a fleeting moment, I feel like I know her, like I had seen her before, but then the feeling is gone, replaced by the dread of the task ahead.

Two thirds of the parking spots are taken already. "Are we late?" I whisper through my teeth without looking at him. Won't make that mistake a mere two minutes into our charade.

"Yes, but that's okay. This way we can minimize mingling. Dinner, meet Josh Cardoza, get out."

Sounds like a plan. Josh Cardoza is one of the few non-servant humans allowed here today, and that would be because he's a politician. While the Founders have either directly taken over positions high up in the government to *facilitate peace and order,* or gotten the human in a position of power pledged to themselves as a New Servant, the lower positions are still left to us. Cardoza's job as the mayor of the forum gives him the unique advantage of access, meaning, he could get to the Masker confiscated by the Founders.

That's all I want. Get in, get the stupid Masker, get out.

I kill the engine. "Showtime," I whisper under my breath and un-click my seatbelt. Okay. I can do this. Get out of the car. Open Jamie's door. Hold it open, head bowed until he is out. Close the door. Keep head down.

Nobody is paying any special attention to us, yet my heart thumps like a sledgehammer. To make sure the slight tremor of my hands doesn't give me away, I press them against my outer thighs as I follow Jamie into the Central Hall, keeping my one meter distance. The soldiers assigned step aside for us—and this time the long, curly blond hair triggers a memory.

Holy cow, is that—

I shake my head. No, can't be. I saw her only a few days ago, with her Founder, her *pledged* Founder, buying magazines. Can't be her. Maybe she's got a sister, that's why I feel I know her.

Plus, it doesn't matter. Not drawing attention does. Focus, Lea.

The sliding doors hiss apart once we approach, and while Jamie has been keeping his wings in tight for our time in the Old

Zoo, now he holds them looser, spread out more. Relaxed.

And it makes him looks spectacular.

Jamie would be beautiful with his wings hidden, but when he holds them slightly extended… he radiates confidence. It's not hard to see why humanity fell for the Angels during their infrequent visits millennia ago. The sheer grace and elegance that comes with carrying wings is mesmerizing. Fascinating. Add Jamie's dimples when he smiles, those eyes shining in the purest blue I've ever seen, and—

Aaannd I better tune it down a notch.

Founder there.

Human here.

Keep it together, Lea.

I dig my nails into my palms to focus. To the left and right of the door, two Watchers stand guard, each in the usual standard outfit including all the accessories. Like Scanners. Crap. If they—

Both their eyes widen when they see Jamie and me, but before I can start panicking, they bow their heads the slightest, and we're past. No scanning us.

Holy cow.

My breath comes out in short puffs, and that was just the beginning. If I don't mess up, I'm still going to have a stroke at one point, I'm sure of it.

As if he'd been here a thousand times—and who knows, maybe he has—Jamie leads the way until we hit another set of double doors.

Jamie stops dead in his tracks.

And waits.

And waits.

Why isn't—

Crap.

I dart forward and get the doors for him, my face beet red. Five minutes in, and I'm already messing up. Jamie lets his head hang. "It will cost you your dinner privileges, human. I expect you to attend to your duties without delay."

The two Watchers behind us snicker, and a hot wave of humiliation washes over me. Not because they heard Jamie chastising me, but because well, Jamie gave me a verbal slap on the hand and he is right, only it will cost me much more than dinner privileges if I mess up.

He walks ahead into the banquet hall, and I'm speechless.

This is grandeur, if I've ever seen it.

Now, granted, I'm a little orphan kid with not much to go by, but this… whoa. This is half a football field with dozens of rows of tables, all set with white linen tablecloths. Even the chairs are covered in white linen, like somebody wrapped them in a sheet and tied a bow in their back. Instead of the usual ceiling lamps, long, front-to-end light channels are integrated into the ceiling. Somehow, they sparkle, as if the photons were flowing in them like in a river, dancing along the path created for them. This place smells of money and magnificence.

It would be awe-inspiring if it wasn't filled with Founders.

Jamie was right. We are late. Most Founders are seated at the tables already, many of them with a human servant standing behind them. Our entrance is mostly unnoticed, and when I say mostly, it means nobody makes a big deal out of our arrival.

I still see their eyes widening as we walk by. The whispered comments to their neighbors. The pointing.

Deep breath in. Deep breath out. Head slightly bowed. Be reverent. Adoring. Keep my focus up.

Doesn't change I'm a nervous wreck. I never liked the quote-unquote fame that came with being the Protégée, but today I hate it. It puts me under a magnifying glass I'd rather avoid.

Jamie stops in front of an available chair, and this time I do my job. "Master." I pull the chair back and wait for him to take a seat. Before I retreat, I fill his glass with water, then step back in line with the other servants to my left and right.

Challenge one? Nailed it.

"My dear fellow Founders." Up front, a Founder has taken the stage. He speaks at a normal volume, which means I can barely hear him. Not that I feel like I'm missing out on something, but the lack of microphone and speakers shows how little the Founders care about us humans. We don't have uber-perfect hearing. Sorry. The Founder is middle-aged and dressed in all white, which truly makes him look like an angel in combination with the wide-spread white wings.

All hushed conversations stop, and he bows. "My dear fellow Founders, I thank you for gracing us with your presence tonight. The California Chapter is proud of its community of Founders and humans alike, and proud of the peace we've brought and sustained over the last decade. Let tonight be about celebrating said peace, love, and of course, our Lord." He raises his glass. "To the Lord, our Father. We are anxiously awaiting His arrival. And He will come. Soon."

Oy. Sounds more like a threat. Plus, for the last decade, they've been waiting for the Lord, and so has humanity. Meeting the man who initiated seeding life on Earth in the Founder's image and who became this mystical figure in almost every religion… A dream of many, but clearly not of all. Once in a while, voices get louder, voices that ask for the Lord, for clarifications, for proof He exists. They get shut down. *It is not our place to question the Lord's schedule. He will come when he so desires.* Oh well. Guess the Lord is busy.

All around me, the Founders in the audience raise their glasses. "Hear, hear!"

Good thing I don't have a glass, because I don't know if I could fake the excitement. A population of Founders is enough. The Lord is welcome to stay wherever he is.

The moment they lower their drinks, a set of double doors opens on either side of the room, admitting servant after servant after servant, all carrying plates with food. Like during a well-coordinated dance they take the room, line up behind every Founder, and serve them at the same time. Put the plate down. Bow. Retreat in the same neat row.

The servants next to me move to attend their duties as soon as the servers are out of the way. I should take my cues from them. They're all older than me, so they probably know what they're doing. I'm looking for the one quote-unquote veteran I can copy, one who must have been in Servitude since Founders arrived on Earth a decade ago, but nobody's *that* old. Early twenties, max. Oh, well. They all wear a Vinculum, meaning, they're all official and know more than I do. So I copy them.

From here on, I'm busy. Put a napkin onto Jamie's lap. Refill the water glass. Cut his food for him. And not a single time do I mess up, despite the other Founders' eyes on me. Once I step back in line and let him eat, the attention is off me, and the atmosphere shifts.

Easy chatter fills the air, laughter, the noise of silverware scraping over plates. Nobody pays us servants any special attention. The Founders around Jamie keep talking to him, everybody who can lean over to catch a word of what he's saying is half on the table. He sure found himself the right crowd, although they look too old to be buddies. But then, anybody would be curious about one of theirs bringing the Protégée for dinner. And while I'd love to listen in, I'm too far way and it's too noisy overall. It's an agitated conversation, but besides the occasional syllable or word floating over, I can't pick up on much. After a while, I stop trying and focus on the next step. I wonder where Josh Cardoza is. He can't be sitting with the—

An elbow pokes into my left side. "Relax. You did well."

My gaze flies to the female servant on my left. "I did—"

She smiles. "You did well. You're new, right? Your Founder is very young, and you're not very old either, so this is probably your first official event?"

"That's fair to say."

Her smile widens. She's a couple of years older than me, a brunette with the most beautiful green eyes I've ever seen. "Figured. You don't have your Vinculum yet."

"Oh. Yes. True." And I don't ever want one.

Her gaze darts over to the Founders at the table and back. "It's tough keeping all the rules in mind, I know. It'll become second nature though, and soon you won't be able to imagine a life without your Founder."

Which would be the day I kill myself. No offense, Jamie. I force a smile in return. "I can't wait."

"If I can give you one piece of advice, don't stress it. Give yourself time, give your Founder time. When they're young, they're under so much pressure." Her gaze shifts to something warmer as it drifts over to the Founder in front of her. "I'm Frances, by the way."

"Lea. And thank you, Frances. I'll bear that in mind." I keep my voice low, like she did, although I don't think we're doing anything forbidden. To our left and right, most servants chat quietly with each other, and neither of the Founders seem to mind. "So, have you been doing this for long?"

"This is my fifth year." She holds up her Vinculum that shines in an iridescent red. "Our relationship has advanced and grown stronger steadily, it's something that I'm very proud of. My master is a beautiful being, and to serve him in any way I can…" She bites her lower lip as her cheeks take on a pinkish hue.

I cock my head to the side. No way. The way she looks at him, and if I didn't completely misinterpret what she said… "You—" *Love him,* I want to say, but I don't get it to cross my lips. Those words, they're blasphemy. *You shall love the Lord and his Founders with all your heart and with all your soul and with all your might—* so, technically yes, we're supposed to love the Founders—but not love-love them. Not physically love them. *And the Lord said, the daughters of men are forbidden to descendants of the Heavens. No human shall desire a Founder, or they shall fear the Lord's judgment and discipline, for it will be eternal.* There's no way what Jamie implied last night is happening in real life. Nu-uh.

"I what?" Frances lowers her head to mine.

Crap. "You, uhh, must have a strong bond with your Founder then," I finish lamely.

Frances doesn't notice. She gives me a shy look under her lashes. "I do. He is wonderful. I dare to think that's why our bond is so strong." She wiggles the hand with the bracelet on.

I force the corners of my lips up some more. "You're probably right. I—"

Frances flinches as her hand shoots up to her nose. "Dang it.

Not again." She sneezes twice. "S'cuse me." A little drop of blood runs from her nose, and she wipes it away with a quick flick of her wrist. She gives me a quick smile. "It's the dry Californian air. I'm from Minnesota originally." She sprays something into her nose, pinches it, and lets go with a relieved ahhh-sound. "Takes care of the headaches too." She winks at me and shoves the spray back into her pocket.

We fall into an easy silence, and the longer it lasts, the more I relax. Jamie is the one working hard right now, chatting with other Founders. I doubt others hear the strain in his voice, but even though I can't make out the exact words he's saying, I do pick up on that. Roomies, like I said.

After dessert has been served, Frances pokes my ribs again. "If you don't mind me asking, are you the Protégée? Do I have that right?"

I suppress a sigh. Here we go. "Yeah, you do."

A little squeal breaks free from her throat. "Amazing! You are so blessed to have your life touched by them."

Ugh. I don't like that phrasing. At all.

She carries on, oblivious to my discomfort. "You'll have to come and visit Benjamin and me, we'd love to have you and...?"

"Jamin." Feels safer to give his official name, more like something a servant would do.

"You and Jamin over," she finishes her sentence. "Maybe this Friday—"

Frances' Founder pushes his chair back and gets up. Like a switch flipped, Frances is back on duty, the relaxed demeanor gone, replaced with the reverent one I can't quite pull off. She darts forward and pulls the chair back, keeping her head bowed. The Founder straightens his clothing as he steps out from the chair, and for the shortest moment, I think—I *think*—I see his fingers brush over her arm as he moves past her, but it must have been a fluke. No Founder touches a human if they can help it.

Frances falls the appropriate two steps behind her Founder without another look at me, and even if she did, I wouldn't have the time to respond, because Jamie is getting up too.

Like the good servant I am, I jump forward and mimic what Frances did.

"Jamin? Will you be staying for a while?" That's one of the older Founders who sat next to Jamie.

"A little while, Joshua. This one is still in training. I'd rather—"

The other Founder chuckles. "Say no more. You should get her back to your place and resume training, that's right."

Jamie's smile stays cool. "Exactly. So please excuse me, I'd like to mingle." With that, he pushes past me and walks down the aisle toward the stage up front. All around us, Founders are getting up, which means I have to stay completely focused to not run into anybody. Wouldn't that be great on my first day as a servant? Killed on the spot for my own stupidity.

Alas, I do fine, at least until a human male in his twenties all but jumps into my way. "Excuse me, but you're the Protégée, ain't that right?" His gaze darts across my face as if he was comparing me to an internal database.

Jamie has stopped, a curious eye on the man and me. I get the slightest nod from him.

"Yes," I say.

"Wonderful." The man beams. "Chris Patterson, L.A. Times. If you don't mind? Founder Jamin, if I may?" Wow, word must spread quickly whom the Protégée is serving now.

The reporter gestures to Jamie and myself, and Jamie gets the hint before I do. He steps behind me, keeping the appropriate distance. Chris Patterson doesn't waste any time and takes at least a dozen pictures of us. Peripherally, I notice the same armada of servants from before swarming in and removing the rows of tables. Once Patterson lowers the camera, he bows. "Thank you, Founder. Thank you, Protégée." And off he scoots. It's so awesome being famous. *Not.*

Somebody passes by us, a Founder barely older than us. "Picture in the newspaper again, huh, Jamin? Looking better this time." He snickers and gets swallowed by the masses.

A shadow crosses Jamie's face before he turns abruptly and walks farther to the front. During this short interruption and distraction, the servants have transformed the banquet hall into a ballroom with hundreds of Founders mingling and socializing. Oh, the fun.

I keep my eyes peeled for the one person we must find today, but so far, no signs of Josh Cardoza. While I'm pretty sure I'd recognize him from the pictures Ice showed us, I doubt he'd just come out and introduce himself. Wouldn't be what I'd consider sneaky. My palms are sweaty, and I'm glad I'm wearing black. Nothing says *afraid* and *overwhelmed* better than sweat stains under my armpits.

Jamie takes a glass of something bubbly from a passing server. Another Founder, blond, straight hair, about middle-aged, does the same. Recognition flares in his eyes. "Jamin. Good to see you here on one of these events."

Jamie bows his head the slightest bit. "Thank you, Isaiah. Good to see you too. I trust things are going well in your district?"

Isaiah claps Jamie's shoulder. "Of course they are. Especially after a certain someone brought up New Servitude. Makes all the difference." He winks at Jamie. "And I've got to say, I'm sure your father is proud to hear that you've chosen to honor the commandments, especially with the Protégée." That's when I get a jerk of his chin.

Jamie takes a sip of his bubbly. "I'm sure he will be, Isaiah. Tell him my regards when you see him." That's a dismissal if I ever heard one.

"Will be my pleasure. I'll be seeing him in—ah, look at that. I guess I'm wanted elsewhere." He winks once more, raises his glass and bows ever so slightly as he makes room for another Founder. A Watcher.

A Watcher who isn't happy at all.

He's taller than Jamie, wider. Probably early to mid-twenties, with long, straight black hair pulled into some kind of mix out of ponytail and man-bun. He'd be attractive, if it wasn't for the scowl on his face and the barely suppressed anger radiating from every pore when he pulls himself to his full height in front of Jamie, arms crossed in front of his chest.

Ever so subtly, Jamie changes his stance too. Straighter. Shoulders back. Chin high. "Bane."

The Watcher's—Bane's—eyes drill into Jamie. "You've picked up a pet." He never looks at me, yet it's clear whom he's referring to.

Jamie shrugs. "You know how it goes. She followed me. What can I do. Shoo-shoo." He waves his hand at me dismissively, but of course I stay. My cheeks flush bright red, yes, but I stay and I don't react. Anything else would be suicidal.

Bane gives Jamie a long, silent look. "I see," he draws out. "No Vinculum. But I trust you have signed up with Michael to take the Pledge, have you not? And *of course* Luke knows, I'm sure."

There's a bite in his tone. Jamie ignores it, but it rubs me the wrong way.

"Luke doesn't need to know everything. And no, Bane, we haven't signed up for the Pledge yet. Training this one is more time-consuming than I thought. We're not ready to commit."

"That's exactly my problem with you, *Jamester.*"

Jamie flinches. "Bane—"

"Heard you were in the area a couple of days ago."

Pause.

Jamie looks straight into Bane's eyes. "I'm all over the place, you know how it is."

Another pause. Both guys stay a hundred percent focused on the other one. I'm missing something here, and I'd bet it's nothing friendly.

After a couple of seconds, Bane holds up his wrist with his scanner attached to it. "Funny story. I lost my favorite scanner."

Jamie's eyes widen, but it looks fake. "No way. Your favorite scanner. How come?"

A muscle in Bane's jaw ticks. "Good question. I guess I'm *all over the place.*"

The way he says it… Wait a second—the Scanner… did Jamie take the Scanner from him? From Bane? Is that why—

Somebody claps Bane's shoulder from behind. "Bane. Can't believe to see you and Jamie at one of—"

Bane raises an eyebrow and steps aside, revealing—me.

The other Founder's mouth drops open to a perfect little *o* as his eyes dart back and forth between Jamie, Bane, and me. "I see." He shakes his head with a small chuckle. "Never thought that day would come. Little Jamie got himself a pet."

Jamie's smile turns icy. "Not just any pet, Peter. I got myself the Protégée, if you haven't noticed."

"No, actually, I haven't—"

"Oh, but I have." Bane's voice is just as icy. "How very fitting for the son of—"

A hard shoulder bumps into me and I stumble forward. Before I can fall, I'm being grabbed by my arm. "Oh, I'm so sorry. I apologize. It's tight in here sometimes."

I turn—and look straight into the eyes of a human male with bright blue eyes and black hair. Josh Cardoza. Yes! The weight of a truck-sized boulder falls off my shoulders. For a moment, I want to get Jamie's attention, but I can't. I'm his servant. And neither can Josh Cardoza. You don't just address a Founder without being spoken to first. But me he can contact.

Play it cool, Lea. Play it cool. I brush his hand off my arm. "Uhh, thank you. Yes, crowded."

He holds out a hand. "Josh Cardoza. Mayor of this little forum community."

"Lea Akiyama. Nice to meet you." We shake hands, and while mine is sweaty, his is warm, with a strong grip.

"The Protégée?" His eyebrows shoot up. Good actor. He must know whom he was supposed to meet tonight. Obviously, this wasn't a coincidental bump-in. "What an honor. When I heard about you being chosen for servant duty, I thought about bringing you a gift to celebrate the occasion, but unfortunately…" He raises his shoulders and lets them drop with a sigh. "Unfortunately, it didn't arrive in time. Maybe later." He winks at me, and my mind scrambles to add one and one. What is he saying—he doesn't have the Masker? My chest squeezes tight, like my throat. No, no, no. We need that thing, or else Ice—

I swallow the lump inside my throat. "Oh, that's… that's nice of you. I'd love to see what it is. When… when could I get it?" Please say later, please say later, please…

His smile widens. "I'm sure it'll arrive soon. If your Founder takes you to the concert in three days, I'll have it, and maybe even a small little extra." He winks at me. "Well, it was nice to meet you, famous Protégée. Hope to see you soon." He raises a hand in greeting and vanishes into the crowd.

Just like that he's gone.

And we don't have a Masker.

CHAPTER ELEVEN

Stigmatized

The ride home is long and silent.

Neither of us is looking forward to telling Ice what a bummer this mission was.

The moment we leave the gates of the forum and reach the freeway, Jamie slides lower in his seat, leaning his head against the head rest, like all tension left his body. He's been wired since we started this trip. Me, I'm still wired. Nervous.

Once we've passed the wind farm, Jamie sighs. "I heard weird stuff today."

Huh? "As in?"

"Tough to say. The Founders are nervous. Things… don't add up."

"And that doesn't add up to me, what you just said."

He grumps. "Same here." He pauses for a moment. "I might read up on the New Scripture."

I cut my eye at him. "Why would you? No Scripture-quizzes for you. Completely irrelevant for a Founder." Not for a human, since we live by this thing. Jamie can do whatever he pleases, kind of at least.

He lifts and drops his shoulders. "Maybe. Maybe not. But anyway, tell me again exactly what Cardoza said." He keeps his eyes closed, hands folded in his lap.

"Only that he'd love to give me a gift, but that it hadn't arrived in time. He would have it for me if you took me to the concert in three days." And he said something about a little extra, although I don't know what that means. Flowers to go with it?

No reaction. Five seconds later Jamie huffs. "I guess we're going to the concert then."

Yeah, I guess so too. "If Ice keeps us alive until then."

"We're still his best hope. He has us on a leash, and he likes it. He'd be stupid viewing this as our failure and leaking the video. That's the moment he'd lose your cooperation—because he'd lose you." He lifts his palm in a crude approximation of shooting his Caeruleum at someone.

Shudder. "And you?"

"I wouldn't be happy about it either."

But it wouldn't kill him. Then why-oh-why does he dance to Ice's tune?

Ice gives me the creeps, although I can't quite judge him. Over the last days I've gotten to know him as ruthless, but also passionate for humanity's freedom. Maybe one must come with the other if you want to survive against the Founders and keep your cool with Watchers everywhere. A shudder runs down my back. Speaking of. That guy that cornered us, Bane. He gave me the creeps even more than Ice.

I sneak a peek at Jamie. "At this concert or whatever, is that Bane guy going to be there?"

Jamie's eyes pop open. "Bane?" A shadow crosses his face. "Of course he'll be there. Bane lives in the forum and is one of our highest-ranking Watchers in the District. He'll be there all right." Bitterness sneaks into his voice, hinting at something other, something deeper.

I fidget with the steering wheel. "Do you, uhh, do you know

him? I mean, the way he talked to you, and, like, the scanner-thing he mentioned—"

"I know him well enough that I don't want you anywhere near him. Do you hear me?" He glares at me as if I did something wrong.

"Easy there, tiger. I'm not keen on running into that man again, and if I do, I'll be on my best servant behavior. I know Founders—"

"Yeah, no. Him you don't. Just do me a favor and stay away from him. With Bane, the rules don't apply." He crosses his arms in front of his chest, closes his eyes, and stays silent for the rest of the trip.

Ice hammers his fingers onto the table in the same irregular, annoying and irritating rhythm as always. "No Masker."

Jamie shakes his head. "Not yet. Three days, Cardoza said."

"Three days."

"Correct." Jamie leans back into his chair, completely relaxed, as if that trip to the forum had been nothing but a social event. I guess he's playing his cards with Ice, and I can't blame him. That man's got enough power over us as it is, adding another weakness isn't really high up my list either.

The drummed rhythm stops. Neither Jamie nor I miss the glance exchanged between Ice, Jezza, and Hud.

"It'll work," Hud says, playing with the cord of his hoodie. That man wears nothing else, or at least I haven't seen him in anything else. "The timing still holds."

Timing for what?

Ice leans forward, supporting his upper body with his arms on the table. "Barely." The drumming picks up again, and I raise my hand as if I was in school.

"He said he'd give it to me at the concert, and it sounded like that was a done-deal. So, I'd say let's plan for that and get it over with." I can do the whole fake it until you make it thing. That sounded as confident as can be. As loyal to the Resistance as I can pull off.

Another glance is exchanged between those three.

Hud gets up. "I'll make arrangements."

Jamie's gaze follows him through the room until he's out. "Arrangements for what?"

"None of your business, Founder." Ice scowls at Jamie, but hey, at least he didn't call him *demon* this time.

Jamie adjusts his wings as he leans forward and folds his hands on the table. "That depends. I'm beginning to wonder if what you have planned for us isn't much worse than whatever the Founders could come up with if you played your cards against us. And if you'd like us to stay cooperative, a bit more information would be appreciated, or else we might decide risking facing my people is the better option." Kudos to Jamie for delivering this like it's no big deal, because if I'm not mistaken, he just threatened to stop playing Ice's game.

Ice mimics Jamie's body posture, minus the wings. "Why would I risk trusting you? You jump through my hoops as it is."

"But then you know I'm not like the others."

Ice narrows his eyes and steps up his tapping rhythm. "Are you saying you'd go against your people?"

"I'm saying I'd like to not get killed for whatever reason, by either party. We can bring you the Masker. In three days, as Cardoza said. Tell me what's going on, and I'll see what else I can find out. You've got to trust me, or else your plans might backfire."

Jezza huffs. He's been sitting next to Ice with a face like we personally offended him, although I'm pretty sure I haven't even talked to him enough to offend him somehow. Or maybe that's it.

Ice's drumming stops again. "You're threatening me. And I don't like it, Demon." Ah, we're back to that loving designation.

"And I understand that. I don't like to be threatened either, yet it's all you do and you're making it clear to Lea and me that we're nothing but your pawns. Maybe that's not the smartest approach." He pauses and nods at me. "The concert is in three days. By that point, rumor about me coming back home with the Protégée will have spread, and the amount of attention on us will be… *different* than today, which can or cannot be good." His gaze flicks over to me.

"Different," Ice repeats.

"Different." Jamie nods. "More attention. More scrutiny. But also, more contact with high-ranking Founders. It's your choice how well we can pay attention."

Finally, I catch on. "True. I might mess up more, and then Jamie can't focus on anything." Meaning, Ice is wasting a good opportunity to spy on the Founders. I like the way Jamie thinks. Turn the tables on Ice. Make him feel that we're the ones holding the cards, not him. "Or I can be really, really good. But that depends on my motivation."

Jamie cocks an eyebrow at Ice. "See? Lea is—"

"Don't you dare pull Lea into those little games of yours," Jezza growls from across the table.

Seriously? "Jezza, what the—?"

"She was pulled into *your little games* the moment you decided to attack me." Jamie gives him a cool look as Jezza shoots forward, both hands on the table.

"*You* are the one manipulating her! Don't think I can't see what you're playing at, Demon! If you as much as get one hair on her out of place—"

"J! Tune it down a notch, man." Ice throws a bottle of water at him that Jezza barely catches before it would've hit his head. "Take a sip and then make sure Lea has everything she needs for tonight. I need to talk to our *friend* here."

Jezza's mouth drops open. "But—"

"Not open for discussion."

"Fine," Jezza growls. He straightens his shirt and walks to the door. "Lea?"

I look over to Jamie, who gives me the slightest nod. I guess Ice is underestimating how much we're in this together at this point. If he thinks Jamie will keep stuff from me just because he removes me from the table, he's mistaken.

I get up and walk out the room, ignoring Jezza's pinched lips and tense body language as I strut past him. "I can find my way, thank you very much." Without looking back, I continue down the hallway. Not many directions to go, and not many people to keep me from it. Ice made sure nobody else but the bare minimum of people were here. Can't have the Founder memorize too many faces. A simple risk assessment.

"Lea!" Jezza jogs after me, grabbing me by the sleeve. "Lea, wait!" He keeps his grip and leads me farther down the hallway away from the main room.

"What?" I yank my arm free. Jezza has changed over the last days. Or maybe he had changed before, and he only kept his old-

Jezza-mask on for my benefit, as his alibi. Before the whole beating-up-a-Founder-incident, I never knew this side of him, the angry side, the aggressive side. It's all I get to see these days, no matter if we speak or not.

He leans against the wall. "Look, I don't know what the Demon is playing at, and… it freakin' makes me nervous. You're spending a lot of time with him, and… maybe you're kind of getting to know him, but…" He presses a palm against his temple. "But you need to keep your distance, Lea."

I jerk back. "What? I am keeping my distance, idiot. In case you haven't realized it, not keeping my distance got me into this position! He's a Founder, Jezza. What else am I supposed to do but keep my distance?"

His jaws tighten. "I'm just saying. I don't trust him, and neither should you."

Well, guess that's the one point we disagree on then. "With that, you're wrong. I can trust Jamie." He has done nothing that would endanger me, and in light of him being a Founder, he's been very considerate with me. More than I'd ever expect any Founder to be toward a human.

"That's what he wants you to think."

I roll my eyes. "Suspicious much, Jezza? Don't worry, I'm pretty sure he's—"

"He's dangerous, Lea. He really is. He might seem nice on the outside, but taking in that Founder was the worst decision Ice could've made. Since when did you of all people forget what Founders are capable of? Since when are you the kind of person to let their guard down around them? He's a liability. We should've cut his head off right there and then, or the latest at the pier, but taking him in…" He shakes his head. "Could be our downfall."

"What the heck are you talking about?" This isn't like Jezza: Jezza doesn't panic, Jezza tackles problems. Jezza keeps a cool head. Always has, *the boy who was there.* "And if you're so worried about me, how 'bout you get me that video Hud took? No video, no evidence, no problem."

Jezza looks at a spot somewhere above my head. "Can't do that."

My jaw drops. Not the answer I expected. *You're sure he's more loyal to you than the Resistance?* No, apparently not. "But, Jezza, that video could mean death for me. I *need* it."

His gaze stays glued to that spot above my head. "It's our only tool to keep the demon in check."

I groan. "Not in the grand scheme of things, Jezza. See what happened in there? It's already not enough. He's challenging Ice. Come on, Jezza! It could get me killed! I need that video, or else I'm always going to be Ice's bitch, you know that!"

Jezza chews on his lower lip.

It's all the answer I need. "He's never going to destroy it, is he?" Because I don't think so. Tears sting in my eyes, but I refuse to let them fall. "I don't want this, Jezza. I don't want to be here."

I hear him swallow twice. He pulls a little device with a screen from his pocket, half the size of a postcard. "You know, first thing I wanted to do is get the video and destroy it, Ice's plan be damned. But then I saw this and… I can't get you the video, Lea. I wish I could, but I can't. The demon needs to be controlled, and Hud's video will do just that. No." He holds up a warning finger. "Believe me. This." He thrusts the pod into my hands. "This is something you need to see. I did some research. Wanted to know what *else* Ice has on him, and now I know. You have to understand that the demon is desperate. He'll do what it takes, and I can guarantee that if you get too close, you'll be part of the fallout. He is a liability. Nothing else."

I blink twice, stunned. "Liab—"

"Just watch it, Lea. Make up your own opinion. And get ready for war." With that, he turns on his heels and walks away, leaving me standing there with the pod in my hand and about a million questions on my mind.

The little pod burns in my back pocket until I take it out and fall down onto my bed. Jamie still isn't here, so…

Do I want to watch this? *Should* I watch this?

I turn the device in my hand. Fact is, Jamie has become a normal person to me, not the Founder I expected him to be. But Jezza is also right. Since when did I forget what Founders are capable of? Since when am I the person to let their guard down around them?

And he's right with one more thing that's been bothering me ever since. There's something about Jamie that doesn't add up. The elephant in the room that made me curious about him in the first place. Why is he behaving like he does? Why is he nice to me? Why didn't he kill me? Why the heck does he follow Ice's bidding?

I sit on my bed with my back to the door, criss-cross-applesauce. Before I can change my mind, I tap the screen and hit play. Here goes nothing.

The footage is shaky, blurry, and without sound, yet I easily recognize the Hollywood Bowl. Nestled into the Hollywood hills its typical armadillo-shaped stage is in the center of the screen, and only peripherally can I make out the audience, and they're all Founders.

Adrenaline shoots through my veins. The Bowl, all Founders—an Assembly. Holy cow, this is an Assembly and I'm holding illegal footage in my hands, recorded by someone spying on the Founders and risking their life to document what was going on. A slight tremor in my hands shakes the screen, until I force them still. This is huge.

A hollow feeling takes over my stomach. An Assembly. Why did Jezza give me this?

The video is patched together and leaves out the beginning, because after three or four seconds of shaking and blurry zooming in and out it focuses on five Watchers flying onto stage to land next to the lone figure in the center of it. The video zooms in, and my heart stops.

Blurry or not, no doubt this is Jamie.

The hollow feeling turns into full-blown nausea. Maybe it's not him—no. Now that I know him, know every line of his face, know the way he holds himself, it's obvious. How Ice recognized and remembered Jamie from this footage though is a mystery to me, because it's *that* blurry.

Unfortunately though, it's not blurry enough. All four Watchers grab either one of Jamie's arms or wings, ripping on them and spreading them as far apart as possible. The bad quality of the video does nothing to hide the pain and despair in Jamie's face, or the fast up and down of his chest. Ice spreads through my veins, freezing me to the core. No, no—this is cruel, what are they doing?

The four Watchers yank on his arms and wings to the point where it must hurt like hell, while a fifth grabs Jamie's face and holds it between his hands, fingers all but digging into Jamie's skin.

Without me noticing my fingers brush over his image on the screen. *Jamie. What are they doing to you?*

An older Founder steps behind Jamie, the black tips of his wings visible behind his back and the only contrast to his otherwise blinding white outfit. He looks somewhat familiar as his long black hair falls into his face as he bends forward and rams his palm next to Jamie's shoulder blade so hard, it throws him forward despite the Watchers holding him.

Oh, hell to the no. A chill snakes around my insides. This is bad in all caps. I know what this is. It took me way too long to figure it out, but in my defense, I don't make it a habit of watching Darknet-footage of anything Founder-related.

This isn't just an Assembly.

This is a Tribunal.

Jamie's Tribunal.

For what did he get a Tribunal? To punish him? For what? What did he do? What could he have done to be one of the handful of Founders a Tribunal has ever been held for?

And it doesn't matter. This is Jamie receiving a Stigma *after he was found guilty.*

I'm glad I'm sitting, because all of a sudden, I don't feel so good. I stare down onto the screen unable to move, unable to breathe.

They're giving Jamie a Stigma.

The older Founder behind him spreads his wings, all black.

All black.

I suck in a gasp of air. That's why he looked familiar: completely black wings, and if this is Jamie getting a Stigma, then this must be Luke, the Luke, leader of all Founders.

The man who killed my parents.

Dark rage fills every cell of my body. *Luke.*

Luke keeps his hand on Jamie's back and calls something into the audience I can't read from his lips.

And then I wish the video was even blurrier, because blue light radiates from Luke's palm, and Jamie…

I swallow hard as nausea rises.

Jamie screams.

His body seizes and twists as the Caeruleum grows in intensity. Only because of the Watchers holding him does he stay on his knees and not fall forward. The camera zooms in onto his face, and I wish it didn't.

Never have I seen somebody in that much agony. The fingers digging into his skin from the fifth Watcher holding his face draw blood—

Wait a second. I hit pause and zoom in. Is that…?

Bane.

Bane is the fifth Watcher holding Jamie's face, helping to get him subdued for the Stigma. No wonder there was animosity between them. Bane's body language screams tension and aggression. It's cruel. I should stop watching—

No.

Cruel as it is, I need to see this. I need to see and remember them for what they are—barbarous, archaic monsters.

I force my eyes open until they tear, but I don't stop watching. It wouldn't be fair. Jamie had to go through this alone, the least I can do is bear it with him.

So, yes. I watch Jamie scream, his body contorting as smoke rises from his back.

I watch Luke giving the Stigma, showing no signs of mercy, no signs of regret. No signs of compassion.

I watch Bane holding his face, wings spread out to the max, as if he wanted to intimidate Jamie even more.

I watch it all.

And it *hurts*.

It hurts for Jamie, my parents, myself, and everything that went wrong since that day.

It just freakin' hurts.

The walls I build around myself crumble and fall as tears drop from my eyes. I don't bother wiping them away. The whole scene might not last longer than thirty or forty seconds, but they feel like an eternity until the blue glow stops and the Watchers let go. All but Bane, that is. Instead of letting Jamie fall forward like the others, he holds on to his face. For a moment, I'm thinking he's letting him down gentle, but when he pulls away I see his eyes filled with hatred.

What an ass.

The camera zooms in on Jamie, lying on his stomach, breathing irregular, smoke rising from his back.

"Now you know," a sad, resigned voice says behind me, and I jump. *Jamie.*

I jerk and drop the pod, heart hammering and skipping a beat. "Jeez, Jamie—" How long has he been there? I turn around and freeze. He looks like crap, and that's saying something for a Founder. Plus, besides the occasional smile Jamie's never been exuberant or bubbly since I met him anyway. He's the quiet type, I figured, and while I saw the sadness shining through, I had no clue where it was coming from.

Now I do.

And I understand the anger, the sadness, the odd behavior. I understand.

It's the same for me.

We're both victims of the Founders. Of Luke.

I peel myself off my bed and stand, reaching out a hand and drawing it back the same second he jerks away from it as if I was the one who gave him the Stigma. "Jamie…" What do you say to somebody who's been through this at the hand of his own people? *Sorry* doesn't quite cut it. "So that's what Ice has on you," I whisper. That's why he can control Jamie. He knew he had one Stigma already, add Hud's video leaking and a second infraction…

If the Founders found out Jamie withheld justice from a human, they'd hold another Tribunal. Jamie's second. Without doubt they'd find him guilty—only that this time it wouldn't be a Stigma. This time it would cost him his wings. And while it only happened twice in the last decade, the illegal Darknet footage of that has been seen by every human in existence, even me: *chop, chop.* Done. Still a Founder, but of the lowest ranks. Without his wings.

A fallen Angel.

Jamie stiffens, his wings drawing closer to his back, as if he was protecting the spot where they burned the Stigma into his skin. He lowers his chin to a slow nod. "That's what he has on me." His voice breaks at the end.

Click, the puzzle pieces fall into place. "Is that why you let Ice beat you up?" It would make sense: his sadness. The way he held himself and all but offered himself to Ice and co., because the pain they could put his body through would never come close to numbing the one in his heart, the one his own people gave him.

Jamie flinches as if I had added another punch to that beating. Ever so slowly he raises his head until his eyes meet mine. "I challenged the Servant Rule. Luke was not pleased."

"What?" My jaw drops open. "*That's* what the Stigma was for?" He *challenged the Servant Rule*? It explains so much, like his distaste for me becoming his servant, why he didn't even want a one. That's why they all looked like they'd seen a ghost yesterday, because the guy who got a Stigma for defying servant laws brought a servant himself. Talk about a change of mind.

When he said I needn't worry about becoming his servant, he meant it, because he doesn't believe in it. He must be the only Founder in existence like that, because this, this is a freakin' big deal. The Founders take their commandments very seriously, and the Servant Rule is part of that. *Humanity shall serve the Founders, so we all can serve the Lord together.*

Challenging that Rule… no wonder they gave him the Stigma. It's as much against Founders as it is pro-humanity, and that changes things. Ice knows he's holding an ace. He knows Jamie isn't the typical Founder and won't kill him—but in return he has the power and no qualms to ruin Jamie.

I stare into the blue eyes in front of me. "How… I mean, why—?"

"Easy." He shrugs. "It never seemed right to me. We're the same, Lea. You know that, right? Our race seeded life on Earth under the Lord's command, millennia ago. You carry our DNA—altered, but ours. Humans are the Founders' children. No child should be forced to serve against their will, or be punished for failure. That's not how society should work. Life, living, thriving—it's a team effort that can't be carried on the shoulder of one people over another."

I have to blink to keep the sudden moisture in my eyes from falling. "That… that was nicely said."

He gives me a small smile in response. "I've had some practice."

"But Luke didn't share your views. Obviously."

"Obviously."

The magnitude of what he did, of what he risked, is overwhelming. "You went against your own people. You were trying to protect humans and—"

"And they punished me for it." His lips press into a thin line. "As I've said before, no matter what Ice or Jezza are trying to tell you, I'm on your side. I'm not the enemy."

No, he definitely isn't the enemy. Not Jamie. We both have a reason to hate Luke. "Do you hate him as much as I do? Luke?"

Jamie's eyes flutter shut, as if the mere mention of his name was too much. "It's complicated."

"Because he's one of your own." And Jamie went against his rules. I bet he feels guilty for that, although he did what was right.

Jamie stays quiet and I chew on the inside of my cheek. "Can I… can I see it? Please?"

For a moment, I fear I've overstepped my boundaries, because Jamie freezes. Completely. No muscle moves, no breath enters or leaves his body. Wouldn't be surprised if his heart stopped as well.

But then he closes his eyes, reaches around his back and grabs his shirt. He turns away from me as he pulls it up his back, the material sliding up, being caught by the roots of his wings. Still, it's enough for me to see the round scar high up between his shoulder blades.

Maybe three inches in diameter it's shaped like a stylized sun, only the flesh looks like it melted and pulled itself together again. It must've hurt like crazy. I'm *this* close to reaching out for it when Jamie drops his shirt and turns to face me again.

Heavy silence hovers between us, before he stretches past me and picks up the pod from the bed, weighing it in his hands as if he wanted to turn it, and yet keeping the screen facing down.

I nod at his back. "Why doesn't it heal?" Anything heals in a Founder, Jamie's recent bullet wound being the proof of that. Nothing should be able to leave a scar.

"Because it's a punishment. Only our Caeruleum can truly harm us. Either it kills, or it gives a Stigma. It's one of the many ways the Founders are completely screwed up."

"No kidding." If I ever meet Luke, I'm going to give him a piece of my mind. Double. For my parents and for Jamie.

We fall silent again, and after a couple of moments of fighting it, Jamie turns the screen over, staring at the image of himself on the ground, stunned, back still smoldering. He doesn't say a word, yet the shallow, harsh breath he sucks in speaks louder than anything he could've said. A pressure builds up in my chest, a lump that's been growing in size since I realized Jamie wasn't an ordinary Founder.

The way he looks, it breaks my heart. "Jamie?"

His eyes stay glued to the screen.

"Jamie. Listen. *Listen to me.* You are going to be okay. Nothing is going to happen. What they did was horrible. Barbaric. Cruel. But it won't happen again. We will be fine." If Jezza thought watching Jamie get a Stigma would open a gap between us, he was wrong. If anything, I understand him better now.

Jamie tears his eyes off the screen, thick lashes sweeping up and down. "Wings are what makes me a Founder, Lee. Without them I am nothing. I'm—"

"First, not going to happen. Not. And second, you're still you, Jamie. The one who challenged the Servant Rule. You're a good guy." If I needed any proof, there it is.

He flinches and his wings tug closer together, as if they wanted to hide the mark he carries.

"*This* won't happen again. It's over." I move my hand forward as careful as I can, reaching for the pod in his hands. Jamie doesn't move. A slow burn crawls up my arm and into my heart. He takes a choppy breath, following the path of my hand with undivided attention. I force myself to breathe in, breathe out, to keep my hand steady until my fingers wrap around the pod opposite from his. Our hands are so close, so close, they'd touch if either of us angled their wrist the slightest bit.

His gaze crashes into mine, the intensity in his stare pulling me in like a magnet.

The air in the room gets heavier, the distance between us smaller. Tension sizzles, bringing the little hairs on my arms to rise. I should probably let go, step back, and put some distance between us, but I can't. I'm rooted to my spot by something deep inside my heart blossoming and connecting to Jamie's in a way I don't quite understand. I've never felt like this—like I couldn't breathe, when obviously my body was fine. Like I was flying, when obviously I'm standing with both feet on the ground. Like I was special, when obviously the only thing special about me are my dead parents.

Static passes from his skin to mine. The apple in Jamie's throat moves up and down before he exhales roughly as all air flees my lungs. "Lee." His voice is rough. Hoarse.

"Yes?" My voice doesn't sound much better than his, because imagination started to take hold and ran wild about ten seconds ago. I can't help but think of Frances and the way she looked at her Founder. Can't help but remember that if I'm not mistaken, he touched her. Can't help but think about what Jamie said, *you've heard the same rumors, haven't you?*

When Jamie speaks, his voice rumbles through me. "Don't do this." His gaze drops on our hands on the pod, and a shudder runs down my skin, be it from his words, or his proximity. He still hasn't moved his hand, but neither have I.

"Do what?" I give him my most innocent look.

Another hard swallow as his gaze drifts up from our hands to meet mine. "You don't want to fall for me."

I jerk back. "What?"

"You don't want to fall in love with me, Lee. I'm trouble."

No, you're not. The words are on the tip of my tongue, but they won't come out. Because he *is* trouble. He spells it with every look at me, with every almost-touch, with every crooked smile.

I put all the conviction I have behind the next words. "'I'm not falling in love with you." And I'm not even lying. I'm not falling in love with Jamie.

At this point it's clear I have fallen already.

Hard.

CHAPTER TWELVE

Concert

Jamie pulls himself up to his full height in front of me. "Again," he growls, eyes narrowed and brows scrunched tight. "You need to know your enemy and your options."

I barely keep from rolling my eyes. We've been over this. It's pointless. "I know my enemy, Jamie. That's why I know there's no way I'm ever going to be able to fight a Watcher, even if it wasn't a sin. That's—"

His eyes soften, the blue losing some of their sting. "Believe me, I don't want you to fight a Watcher. Or anybody, Founder or not. Not if I can help it, not if I'm around. But with the Mark still at…" He looks down to the scanner on his wrist. "At a steady tangerine, plus us going to the concert, plus us trying to smuggle out a Masker… I'd say better safe than sorry."

Not quite true. There is no *safe* for me. "I'll be sorry either way. I hit a Watcher—any Founder—I'm as good as dead." I lose, no matter what. If they wanted to kill me, they could. If I fight them, they'll only have more reason to kill me even deader.

Jamie tips his head to the side. "True. Generally speaking, you don't stand a chance. What I'm trying to do here is prolong your life."

"Wow. You really have a way with words, you know that?"

Jamie grins, and that grin… dang if it didn't make me proud I was the one who put it there. "One of my many talents. And keep in mind, whatever we practice, you can also use on humans. It never hurts to know how to defend yourself." He cuts his eyes at me and I get it. We're in deep.

I blow a raspberry. "So, Ice didn't say anything else but that the Resistance had intel something big was about to happen?" Couldn't be much more vague than that.

"Nothing else. Thing is, I have my ear pretty close to the ground most days, and I haven't picked up on anything lately."

"Is that good or bad?"

He shrugs. "Tough to say. Good, because I'd say I'd know otherwise. Bad, because if I don't know about it, it's pretty high up and top-secret, which then by definition is bad."

I lift my chin and look at him down my nose. "If you don't know about it—good to see your ego is at least still intact, Mr. I'm-so-Important." I stick out my tongue at him, and Jamie grins, dimples and all.

"Shut up, you. Just telling it as it is, I've got my contacts.

"Right. *The Jamin works in mysterious ways.*" Misquoted, used in the completely wrong context, but hey, I quoted the New Scripture. Kind of.

Jamie rips a pillow off the bed, sending his copy of the New Scripture he's been reading to the floor. "Shut up, I said. That's the Lord's line, not mine." He throws the pillow at me, but I deflect it.

Huh. Speaking of. "Have you ever met the Lord?" Lord knows—hardy-harr-harr—humanity hasn't seen Him in millennia.

Jamie picks up the pillow. "No. I was born shortly before we started our route to Earth. My father has worked with him—on Earth actually. Centuries ago."

Whoa. "Seriously?" I can say what I want, eternal critic and non-believer that I am, but *the Lord*, the person who initiated seeding life here… he is God, by definition. Bringer of life. Meeting Him must be pretty cool.

Jamie turns the pillow in his hands. "Yup. They didn't get along, I hear. I often wondered…" He throws the pillow back onto my bed.

"Wondered what?"

A sigh. "Nothing. Anyway, time for action. Show me what you've got. May peace be victorious," he quotes the Rebellion's mantra. "But no peace without fight."

Aww, dang. Back to that.

He spreads his wings out as far as possible in our tight quarters and keeps his hands close to his sides. "No Watcher is going to feel the need to go into a full fighting stance with you. Not with a human. Maybe with a Resistance fighter, but probably not even that. They might not even feel threatened enough to activate their Black Box. If at all, they'd maybe use their Raptor to catch and control you." He taps the side of his hip, where a Watcher would carry their Black Box and the inconspicuous piece of metal that could turn into a hungry snake and wrap around any body part, controlling it. "Or they could of course unleash their Caeruleum at the attacker, and they're history."

He raises a palm, and I swallow dry. It's been a decade, but unsurprisingly I'm still PTSD'd from that one fateful afternoon. One quick stretch of his fingers and Jamie's palm begins to glow in a faint blue light.

"This is when you need to be fast, but we'll play it through slowly, for obvious reasons." His voice is gentler now. Calming.

"Okay," I squeak.

"Go."

I bring both hands up in front of my face and step forward in slow motion. "Protect." Both my hands stop an inch in front of Jamie's extended arm. "Deflect." This is where he pretends I pushed his arm out of the way and he reacts in slow-mo to my pretend-attack. I lift my right knee and flick a kick in the direction of his groin. "Attack."

"Good." Jamie fake-doubles over. "Don't stop. What's next?"

Next, next… "Scanner!" I reach for his wrist and pretend to rip off the disc on his leather band. No Scanner, no Watcher trailing me.

"Next!" Jamie gets up in slow-mo, and I dart forward at a snail's pace, hand outstretched for the belt around his waist.

"Snap!" I pop my lips in an approximation of the sound I imagine ripping off the Black Box would make. Losing that little thing won't hurt the Watcher, but it'll make his work way more difficult when it's gone. Since Jamie started training me yesterday in preparation for what might be coming our way, I've learned more about Watchers than I ever wanted to know. They're trained for battle from early childhood. Altered pain receptors. Loyal to the core. And equipped with enough technology to make NASA envious. That little Black Box on their belt connects to receptors in their uniform. In addition to generating a protective force field around the Founder that would allow him to touch us humans without repercussions, it also holds enough power to continuously emit a similar force field that protects Watchers against bullets and other mechanical threats. Must be a pretty good AI powering that little feature, given that a Founder can touch whatever he wants and can be touched himself—without a force field springing to life. Pity you can't beat them to death, or the Resistance would've tried. Must be nice to have healing powers. The Black Box also records whenever one of their little tools is used and sends the data to the hives for analysis. If I got scanned, that data would be saved and uploaded a millisecond later, and even if I disabled that Watcher, the information would be out there and me eventually screwed. I hear some of the Resistance are wearing technology messing with that data upload, not that Ice upgraded Jamie or me with any such tools.

Hence, my goal is to take off the Scanner and disable the belt. It's almost more important than disabling the Watcher. It makes all the difference between dealing with one person or a battalion.

"Next," Jamie orders.

Next? Wait, we didn't talk about what's—

Lightning fast, Jamie jumps up and forward so close, only an inch separates us. His wings stretch out and then curl around behind my back as his arms move in as if he was going to grab me, only stopping a hair's breadth before contact.

Holy cow.

My next breath comes out chopped. I'm trapped between Jamie's arms and his wings, like in a hug without contact. I'm positive that even if I did nothing but take a big breath, the movement would be enough to touch Jamie. Enough to worsen my mark.

We're both frozen, motionless, trapped in a dance that came to a sudden halt when the music stopped. Even though Jamie doesn't move, his body is wound tight, every muscle tense, every breath harsh and short, like mine.

"*Boom*," he whispers, "in real life, the Watcher just killed you." His gentle breath caresses my ear as he speaks. A series of shivers dances across my skin, so overwhelming my eyes fall shut. My body tingles head to toe, and we're not even touching. Jamie's vanilla-scent is everywhere, surrounding me, cocooning me.

I should feel bad that I messed up again, that I let Jamie get the upper hand, but I'm not capable of feeling anything but this, this light, happy, warm feeling that lifts me up as if I had wings myself.

"You hear me?" This time his breath stirs my hair, and I squeeze my eyes shut so hard, stars dance behind my closed lids—because if I didn't, if I looked, I'd see Jamie so near it would be easy to turn into him. To touch him.

And that can't happen.

"Mh-hm," I mutter.

I hear him swallow. "After this, you need to run, Lee. It's your only chance."

"Run, got it." Like I probably should right now, only I can't move. Don't want to move.

"Lee?"

"Huh?"

"Open your eyes."

I do, and *whoa*, Jamie is *right there*! His head is next to mine, turned, so he can look at me. A lock of his black hair falls into his face, and pathetic as it is, all I want to do is swipe it away.

All I can risk is a slight tilt of my head, or our cheeks would connect.

That thought alone unleashes sparks of an unknown magnitude inside my stomach.

A ragged breath leaves his throat. "I—"

Pause.

Somehow, the ground seems to be shaking. Can't be my knees. "Yes?"

His thick lashes sweep down as his chest rises sharply. "Nothing."

In the blink of an eye, he's at a safe distance of at least four feet. He curls his fingers to fists at his sides and relaxes, then curls up again as he's dragging up deep breaths. "We're dangerous. Just… just keep that in mind." He folds his wings in tight and turns away from me. "Or else I can't guarantee I'll behave."

I wrap my arms around my chest, cold from the sudden loss of his warmth and sudden realization that Jamie is just as affected by whatever is between us as me.

Dangerous.

I agree.

Only I don't know who's more dangerous to me at this moment: a Watcher, or Jamie.

The forum is way more crowded this time around.

What were empty streets are now a buzzing town square filled with Founders. No matter where I look, wings are everywhere. Founders, Founders, Founders. Granted, a good fifty percent bring their very own human servant, but the few young human males and females do nothing to break up the sea of Founders. The ones without a servant walk around in groups of two or more, some of them holding hands. Once or twice, I see Founder-couples hugging or kissing, and by Founder-couples, I mean two males.

That's maybe the one good thing about Founders. They don't discriminate. *There is to be no sin where there is love, for all of His creations are made equal,* New Scripture, New Book of Luke something-something. Yup. Love is love, no matter what. Perhaps that's also their only option considering their hives only carry males, but for once, I refuse to see them in a bad light. The fall of all homosexuality laws was the best thing the Founders brought us or will ever bring us.

Jamie leads us from the parking lot down the main road toward the outdoor stage. It's staggering how much cleaner the forum looks. Compared to the human cities, I mean. On the way over, we passed one of those little towns close to the freeway, and a whole block of houses was destroyed. Burned, torn down, whatnot—the Founders cracking down on Resistance hideouts. Gave me the chills, for more reasons than one.

Plus, the Founders had the advantage of planning a village in the middle of nowhere, meaning, space is not an issue. Not only are the houses bigger than anything in L.A., but also the park in the middle of the forum is movie-worthy with its fountains, fruit trees and birds en masse. It's a little bit as if they had replicated a little bit of Eden here, although who knows if that ever existed. If it did though, it must've looked like this park, minus the dark, heavy clouds looming above threatening with rain.

Oh, well. Kinda glad not everything's perfect for the Lord's creatures.

Up on stage, a couple of human musicians tune their instruments. *Hollywood Bowl Orchestra*, it says on a sign next to the stage. I hear they have an amazing viola-player. Only the best for the Founders.

I keep my eyes peeled for Josh Cardoza, but if he's here already, he's hidden by the crowd. It's not so easy picking out a human male among a sea of Founders. The majority of them aren't pledged, which means I've got to check a lot of single males, hoping Cardoza is one of them.

Once in a while, Jamie stops here and there, chatting with

Founders he knows—or rather, who know him. Now that I've seen how he's come to his fame, I get why they all do and why he's so on edge. More than once a fellow Founder takes him by the sleeve and angles him away from me while speaking, and every time Jamie's face pinches a little bit more.

Whatever they're telling him, he doesn't like it.

I pick up on a couple of cut-off words—war, Lord, Commander, inevitable—and while I'm missing out on all context, those few crumbs are enough to bring the small hairs in my neck to a raise. So, Ice was right, something is going on, the way it seems.

A slight breeze picks up as the sun disappears behind some clouds. If we're lucky, it's not going to rain, although I should probably rephrase that, because California does need the rain. This concert doesn't.

"Lea!"

My gaze flies to the left—Frances, trailed by the Founder she served during the dinner. Benjamin, I guess. I fall into automatic servant-mode. "Founder." I bow, nice'n deep. Ice would be proud of me. The Founder gives me a quick nod before he joins Jamie and the other Founder a few steps away from us.

Frances smiles ear to ear and takes my shoulders. "So good to see you again. I'm glad your Jamin decided to come. Provided the weather holds up, this should be fun." She points a thumb over her shoulder at the stage, the bracelet on her wrist glowing in bright, deep red. With all the Founder-human couples I've seen today, I'd say hers is the reddest. Everybody else's has a slighter red or even only a rosé-tone.

Guess some are more motivated to *connect* with their Founder than others.

But anyway: "I'm also happy to experience it with him." That sounds right, doesn't it? A servant thing?

Frances' smile widens, if that's even possible. She's so at ease in her role, but so is her Founder. I mean, he let her lead the way over, not the other way around. "One of the many things you both will have in common and that will bring you closer together." Her gaze drifts over to Benjamin. Only a blind person wouldn't see the love she holds for him, but they'd hear the adoration in her voice. It's that obvious. I wonder if they really… I mean, are they truly—

Anyway. I clear my throat. "Yeah. Uhh, I hope so." Can't help the red crawling up my neck.

The wind picks up in a strong gust, throwing twigs and leaves on the ground into a swirl.

Somebody taps me on the shoulder. "Looks like it's gonna come down pretty soon, eh?"

Bull's eye! "Mr. Cardoza." I hold out my hand. "Good to see you again."

"Likewise." He shakes hands with me, then with Frances. "You and Benjamin ready for the concert?"

"Yes, sir. Looking forward to it."

Cardoza nods. "Me, too. Oh, but Lea—I was hoping I'd run into you. And before I forget it." He holds up a finger. "It's not much, but I feel like going into Servitude should be celebrated. After all, you're devoting your life to the angels descended from Heaven." He reaches into the large bag slung across his body, and my heart rate spikes up.

The Masker—he really brought us the Masker.

Cardoza pulls a large candy jar from his bag, filled to the brim with round, flat, wrapped sweets in the colors of the rainbow. "From one of my most favorite stores up in Vegas. You've got to try—"

"Now look at that. Are we giving out gifts today, Mayor?" The voice is full of snide and sarcasm. Bane, arms crossed in front of his chest, the trademark annoyed scowl on his face.

Crap.

To his credit, Cardoza has himself way better under control than me. I probably would've dropped the jar, because as it is, I have a hard time to keep on playing along and bow deep, like nothing's happening here.

Cardoza smiles at Bane. "Watcher. May your day be blessed by the Lord. Yes, indeed, I am giving a gift to the Protégée. Her dedication to Servitude is commendable and should be celebrated." He hands me the jar with a slight bow.

"Th-thank you." I take it and press it against my chest. Not taking any chances.

Frances just stands there, looking from one of us to the other, but probably wishing she were somewhere else. Feels pretty chilly here all of a sudden.

Cardoza's smile widens. "I'd keep them to myself if I were you. You wouldn't want people digging in there and picking out the best ones." Translation: the Masker is in there. Don't let people find it. Still, he keeps up the charade, winking at me and lowering his voice to a conspirator whisper. "The pink ones are the best."

"I—I'll keep that in mind."

Bane glowers at me, and while it scares me to the core, it also makes me mad. Angry. That's one of the guys who held Jamie during his Tribunal. I remember how hard he grabbed his face. I remember the hate in his eyes.

I remember.

Keeping that soft smile on my face is more than hard work.

Bane narrows his eyes. "Pink, you say? Let me try one." He reaches for the jar, and before I can suppress the reaction, I've twisted my upper body away from him.

It doesn't need Cardoza's and Frances' sharp intake of air, or the thinning of Bane's lips to know I just made a mistake.

It's not my place to deny a Founder anything.

"Give that to me, pet," Bane hisses. He reaches for the jar and—

"Bane." Jamie sighs his name more than he says it. "Still can't take no for an answer?" The person Jamie talked to takes one look at Bane and scurries off, wings curled up as if they could protect him from the Watcher's wrath, while Benjamin comes over to stand next to Frances. We must be giving them a fun little show here.

Bane's hand drops, and for a moment a shadow crosses his face, gone as quickly as it came. "Actually, I can work with a no I can see the reason for. Otherwise, not so much."

Jamie stands tall, hands crossed behind his back. "So, I've noticed. You're giving my servant a hard time?" He nods his chin at me, my cue.

"Master, I apologize." I bow as deep as I can, keeping the jar pressed to my chest. Excuse coming up in three, two… "I grew up in an orphanage. Candy was scarce. I'm used to protecting what's mine." I stay down low, heart seizing more than beating. If Bane takes the jar… we're all history.

As it is, the Watcher looks at me with disgust. "It talks."

Jamie steps forward, closer to Bane. Even from my bowed position, I can see the look he gives him. Challenging. Hard. "I don't mind her talking. Get over your superiority complex, Bane. Rise, servant."

I straighten.

Cardoza bows before he addresses Bane. "If you so desired, it would be my honor to order you some—"

"No." Bane makes a cutting motion with his hand. "I'd rather try this." His eyes bore into Jamie's.

A gust of wind plays with the two men's feathers and cranks up the goosebumps on my skin. Yes, the temperature dropped, but it could very well be because of the icy atmosphere between those two. No love lost there, for obvious reasons.

Jamie is the first to react. A cool smile plays around his lips. "Well then. In the interest of good old times, why don't you try one? Lea, please offer Bane some candy. He gets hangry when his sugar drops."

Oh, holy cow. "Of course, Master." I bow again, then screw open the lid and offer the jar to Bane. "Founder."

Bane's glare could kill on sight as he reaches for the candy.

Cardoza's fake smile freezes, but Jamie's self-assured, cocky grin never changes.

I hold the jar steady as Bane's hand dives in… in… deeper… searches—

"You might want to pick one and move on. That's good advice, for now and for life."

If I wasn't so attuned to the Founder in front of me, I might have missed the small twitch of Bane's jaw, the widening of his eyes, or the short moment his hand freezes inside the jar. As it is, it lasts no more than a split second, but I see it.

And I get it.

Jamie's needling him to distract him from searching the jar.

I can help. After all, I'm a servant. "Founder," I say with all the reverence I can muster and bow, effectively lowering the jar from Bane's hand until all he can do is pull it out with a random candy between his fingers.

I could swear I hear a sigh of relief from Cardoza.

Bane's nostrils flare, his expression hardening. "You're the last one to give life advice, *Jamester*. I'm watching you. Always watching." He points two fingers at his eyes, then at Jamie.

"I know, Bane. I know." There's something in his voice I can't quite interpret, a certain heaviness that adds to the terse silence hanging between us.

This is *so* not about candy anymore, or rather, it never was. Not the way Bane's eyes drill into Jamie. Not the way Jamie's pulse in his neck speeds up. Nope. This is about the Stigma Bane helped give him.

A heavy drop of rain falls onto my head. And another one. Another one.

Frances squeaks and covers her head with her hands.

"Let's go." That's Benjamin, leading her away before I can say goodbye, not that I'm too terribly sorry about that.

Jamie sighs and looks up to the sky. "Yeah. Not staying for that either." He turns on his heels. "Servant."

To my surprise, I fall right into step with him. "Master."

Without a second look back, Jamie walks away from Cardoza and Bane. The rain picks up, tapping a fast drum-rhythm onto the asphalt. Jamie spreads his wings like an umbrella and brings them together above his head, protecting him from the rain like he did for us at the carousel. Only today, I'm his servant, and I get drenched.

"Jamie?"

Jamie stops dead in his tracks and turns around. "Bane?"

Bane's white wings are spread over his head, like every other Founder's. "Luke knows." He points his index- and middle-finger at his eyes again, then at Jamie. "Always watching."

CHAPTER THIRTEEN

Turbine

The moment I close the car door, Jamie talks under his breath. "I want you to drive out of here like nothing was wrong. Obey all traffic laws. Take your time. Smile when you see a Founder. Keep up the Charade." He takes the jar from me and sets it between his legs on the ground, his fingers shaking. "I promise you Bane is going to follow us, and I don't want to give him any reason to get his hands on this." He nudges the jar with his foot.

"Okay," I say hoarsely between my lips as we pull out of the parking lot.

Never have I driven more carefully than I do now. The rain is coming down hard, which is a good explanation for why I'm driving like an old lady, but also for why nobody pays any special attention to us. They're all running away from the rain, finding shelter.

So much for the concert.

The one day it rains in California, it pours.

I stay on the main road that brings us right to the Freeway.

"Floor it." Jamie twists his upper body and looks back. "This is our only chance to have him lose us."

I punch the pedal to the metal and grip the steering wheel so tight, my fingers hurt. Bane following us is not good. So. Not. Good.

Speaking of not good. "He said Luke knows. Knows what? And what's with him and Luke anyway?" I've met him twice, both times he brought up Luke. Needless to say, that doesn't make me like him more.

Jamie chokes on his next breath and coughs twice. "*Luke.*" He spits it out more than he says it. "Like I said, Bane is one of our highest-ranking Watchers. Him and Luke are tight, and Bane likes to follow rules." He all but spits out that part. "And since we haven't registered yet to pledge our loyalties in front of Michael—"

"Which we'll never do. No offense to you as my master."

"None taken. We won't pledge, no offense to you as my servant either." He gives me one of those rare, wild smiles. "But anyway, most Founders register as soon as they agree to take a servant. Obviously, we didn't, and I really would've preferred to keep Luke out of this, but Bane is a tattle-tale. So yeah, at this point, the boss knows."

"Crap." There is no good attention that comes from Luke, not in our position. Any attention is bad attention.

"Pretty much."

Ugh. Okay, maybe it's not that bad. Maybe we can make it work for us. "But maybe that's good, because…" I don't know if I should mention it or not, but… "because you got the Stigma for being against the Servant Rule. So, won't this improve your standing with your peeps and with him?" And that would be good for us again, right? Less scrutiny?

His forehead creases with tension. "I couldn't care less what Luke thinks of me. I'm more worried about what he might want us to do. Hint, hint: pledge. Anyway." He bends down, and picks up the candy jar, jamming his hand in there and fishing around. "There. Almost on the bottom. I—" He pulls out his hand, a little clear plastic bag between his fingers. "Whoa." He whistles through his teeth. "Three Maskers."

Three?

For one quick second, I look over at the bag in Jamie's hand. "Three," he repeats, the apple in his throat moving up and down.

"What the hell does the Resistance want with three Maskers? What are they planning?" One is bad enough, three…

"I don't know." Jamie lets out a shaky laugh. "But whatever it is, it's not good."

I throw him a quick glance. "What did you find out from the other Founders?"

He massages the back of his neck. "Nothing but general blah. Quite disappointing, actually."

Huh. "Sounded different from what I picked up. I heard one of them mention something about war, the Lord, Commanders—"

He gives me a sideway glance. "You've got good ears. Part Founder, eh?" He winks. "Yes, that's what I got as well, but nothing concrete. A couple of the older Founders remembering their glorious days, but nothing definite. I agree they're all… quite nervous, so maybe the Resistance is on to something. They all asked me if I knew something, which obviously I don't."

"Maybe the higher-ranking Founders know, and the ones you talked to don't?" They could pick up on the general mood though.

"Sure, although usually I'd say I'd know if that was the case." He opens the window on his side. "But then, I'm not quite as *integrated* anymore as I was before. We'll see."

Integrated. Jamie has a good sense of self-worth, little fledgling he is in comparison to all those older Founders.

He twists his body and looks out the window, checking our

behind. The rain is not just falling anymore, but hammering down with a vengeance, the gusting wind carrying it in wild vortices for one moment, then almost diagonally the next. Jamie's head and shoulders are drenched within seconds. Water drops from him when he pulls in again and closes the window.

"He's behind us. Barely enough distance that we can lose him."

"But I can't go any faster!" I'm flooring it as it is, disregarding speed limits and all. "He can't catch us—"

"And he won't. Bane hates rain. Always has." His tone becomes pensive. "Okay, listen, here's the plan. Remember the wind farm in another couple of minutes, on the right?"

"The turbines?"

"Exactly. There's a solar farm next to it. You keep up the speed until we get there. That'll at least keep the distance between us and Bane. Once we hit the solar panels, you're going to go off road and park the car as close behind one of the panels as you can. Then we get out and run over to the turbines—"

"We leave the car? He's gonna catch up in no time—"

"And he's not going to find us. The power generated by the solar farm and wind turbines disturbs his scanner." Jamie pats his belt where Bane's disk would be.

"So, we hide?" A wave of cold rolls over me. This is so not good.

A grim expression sets in Jamie's face. "For now."

James Bond has nothing on me as I pull off the Freeway at a dizzying speed and dart toward the solar panels. The car jumps and bucks over the few bushes and uneven surface, and I nearly crash into the first solar panel. They're way bigger from up close, like truck-sized.

"Farther, farther!" Jamie jots a finger into the distance. "The less we have to run!"

The wipers swish water off my windshield at the highest setting, yet it doesn't do much to improve visibility. It's not plain rain anymore, it's a full-blown storm.

"There!" Jamie points at a panel that looks no different than the others. "Far enough from the street he won't fly over here. Rain's gonna wash away our tracks. Park!"

I throw the car into an almost 90-degree bend and barely get it to stop behind the solar panel.

"Out!" Jamie throws his door open, leaving the candy behind. The Maskers have long been tucked away in the pocket of his tactical pants.

The moment I leave the car, rain assaults me. It runs into my eyes, blinds me, pummels my body like little needles, and drenches me to the skin within seconds. "Crap," I yell, although it sounds like a whisper against nature's sound.

"Come on!" Jamie calls out and waves a hand. He runs ahead so fast, I have a hard time keeping up. Can't fall. Every misstep could cost me valuable time. I check behind me, but nothing. Not seeing Bane. Still that doesn't make me feel better. Quite the opposite: it scares me more. Bane is mean. One of the best Watchers, Jamie said. Yeah, he might hate flying in the rain, but he hates Jamie more.

And, by proxy, me.

"Where are you going?" There's nowhere to run out here. No houses, no nothing. Turbine after turbine after turbine—but nothing that could be used as a shelter.

"Trust me," he yells back over his shoulder, words partially swallowed by his wings. He'd be way faster flying, but he'd also be more visible to Bane.

Jamie leads us through a maze of turbines, all buzzing and turning like crazy, some of them farther away from the hills where the winds hit harder.

My sides sting, my heart has never worked so hard in its life, and my lungs burn—and I'm a good runner. More than once do I slip and almost fall, only sheer luck keeping me from sprawling face forward.

"There!" Jamie points to a turbine like all the others, the only difference being this one's blades are standing still. He runs up the few steps to the small door in its stem for service workers and hammers a code into the numeric lock, then rips the door open. "In!"

He doesn't have to say it twice. I dart in and Jamie follows, slamming the door.

Silence.

Well, besides the howling of the wind outside and our heavy breathing inside.

"Oh, hell." I pant and bend forward, supporting my weight with my hands on my knees. "How did you… I mean, why—"

"This is my turbine." Jamie coughs and wipes the wet hair from his face. "I'll show you." He points up the narrow ladder leading up all the way to the top of the shaft. "Usually I'd fly up to the top, but I don't want to risk Bane seeing me. Let him follow the Freeway and look for us. Good luck." He grabs the rungs of the ladder. "Let's go."

Usually he'd fly up to the top? "How often have you been here?"

"Often." He climbs ahead of me, water dripping off his wings. "Remember when I met you at the pier? I'd been living here for a couple of weeks."

"You'd been living here? Inside a turbine?"

"Quite comfortable, actually. When you make it work for you, that is." He pauses long enough to give me a quick wink and smile. "And remember, that was after my Tribunal. I wasn't really keen on staying in the forum at that point, but I didn't have any money to rent in the city."

"And you didn't want to impose on anybody." Like he didn't get himself much food either.

"Nope."

We fall silent again and continue climbing. My hands are cold, my feet are cold, heck, I am cold. More than once I need to check where I'm placing my hands to make sure I'm actually grabbing a rung and not just air. Most sensation has fled my hands and feet, and I'm shivering like crazy.

"We're here." Jamie reaches up and pulls himself through a little hatch. I follow his lead and reach up once he's out of sight, force my stiff, cold body through the tight opening, and collapse on the cold metal floor.

That was close.

Too close.

While I'm working on catching my breath, Jamie crosses the small cabin to the very front. At one point a huge, electricity-generating engine must've been in here and at least part of the mechanism is still here. Some kind of gears stick out of the floor in the middle, panels quote-unquote *decorate* the side, and the little front hatch Jamie's opening now to lean out and check our surroundings must be where the gear shaft ran through.

This whole thing isn't very wide, maybe the size of a short school bus, but it's obvious Jamie's been here. I can make out blankets, pillows, a couple of books, empty bottles of water, and a couple of power bar wrappers farther up front. Plus, I could swear it smells like him.

I push myself up to standing. The cold floor is sucking out all the heat I have left.

A flash of light, a crashing thunder—I jump and squeak. Thunderstorm. Great. These things act like a Faraday cage, right?

Jamie pulls the front hatch closed, still looking out the broken panel, the only source of light in this otherwise dark cabin. "I think we're alone now. Bane won't fly during lightning." He turns around. "We can stay here until—" Jamie sucks a sharp breath in when his eyes fall on me. His gaze sweeps over my wet body, down my chest, my stomach, to my legs, every inch burning as if he touched me with fire. A deep sound rumbles from his throat, and it does amazing things to my stomach.

He takes a step forward.

And stops.

Another one.

And stops.

His lips part, eyes vibrant behind his thick lashes. "You're soaked." The apple in his throat moves up and down.

"So are you." My voice wavers just a little, because yes, I noticed. How could I not? Jamie is beautiful any time of the day, but with his clothing clinging to every muscle… spectacular.

For an eternal second, we stare at each other. A flush rises in his cheeks, and it makes him look younger. He swallows again. Hard. "Get out of that wet clothing," he says, voice rough and heavy.

Get out—

I cross my arms in front of my chest. "No." Hell no. I'm not getting out of my—

Smooth as a panther, Jamie prowls forward until he's in front of me. "Take. Off. Your. Clothes." His eyes bore into mine with an intensity that doesn't leave room for imagination. All of a sudden, the air is heated between us. Burning. Scalding.

He lifts up his palms. "You know these will behave."

It's my time to work on a dry swallow. Yeah. I know that. He won't risk touching me. The Mark has begun to fade, and both our freedoms depends on it. A shiver runs down my body, one brought on by the thought of undressing in front of Jamie. Well, maybe being soaked plays its part too.

Jamie keeps his gaze glued to me. "Blankets. Over there. But not in your wet clothing."

It… it kinda makes sense. Right? Totally does. "You first." My voice is a hoarse whisper. Him first, and then… I don't know.

For a moment, Jamie cocks his head, a surprised look on his face, but then he takes a step back and unfurls his wings as far as he can in this tight room. With one quick move, he reaches for the shirt on his back and pulls his off, the material giving at the roots of his wings.

Holy. Freakin'. Cow.

Not much light shines into this tiny room, but it's enough. Way enough. Jamie… is stunning. I mean, I knew that but… this is breathtaking. The little bit of light throws shadows over his chest, emphasizing the muscles and his six-pack. Correction, eight-pack. Of course. Wouldn't want a Founder to be less than uber-perfect. And while his body calls to me, it's not what makes my stomach cramp up and my knees wobbly. It's the way he looks at me: challenging, his mouth slightly open, breath coming in and out quicker than normal. Ever so slowly, he moves his hands to the buttons of his pants, but his eyes stay on me, holding me captive, daring me to not look away.

Pop.

That was the first button of his pants.

Pop.

The second.

Pop.

The third.

Pop—and he slides his pants down to his ankles and steps out of them. A gust of air hisses in through the broken panel, and automatically his wings spread the slightest bit, catching the draft.

I know I'm pathetic, but… I'm drinking in the sight of him: his long, lean body clad only in black boxer briefs, the black hair messed up by wind and rain, and all of that framed by two strong wings, so white they illuminate the darkness.

"Your turn." It's a mere hoarse whisper, yet it resonates like thunder.

My turn.

Okay. I can do this. I can do this. I've walked the whole mile with Jezza, but never during that time did I feel like I was about to explode, become a victim to spontaneous combustion and faint, all at the same time. That's what the idea of experiencing any of that with Jamie does to me.

There's no denying it. I want this. I want to go there with Jamie, although I know I can't. *We* can't. So maybe this, this little game, whatever it is, is all we can have.

And I'm not about to be a spoilsport.

I grab the hem of my shirt and pull it over my head, only

breaking eye contact when the shirt covers my eyes.

Gone.

Goosebumps run down my skin, and while I'm definitely more affected by the cold than a Founder, this time they have nothing to do with the freezing temperatures. They're all courtesy of the small gasp coming from Jamie. It's all I need to keep me going.

Pop—the button.

Zip—the zipper.

A short moment of hesitation, and then I wiggle myself out of my pants, until I'm in my underwear. Black bra, black panties. Nothing else. Yes, we've been roomies, but both of us have changed in the bathroom. This is new, to both of us.

My heart hammers like crazy. Like desperate. Like it wanted to burst out of my chest and hurl itself at Jamie. And that is scary—no, terrifying, because here I am, standing almost naked in front of a Founder. A *Founder*. I'm throwing away all caution, all lessons learned the hard way, and yet it feels right.

Wordlessly, Jamie turns and motions to the heap of blankets. He straightens three of them out on top of each other, kind of as a mattress, then holds up the thickest and largest of them. "Come here."

Walking toward a guy in underwear is something they should teach as girl-101-skills. Do I sway? Do I walk normally? Do I cross my arms in front of my chest? Luckily for me, Jamie is busy sorting out the blanket, so I don't embarrass myself too much.

"Lay down," he rasps, and I almost faint right there.

"Okay," I breathe and lay on the side of the heap of blankets. Jamie sits next to me, keeping distance of about an arm's length, and drapes the blanket over me, careful not to touch me.

Still I'm about to have a stroke.

I'm sharing a pseudo-bed with Jamie.

My heart pounds so hard it hurts, and every breath brings more and more of his vanilla-scent until it fills my senses and drives me crazy.

Neither of us has said another word.

Jamie lowers himself onto his side, facing me, one hand supporting his head, the other one lying between us, as if he waited for me to take it. His upper wing is draped over his body like a blanket, and once in a while, when another gust of wind enters the turbine, he angles it slightly to deflect the wind. I'd be freezing, but his body is adapted to cold much better than mine.

His gaze shifts to me, and the pulse in his neck speeds up just like mine as awareness spreads between us.

This is torture.

I want him. There's no doubt about it. It's crazy and reckless and idiotic and whatnot, but I want Jamie.

And judging by the way he looks at me, he wants me too.

He curls the hand on the blanket between us into a fist, balling up the fabric with it.

I wish it would do that on my stomach.

That thought, it unleashes an onslaught of butterflies. A breathy sound escapes me, mingling with Jamie's ragged exhale.

Slowly, like it cost him a lot of strength, he relaxes his fingers. His eyes dart to the left, and he picks up a long, black feather. It could be one of his, if it wasn't dark.

He twirls the shaft between his fingers.

"Just like yours," I whisper.

He keeps his eyes trained on it as it moves between his fingers and harrumphs once. "I wish". A muscle in his jaw twitches. "Close your eyes," he whispers back.

"Huh?"

"Close your eyes, Lee."

I don't know what it is, but all of a sudden, I'm not cold anymore. With this one command—and let's be honest, it was one—with this one command the temperature in this room has changed from freezing to… something else.

My heart hammers inside my chest, but I do as he says.

I hear him take in a sharp breath on my left—and then a touch, feathery light, dances up the inside of my right arm. A gasp breaks free. What—

"Keep your eyes closed." Jamie's voice is hoarse. Raw. "Imagine… imagine it's me."

Imagine it's me.

Not a problem.

Not a problem at all.

The feather dances across my skin, up to the crook of my elbow, across my bicep, and toward my shoulder. I imagine Jamie's wing, angled inward and toward me, how it glides up my arm. How he needed to be even closer than now to do so. How he'd hopefully be wearing even less. How *I'd* hopefully be wearing even less.

My lips part and a soft sigh escapes.

Jamie lets the feather circle twice around the strap of my bra, and then… it dips along my collarbone to the hollow of my neck.

Oh, in the name of all that's holy…

He must see my pulse hammering. He *must*.

I hear him swallow next to me. Another whisper, rougher, the same mantra repeated: "Imagine it's me."

The feather dips down between my breasts, and my back arches off the ground. "Jamie—"

"Shh."

Despite his order, my eyes fly open, and there he is, a mere three inches above my face, his index finger hovering above my lips.

Almost touching.

Even better than in my imagination.

He's so close, I can feel the warmth radiating from his body. So close, I can see the clouds of gold in his blue eyes. So close, I want to pull him in and touch him.

And I can't.

The feather hovers right between my breasts, and it takes all the restraint I have to stay still.

Well, *I* am.

My chest isn't. In fact, it's heaving up and down as if I just ran a marathon. Out of the corner of my eye, even I can see my left boob wiggling with every single one of my rapid heartbeats.

And I know Jamie sees it too.

His lips part before he sucks in his lower lip and captures it between his teeth. He holds my eyes, the same longing in his I'm sure he sees in mine.

So close.

So. Unbelievably. Close.

And yet forever out of reach.

His throat works on a dry swallow. "Me."

The feather moves up over the swell of my right breast, tracing the outline of my bra. Holy—

I suck in a deep breath. It's a feather, for heaven's sake, it shouldn't come with barbed wire tearing me apart from the inside, but that's exactly what's happening. And it's not only because of the feather—it's mainly because of his words. *Imagine it's me.* It's the fact that he feels exactly as I do: torn. Held back. Cheated.

A move to my left breast, a circle over the cup—and I don't know how I'm still alive. My whole world has turned into Jamie. His scent engulfs me, his presence warms me, his touch burns me alive.

The feather dips down, following the contour of my bra—and stops. With a quick flick of his wrist, Jamie turns the feather over, using the hardened end to move the fabric of my bra down.

My tattoo. My *forbidden* tattoo.

"Freedom," he whispers. "Right?" The feather's shaft traces the outline of the small x with its inconspicuous dot on top of it. It's Chinese, and yes, I should've chosen something Japanese to honor my dad's heritage, but it would've made me too sad to be reminded every time I took a shower. This is safer. Nobody knows what it means. Usually, at least. I doodled it into all my assignments in the weeks prior to getting it. If any of the Sisters had known it meant freedom, I would've served detention for *lack of faith in the Lord's way*. And that is after they called it in to the Watchers and had me get it lasered off my skin.

"Yes," I whisper back. "Freedom. You're going to report me?" He could add it to the list of things I've done wrong lately, like touching a Founder.

Or, like playing with fire with a Founder.

Jamie chuckles deep. "And tell them how I saw it? No way in hell." He winks and pulls the shaft back, the bra snapping back in its place. "Any more surprises?" His hand moves toward the blanket covering my lower two thirds.

"Why don't you see for yourself?" Heat thrums through my veins, making me itch for more of this—more of Jamie. It makes me reckless; it makes me yearn for more.

"Oh, I will," he breathes hoarsely. Two fingers take the blanket and slowly, ever so slowly, pull it down.

Down to my belly button.

Down to the hem of my undies

Down to my upper thighs.

My brain whirls with the overwhelming input it receives. Jamie's mouth, slightly open, lower lip captured between his teeth. The widening of his pupils. His wing lowering, protecting us. His sharp inhale when I arch my back toward him.

The feather is back and skimming over my skin, leaving fire in its trails. With a slight shake to his hand he moves it down onto my stomach and circles it around my bellybutton, dipping it in once or twice.

I don't have to exert my power of imagination to know what he's thinking.

And I like it.

I want more.

So much more.

He gives me a hundred percent of his attention, picking up on every widening of my pupils, every move of my facial muscles. The world around me melts into nothingness. Nothing exists but Jamie, his touch on my bare stomach as the feather circles around my bellybutton, then lower and lower—

Ever so slowly, I lift my hand toward this cheek. I need to feel him. Him, him, him. His skin, his warmth. Not a feather. I want to touch him.

His chest rises more and more unsteady the closer my palm comes to his cheek. He wants this just as badly as I do. "I want to feel you," I breathe.

And it breaks the spell.

With a strangulated grunt, Jamie drops the feather, jumps to his feet, and stumbles a good two feet away from me. "No."

CHAPTER FOURTEEN

Aftermath

Like a bucket of ice water was emptied over my head, I jerk my hand back.

What have I done?

What in the name of all that's holy did I almost do?

Nausea rises, and it brings the taste of bile with it. "Jamie—"

His chest heaves up and down as he gulps down air like a drowning man. "Heavens, Lee…" He works a shaking hand through his hair. "Don't… don't do that. Don't say that. Don't tempt me like that. I—" His eyes fall shut, and when they open again, regret shines from them. "I almost let you touch me. And believe me, then I would have touched you, and then…" He blows out a puff of air through pursed lips.

Yeah. And then I doubt either of us would've stopped.

With Jamie, it's too easy to forget he's a Founder. Who knows if touching his wings would've brought me to my senses.

Probably not.

At least he had the sense to back off. I on the other hand couldn't hear reality screaming at me over the roaring sound of my hormones.

My face burns bright red. I push up onto my side, pulling the blanket a tad higher, because suddenly I'm cold. Happens when your body drops from hundred to zero in a split second. Or when your brain catches up with your body and realizes what an enormous blunder it almost let happen. "I'm sorry, I… I—"

The regret in his eyes changes into something else, something warmer. "Don't apologize. I started it. I mean, I shouldn't have. Shouldn't. I should've been a gentleman and given you a blanket and be done with it. But…" He looks at me with such tenderness, I almost melt right here and now. "But obviously, my chivalry isn't quite at the level I'd like it to be."

I cock my head at him and wink. "Well, you're only human after all, Jamie."

He chuckles, and it breaks the last bit of tension hovering between us. "So *the Lord created mankind in his Founders' image.* You know, since I've been reading New Scripture, things start to make sense." He winks and tugs his wings in closer. Small step by small step, he comes back to the heap of blankets and sits next to me, legs crossed and careful to not come too close.

And still I feel drawn to him.

Jamie picks up the black feather from where he dropped it and twirls it. "Okay, let's get this out in the open, Lee. This is not going to lead anywhere. Us. It can't happen."

But I want it to. The words are on the tip of my tongue but won't come out. Good to see common sense hasn't left me completely. I push up higher. "I know. Believe me, I know." I drop my gaze onto the feather between his fingers and my voice to a whisper. "But it's not fair." Nothing is, especially fate. Come on, why would she make me fall for a Founder of all people? A guy whom I can never have? A guy who stops in the middle of a make-out session. A *Founder* who stops. They take what they want, and, as we've kind of established, and at this point, I'm pretty sure that includes women—with not much of a risk for themselves. The fact that he's holding himself back, it means way more than if we had sex right now and here, although it feels like a letdown of ginormous proportions.

But it also means he cares.

Jamie stretches himself out, propped up on one elbow to face me. "No, it's not fair. But I'd be an egoistic ass if I let this progress any further." He pulls the blanket higher for me and slips under his own. "Because they will know. They will. No doubt about it, which is why we can't have each other, no matter how much we think we should. The Mark, virginity—everything the Founders emphasize will be our downfall." His eyes drop to my bra strap that's slipped off my shoulder, and his Adam's apple bops up and down. His voice turns husky. "No matter what I want to do with you right now, it's not going to happen. I'm not putting you in harm's way."

A strange kind of heat pools deep inside my body unlike the one I felt a mere two minutes ago. Deeper. Steadier. Headier.

I lay my hand out in the middle between us, a mere inch separating his with the feather and mine. "So… where does that leave us?"

Jamie sighs, a sound full of regret. "Alone." He dips the feather once, so that it brushes over the back of my hand.

Alone.

"Alone together." Because we're in this together, and I do feel better with Jamie with me. Oxymoron, at least for the old Lea, the one from before she touched a Founder.

"Alone together," he repeats after me. "Now go to sleep, Lee. Tomorrow, we'll bring the Maskers to Ice, and then… then we'll see." With that, he closes his eyes, and while his breathing turns regular within seconds, he still keeps the feather between his fingers.

Despite the low-light conditions in here, I can make out the profile of his face: the high cheekbones, strong chin, full lips. I'm an idiot for falling for him. A complete idiot. If Jamie hadn't been so level-headed, I'd have thrown myself at him even more, and then? Yeah. SOL.

When exactly did those feelings for him start? And why? With my history, the last thing I expected was this, was Jamie. Yes, he's attractive, but all Founders are. Yes, he's cute. More than cute. But again, it comes with the job description for a Founder. But lying next to him, all I can think of is what it would feel like to actually touch him. What it would feel like to be touched by him, not a feather. *Him.*

So yes, I cater to the whims of the pathetic and look at him until my eyes grow heavy and I drift off to sleep, the image of him burned into my retinas.

In the very last moment before the darkness claims me, I could swear the touch of a feather brushes over my cheek.

Three days later, the Old Zoo still doesn't feel the same after the night up in the Turbine.

It feels tighter.

Too tight, because no matter where I go, there's Jamie.

And I'd be lying if I said that didn't put my self-control to the test.

But hey, at least I'm not the only one affected. Whenever I enter the room, Jamie's gaze flitters over my body. Whenever I stand a tad too close, his throat bobs with a hard swallow. Whenever we're alone together, he's wound so tightly it's a wonder he doesn't lose control.

It's heaven and hell at the same time.

Heaven, because it's Jamie. Close to me. On my team, feeling the same, wanting the same.

Hell, because even if we were the last people on Earth, we couldn't have each other. Well, okay, maybe then, but not in any other scenario.

The whole thing is a real mind f-ck, to be honest. It gives me a headache. No, really, it does. The Protégée—the First—has fallen for a Founder. Even worse, a Founder has fallen for a human. Twice, the tension between us was so thick, Jamie walked out on me late in the evening, only to come back when he thought I was asleep already.

Today is no different. We've practiced my Servitude all morning and all afternoon, and the whole session I had a hard time taking my eyes off him. In my defense, Jamie did make it difficult for me. He had me repeat helping him into a jacket five times in a row. Because I *wasn't reverent enough*. Hardy-harr-harr. I bet it was because for me to zip up the jacket by the elongated zipper—to avoid accidental touch, of course—I still had to stand real close. So close, I could see the pulse in his neck speed up. Same for his breathing. Guess for two people who can't touch, we're desperately clinging to every excuse to be near each other.

Nobody seemed to notice though, which is a blessing in itself. No need to give Ice any more ammo than he already has. If he thought he could blackmail us even more than he does now… Yeah. Exactly.

Still, today wasn't all fun and games. Jezza was in a bad mood since we met and even worse after Ice showed him something on the Pad about an hour ago. Since then, he's been staring at Jamie with anger written all across his face, while Ice is totally preoccupied with his Pad, tapping and swiping until he curses under his breath.

"Okay, guys. Take a break. Have a seat." Ice points at the chairs across from him and gives the Pad a shove to slide it over to our side of the table. "This might complicate things." He really isn't a happy camper today, and hasn't been since we got back three days ago, but I doubt it's because of us. Well, I hope. I'd like to stay under his radar as much as possible until this whole thing blows over or Jezza mans up and gets me the video. If Ice forgot about us, I'd be the happier.

Jamie cocks an eyebrow, catches the Pad and turns it for us to see. A groan breaks from his throat before I have read the—

Protégée Expected at Tuesday's Pledge Ceremony.

My heart plummets into a bottomless abyss. No, no, no.

"The Pledge Ceremony?" It's a mere squeak. "Not going to happen. We said it's not going to happen. No Oath. No Vinculum. Only training. Pretend training. Nothing more." I can't help the edge of panic creeping into my voice, but this is a biggie. The only reason why I coped okay-ishly with the whole servant thing is that the last step, the Pledge, was off the table. I can check my ego at the door for a while and pretend I'm a servant, but becoming one?

I point an accusing finger at Ice. "You said you weren't going to make us take the Pledge!" My gaze hops from the Pad to Jamie and back. That's not how we planned it. Sit this out. Go our separate ways. Stay under the radar. Not get bound together.

Instead of Ice answering, Jezza huffs dry as Jamie scans over the article. "Surprisingly, Ice didn't have anything to do with that." His lips thin the further he reads. "But that tattle-tale Bane did." He points to a paragraph under a picture of me.

"What?" Bane? I massage my temples. Not making the headache any better. At all.

"Bane. '*A high-ranking Watcher from the Los Angeles Hive confirmed the Protégée was progressing very well in her training sessions and would be present during the next Pledge Ceremony. 'We're looking forward to seeing Jamin and the Protégée make it official,' the Watcher said. 'Both of them need to commit to a future in the name of the Lord.'*" He lets the pad sink down as I push back my chair and pace.

"How'd that happen? Although, who cares? Everybody who knows me knows I'm a screw-up. Nobody would expect me to last through training. Our plan was good. Failed training. That's so me. Move on, done." I'm rambling, I know, but that's the panic speaking, looking for a way out.

"That's Bane's way of controlling us, of forcing our hand. He knows something is off. It's like a game of chess, and he just made his next move, waiting for ours." Jamie picks up an invisible chess piece and moves it diagonally.

"Then he'll be glad to hear this round goes to him, because I ain't playing." Pledging goes against everything that's me. Pretending to serve was a stretch, but committing? No matter it's Jamie, it's still official, i.e., a no-no.

Ice taps his fingers on the table in the same annoying rhythm he seems to prefer. "I don't like the fact that you're getting so much attention—"

A harsh laugh breaks from Jamie's throat. "Good one. Told you from the get-go if you throw the Protégée in with me it was guaranteed to happen." Jamie drops the Pad onto the table.

"Still was hoping it would take longer. But anyway. Yes, you're more under the spotlight than I thought, which means this," he makes a circular gesture around the room with his finger, "won't work as a hiding spot much longer. Once you're officially pledged, training is over, and then—"

I stop dead in my tracks. "Once we're officially pledged? Not going to happen. Forget about it!" I cross my arms in front of my chest. Yes, I agreed to this charade, but only because I had no other option and it was a hoax, not official, but with a set expiration date.

Ice sighs in this exaggerated way of his. "I don't think we—you—have a choice. They're calling for you to take the Pledge, and if you don't, it'll be suspicious."

Jamie sits up straighter. "Nope. We call it off. Lea failed training, period. We offer an interview, we both state it wasn't the right fit, and done." He doesn't want a servant any more than I want to be one.

"Yeah, won't happen." Ice reaches for the pad.

"It totally will." I dart forward and slide half onto my chair. "We'll give the interview today, say my behavior at the concert was unacceptable—"

"I said it won't happen." Ice taps onto the Pad. "Both of you will go up to the hive and take the Pledge in front of Michael."

Hot anger shoots through my veins. "You're freakin—"

"And why would that be?" Jamie's eyes narrow.

"Easy. Because you both still work for me, and because I need you up in the hive." He turns the Pad around again, the image of the tear-shaped ship over the Los Angeles desert displayed on it. "I want you at the ceremony, and I want you to place this onto any access console, computer panel, or whatnot you can find." He fishes for something in his pocket and throws over a small leather satchel.

Jamie catches it with ease and looks inside. "A splitter?" Disbelief makes his voice crack at the end.

A splitter? Oh, hell to the no! "Now, wait a second. You want us to install an illegal access device on board of a freakin' hive? While there for a Pledge Ceremony? Are you crazy?" They find this thing on us, we're dead. And this time, if we're found out, it's not only me who's going to be dead.

It's Jamie as well.

The Masker was bad, but this is worse. *This* is going to implant a computer virus that can be used for an attack against the Founders, and they won't have any mercy with us if they discover us. None.

Anger tightens Jamie's features. "You're expecting me to open the door for you to attack my own people?"

Ice holds his gaze. If Jamie's making him nervous, he doesn't show it. "Yes. You and the Protégée have access. She is liked. She is their golden child, saved from her cruel fate by the Lord's grace. Lea's invitation to the hive is serving us this opportunity on a silver platter, especially because… because we *know* something is about to happen." He slaps the table. "Something is off, you said so yourself. The Founders have recruited twice the normal amount of soldiers over the last six months. The hives have been buzzing with coded communications. Little infractions by humans are being punished harder than before. The signs are there, and getting that virus into their system is our only chance to find out what it is."

Jamie lets his head hang. "I told you there's nothing concrete going on. I'd know—"

"Then maybe you're not quite as well connected or informed as you think. I don't trust your intel. You're not initiated yet, so why would you know. Did I get that right?" He glares at Jamie then points a finger at the two of us. "You're going up to the hive. Take the Pledge, place the splitter. Done."

The headache cranks it up behind my forehead. Every thought hurts. I massage my temples. "So, you're sending us up into potential death on a whim?"

"Not a whim. Intel. We—"

"But Jamie is one of *them*! And he says—"

Ice slams a palm onto the table, much harder this time. "I don't care! You think I'm going to risk the fate of humanity on a single Founder's word? This is non-negotiable! I said it before and I meant it, I will leak the video, never doubt that, and I will send you up there. Do well and survive, or mess up and don't. Your choice."

Whoa. My knees wobble and give in, planting my butt barely on the edge of my seat. A sudden epiphany paints my future in black and grey. Even if we survive this, Ice is never going to let us go. It's too nice to have the Protégée under his thumb, too tempting not to use her.

"If I do this, I want out," I croak. "Out. This is the last thing I do for you, Ice. I want out." I'm trying my very best to neglect the tiny but crucial piece of information that if he lets me out after this I'm still pledged to Jamie.

Still a servant.

Ice rubs a hand along his jaw. "Look, I know this isn't what either of you wanted, but please see it from my point of view. Ten years of oppression. Ten long years of living in the name of the Lord, obeying the Founders' every word, throwing out centuries of culture and beliefs because of them. You know exactly what I'm talking about." He nods at me, then looks at Jamie. "And you,

you've tried to make things better for us, and yet your own people turned against you. You know why we need this installed. You know why we need you two."

A muscle thrums along Jamie's jaw. "You're overestimating me. Maybe I'm not as good a guy as you think I am."

"Or maybe I don't care as long as you dance to my tune."

I wonder how long Jamie is going to take this. The teasing. The orders. When is it enough? When is giving up his wings not going to be too high a price anymore? Whenever that is, it's the moment Ice loses. Big time.

Jamie's wings bristle. "Then let's cut a deal. If Lea and I place that virus for you, you give us the video. All the copies. Nothing will be left of it." He cuts a challenging glance at Ice.

"That's the one thing I have to control you." Ice taps a finger to his temple. Translation, you must be crazy.

"Exactly." Jamie leans back. "We have cooperated. Maskers. Training. Taking the Pledge is more than we agreed upon. We do this for you, you set us free. If we want to work with you afterwards, it will be on our terms."

Fat chance.

"I don't trust him," says Jezza. He hasn't said a total of five words today as far as I can tell. All he did was scowl at Jamie and ignore me.

Very mature behavior.

Ice pinches the bridge of his nose. "Neither do I, but he has enough incentive to help us here." He folds his hands together in a crude resemblance of two wings, flapping them twice. "Still, I'll have Lea carry the splitter. Better safe—"

Jamie shakes his head. "Lea shouldn't be exposed to that. Watchers do conduct sample searches. If they find—"

"Then, my dear Demon, you want to make sure no Watcher lays a hand on her."

Wait, that could also happen? "This idea is getting more and more stupid. I ain't—"

"I'll carry the splitter. Less risk for Lea—"

Ice sighs. "Children, listen to me. Lea is carrying the splitter, over and out. My trust in a Founder only goes so far. If you truly think she's in danger, then I advise you to keep an eye on your precious little Protégée, or else—"

Jamie stands so fast the chair topples over and falls to the floor with a bang. "Listen, Issaac. I've said it before and I'll repeat it again, since you seem to be on the slower side of uptake. You don't know what or whom you're messing with. I—" Blue light pops up on his palms before he balls them into fists a split second later. "Shit." He spins around on his heels and storms out, almost ripping the door out of its hinges, the Caeruleum still glowing in his palms.

"Jamie!" I'm about to follow, but Ice holds me back.

"You stay. I need to talk to that idiot before he brings down the whole lair." He follows Jamie, his fast steps turning softer and softer the farther he jogs from our room.

Which leaves me alone with Jezza.

Oh joy.

Ten seconds.

Twenty seconds.

Thirty seconds.

The silence between us is more than awkward.

Jezza glares at me with his arms crossed in front of his chest, a deep scowl etched into the lines of his face.

And it annoys me. "What?" I throw up my hands. "What is it with you these days? Seriously, Jezza, I—"

"I honestly don't quite know where to start, Lea."

Whoa. "Wow, Jezza. So helpful. Really—"

"Have you ever thought about what kind of power you have? You, the freakin' First?" He holds his index finger up like it's a weapon.

Oh, don't get me started! "Power? Me? Have you maybe ever thought about how I am a nobody with no future? Under the observation and scrutiny of everybody and their grandma? Who the frack cares about the stupid First, Protégée, whatever? It's all a load of bull—"

He slams his fist into his palm. "Do you even hear yourself? You're whining like a kindergartner! Yes, I get it, what happened to you was horrible! I was there, I saw it, and I still have nightmares from it! But that was ten years ago! I'm not asking you to forget it, I'm asking you to get over it and finally get your ass in gear!" He kicks against the table, for emphasis.

My mouth drops open. Whoa. Just… whoa. "My ass—"

"Yes, for crying out loud! You're so unbelievably blind when it comes to anything Founder related it's ridiculous. To them, you are the Protégée, their little puppet they don't really care about, but shlep around for PR reasons. Sorry. You know it's true. But then you're also the First, the first victim who *still lives*. People know you all over the world. They look up to you, they want to know how you're doing, because you're the example that we can survive *them*—and all you've ever done is run away from that."

I jerk back. "I didn't ask for any of it."

"I know, but you got it and now you have to deal with it. You have a responsibility, Lea. You are the First. Your actions can change things. Not like me. Maybe I can get into their army, maybe I can make a tiny bit of a difference, but you, with your reach…" He shakes his head. "You can reach millions. You can give hope to millions. And instead, you're hiding and looking for the easy way out."

I blink to keep the tears from falling. "Is that what you think of me? That I'm hiding?"

Jezza rubs a hand across his eyes. He looks tired. "Yes. Kind of. Maybe. Don't pretend like you're going to be helping us here when—if—Ice gives you that video. You're not going to join the Resistance, let's not kid ourselves."

"You know me well."

He harrumphs. "I do. And yet I only agree with you on one thing, it appears. I don't want you pledged to the Demon. It'll send a message to humanity stronger than anything the Rebellion can pull off to counter. It'll tell people pledging yourself to a Founder is a good idea, and we all know it isn't. That's the kind of power your actions carry, Lea. You are the freakin' Protégée, and whatever you do, it comes with consequences. Like I've been trying to tell you, you can—and you should—choose your destiny, but at the same time, you shouldn't pledge to the Demon."

The tears start to sting. "But what if it's my only chance to get that video—"

"And what if it's not? Ice has never had a Founder under his thumb, he's flying by the seat of his pants half the time! Maybe we can stall, come up with another idea—I dunno! Something big is about to happen no matter what the Demon says, and I don't know if humanity is going to come out better for it. I want you in the right position and mindset when the time comes, and as far away from him as possible. I never meant for you to pledge to a Demon. It never ends well." His lips press down into a fine line.

"Then at least we're on the same page there. I never meant that either, but I guess it could've been worse." At least I got to know Jamie before the Pledge. And it's him—it's Jamie.

Pause.

Jezza drums an annoying rhythm onto the table, just like Ice usually does. "This is not like you. Being so cavalier about pledging your life to a Founder."

"I know. I've come a long way, haven't I?" The joke falls flat.

More drumming. "You know he's just like any other demon, don't you?"

"What?" I shake my head. Where's that coming from?

"That even if you're pledged together for this, he's still like any other Founder. New Servitude, traditional, whatever. He'll use you for whatever he needs you for, and then he won't care what happens to you. Like any other Founder."

Not true. "Jamie's not like them, Jezza! You should've noticed that by now."

He huffs. "All I noticed is even more reason to not trust him, because he's like. Every. Other. Founder." The way he emphasizes each word makes me even madder.

"Screw you, Jezza! You don't know squat. Jamie is not like any Founder. If he were, he'd already—" I snap my mouth shut. Crap.

Jezza turns his palms up. "He what, Lea? What in the world makes Jamie so damn special and different from the others?"

I shake my head. "Nothing." *Everything.* If he were like the others, he'd have already touched me. Kissed me. But he's not like the others. Jamie holds back, because of me. Because he cares for me and what becomes of me.

He crashes his fist onto the table, making me jump. "Damn it, Lea! I see the way he looks at you! I see the way you look at him! How can you be so stupid—?"

"Shut up, Jezza!" I yell. "It's not your place—"

"It's damn well my place! I'm your oldest friend! You shouldn't need me to remind you what happens with Founders! You should keep him away with a ten-foot Raptor-pole, pledged or not! Instead you look at him with googley eyes and follow him like a puppy dog waiting for a treat!" He breathes heavy.

I open my mouth to throw a good string of curses at him— but no. Too much hurt. Too much. I let my eyes fall shut for a moment to collect myself. Denial. I need to deny everything, because nothing is going on, and because even the suspicion will already be additional ammo to Ice.

Jezza is faster than me though. The anger is gone from his voice when he speaks again, replaced by worry. "Lea, I… I trust you know that nothing can happen between the two of you, right? No matter what you think of him—heck, what I think of him— it cannot. Not now, not ever, pledged or not."

When I open my eyes, I find Jezza's brown eyes fixed on me. "I know," I whisper. "And nothing is." Because Jamie is good. Jamie is not like any of his people. Jamie is different. I swallow dry. "But it doesn't stop me from wanting it."

Pity washes over Jezza's face. "Lea…"

I shrug and turn away from him. How low have I sunken? Admitting I care for a Founder in front of Jezza? Jezza, who held me when my parents were killed by the black-winged monster—

Jezza wraps his arms around me from behind and pulls me against his wide, hard chest. He snuggles his face next to mine, nose rubbing over my cheek, just like he did when we were still a couple. Warm breath dances down my face, and for one single blissful second I allow myself to think it was Jamie holding me.

"I'm sorry," Jezza breathes. "I never wanted for any of that to happen. Whatever comes after the Pledge, I'll do my very best to protect you. To keep you safe."

Goosebumps erupt on my neck and travel down my spine. "Why does that sound so scary, Jezza? Is there something I should know?" Because it sure carries a whole buttload of foreshadowing, seriously.

He reaches for my hands and pulls them into the hug, thumb smoothing over the back of my hands. "Besides that I would prefer you un-pledged?" He pauses, and I feel his chest expand with a slow inhale. "Don't worry about it. I'm here. We'll make it through, as we always do." He presses his lips against the side of my head.

Maybe it's the barely disguised foreboding in his words, maybe his tenderness, maybe the fact that I really wish he were Jamie—but no matter what breaks the dam, my eyes turn moist and the first tears fall before I've completely turned around and buried my face into Jezza's shoulder.

Then, I cry.

CHAPTER FIFTEEN

Carousel, Reprise

When I get back to our room, Jamie isn't there. For the first time in a while, I'm kind of thankful for that. I have a lot to swallow. Taking the Oath, pledging myself to be a servant, planting a virus, and oh, right—admitting my feelings for Jamie to Jezza.

One heck of an evening.

I fall onto my bed backwards.

Ugh.

Gotta say, I have felt better before. Headache. Body ache. Everything-ache.

Worst of all is actually none of the above. It's the fact that I understand why Ice is forcing us to do this. Why I need to be doing this, no matter what Jezza says. Or maybe because of what Jezza said.

And I don't like it.

My life has been touched enough by the Founders, pun intended. I've paid my dues, taken my bows and my curtain calls—whatever you want to call it, I've done enough of it to cover a whole lifetime. I think I've earned the right to sit out whatever has to do with them.

I *thought* I earned the right to sit out whatever has to do with them.

Problem is, Jezza is right. I didn't.

Him and Ice have a point, as much as it pains me to admit. The Protégée has access. Better, what *the First* does is important to many people and has the potential of influencing them. Plus, the Protégée gives me a great cover. Not playing along and retreating back into the orphanage and hiding as I've been trying to do all my life… I'd be a coward. Not to mention the orphanage is out—it's the forum with Jamie for me once we're pledged. Founder-central.

As much as that thought makes me nauseous, it also ignites a spark. Josh Cardoza does it. He plays for both sides. With my reach… Maybe I could do it too. Question is, would I tell Jamie? He has enough reason to hate his people—but they're still his people. Would he ever be okay working against them? Not just under threat of extortion?

I chew on the inside of my cheek. Don't think so. He's doing what he has to—what Ice wants him to—to survive. To keep his wings. When that pressure is gone, I doubt he's going to be voted the Resistance's next all-star recruit. Oh, don't get me wrong, he's still going to be the same Jamie—against Servitude and pro-humanity. But I doubt we're going to be with the Resistance.

So where does that leave me?

In the forum, with Jamie, hiding our unusual approach to Servitude in plain sight?

And what if… I mean what if Jamie is right? What if taking the Pledge means the Eleventh Commandment turns more into a suggestion? Would I… would we… would something happen between Jamie and me? Could I let it, knowing that every touch is violating the very rule that got my parents killed? What if somebody found out? Oh. Easy. The punishment would be on me. Most of it, at least. The part with the bigger impact.

I press both palms into my eyes. Ugh. "Damn you, Jezza," I whisper-curse. Damn him for getting me into this. For talking to me and pushing all the right buttons. For taking away my blissful ignorance and tearing down my walls. Damn him. I swipe a quick hand over my eyes to get rid of the moisture.

No matter which way I look at it, my life is over. Working for the Resistance is going to get me killed. Being a servant, even to Jamie, is going to break my spirit, because at one point I won't be able to play along anymore. No matter if… something happened between us or not. Reverence. Adoration. *Gag.* The Founders will get rid of me then, and no amount of intervention from Jamie could keep them from it.

Meaning, all roads lead to Rome—in the end I'm going to be dead, and way sooner than I thought or hoped I would.

Shoulda kept running when I heard Jamie scream that night.

I didn't though—so what does that say about me? That I don't back out? That I do the right thing? If that's the case, then I should take the Pledge tomorrow and see where it takes me. Make the best out of it, step in front of Michael—

My heart skips a painful beat.

Step in front of Michael and pledge my life and Servitude to Jamie.

Holy freakin' cow.

The next breath comes in wheezy, devoid of oxygen. A wave of dizziness passes over me and brings new fuel for the headache pounding behind my temples.

I'll pledge my life to Jamie.

It sounds so wrong. So unbelievably wrong.

So why then does part of it somehow feel… so unbelievably right?

About five minutes later, the door opens and closes softly.

Jamie. He has this way of moving like a panther, smooth and silent, not like any of us humans, stumbling through life like the brutes we are.

I push up onto my elbows. "Hey."

"Hey." He gives me a small smile but stays in the middle of the room, playing with something in his hands, eyes fixed on it. A shawl of sorts?

"Ice talked you down from tearing apart the evil lair?"

A small smile tugs on the corners of his lips. "He did. I still don't like his plan, but…" He sighs, his shoulders heaving up and down once. "If he gives us the video…"

The video.

If he ever does.

Still, I force a smile. "Okay then. If he agreed to the deal, we're going to plant the virus for him and see what your people are hiding."

Jamie absentmindedly wraps the shawl around his knuckles, like a boxer before the fight. "Yeah. Listen, I'll have to take care of it once we're up there. The hives are huge, and after a reasonable discussion of the facts, Ice thinks you're *lacking the training to recognize a console where you should place it.*" He rolls his eyes when he imitates Ice's voice. "But at least that keeps you out of the crosshairs."

I raise an eyebrow. "So, Ice changed his mind? He's okay with you placing the virus? You're okay with it?"

He nods. "Yes and… kind of. I've… never been one to play by the rules. As you know. But, what about you? The whole becoming a servant thing?"

I sit up completely and swipe a strand of hair out of my face. Showtime. "I'm surprisingly okay with it, all things considered. Better pledged to you than to anybody else." My face heats up. Guess the cat's out of the bag in regards to my feelings for him, but still. Tad too sappy for my taste.

"I'll take that as a compliment." Jamie tugs on that shawl around his knuckles. "But I can't believe they talked us into taking the Pledge." He uses air quotes. "And if I had the choice, I'd rather not Pledge to you."

"Ouch, Jamie." I place one hand over my heart. "You know your way with girls, really."

He chuckles. "Not the way I meant it, Lee. I'm just... worried."

Well, duh. So am I. Comes with the territory of pledging your life away. "Anything specific?"

He tugs the shawl again. "Not really. More an overall sensation that we're missing something. Getting a Vinculum is a big deal, and it feels... I don't know. Whatever. Just has my spidey-senses tingling."

I laugh out once. "Your spidey-senses? Really?"

"Sixth sense, whatever. You know what I mean."

I nod. "Yes. Yes, I do. Can't say I'm a hundred percent comfortable, but that ship has sailed the moment we met, I'd say. We're in, for better or for worse. Plus, you need a reason to go up to the hive, and I'm the reason for us to go. I see the Resistance's point of view, it's an opportunity too good to pass for them." And it looks like I'm getting with the Program.

Jamie huffs. "Reason to go up. We don't need a reason, but Ice won't listen to me. I can get into the hive at any time. My father lives there."

That gets my attention. "Your dad? Wait, but you said you grew up in the forum."

"I did. My father didn't stay there though."

"What the what? He left you alone?" That would explain why Jamie hasn't spoken one positive word about him.

"Not alone. With one of my older brothers. Father was busy in the hive." He balls the fist wrapped in the shawl. "But anyway, Ice thinks you are the perfect distraction and carte blanche, so even if I could get in alone, he'd prefer you there." I doubt it's only that and nothing more. It's also Ice's paranoia and distrust of anything Founder related.

"He doesn't know you, Jamie. He doesn't trust you like I do."

"You trust me?" A sheepish smile pops up on his face.

"I do." Like he trusts me. I wouldn't even consider taking the Pledge otherwise, for show or not.

Jamie prowls a step closer to my bed. Another one. "Are you sure?" The smile turns impish. Mischievous.

"Uhh, yes?"

He stops a mere arm's length from me, shawl now unwrapped from his knuckles. "Prove it," he whispers, a daring gleam in his eyes.

I swallow hard. "Prove it—how?"

He throws one end of the shawl over to me and nods at in. "Come on."

I grab the end he threw and let him pull me up to standing. "You didn't drop me. Woo. Big deal. Trust definitely established."

Jamie chuckles that deep, rich sound that makes me feel warm from head to toe. "Oh no, that wasn't it. Turn around." He twirls his finger through the air.

Turn. Okay. "Showing you my back isn't really a huge exercise in trust either."

"True. Hold your horses there, young lady." He tugs on the shawl I'm still holding onto until I let go. "Close your eyes."

"I feel daring." But I do as he says, and to be honest, I do feel daring, because Jamie has something planned. And I'd be lying if I said my heart wasn't beating faster and I wasn't excited.

I hear some rustling behind me, then feel soft, cool fabric covering my eyes. The shawl. Jamie wraps it around my head to cover my eyes, careful to not touch me, only the fabric.

"Don't move," he whispers, and that soft sound stirring the hair on my neck together with the shawl taking my vision from me… it brings a whole motherlode of butterflies to a flutter. Jamie ties a knot in the back, then, three seconds later, something hard knocks against my hand.

"Here. Hold on to this."

I grab it. "A stick?" Why the heck would he give me a stick?

"Yes. If I weren't a Founder, but a human, I'd take you by the shoulders or hands and guide you. Maybe I'd bump you into something here and there on purpose, gently, of course, but I'd guide you. The way it is, I can't. You hold on to that end, me to the other." He gives the stick a short tug.

Something else rises up with the butterflies, something very inappropriate, but also very, very exciting. "Where are we going?" I yield to the tug and follow its lead.

I hear Jamie smile. "Now, that's where trust comes in."

Honestly, right now, in this very moment, he could lead me wherever and I'd follow him.

I'd follow him.

I'm pretty sure Jamie leads me in circles. We've gone up some stairs, down some stairs. We've turned corners I'm sure lead nowhere but back to where we started. After two minutes, I have no clue where in the Old Zoo we are. Even when we leave the lair and go topside, I have no clue which of the dozens of entrances-slash-exits he took.

The night air is cool and damp, the sounds of the city muffled. Here and there, I pick up on noises the wind must've carried over, or I wouldn't have picked up on them, but overall I'd say it must be close to curfew, or beyond. L.A. doesn't sleep unless it has to.

"Careful here." Jamie slows us down as leaves and twigs brush over my arms.

"Okay, now the whole trust-thing is getting a bit of a creepy mass-murderer-feel." I stumble over a root. Where is he taking me? There's nothing but trees, bushes, and plain old nature around the Old Zoo.

I hear Jamie's grin in his words. "That's why it's an exercise in trust, Lee. Not much longer." He falls silent again, directing me through the night until he stops. "Okay. There's a step here. Lift your foot—there you go… and stop."

Okay. "What now?"

"Now you wait." I hear him walk away from me, his steps soft on a ground that's definitely not covered with leaves and twigs. There might or might not be a small click and humming sound, or a little change in the light around us. Can't tell. At this point, little stars dance behind my lids anyway from the shawl's pressure on them.

Jamie comes back. "Let go of the stick and reach forward, straight in front of you. Hold on to it."

Curiosity shoots through me. What is he up to? I reach, my knuckles brushing against cold metal. "This?"

"Yup."

A smooth, cold, vertical metal rod. My fingers travel over it. "What—"

I feel the rush of air as Jamie reaches past my face and removes the blindfold with one pull on the shawl's end. It falls from my eyes, and—

The next breath gets stuck in my lungs. "Whoa." I blink once. Twice. "Jamie, that's… that's…" I'm at a loss of words. Thick emotion assaults me together with memories of better years, of family, of love. It clogs my throat and makes my voice thick. "You fixed it."

He fixed the merry-go-round. The lights are on—most of them at least, the ones that aren't broken. Hundreds of little bulbs illuminate and frame the carousel's outline, bathing everything into a warm, yellow shine: the horses, freed of their decade-old patina of dust and dirt, the reliefs on the center piece of the carousel. The intricately decorated ceiling—well, what's left of it anyway.

Jamie flashes a wild sort of grin, one that makes me feel all warm and fuzzy. "Yeah. Fixed it. Took me a while to find what's wrong with it, but once I did, it wasn't so bad."

I glide a hand up and down the pole I'm holding on to. "That's what you did at night? When you left?"

He nods. "Yeah. I figured, I… I might as well use my frustration and make something out of it. Thought you might like it." His gaze drifts off, looking over the horses to our right.

There's something in his voice that makes my insides melt a little. "I don't just like it. I love it. It's beautiful," I breathe. Beautiful, breathtaking, awe-inspiring—and I'm not talking about the carousel. I'm talking about Jamie doing this for me, because he knew what it once meant to me.

A mere couple of days ago, Jamie was a Founder. The enemy. Then he became a guy trapped in the same web as me. Then he became an accomplice, then maybe even more. Now… now he's the rock in my life. The one person I can trust. Times, they are a-changin'.

This is where I want to be. Here and now. With Jamie.

Jamie steps closer, wrapping his hand around the same pole, only inches above mine. "It gets better," he whispers.

"How so?" I doubt there's anything that could improve on what he did. As it is, I'm brimming with a happiness I haven't felt in… forever.

The smile travels up to his eyes. "Hold on." The hand not on the pole pushes a button crudely attached to a power cord draped over the horse next to him.

Magic happens around us.

With a slight jolt, the carousel begins to move counter-clockwise. Every other horse rises up and down its pole, like a whole herd had sprung to life. The lights flash in a mesmerizing rhythm to music that isn't there as we ride through the night, a cool breeze brushing past us.

Un-be-lievable.

"It works!" Jamie fixed it—*he fixed it*! "It works!" A wild laugh breaks free from my throat. I'm five years old again, on my second or third ride in a row, my dad waiting at the popcorn stand, taking a video of me and Jezza as we fly past him again and again and again.

"I couldn't get the music to work. And then I thought it's probably safer without it anyway, curfew and all. Sorry though—"

My finger shoots up to his lips, stopping a hair's breadth before I'd touch him. "Shush. I don't care about the music.

This…" I work on a hard swallow to get rid of that stupid lump inside my throat. "This is wonderful. Thank you, Jamie."

"You're welcome." The warm breath of his caresses my finger. His gaze lands on my mouth, and his chest rises sharply. Once. Twice.

Still I hold my finger right where it was. Close to Jamie's lips. I want nothing more than to brush over them. To step closer, wrap my arms around him and feel his around me.

His chest rises unsteadily. "Take away your finger, Lee. Or I can't guarantee I won't light up that Mark again."

For a moment, I don't.

For a moment, I'm about to ignore all reason. Life's too short to play by the rules, especially mine.

For a moment, I wish he'd throw the Eleventh Commandment and caution to the wind and kiss my finger. Then me. Then—

But in the end, my higher brain functions kick in and I withdraw the finger. All this bogus about Founder-human couples breaking the Eleventh Commandment, it only lets me hope for something impossible.

He breathes a sigh of relief, eyelids fluttering shut for a second. When he opens them again, they shine even warmer than before. "Come on, Lee. Let's have a ride." He taps one of the horse's backs and makes room for me.

I'm on it in no time, while Jamie stands a bit farther away, wings spread as far as he can without bumping into me. The wind plays with his feathers, ruffling them until he adjusts the angle and the wind smooths them out.

We stay like this for what feels like hours, riding to a music only we can hear; the human girl on the horse, and the angel standing guard next to her.

CHAPTER SIXTEEN

Hive

The shuttle for the transport up to the hive is parked a good twenty meters away from the fence and ID control station smack in the middle of the desert. When the Founders arrived, their tear-shaped hive hovered directly above Los Angeles, but turns out, the constant shade messed with solar power on people's roofs, not to mention LAX's busy airplane traffic.

In a surprisingly thoughtful move considering we're talking about Founders, they relocated the hive to hover above the northern outreach of L.A., the Santa Clarita area. Conveniently, there's more desert, less people, and enough sun for everybody. Because of its size, the hive is still visible from L.A., at least when the weather is good and the air nice'n clear. I guess, for the Founders, it's enough of a reminder of their presence, not that we'd forget otherwise.

Getting onto the hive is complicated. After all, it's considered a privilege, and not many humans can say they've gone up more than once, if at all. Regular people will never go, but if they're a servant or soldier, they will to pledge. But without a Founder vowing for our integrity, none of us humans would go up.

About twenty other females between late teen years and early twenties get dropped off by their masters, just like me. The whole thing feels a bit like parents dropping off their kids at the bus for a school trip, only that my quote-unquote parent isn't very happy.

Still isn't very happy.

"Listen," Jamie whispers and motions at me to stop. "The flight up there won't be more than five minutes. I'll be meeting you in the hive, and from there on, every move we make is going to be under scrutiny. I will have to act it out." He looks apologetic, but I get it.

"It's fine. I can pull off a convincing show. You have the splitter already, so we get this over with, you place it, we get off, done." My stomach cramps.

He looks over the assembled Founders around us. One of them leads a group of new soldiers to the shuttle, all young, all female. They're getting sworn in just as we do. Yay, a party! *Not.*

Jamie's focus is back on me. "You're down to mustard-yellow on the scanner. Not suspicious for somebody who just completed training. You'll be fine. Just remember we're in this together, okay? The hive, Michael, the Pledge… It can be overwhelming." A shaky smile tugs on the corners of his lips.

I give Jamie a smile back I want to feel but can't. Nerves. "You'll watch out for me. We got this." I hope. "And you know what? You might see your dad up there."

A muscle in his temple twitches once. "Not high up on my list. But anyway," he casts me a worried glance, "please keep in mind that… Oh, whatever. Okay then. Off you go." He makes a dismissive gesture and I bow.

"Yes, Master." See? Perfect servant, right here. The performance of my life, and I better make it my best, or else it might be my last.

I get in line right behind the newly minted soldiers, show my ID and get into the shuttle. I've never been in one—and why would I—so yeah, that part's kind of cool. The soldiers in front of me fill up the rows in the back, one seat after another, until it's my turn to take a window seat. I'm glad I can get off my feet for a few precious minutes. Probably my nerves giving me wobbly knees and all. Coming down with the flu must feel similar to all the aches and wobbliness annoying me for the last days. Oh, the joys of living on the edge.

I fasten my seat belt. The school trip-analogy still holds, because the rows and rows of seats in here makes it look more like the inside of a large school bus, only it's grey, not yellow. It looks very human-made, not quite angelic, but obviously that makes sense. Founders don't need shuttles. Jamie and the others are flying up to the hive under the power of their wings. Only us poor humans, we need help with transportation, which is why they built shuttles.

I tug the seat belt tighter and accidentally bump the female soldier sitting next to me with my elbow. "Oops, sorry, I didn't mean to—"

The rest of my sentence gets stuck in my throat: the greenest eyes I've ever seen. Blond hair, not long and wavy, but cut short. Still, this is Frances. I shake my head. "What are you doing here?" She has taken the Pledge already. She's been Benjamin's servant for five years or something.

Frances shows no sign of recognition. "I'm a new soldier. My Pledge ceremony is today."

What the what? My gaze glides down her body: Soldier garb. I don't get it. "Why are you a soldier? What happened to Benjamin?"

Her face stays blank. "Benjamin?"

"Ben—" My heart skips a beat. Something's not right here. Is it me, or— "Benjamin. Your Founder, Frances?"

She turns halfway in her seat to get a better look at me. "Do we know each other?"

"I'm Lea." No reaction. "Lea. The Protégée?"

Still no smile, no nothing—only the slightest bow of her head. "The Protégée. You are so blessed to have your life touched by them."

I barely keep from rolling my eyes. That's what she said at the forum, and I already didn't like the phrasing back then. Anyway, speaking of. "Yes, thank you, I know. You and I, we've met at the forum. I was there with my Founder, you were serving Benjamin."

She cocks her head to the side. "I'm to become a soldier." And with that, she turns away from me and busies herself with her cuticles.

An icy feeling takes hold of my stomach. What the heck? This is Frances—the same Frances I've met twice. The same Frances, who was *in freakin' love* with her Founder. Now she sounds like she got hit over the head. What the—?

Frances scratches her head and her sleeve falls down a bit, something deep red popping up. Her Vinculum.

Yeah. This is Frances all right.

But something about her is very, very wrong.

Once the shuttle touches down in the hive's hangar bay, I lose sight of Frances. She creeped me out, and I'm creeped out enough already as it is. Weird woman, whatever was going on with her.

A dark-skinned Founder with beautiful long, black hair directs the incoming humans. "Prospective servants to the left. Soldiers to be sworn in, to the right." His wings stay up and three-quarters extended, a clear benefit of the high ceilings and wide, roomy area here.

The landing bay or whatever you want to call it isn't as big as countless sci-fi movies tried to teach me over the years. It's actually smaller than the dining hall in the forum was, but then, it only needs to fit a couple of shuttles for us wingless humans. Behind us, the hatch that opened to let us in closes without a sound. All the other openings in the hive's hull—horizontal slits wide and high enough to accommodate an incoming flying Founder—remain open to admit angel after angel as they return to their home. I wonder how many of them live up here. The hives are gigantic, and there are sixty of these huge spaceships. Sixty times however many tens of thousands of Founders fit in here… equals a lot.

Despite the busy traffic, I pick up on Jamie the moment he enters through one of the slits straight ahead from the shuttle, and it's not only because many of the other Founders direct their attention toward him when he's flying in.

Nope.

It's because every cell in pathetic little me gets excited when he flies in, as if they were magnetized and attuned to his presence. Jamie flying is a sight both magnificent and humbling. It makes me fall for him a little bit more every time I see it.

Apparently, I like to live dangerously.

Jamie lands smoothly, shakes out his wings, and folds them close to his back as he comes over to me. I get one tiny hint of a smile before he jerks his head at me. "Servant."

I bow. Deeply. "Yes, Master." This is showtime.

All around me, Founders pick up their human servants while the soldiers are being led away by several Watchers. One of them, the last one, stops and turns, scanning over the mass of humans and Founders until his eyes fall on us: Bane.

Crap.

His lips twitch once when he sees us. He crosses the distance between us in a casual stroll, hands folded behind his back. "Bringing your new toy, Jamie? About time. Thought something wasn't working right." He grabs his crotch and rocks his hips forward.

My jaw drops from his innuendo, but Jamie shrugs it off. "Classy, Bane. Really. Unlike you, I'm able to keep it in my pants. She's here as my servant, and that's it. I don't swing that way. Humans." He shudders, and Bane laughs.

"I know exactly which way you swing. Wait till you got a taste." His eyes narrow. "And I'll make sure to keep an eye on you. You decided to play it that way. Don't think I'm not keeping up."

"Whatever, Bane." Jamie shoulders past him, and I follow. So does Bane's gaze, and it's burning a hole into my back. Walking straight and appearing unaffected is hard. I'd rather curl up somewhere and rock in a corner, but I can't, for obvious reasons. Duh.

If we weren't in the hive, I'd ask Jamie about Bane, but of course I'm not allowed to speak to him as his servant, and the one question I needed to ask I couldn't anyway with ears behind every corner: does Bane think something is going on between us?

Because to me, it sure seemed that way—but why was he so casual about it? He's a Watcher, he should've whipped out his scanner and checked me if that's what he suspected. What the heck?

Jamie leads me down the empty, spacious, white hallways and around dozens of corners. We pass access console after access console, and he still hasn't stuck the small splitter to any of them.

Another computer panel, this time nobody else is around. Okay, it's all on me. I fake a small stumble. "Ow!" Limping two steps to the side of the hallway I bend down and massage my left ankle.

"Servant." Jamie's voice is stern.

"Master, I apologize. I twisted my ankle." Rub, rub, fake, fake. My left hand is taking care of the ankle, my right stabilizes my body on that access panel—the access panel I tap with my index finger: hint, hint.

And nothing happens.

"We are late. I trust you can make it down the hallway? Or do we need to amputate?" His voice drips with sarcasm. Geez.

"No, Master, I'm fine." I growl it out more than anything else. Man! Get it done and over with, or—

Oh. Okay. Heat invades my cheeks. Jamie is supposed to place the virus because I lack the skills to recognize the right panel, as Ice said.

Which I've probably just proven.

Ugh.

Anyway. I follow Jamie, now a little less eager to show off. Not much longer and we come to stop at a wide, closed sliding door guarded by two Watchers with their wings extended to the max. We're not the first ones to arrive, but neither the last. Michael's popular today, it appears. Everybody arriving lines up neatly behind the person in front of them. Proves humans descended from Founders—queuing comes natural to both races, it appears.

Every couple of minutes, the Watchers step aside and retract the wings blocking the door. Then a Founder-Human couple steps forward, the doors slide apart, and the prospective master-ervant-couple enters the atrium, where Michael is waiting for their pledges.

The longer we wait, the antsier I get. Jamie, though, is a rock—my rock, my stabilizer—no matter the show he pulls off. He stays to my right like all the other Founders with their humans. He doesn't talk. He doesn't look at me. Same with everybody else. My hands shake and I cross my arms behind my back. He'd fool me with his behavior if I didn't know differently.

After about thirty minutes of waiting, it eventually is our turn. The Watchers step aside, the doors open, and my last minutes of life as I know it have been initiated.

Must walk strong.

Must keep my cool.

We enter the room, a wide, open hall with black, sparkling floors and walls decorated with flowing, soft curtains in white and grey. In the middle of the room is a pedestal with a throne-like chair on it, and a Founder in it.

Now, wait—

Jamie's step falters the slightest bit.

He moves to the side, revealing the view of—

Black wings.

Black.

Complete, utter black. Not a single white feather. They're all black.

Black.

Black.

Black.

My head spins, I'm six years old again, and the spheres have just arrived.

I'm six years old and have witnessed my parents getting killed by the angel with the black wings.

This isn't Michael.

This is Luke.

This is the man who killed my parents.

Luke.

Luke. Luke. Luke.

The man who killed my parents and burned Jamie's Stigma into his back.

Luke.

The nervousness I had a moment ago is washed away by a nice serving of good ol' hate. Behind my back my fingers curl into fists, and I could swear that Jamie's movements become stiffer with every step we get closer to *him.*

As the distance between us and him shrinks down, the more details I can make out: the all-white clothing, the black wings tucked in behind his back. The heavenly features, so beautiful when smiling and so horrifying when angry. I remember it all.

I remember.

And if I didn't know better, I'd say this man could do no harm. But I do know better.

Jamie and I walk forward, him straight and stiff, me devout and humble, an award-worthy performance on my part. I follow Jamie's lead when he stops a few meters in front of Luke on his throne and bows.

I bite down hard and bow as deep as I can. *Reverence.*

A smile graces Luke's face. "Jamin and Lea. The Protégée. What a pleasure to see you both. You have grown a lot since I last saw you, Lea Akiyama."

Something hardens inside my stomach. "Yes, Founder," I

reply nonetheless, because it's the only valid answer.

Luke addresses Jamie. "It is good to see you again, Jamin."

"It is good to see you too, sir." Jamie stands ramrod straight, hands folded behind his back, wings spread the slightest bit, so that they extend past my back.

Luke tilts his head, fingers drumming onto the throne's armrest. "I would have expected updates from you."

"And I would have expected to be left alone to train my servant."

Luke chuckles. "Had I known you chose a servant, yes. If Bane hadn't come to me, I wouldn't have known you changed your mind."

Bane, that snitch. I could swear Jamie stiffens even more.

"I have come to see the errors of my ways."

"That is as commendable as it was well overdue. Still I would've appreciated a heads-up. I think it more fitting for me to take your pledge than Michael. Also, if I may remind you, you haven't been initiated yet." He gives Jamie a hard glance.

"An oversight, sir. I'm sure the situation can be remediated."

"Yes, it can. Alas, not today, I am busy. You will have to come back."

"Of course, sir."

Of course—or not, as in never-ever-ever, if I can help it.

"All right then, before you change your mind again, let's begin the Pledge." Luke raises both his hands, palms facing toward us. "Do you, Lea Akiyama, swear yourself to your Founder until the end of your days to your best knowledge and abilities? Do you swear to honor and respect him—"

All I see are his palms. Glowing, blue palms.

How they fire on my mom.

My dad.

How they burn into Jamie's skin until smoke rises.

"—to pledge your life as an obedient servant to your Founder?"

Blue fire, cold eyes, my parents gone, Jamie in agony. All I see are the palms of a heartless monster.

My breath comes out short and puffy, my fingers tingle and turn numb. Panicking is around the corner. I—

"Lea?" Two pairs of eyes look at me expectantly, one of them with the silent reminder to keep it together.

"Y-yes. Yes, I do. I swear myself to you. I pledge to you, my Founder, my life as an obedient servant." It comes out with a wheeze.

Luke turns toward Jamie. "Jamin, do you swear to stay at your servant's side from now until the end?" His pledge is so much shorter.

"I do." Jamie's voice doesn't break, like mine did. It's strong and sure of itself. A typical Founder accepting the Servitude of a human. Nothing more.

Luke nods. "Then you are hereby united by the power invested in me by the Lord himself. We shall not destroy what He united. You are from here on bound together." Luke raises both hands higher, palms facing forward, like a preacher in church. "Let the Vinculum tell the story of your bond as it grows stronger over the years."

From the left and right of us Founders walk over. "Hold out your right wrists."

Like in a trance I do as they say.

Snap!

The Founders attach the bracelets to our wrists, mine thinner, with intricately designed elements, Jamie's simpler, like a band, both glowing in a faint silver color.

"Congratulations, Lea and Jamin." Luke claps. "And now that that's taken care of, more urgent matters of business. Jamin, have you considered my proposal?"

Proposal?

Jamie's shoulders pull straight. "No, sir. I was busy with the servant."

Luke sighs and rubs the bridge of his nose. "While I appreciate you taking a step in the right direction, I need you to keep your head in the game. It was your idea, and at this point, the only thing keeping us from implementing it is your missing input. Bane would be happy to assist—"

"I said I'm thinking about it."

Something passes between them, something that speaks of more than one unresolved issue. Eventually, Luke nods as he stands up and steps down the pedestal closer to us. He spreads his all-black wings, the ones my nightmares are made of.

"Very well then. I trust you will give this matter the urgent thought it deserves, Jamin." He lays one hand onto Jamie's shoulder and a smile crosses Luke's face as he looks at Jamie, the same smile I got after he killed my parents. Nausea rises, and it brings a wave of dizziness. What a despicable being.

The doors hiss apart behind us. "Luke."

Luke's gaze pops up to the newcomer. "Ah, Michael. I wondered if you'd come."

"Of course. The boss takes over the pledges I know something is going on. Wouldn't want to miss this special occasion, and I surely wouldn't want to miss this." He walks over with long strides, more a gliding than a walking and stops next to Luke in front of us. "Congratulations, Jamin. Well done."

"Thank you, Michael." Jamie bows, and so do I. When this became automatic, I don't know.

Michael shakes his wings out and gives me a long, good look that bring the goosebumps to a raise. Must keep my head low. Must seem unaffected. Devout. Reverent.

Michael chuckles once, a teasing gleam in his eyes when he addresses Luke. "So, old man, how does it feel seeing your youngest take the Pledge?"

Jamie twitches next to me and Luke laughs once. "Don't rub it in, Michael. I think I'll be skipping procreation for a couple of generations. Things have changed since the good old days. But…" He squeezes Jamie's shoulder. "I must say, I'm still proud it was Jamin of all people coming up with the idea and plan. And then he sets an example and gets himself the Protégée. You did well, my son."

Jamie takes a sharp breath in. "Thank you, Father."

What—

Son?

Father?

As if slapped, my head jerks back. That must be a mix-up, a—

"I didn't expect anything else from a son of Luke." Michael shakes out his wings.

Son of Luke.

No.

No, no, no. That can't be. Jamie can't be Luke's son.

Cannot.

My heart beats so fast, it stumbles over its own feet. Jamie would've told me something so big. Why didn't he tell me? Why—

It must be a mix-up, it—

"Anyway. I have business to attend to. Michael?" Luke turns away from us and walks up the pedestal again. At the same time, two Watchers open a door on the other side of the one we entered in to. "I'll be looking forward to seeing you more often, son."

Jamie bows again. "Same here, Father."

Father.

Father.

Father.

Jamie is Luke's son.

Jamie, whom I saved.

Jamie, who saved me.

Jamie, whom I trusted. Who fixed the carousel for me.

Jamie.

It was *Jamie's father* who killed my parents.

And Jamie knew it all along.

CHAPTER SEVENTEEN

Overload

The door closes behind us with a slight swooshing sound. Only peripherally do I register the two Watchers standing guard widening their stance as soon as we've passed into another bright, white, and empty hallway.

The air is too thin to breathe. Way too thin. Every breath goes in raspy and comes out wheezy.

Jamie is Luke's son.

He knew *his father* killed my parents.

He knew it.

I let myself get pledged to the son of my parents' murderer.

I'm breathing through the sharp rise of nausea that will overwhelm me if I let it. Must focus. Must keep it together. Must—

"Lea," Jamie hisses under his breath. "Slow down. You're attracting attention. Slow down!"

I don't slow down.

I walk, walk, walk at a fast pace to get away from that room, from that boy I'm now legally bound to, who is nothing like I thought he was. I know nothing. *Nothing.*

I walk faster, past closed white doors, around corners, past the occasional other newly-pledged human-Founder couples. I walk, walk, walk, clawing at my Vinculum, but it won't come off. Of course it won't, it's on there for freakin' *life*!

231

"Lee, dammit, stop!" Jamie does his best to pretend he's leading the way, but he isn't. He's following me, *stalking* me, like he's done for the last weeks.

"Lee!" He reaches for me, but in the very last second withdraws his hand.

It makes me speed up even more. I'm dizzy and my mind's a maelstrom of garbled thoughts and hurt emotions. *He knew. He knew.* The next couple of breaths come out choked.

"Jamin, what's going on with your servant?" asks some Founder, I wouldn't know who, and I wouldn't care.

All I care about is that Jamie stops.

"Nerves, Paul. We just took the Pledge," says Jamie.

"Ah. Okay. Happens."

"Yeah, it does. Now——"

The rest I don't hear, because I rush around a corner into a blissfully empty hallway.

The urge to run, to flee, to get away from the Founder who betrayed me, is so strong it physically hurts.

Yet, to my surprise, logic prevails, for once, maybe. Running means being suspicious, means trouble, means death. With the Founders, those equations are easy to calculate.

I lean against the cool wall, hands balled into fists, sucking in deep breath after deep breath, as if it could cleanse me of what just happened and calm me down.

I need time.

Space.

I need to think.

Luke's son. Luke's son. Luke's son.

What does that mean?

He didn't tell me—why?

Why, why, why?

Need a minute. Or two. Or a century.

Did he play me? Why would he? What's his game?

The only answer I can come up with is that Jamie *did* play me. He played me. He knew my story—and yet no full disclosure. Why? Easy. Because at the heart Jamie is a Founder, like all of them. *He sets an example and gets himself the Protégée.* Only I was too stupid to see it. Jezza was right, all along. *He'll still use you, like any other Founder.* And he did. The Protégée's influence and name, now conveniently tied to a Founder—the son of Luke, of all people.

Jezza was right, and boy, does that hurt. I let my senses get clouded and fell for a freakin' Founder. Me. The First. And now I'm pledged to Jamie, who's no better than the rest.

The sound of fast steps comes around the corner behind me. I hear a hurriedly spoken, hissed word: "Lea!"

Then, Jamie is in front of me, letting go of a deflated breath when his gaze falls onto me, flattened against the wall. "Lee. I'm sorry. It's not what you think. I—"

"Stay away from me. You used me," I hiss. The sound of my pulse swells in my ears.

He bites his lower lip. "No, I didn't use you. Let me explain—"

"You knew." How could he not have told me? I opened my heart to him about my parents. I trusted him.

Trusted. Him. A Founder. What a blithering idiot I was.

This one shuts him up. His shoulders slump forward. "Yes." He pauses. "Yes, I knew. Of course, I did. But I was hoping you'd never find out." He angles his body to the side and points in the direction we came from. "Come on, Lee. We've got to get off the hive."

I shake my head so hard, I hit it against some kind of metal-thing on my right. "No." I mean, yes, I need to get off the hive, but without Jamie, preferably.

"I promise you I'm still the same—"

A crazy, way too loud laugh breaks free and echoes through the hallway. "The same? The same guy who lied—"

"Shh!" Jamie looks from left to right. "You've got to stay quiet! You're supposed to be my servant, Lee!"

Oh, really? I unclench my fists and flatten my palms against the cool metal behind me, the Vinculum chiming once when it hits the wall. "Your servant? The last thing I want to be is your servant," I yell. Screw him! Screw whatever game he played—I'm out!

"Lee—"

"Screw you, Jamie!"

...eeew uu meee... eee... ee! My yell echoes until it fades into silence.

Jamie pinches his lips. "Okay. I see this here is not working." He nods his chin at a larger door to my right. "Come on."

"Yeah. *This here* is so not working." I growl, pointing from him to me and back.

He looks to the ceiling in an exasperated way, then points to the door on my right side. "In here. Less echo, more privacy. Much better to yell at me." He steps closer and presses his palm onto a reader next to it. A beep chimes from the door, prompting Jamie to press his other palm against the reader, until finally it opens. "Seriously. Get. In. Here!" Every word is accentuated by him pointing a finger into the room.

Not that I specifically want to be alone in a room with Jamie, but more yelling? I cross my arms in front of my chest. Count me in.

As soon as Jamie and I have entered, the doors close with a swooshing sound behind us, leaving us in a large and wide room. It's dimly lit, at least two stories high, and equipped with a semi-circular table with wide seats made for Founders in the middle and consoles lining all four walls, all of them man-high or bigger. At the far end, one is angled off the wall, pulled forward for repairs or whatever. Cables and power cords and whatnot are coming from its rear, so my hunch regarding maintenance is probably only half bad. That's the one Jamie strides toward without looking back.

I scramble to keep up with him, momentarily caught off guard by him leading me here, and then leaving me standing at the door like an unwanted visitor. "Hey!" I yell. "Really? And now you walk away from me?"

He types something into the console. "You happen to speak more than loud enough for me to hear you. Superior hearing, remember?" The mocking tone does nothing to calm me down, quite the contrary.

I dart forward until I'm next to him. "Oh, sure, ignore me, that's so mature! What the heck are you doing, Jamie?" I'm *this* close to grabbing him by the sleeve and yanking him around.

"I'm looking up a phone number," he deadpans. "Take a guess."

Ugh! I stomp my foot. "You are the most obnoxious—"

A beep comes from the door.

Jamie and I tense at the same time—somebody is coming.

"Shit," he whispers. "Lee, behind the console!"

I groan. "Why?" I'm standing far enough away for a servant, we're not touching—

"Because this is a senior level operations room and we're not supposed to be in here!" For a moment I think Jamie's going to touch me and shove me behind the console he's been working on, but he thinks better of it. And thanks to his last words and my survival instincts kicking in, I'm already on it, shimmying into the slim room behind it. As angry as I am, I'm also very likely to die a fast and fiery death if I'm caught disobeying regulations.

I press my back into the console, doing my best to ignore the connections, plugs, and cables poking me in the back, heart hammering, and sucking in one ragged breath after the next. Anger, fear, sense of betrayal, they're all mixed together into a truly breathtaking combination.

No more than a split second before the door beeps a second time and opens, Jamie slips into my hiding spot with me, one arm planted on the right of my face, one on the left, only a couple of very important inches between our bodies.

"Don't move," he whispers, as if I had any room for that or any desire to bump into him. Hint: I have neither nor.

"Hide somewhere else," I whisper at him. "Shush, get away—"

Somebody enters the room in mid-sentence. "… we're definitely up and running. Aren't we?"

Jamie's eyes widen. "Luke."

Like an icy fist wrapped itself around me, I snap my mouth shut. I don't breathe. I don't blink. Maybe even my heart stops.

Still it's not enough.

"Don't make a sound," Jamie whispers under his breath and tucks in his wings tighter, so close that every desperate breath I suck in brings his scent. So close my body warms from his proximity. So close I imagine I hear his heart beat as fast as mine.

Oh, holy hell.

An hour ago—hell, fifteen minutes ago—I would've been all for it, but not now. Not now that I know he's one of *them*. All I want is a continent between me and Jamie, at least.

My gaze darts to the opening on my left. If I'm fast—

Jamie catches my glimpse. "Don't," he whispers again, "it won't end well." Something urgent creeps into his voice. "*Please.*"

I don't care. His word means nothing anymore. If I stay low, down to the ground, I can hide in the shadows and wait out Luke *without* being way too close to Jamie. A win-win.

A second voice: "Yes. And preparations are sufficient at this point. All we're waiting for is—"

Jamie's eyes widen as he too recognizes the voice: Michael. *Freakin'* Luke and *freakin'* Michael are in the room. For a moment, Jamie's distracted, and I take my chance. It's the only one I'll get.

My muscles contract, about to propel me forward and duck under Jamie's arm, but still Jamie is faster. With a curse that sounds like a groan he angles his body, wings spread as far as possible in this tight space, blocking my way.

A surprised gasp breaks free from my throat—and is snuffed out by Jamie's right hand covering my mouth.

Repeat: *his hand covering my mouth.*

As in, skin-on-skin.

For a moment, I'm too shocked to move, too shocked to do anything, and Jamie makes use of it. Within a split second, he has me pushed into the wall behind me, his body pressed snug into mine, keeping me in place as his wings wrap around the two of us, cocooning us.

My heart stops beating, shocked into arrest by the onslaught of endorphins and adrenaline. The ensuing silence is only disturbed by Jamie's chopped breaths and my panicky ones, because Jamie…

Jamie is touching me everywhere.

Jamie.

Is.

Touching.

Me.

Everywhere.

Holy freakin—

Luke: "What was that?"

Michael: "They're repairing the control panel. It's been acting up. Probably short-circuited or something."

Luke: "Whatever. I want the plan set in motion sooner rather than later."

Jamie whispers, soft against my ear, urgency creeping into his voice, "Not one sound, Lee. You can hate me, you can run from me, but right now, not a single sound, or we're both dead."

Both dead—who cares? I'm pledged to a freakin' Founder, doesn't that mean I'm already dead? I try to struggle, but Jamie is too strong.

He pushes into me harder, wrapping his wings tighter around us. "Remember what you said at the carousel? You don't believe the son should pay for the sins of his father. I have nothing to do with Luke. Nothing." His warm breath stirs the hairs next to my ear, and a series of shivers dances over my skin.

I hate my body for reacting to his touch, because he has *everything* to do with Luke. He's Luke's son—and I trusted him! I trusted him!

We're so close, we're breathing the same air. I can feel his heartbeat through his chest all the way into mine. My body rejoices to finally feel him on me, his skin on mine, but my brain won't join the celebration. Jamie is one of *them.* He—

Jamie swipes his thumb across my lip. It halts all conscious thought. Only now do I realize he's staring at me—staring at me through the darkness, right into my soul. He bends lower, so his lips brush across my ear when he whispers, "Silence." He tugs his wings tighter around us. "Do you understand?"

Yes, I do. I nod against his hand, the movement rubbing my lips across his palm.

Jamie lets go of a shaky breath and leans his forehead against mine. He *freakin' leans his forehead against mine.*

His next shaky exhale dances down my face as he slowly lowers the hand that covers my mouth, and it slides down my chin and up my cheek until it cups my face. I close my eyes so hard stars dance in the darkness.

Behind us in the room Luke continues the conversation. "What's the latest on the fleet's arrival?"

"Sensors have them out by another week at the most, depending on speed adjustments."

Luke curses. "How did he find out? The old man usually wouldn't recognize somebody stealing the food from under his fork."

"Unclear, and it won't change the outcome. We have to be ready for battle sooner than expected."

"Are we?"

"Ready for battle? I believe so. We have recruited triple the amount of soldiers over the last months. Our people are high up in government positions together with their pledged human counterparts."

Luke sighs. "Who's going to lead?"

"You, obviously. Me. All your sons will be in leadership positions. Where do you want Korim?"

"The South."

"All right." Michael hesitates. "Question is, what do you want to do with Jamin now that he brought in the Protégée? He's ready. He was trained his whole life for this. But do you trust him after the stunt he pulled with the servant laws?"

"Good question," Luke replies. "I must admit, he surprised me. Getting himself bound to the Protégée was a smart move. She will be a valuable asset for us when it comes to leading humanity. My son and the Protégée—it doesn't get much better than that."

I stiffen under Jamie as the ground opens to swallow me whole. Jezza was right. Jamie played me, he used me, but I was too busy being swept off my feet.

"I agree. It is a very fortunate combination. He must've worked hard to gain her trust. I hear she's not really servant material."

"And he will use her well, I'm sure of it." Luke chuckles.

"Look at that, your youngest learning our ways. He's almost of age, Luke. He should've been initiated before the Pledge. He needs to know."

Luke's voice takes on a bit of an edge. "And had I known sooner, I would've initiated him already, but today—"

"No time."

"Agreed." He sighs. "It will happen. Soon, because we need him at his best. We have Founders in most high positions. What was missing was our influence of the base. His Pledge to the Protégée will take care of that. It will shift the balance of power in our favor."

Numbness settles in my bones. There it is. I was a plan.

Nothing but a freakin' chess piece. Should've known it when he agreed to Ice's plan as soon as he knew I was the Protégée. Tears shoot to my eyes, but I force them down.

Mustn't let Jamie see what he did to me.

I shove all the raw emotion away from my heart and lock it up.

Mustn't cry.

"Exactly my thinking, Luke. By controlling her, we control the majority of humans. But that still doesn't mean you trust Jamin."

Jamie tenses against me, the hand on the wall next to my head balled into a fist. How the other one can stay so gentle on my cheek, I don't know.

But I want if off.

Luke pauses. "A double-edged sword. He's showing potential, but his track record speaks against him."

A low growl escapes Jamie.

"But he's still your son, Luke."

"That he is. But he's always been the odd one out. Not as determined as the others. Now that he has the Protégée, people will follow him, even the ones we couldn't program, and—"

Program?

"—we'll need those numbers. I expect about a hundred human soldiers are necessary to kill one of their Founders. As it is, we will lose millions of humans."

My heart freezes in my chest. Lose millions of humans—

"But that's what they're there for. Their only purpose. Well, almost." He snickers. "Anyway, I have to admit I'm glad war is about to happen now. We've seen more uprising, more protests—"

"Should we hunt them down more? We've taken apart more

Resistance splinter groups over the last months, if we—"

"No. The more violence we use, the more we're going to turn humanity against us. We're continuing this angle—the loving, guiding Founders—and I assume once half of humanity is dead, we can change gears then. Because once the Fleet is out of the picture, Earth will be ours alone. And so will the other colonies."

"That's the plan."

Jamie exhales choppily. His lips move next to my ear, the sound barely audible. "*And no wonder, for even Satan disguises himself as an angel of light.*" I hear him swallow.

Too close. Too close.

Luke and Michael both chuckle. "A war to remember. It's going to be bloody, like the good old times. Earth has been there before, but this time we won't let the old man see the light of day. We will crush him."

"We will."

Oh my G—

This is *bad,* as in Bad with a capital B. Heck, *all* caps! A war against more Founders—Founders against Founders, using Earth as their battleground.

The sound of shoulder slapping crosses the room, then Luke clears his throat. "All right, I could use your help, old friend. Today's batch of new soldiers needs their programming done. Would you mind?"

There's that word again, programming.

"Not at all. I like to do this myself, so I know it's done correctly. Don't worry. All soldiers will listen to you. The family of Luke controls the armies. As it should be."

"As it should be. Are the hallways cleared?"

"Of course. Wouldn't want word to get out, would we?"

A short laugh. "No, my friend. The way it is is perfect." Steps lead away from our hiding spot until the door opens and closes behind them.

Tense silence stretches. A twisting and churning motion spreads from my stomach all over my body, infesting my heart and my soul until all I feel is nausea at a level there's no breathing through it.

My whole life, I knew Founders were bad news. I lived, breathed, existed only to carry that grudge against them in my heart. I took a ginormous step opening said heart for Jamie—only to have it ripped out and crushed right in front of me.

I knew it my whole life. Founders are evil.

They're no angels, and now I have the proof. They're planning war, and I'm going to be an accessory to murder.

The hand on my cheek slides down my face with a slight jitter to it.

All the tiny hairs on my body rise in response, and not in a good way.

Jamie lifts his forehead off mine.

Takes one small step back, as much as he can, leaving my body cold where his kept me warm.

Unfurls his wings that locked me in.

I stare up into the face I thought I knew, the same face that has looked at me in wonder before.

This is Luke's son.

Luke may have taken my parents' lives, but I won't let his son take mine.

I raise my chin, then slap both of Jamie's hands off my shoulders. "Don't. Touch. Me." I growl and glare at him. "I need you to get out of here alive, but that's all. After that, I never want to see you again."

"Lee—"

I resist the urge to shove him against the wall less than five inches behind him. "Shut. Up. You make one wrong move, and I swear I'm going to be the first human killing a Founder with her bare hands."

Because as of fifteen minutes ago, our little alliance here is over.

From now on, it's back to the way it was all my life. Me, on one side, Founders on the other.

CHAPTER EIGHTEEN

Intercepted

Jamie leads the way out of the control room via the opposite door of the one Luke and Michael just took and walks us through the bowels of the hive.

I stay behind him like a good servant. How convenient, because I won't show him my back. Nu-uh. I keep my eyes trained on him, since I'm fresh out of trust for Jamie. What do I do if he turns on me? More than he already has, I mean. If he decides I'm worthless now? My mind scrambles to come up with a plan, because I must get out of the hive. There must be a way that doesn't include Jamie. Maybe board a shuttle. The other humans need to get flown down too. I could sneak in between the soldiers and the other newly-pledged servants and leave the hive. Once I'm on Earth, I'll let the Resistance know what they're planning. Then I'll hide. The mountains. Or maybe one of those ruined, abandoned western towns. Somewhere. Maybe even stay close to the wind and solar farms, beat Jamie at his own game, with his own idea.

I don't know. If I have to, I'll figure it out. All I know is once I'm off the hive, I cannot stay with Jamie. With Luke's son. Who's supposed to lead Founders against Earth. With my face and name endorsing it.

It's hard to understand: war. War is coming. Jezza was right—

again—and they need to know. They—

Voices. Steps. Lots of them. Crap.

I skid to a halt at the same time as Jamie does. For a moment he seems torn—body coiled tight, gaze darting across the doors to the left and right in front of us—until he relaxes only a moment before a Founder comes around a corner.

Michael.

Michael, followed by at least… I don't know, ten… twenty… more like thirty… crap, at least fifty human soldiers.

"Jamin!" Michael lifts a hand in greeting. "That's unexpected." At least I think that's what he says. He doesn't raise his voice much, and while it's enough for Jamie's super hearing, my human ears have a hard time understanding him over the sound of who knows how many feet marching behind him.

Jamie returns the greeting gesture. "Michael."

The older Founder stops about ten meters in front of us, the soldiers halting in their steps the very second he does. "I'm surprised to see you here. Who told you?"

"Rumor has it, you know?" Jamie shrugs in a nonchalant way, but because I've spent way too much time with him over the last weeks I pick up on the delay between Michael's question and Jamie's answer.

Michael doesn't. "Well then, it's good you're here. Come on, it's about time."

Jamie falls into a quick stride toward the older Founder. "Of course."

Of course, I mock him in my mind. So eager. How I could ever believe his BS is beyond me.

Michael leads the soldiers into the room he stopped in front of. As soon as the last one has marched in, we follow. I mean,

Jamie follows, and I follow him.

The room looks medical with several consoles and dozens of gurney-style beds pushed to the sides to make room for the like fifty humans in soldier garb lined up in rows, shoulder to shoulder.

"Jamin." Michael gestures for Jamie to join him at the far end in front of the aligned soldiers. "Leave your servant over there."

Dutiful little me bows before Jamie can even command me to stay. "Of course, Master. It will be my pleasure." The last sentence I lace with sarcasm, enough for Jamie to pick up on, but not too much for Michael to think I'm out of line. Just a servant voicing her obedience, the way they like it. A muscle in Jamie's jaw twitches, but other than that he doesn't react to my jibe.

Good to see he has some decency left and isn't throwing me to the wolves. But then, if I got killed, he loses his precious Protégée, and wouldn't that be sad?

He leaves me to the side of the last row of soldiers and strides through the center of the room toward the front, like the Founder he is. As if they'd practiced it, the soldiers left enough space in the middle for people to pass. And who knows, maybe they did practice, at least they're all standing tall, at attention, eyes trained straight ahead and arms pressed to their sides. Some of them—

I suck in a harsh breath when I spot blonde hair: Frances! Close to me, in the second-to-last row, a little to my left—it's definitely her! Like everybody else, she stares straight ahead, focused on— No. On second thought, none of them are *at attention* or *focused*. There's no spark in their eyes, for a lack of a better term. They look dull. Like after a boring morning of school. Out of it.

Michael walks over to stand beside Jamie at the front of the formation. "I know you're missing your initiation, but this is part of what you're going to learn about. Those soldiers are ready to be sworn in."

Since I'm small and in the far back I can't see either of them, but the rustling of his feathers I pick up on makes me think Jamie is spreading his wings, the way he likes to do when there's room. "Two ceremonies in one day. A pledge and soldiers. Lucky me." He chuckles.

"Indeed." Michael chuckles as well. "As a matter of fact—"

Movement on my left side catches my eye: Luke enters the room, shaking out his black wings. "Sorry I'm late, Michael. Are they set?"

A wheezy breath leaves my throat. Luke. Is there no rest for the wicked?

"As good as ready. Vinculums are off—"

Wait, what—*off?* Vinculums are *off?*

"… last round of injections are in. They're primed. You want to get in position so they can get the pheromones? Double the dose, since we have Jamin here."

"Ah, fantastic. Jamin. I appreciate the initiative."

"Privileged to be here, Father."

Puke.

Luke walks up to the front of the lines and steps onto a small podium. "Watch and learn. Soon this will be your task." He spreads his wings to the max, raised slightly higher than his head.

"Soldiers." Michael's voice is full of authority. "Ready your packs."

What the what?

Like synchronized, all soldiers release something from a hook on their belts.

"Inhale."

My decision is made in the same second it takes the soldiers to raise their hands to their mouth. Keeping my body bent at the waist, I dart forward and to the left, duck past the first soldier in the row and stretch to catch Frances' arm before she can breathe in whatever is in those inhalers.

The sound of dozens of lungs sucking in air fills the room.

"Perfect," Michael says, as silence takes over. "Luke, you should start—"

"I need this," Frances whines, and tries to tug her arm out of my hold like an uncoordinated toddler.

"What? Why are they talking? Michael?" That's Luke, and he doesn't sound pleased.

"You know how it is. For some, the priming begins to lift before they inhale. It should kick in soon."

Frances tugs once more. "I need this."

Crap—

"Maybe we should give that one a double portion, if they metabolized the primer already." Luke sounds annoyed, and sweat breaks out on my brow. Frances is strong.

Michael sighs. "We can. Do the swearing in, that might override whatever's still going on in that pea-sized brain."

Frances struggles to lift her arm higher, giving me a nice shake that comes close to sending me into the soldier next to her.

"Frances!" I hiss-whisper, clinging onto her arm with both of mine. She doesn't use the other one to take the spray or to punch me—not that it wasn't obvious, but something is really wrong with her.

She repeats a third time, "I need—"

Oh, shut up! I let go of her with my left hand and reach for the used inhaler held loosely by the soldier next to her. "Here."

With one quick switch I replace Frances's inhaler with the used one from the other soldier. As soon as I let go, she brings it up to her mouth and sucks in a deep breath through the mouthpiece.

Maybe it's my imagination, but I feel it sounds emptier than the other ones.

The tips of Luke's black, uplifted wings are visible even from back here. "Jamin, spread your wings."

"Yes, Father." Jamie's white feathers reach higher than Luke's darker ones.

Luke clears his voice. "Soldiers. You are to serve the Founders, and the Founders only. You take your orders from the clan of Luke only. You will obey each and every one of us, and you forfeit your life should you disobey." He looks over the crowd of soldiers. "Do you understand?"

"Yes, sir!" Two words, spoken simultaneously by dozens of voices—dozens of voices that sounded like… robots. No emotion. No soul. No heart. It brings goosebumps to my skin, hearing Frances like that.

Slowly, because it would really be a bummer being caught now, I back up until my body meets the wall.

Luke claps Jamie's shoulder. "Thank you. Another batch of soldiers loyal to us. We're getting up there with the numbers. We'll be ready way before we need to. Good work."

"Th-thank you, Father." Jamie clears his throat. "When you say that, what do you mean by *ready before we need to?*"

Silence hovers, broken by a lip-smacking sound a good ten seconds later. "Well, I have no time to go through your complete initiation right now, but this, I agree, you need to know. Send your servant out."

Wait, why—

"No need to worry about her, Father."

"Still, she needs to leave. I wouldn't want her to… let's just say, get the wrong impression."

The wrong impression? Like, figuring out freakin' war is going to happen?

Jamie laughs out. "Please. This one's never shown any signs of caring for her race. All she ever does is waddle in self-pity about her own fate."

As if punched in the gut, my stomach muscles tighten. That bastard—

"Nonetheless, send her out." Luke's voice hardens.

"If you wish so." Jamie pushes off the ground. With a few easy beats of his wings he hovers in the air so he can see me over the rows of soldiers. "Lea, wait outside." He sounds bored. Arrogant.

Grinding my teeth I force myself to say, "Yes, Master." I bow and retreat until I'm in the hallway and the doors close behind me. Ugh. I wonder what they're talking about. Initiation whatever. Those soldiers are creepy though. The way Frances didn't react normal—

The sound of beating wings comes from around the corner, and two seconds later I recognize the Founder: Bane. Crap, crap, crap. Just my luck.

"There, there. If that isn't Jamie's little toy?" Bane lands in front of me, trapping me between the wall and himself.

"F-Founder." I bow, my heart running ahead and fleeing away from this guy without me.

Bane shakes out his wings and pulls them closer. A predatory gleam lights up in his eyes. "All by yourself. So that's how you serve your Founder. How you honor your Pledge." He spits out the last word.

"Founder, Jamin is in the room behind me. I was ordered to wait outside." I keep my gaze down, my posture demure.

"And it speaks without permission. That's not a good pet."

I grimace. Dang it. Technically, he's right, but most Founders take this rule a bit lighter. A good reminder Bane isn't Jamie. I swallow my response and suck in my lower lip to bite on, just to be sure.

"There you go. A silent servant is a good servant." He folds his wings tight to his back. "Although, I still wonder, what do you have that—" He clears his throat once. "What does he see in you? I don't trust you, little pet."

Deep breaths, Lea, deep breaths. Don't react, don't react. I press my sweaty palms against my outer thighs, hoping he can't see my pulse hammering in my neck.

Bane raises his left forearm with the round disk attached to the leather cuff. "I must be missing something. Alas, that's what scanners are for."

Instinct kicks in. If he scans me, I'm as good as dead. Less than two minutes ago, Jamie was all over me. His hand on my mouth, his lips on my ear, his body pressed into mine. No way I'm still mustard-yellow. This is lobster-red all over again.

Distraction is all I have. I lift my chin. "It's not like that. I live to serve. It's how I was raised. My parents gave their life for the Founders." Also technically true.

"And it speaks again, more than it's supposed to." He cocks his head to the side and lets his left arm sink lower again. "Something is off with you. Something is off with Jamie. And I don't like it." He takes another step closer, backing me up until I'm pressed tight against the wall.

"Founder, I—"

"I mean it, pet. Whatever you're playing at, I will find out. You're failing your servitude less than an hour after getting bonded. It's not right." Bane stops a mere meter in front of me. He's massive, especially with his wings almost completely unfurled. Threatening. Which is probably the point, come to think about it.

"I serve Jamin with my life, Founder. It's what I pledged to do." It comes out harsher than I planned, and Bane doesn't like it, or the fact that I'm talking, who knows.

"And I'm very much willing to give you the benefit of the doubt, Protégée. *After* I scan you. Because if you're using Jamie, your life is over." He lifts the wrist with the scanner attached to it.

Oh, hell no.

I react before I think.

My left leg shoots up and forward, right into his groin. As if hit by lighting, Bane doubles over, a choking *oomph* breaking from his throat.

Me, I can't get any air in, my lungs won't work.

But my legs do.

I duck under his wings, and run.

I run.

It's what I'm good at, running.

I race away from sure death and down the hallway. Probably shouldn't have kicked him. *Definitely* shouldn't have kicked him.

Stupid reflex—now what? He scans me, I'm dead. He doesn't—I'm also dead. I attacked a freakin' Founder.

Must get away from Bane, must hide, leave the ship—

Alas, I'm not fast enough.

A grunt, a fast swooshing sound—and a burning, sharp pain explodes in the right side of my right back. I yelp and stumble, sheer adrenaline keeping me from falling. Every step is pain, every breath is agony, but some primal fight-or-flight mechanism engrained over thousands of generations keeps me pushing forward.

Because if I didn't, I'd be dead for sure.

I reach back as I keep forcing myself to move, move, move, to not stop, to be faster. *A hilt. Knife.* Bane threw a knife at me. And from what I can feel, it's in deep.

My hand comes back sticky and wet.

Hurts.

Every breath hurts.

Every step is agony.

I pass by a Founder-servant couple that eyes me suspiciously, although I doubt they see the knife.

Must be faster, must run faster, must get out of here faster.

I dart through the hallways, limping on my right, waiting to hear Bane's steps behind me, his shouts, his Caeruleum lightning up and incinerating me, but nothing.

Yet.

My right back is bad.

Bad.

Within twenty more steps, the pain turns from bad to worse to blinding until my steps falter and I stop.

Must get the knife out.

Oh, crap.

I wrap my fingers around the hilt—

Can't do it. Tears stream down my face. Every breath is raspier than the one before. Wheezy.

I grab tighter and pull—

Oh, *f*—

This is pain on a level I've never felt before. Hot, burning, agonizing.

But if I don't pull it out, I'll never make it off the hive. A human with a knife in their back is suspicious.

Three, two, one—

I suck a big breath in and pull.

"Nnnghhh!" My grunt of pain breaks through my clenched teeth, no matter how hard I try to keep it in, but the knife comes out, a loud gush of blood with it.

Don't care. Must find a way out. Now.

I pocket the knife and stumble on forward. Can't leave it lying here.

Every left step is bigger than the one on the right. Less pain.

Around a corner, another one.

To the left. I need the shuttle bay, I need—

I turn around the corner and almost crash into—

Jamie.

The hive is huge, how'd he find—?

"Whoa!" He jumps back, arms wide, wings extended, to keep himself and inertia from carrying forward and into me. "Lea!" he hisses. "Damn it, where've you been? You were supposed to wait—" His eyes fall on my tears, then the torn shirt. "What happened?"

My mind can't make sense of what he's saying. So dizzy. Headache. My life is made out of pain, and its center is in my right back.

Jamie reaches for me, and for one tiny moment, I think he's going to wipe away that tear, but no. He cramps his fingers into a fist and pulls back. No touching. Never. And I don't want him to. Ever.

"What happened?" The second time his tone is more urgent, and it penetrates the fog surrounding me.

"Bane," I wheeze.

Jamie's features harden. "Bane," he hisses—but he doesn't ask. Maybe he doesn't have to. No matter what happened with Bane, the fact that I'm here, running from him, is proof enough I'm in trouble.

"Bastard! That changes things. We can't leave via shuttle. He'll be waiting for us, easy catch. Follow me." This time, he jogs in the direction I was going.

Funny how priorities shift. Ten minutes ago, I wanted nothing to do with Jamie. Now I have worse to worry about.

Much worse—and I don't mean Bane.

I mean my back.

Warm blood runs down my side and soaks my shirt and pants. It's a wonder I'm not leaving drops of blood all over the place, but maybe that's because most blood is pooling internally.

Would explain the dizziness.

The shortness of breath.

The—

"Faster, Lea!" Jamie waits in front of a large, wide window for me and waves me over. I pant as I wobble there. Breathe in. Out.

In.

Out.

In.

Every breath reverberates through my skull like Darth Vader stood next to me. Every breath is pain. Every breath is bringing less and less oxygen to my lungs.

This is not good.

Jamie presses his hand into a reader next to the window, which slides aside like a door, so it's more like a hatch. A muscle in his jaw twitches. "Do you trust me?"

I lean against the wall.

Breathe in.

Out.

In—

"Lee! Do you trust me?" His gaze holds mine with a sincerity I haven't seen in him before. Or maybe I have, and I forgot. So blurry. Everything.

"Lea, do you trust me, damn it?" He punches the wall next to my head.

I jerk. "I—" I don't know. Can't think. My instincts scream yes, I trust him, my brain says *hell no* at the same time. "I—"

"Oh, for heaven's sake," Jamie growls—and then he grabs me by the hips and throws me over the sill and out into the open sky.

I fall.

I fall, fall, fall.

Air rushes past me and steals my last breath, my silent scream, my hope that this isn't real.

But it is.

Jamie threw me out the hatch.

Jamie got rid of me.

Jamie lied.

My body rushes down the five thousand meters toward the surface, accelerated by gravity and held back by nothing. I see the moon, stars, surface, moon, stars, surface, moon, stars, surface—

I don't stop spinning.

I don't stop panicking.

If I could, I'd scream. But no air.

No strength.

Little strength I had got stabbed when I did. Withered away when Jamie betrayed me, over and over again.

Will hit the ground soon. It's rushing to meet me, to smash me into a pulp.

Maybe that's best. Then it's over.

Over.

The ground comes closer. Not much longer and—

A stronger rush of air—arms, wings, a soft body—

With a grunt, Jamie catches me. I cry out from the pain in my back. Feels like being stabbed all over again.

"I got you, Lee. I got you." He cradles me to his chest like a baby, one arm around my shoulders, the other under my legs. "Good thing I know Luke's favorite way of leaving the hive without cameras tracking his coming and going."

My fists pummel his chest, weak. "Lemme go! Lemme go!" More a mumble than anything else, but he understands. Holds on even tighter.

"Yeah? That really what you want? We're hundreds of meters high, good luck making it down in one piece, or in one that's not smeared over a football field."

He's got a point.

Plus, can't keep up the fight. Too tired.

In some far away corner of my mind, I know this is bad. Bane, out for revenge. Me, dizzy, sucking in one desperate breath after another. Jamie's hands on me, again, in a major way. Not a brush of fingers. Full on body contact, like in the hiding spot in the hive.

A problem.

But not for now. Nothing is.

Oy.

Can't focus.

Next breath is shaky. Brings way too little oxygen to my starving brain. Things get blurry around me. The wind dries my eyes. Blinking is too hard.

I look up and—

The little bit of breath I have left catches in my throat.

Jamie.

Jamie flying.

Looking like an angel. White wings. Spread far, can't make out their tips. Lift and lower, lift and lower—magnificent. Moon's giving him a halo. Blurry.

Heart's beating too fast. Strange kind of tingling runs over my body.

I remember though. He's using me.

Using me.

Using—

Touch down. Gentle. Still hurts. I grunt.

He lets me down on something metallic and curved. "Wait."

Couldn't do anything but. I double over. Jamie flies down onto the wings of this—

"Plane?" I wheeze. This is… plane. Am on top of a pla—

A cramp. Through my side. Ow—

Jamie swoops up from below. Picks me up like a child. "It's a plane graveyard. Out in the desert. Nice and dry, and very private." He flies us down to the wing. Lands. "This is my favorite one." He stands me up. Difficult. Must walk forward. One step. Two. Three. Over the threshold. Into the plane.

Jamie pulls the door closed behind us. Folds his wings in tighter. "And by the way, Lee, don't you ever think I'll throw you to the wolves, whatever the idiots say." Puts both hands on his hips. Glares at me.

Dizzy. Blurry.

A seat. Sit on the armrest.

The glare stays. Blue emergency light spring to life. "I'm on your side. Trust me. I—"

Trust. Hard. Talking. Harder. "B't... L'ke sai— no, M'chael..." Can't get sentence out.

"Yes?" Both eyebrows up. Waiting. Blue light bathing him into a strange, alien light.

Tongue so heavy. "Use... Pr't'gée." He said. Luke said. I rub one heavy palm over my eyes. Can't see straight. Warm here. No, cold. Freezing.

Jamie rolls his eyes. "Yeah, and did you maybe remember all the stuff I told you about him? Like, for example the little fact that we don't get along at all? That he hates me? That he is the one who gave me the Stigma, son or not? Hell, you heard him. He doesn't trust me." He throws his arms up. Deflates. "You should know me by now, Lee." Pinches the bridge of his nose. "I'm sorry I lied to you. Of course, I knew it was my dad who killed your parents the moment I found out you're the Protégée. Even if your story wasn't common knowledge, I'd have known. There's only one of him. Only one with all-black wings. But..." He lets go of a sad breath. "You would've hated me from the beginning. I didn't want that. And for once, I didn't want to be Luke's son. Or a Founder. For once I wanted... I wanted to be me."

"Ugh." Lips are numb. Came out wrong. Wanted to say more. Wanted to say I understand. Wanted—

Sad smile, wider. "I know, huh? Kind of sad. But you saw a person in me when everybody else saw Luke's son. A Founder. A demon. You saw me, and it meant the world, Lee. I didn't want it to change." The look he gives me. Warm. Soft. Feels good.

I—

Knees too weak. Give in. I fall to the ground. Chin barely misses the armrest of the seat one over.

Ow.

Pain on my knees not bad. Pain in my side—hell.

Jamie, next to me in a heartbeat. "Lee? Lee, what's going on?"

A hand on my arm, one on my right side. Digging into my injury. *Torture.*

"Lee?" Like through fog.

Would tell him, but can't. Side is killing me. Literally, probably.

Heart doesn't beat, it flutters. Not in a good way.

Jamie gasps. Pulls his hand from my side.

Stares down at it.

Looks down his body. *Blood.* My blood. Everywhere.

A roar. Darts forward. Guides me to the ground. Gentle.

Pain gets less. A tad.

"Where, Lee?" Hands roam over my body. "Tell me where!"

Hands travel over my shoulders. Arms. Chest. Sides—

I flinch and grunt. Ow. Ow, ow, ow.

He rolls me to the side lightning quick. Yanks up my shirt, pulls in a sharp breath of air through his teeth.

Not good.

But I'm warm. Comfortable. Dull pain. Peace. Blurry peace, but peace.

Rolls me on my back. "Lea," he whispers. Single tear, down

his cheek. "Fuck, Lee… This is bad." He lowers his forehead against mine.

Heaven.

Feels good.

Feel right.

Always wanted this. *Him.*

Something wet drips onto my face.

Arms sneak under my shoulders and legs. Careful. I feel lifted up. Feel carried. Feel squished through a narrow staircase. Feel lowered onto a soft mattress.

Sticky hair on my forehead. A hand swipes it away.

"I'm sorry. I'm so, so sorry." Warm palm on my stomach. "I'm so sorry." Once more, hoarse. "So sorry."

Want to raise my hand. Want to tell him—

Lightning.

Lightning hits me in the center of my stomach, turns me into a supernova of heat. Heat, pain, heat, pain—nothing else. A strangulated choking sound leaves my throat. Body bends into unnatural positions, torn by a force can't comprehend, can't understand, can't handle. Can't breathe. Can't move. Can't think—all I am is *pain*, all I'll ever be is pain.

Jamie's hand stays glued to my body. Burning like fire, heavy as lead, sour as acid.

A mangled scream breaks free, but he doesn't let go. His face contorts into a mask of pain, but unlike me he stays quiet. Focused. The world consists of nothing else than the blinding hot pain and Jamie in the center of it, hovering above me, hand pressed into me.

That is, until it isn't anymore.

The pain tunes down.

The fuzziness retreats, taking the darkness with it.

Little by little, my heart beats stronger, my lungs inhale more air, my mind clears up.

The pain is gone, but Jamie is still there.

Jamie.

His fingers have cramped into my stomach and surely left scratch marks. His chest heaves up and down like after a marathon, and his eyes… his eyes are as large as the moon when he blinks once. Twice.

He falls back on his butt, holding his hands out in front of his face, eyes darting from them to me and back. The apple in his throat moves up and down. "I'm sorry." It's a croak. "I…"

I push up on my elbow.

No pain. I draw in a sweet lungful of air. Still no pain. The fuzz that had my brain wrapped tightly is gone. What… where—?

Oh.

Concave ceiling, no windows, mattresses covering almost the complete surface. The rest area for flight attendants, I assume.

Jamie's attention stays glued to every move I make, sorrow radiating off his body like heat from the sun. Don't get it. Why is he sorry? I feel better. Like me. Like before Bane stabbed me almost to death—

The short bout of elation shooting through me is drowned by reality in an instant.

"Oh, God," I rasp. Doesn't sound like me, but it is. It's me, alive and, well, *well*—if it wasn't for one small caveat. Like in slow-motion, I lift my head and look at Jamie.

A heartbeat passes as our gazes lock, the pain in his eyes similar to the day they gave him the Stigma.

"I'm sorry. Lee, I'm sorry. But I couldn't let you die. I

couldn't. I—" Tears stream down his face as he works himself onto all fours and he crawls over to me. My arms open and cradle him to my chest as he cradled me a few minutes ago, like it was the most natural thing to do. Sobs shake Jamie's body and burrow their way into my soul.

I'm alive.

The fall didn't kill me, because Jamie caught me.

And Bane's knife didn't kill me, because Jamie healed me.

Jamie.

Healed.

Me.

A human.

Jamie broke the biggest law there is: he healed a human.

Jamie marked me.

Permanently.

Permanently.

CHAPTER NINETEEN

Boundaries, Lost

Jamie healed me.

I'm alive thanks to him, but thanks to him, that life might be shorter than I planned.

And yet I'm not mad.

Not angry at how my life turned out.

No. I'm strangely calm.

Maybe because I came back from death's doorstep, maybe because of what Jamie said. His apology. His explanation. *You saw me and it meant the world.* I heard that. Now that I can think again, I understand it.

And it patches my soul, one tear at a time.

We're both pawns in a game played around us. And we both have to deal with it. We both have to carry our burden, and his is as heavy as mine, Founder or not.

Oh, Jamie…

His face is burrowed into my chest, and whatever little sounds he makes is drowned out by my clothing. I stroke over his hair, so soft, and little by little the sobs get less frequent, less violent.

I'm the first to break the silence. "It will never go away." A statement, not a question. A life-altering statement.

Jamie rolls onto his back, head in my lap. "It will never go away." He wipes the tears away with the sleeve of his shirt.

Never. Marked for life, however long that will be. I close my eyes so tight, stars dance in front of my lids. "So, it didn't matter," I whisper. "Nothing did."

"What?"

I shrug. What a waste of energy trying to keep me alive and the Mark to disappear. "A waste. All the effort. All the hiding. All the—"

Jamie sits up like pulled by a string. "Shut up, Lee! It mattered! It matters! Everything does, and yes, I would've loved not to mark you permanently, because it spells a buttload of trouble, but I'm glad I did it! I'm glad I found you, or you'd have bled to death up there. Gosh, if I hadn't had this hunch where you were…" He shakes his head to himself. "And don't you dare say it didn't matter. It did, and so do you. And I couldn't let you die." His eyes bore into me as he takes my hand, fingers slipping through mine. "Do you get it? I couldn't let you die."

The way he looks at me… The air around us warms. Sizzles with electricity. I feel a tug deep in my belly, the kind I've tried to ignore for the last weeks, because I had to.

Only now, the tables have turned on us. My gaze drop down to our entwined hands. "So, it doesn't matter."

"It does—" He stops mid-sentence when he feels the shy brush of my thumb over the back of his hand.

"It doesn't matter," I whisper. It doesn't matter. Touch doesn't matter anymore. What's it gonna do? Bring me from supernova-red on the scanner to… still supernova-red? I'm marked for good. Eternally. With all the consequences that come with it.

Might as well start living, before it's cut short.

I give his hand another sweep of my thumb.

And another one.

One more.

The blue emergency light is enough to show his pulse jumping in his throat. "It does matter," he breathes back. "Everything about you matters." He takes my other hand and pulls me to my knees. His wings spread wider behind him, catching the little light illuminating the darkness. Our bodies are separated by scant inches—so few, I would've been nervous not long ago. Now I want them gone.

Jamie sweeps his thumb over my hands like mine did before. A small step for anybody else but us. We're touching. *Willingly.* This is huge.

His throat bops with a hard swallow—and he takes my hands and places them on each side of his waist. "Feel me," he whispers.

My palms feel the hard muscle of his sides, and my senses switch from alert to hyperaware in less than a split-second. Because we're doing this. We're starting something we won't be able to stop.

There's no going back, I know it.

Once I get a taste of Jamie, how could I stop?

Easy.

I couldn't.

But then, I don't have to. I'm marked forever.

And right now, I don't care.

My hands slip under his shirt, fingers skimming over his skin, bringing up goosebumps. A breathy sound leaves his throat and it fuels me. I scoot closer and push my body into his. He said once he never had a girlfriend before, so I probably shouldn't go too fast, but it's difficult. My heart hammers and cheers me on, and all I want is to feel more of Jamie. More.

Jamie glides his hands over my arms and down my back,

taking their sweet time. His body melts into mine with a natural ease that calls the Founders' laws hearsay. Humans and Founders, we are made for this. Jamie and I are made for this, and our bodies more than eager to take what was denied to them since the moment we met.

I flatten my palms against his back and feel my way up over velvety soft skin and hard, lean muscle. When I skim against the roots of his wings, he moans softly. So I do it again.

And again.

Jamie pushes harder into me, fingers digging into my back, as if he wanted to make sure I didn't stop, I didn't let go.

I wouldn't, even if the world ended around us.

With every brush of my nails over the roots of his wings, Jamie's breathing speeds up. So does his exploration. His fingers glide upward and grasp the back of my neck, holding me right where I am. Like in the hive, he leans his forehead against mine.

His eyes fall shut and his lips part. "Lee." His gentle breath caresses my face, and that sound, my name whispered like that, it sets me on fire one cell at a time. Every little pent-up, denied emotion—the craving, the hunger, the longing—is released in this very moment. And it's beautiful. The way he holds me. How his other hand brushes over my body, so gentle, so full of wonder.

I still my fingers and let him hold me, feel me. I don't want to overwhelm him. His pace, not mine.

We're so close, each breath I take is Jamie's, each of his is mine.

Then, he dips his head the slightest.

Anticipation shoots through me like an arrow. Is he—

His lips hover above my mouth, every choppy breath teasing me, taunting me, speaking of things about to come.

A tentative brush of his lips against mine—and it comes with a jolt of electricity.

And I want more.

I push forward and into him. More. Screw going slow. My hands tangle in his hair as I bring my mouth to his for a soft kiss. A low moan breaks from Jamie's throat when I coax his lips apart with my tongue, and it hits me like lightning.

This.

This is everything.

Jamie wraps his arms around me, deepening the kiss. Our tongues play, our breaths mingle, our hearts beat as one. Not lying, I can feel it in his chest.

This kiss… it could make me believe in a life without consequences. It speaks of hope, of a future together, of a promise and redemption and salvation. And for now, I choose to believe it.

His arms tighten around me. One hand clutches a fistful of my torn shirt. "I need this off," he whispers against my neck, the words burning on my skin like lit by fire.

And I'm happy to oblige. I like that pace he's setting.

The shirt is gone in less than a second, and I feel daring. Jamie's eyes roam over my body, their heated gleam warming me up against the cool air's chill. For one moment, they dim as they brush over my right side and the caked blood, but when he looks back at me, the moment's passed.

His chest heaves up in heavy breaths. One fast reach and pull, and his shirt is off. He spreads his wings wider, touching both walls in this cabin, and I swear a firework explodes inside my stomach. Must be. No other explanation for the fire rushing from my center down to every last cell in my body, igniting it and burning it until nothing's left but an inferno.

All for Jamie.

On his knees, wings spread, every muscle toned on his uber-perfect eight-pack body he is more than beautiful. No, beautiful doesn't cut it, because that would only describe his looks. But Jamie is more. Much more. He's stunning. Mesmerizing. Enthralling. Extraordinary. Staggering. Incredible.

And he's mine.

Ever so slowly, he reaches out for me, one finger extended until it lays on my shoulder. He works on a dry swallow. "Me," he says. "Imagine it's me." And with that he glides his finger along my clavicle, down the middle of my sternum, over the clasp of my bra, all the way down to my bellybutton until it hooks behind the hem of my pants.

With one quick yank, I'm against him, skin on skin.

For a moment we both freeze.

"Whoa," I breathe. Skin on skin is awesome.

"Whoa indeed," Jamie whispers back. "Watch out." He scoops me up, and not even one second later I'm on my back, Jamie hovering above me. "Thought we'd mix it up." A mischievous smile graces his face as he lowers his weight onto me, rocking his hips against mine. *Whoa*, again. Stars dance in front of my eyes.

Jamie showers me with hot little kisses to my lips, my jaw, then down my neck, all while keeping that delicious pressure in all the right places. His touch teases my senses, ensnares my mind, and turns me into nothing but feeling. The way he circles his hips—

A soft gasp breaks from my throat. "Where'd you learn that?" I whisper at him. A-mazing. Never knew the human body could feel something like this. Sorry, Jezza.

Jamie gives me a cock-sure smirk. "You'd like to know that, wouldn't you?" His answer comes with another circle of his hips, and it spins my world upside down. Touch becomes natural, an instinct I follow, as my arms roam up and down his back, play with his wings. Don't know when I hooked my legs behind his, but it does wonders to keep me closer to him, glued together into one—tangled together, touching everywhere, a Gordian Knot of extremities.

All the control we exercised over the last weeks, all the little pull-backs, the careful work-arounds, the moments not given in to—all gone. Gone. The walls are down, destroyed forever, turned into rubble by a gesture that saved me but will also be my downfall, since—

Shit.

Realization strikes, and it comes with an ice-cold rush of terror through my veins.

I jerk back, breaking our connection.

Jamie tries to kiss me again, but I hold him back. Something in my body language must've tipped him off, because one look at my face is enough for him to sober up. "What?"

My breath comes out in short little pants thanks to the make-out session and the sheer terror that found its way into my heart, making it stumble and stutter.

I shake my head. "It's not just me."

Jamie tilts his head.

He doesn't get it. "It's not just me, Jamie. I'm marked, and we know how that will end eventually. But you—" I swallow hard. How could I not think of that before? Egoistic little bitch than I am. "You're going to be punished as well."

He holds my eyes and gives me a small nod. "Yes."

No fear, no worry, no nothing. "Wait—that's it? *Yes?*"

He lowers his head and kisses my jaw. "Yes."

Man of many words. I groan and buck my hips into him, but not in a nice way. Talk, for heaven's sake! "*Yes,* what?"

Jamie chuckles as my movement rocks him up. "Yes, Lee. I knew that."

"And you still healed me."

"Yes." Another kiss for my jaw. "There was no other option if I didn't want to lose you. And I didn't. *For there is eternal fire waiting for those who cannot obey the Lord's command.* You know, I like it warm." I feel his lips pull into a smile.

Boy...! "So, we're both doomed."

He sighs. "Kind of. But you're the only one I ever want to be doomed with." He trails soft little kisses down my neck, over my collarbone—

My eyes roll into their sockets. "Okay. Okay then."

"Okay what?" he mumbles between kisses.

I sneak my right hand down his back and slip it under the seam of his pants directly onto his butt. "Let's be doomed together."

Jamie groans and presses his hips down into mine. A mischievous smile lights up his face. "I like the way you think. Let's be doomed together."

CHAPTER TWENTY

Planning

I't's late at night when we both are finally wearing all our clothes again, bloody as they may be, in my case.

Jamie's on his back, left arm propped behind his head, right holding me cuddled close to his chest. His heart is beating its strong rhythm against my palm on his ribs, a reassuring double-dub that calms my soul, no matter the situation we've gotten ourselves into.

A blanket is draped over our lower bodies. Leave it to Jamie to think of a plane graveyard to hide and the flight attendants' rest area as a make-out place. Okay, more like an improvised emergency room first, then a make-out place, but I'll take it. Because, it was a mighty good make-out session. One that led way further than I would've thought. Not the whole mile, but we came close. Pun intended.

His fingers play with my neck and hair, brushing over the skin or twisting the few longer strands I have. He extended his right wing fully, and after a bit of hesitation, I lay down on it. I didn't… I mean, it's not as if I had done that before. Don't want to hurt him, although the wing is way more flexible than I thought. The moment I curled into Jamie's side, he wrapped it over me like a blankie.

Or rather, like a guardian angel.

And while I feel more at home and protected than I have in

over a decade, we need to talk about the elephant in the room. *Elephants.* Plural. Definitely plural.

I sigh. "So. That's why everybody has been looking at us. And why you said we'd draw attention at the dinner. And why you were so convinced you'd know what the higher-ups are planning. You're Luke's son." That came out of left field, no doubt about it. Egocentric little me only assumed the attention was because of my Protégée fame, and his little one-liners from an inflated ego. Think again, honey, you've got the cart before the horse.

Jamie stills his fingers. "Yes. Because I'm Luke's son."

"And you guys don't get along." Didn't take a rocket scientist to figure out even before I met his dad or heard his apology why he neglected to mention this particular family connection.

Jamie pauses. "No. Everything I told you is true. I'm child number seventy-six. I'm old news and nowhere close to what he feels for some of my brothers."

Huh. "Maybe you haven't been around long enough. You're what—eighteen? Nineteen?" We've already established he doesn't have a birthday—bogus, but whatever—but eighteen-ish makes sense. "Your brothers must be way older. He had more time to bond."

He resumes his play with my hair. "Thank you for defending my father, but I doubt there's anything that could change his mind. His opinion of me was set the moment I was born with white wings."

"Ouch." I cringe. "*That's* his issue with you?" Wing color?

"My father is much shallower than many think. Black wings are his pride. The fact that I don't have any black in mine is a slap in his face."

"But your people are great at inclusion." Seriously, they are.

The Founders' skin colors range from the lightest, palest white to the fullest black, and yet they don't discriminate. I feel like wing color shouldn't matter either.

Jamie wraps a strand of my hair around his fingers. "Luke is the only Founder *ever* born with all-black wings. Only his sons carry the gene. Depending on our mothers, we all display it to a different amount. All but me, that is." He pauses and holds his breath. "I disappointed him the second I was born, and he hasn't let a day pass without reminding me of what a failure I am. And even if it wasn't for the obvious flaw, me trying to change his precious servant laws didn't help." He sounds bitter.

I think back to the hive. "He seemed happy you got yourself a servant, though. In the evil mastermind kinda way."

Jamie chuckles. "Interesting phrasing. You know, I've been reading the New Scripture, and..."

"Yeah?"

He wraps a lock of my hair around his finger. "Nothing. Just interesting finding the true parts of family history in there. But anyway, yes, *Luke* was happy about me getting a servant." He gives his father's name a weird intonation. "It's a good move to keep him satisfied, but it won't last for long. My father always wants more."

Speaking of... "So, what now?" Now that we're doomed, as we put it earlier. In the heat of the moment, it seemed kind of funny. Now, not so much anymore. One word: "Bane."

Jamie's body tenses. "Bane." It comes out part angry, part... I don't know. Helpless. "Tell me what happened up there."

"Short version? I talk too much, he wanted to scan me, I short-circuited, kicked him between the legs, and he threw a knife at me. The rest you know."

"Ugh." Jamie groans. "But it's not as if that bit of contamination from the kick mattered. Not after *this*." He gives me a squeeze, and he's right. Supernova-red is supernova-red, and that short, one-second contact is not going to make a difference. But it's also not what I'm worried about.

"Never mind the contamination. I attacked a Founder. Bane is going to kill me, Jamie. He hates me anyway—"

"I don't think he hates you. It's not you he's got on his radar, no offense."

"None taken, but well, then he hates me because he hates you, but—"

"He doesn't hate me either." Jamie bangs his head onto the mattress twice and groans.

"Yeah, right. Sure. He loves you, clearly." I give his forehead a light smack with my palm. "He needs to learn how to better show his feelings then. But anyway, no matter his emotions, I still kicked him. He'll report it, tell everybody, or whatever Watchers do, and *boom*, I'll be on the kill-list for attacking a Founder. Can you really imagine Bane letting that go?" Like, meh, no big deal, let's call it a day?"

"Actually, I can."

What the what? "Are we talking about the same person?"

Jamie chuckles. "Yes. I know how he ticks. One, I can promise you he isn't going to report it. A little pet getting the best of him? One of our best Watchers? No way. Too humiliating. Two, he's going to wait and see what happens next. Everything's like a game of chess with Bane, and he's observing our every move. And I'm not saying he is going to forget what you did, but in general, I worry more about you lighting up on a scanner than about Bane."

"Can I just say I worry equally about both?"

Jamie tucks me against him once. "That's fair enough, but really, I'll handle Bane if—if—we run into him again. In general, though, we need to focus on not getting scanned, because once we do, it will be obvious. This is beyond contamination, it'd be down to the cellular level for both of us."

I suck in my lower lip. "So what do we do?"

"Not much to do about it unfortunately. Besides not get scanned." He wraps his wing tighter around me, feathers tickling my butt. I swear he does that on purpose. "Which means, we have to hide. You and me. We can choose any place you like. A different country. The mountains. Desert. I don't care. We hide, we stay away from Watchers, even Bane, and humans, and we live life the way it was meant to be. Free."

Free.

Free-ish, because we'll always be watching our backs.

I trace my finger down a line on his black shirt. It sounds tempting. Really, it does. But I don't think I can do it. Not after the talk Jezza and I had. Not after what I heard in the hive. What I saw. "And if I don't want to hide?"

The hand in my neck stills. "Why would you not want to hide? You know what's at stake."

And that's exactly the problem. "I do. I know what's at stake for you. For me. But thanks to a certain few minutes of eavesdropping, I also know what's at stake for humanity, Jamie. The Fleet? Another Fleet of Founders, like, I dunno, another tribe Luke can't stand? War? One hundred humans to kill one Founder, losses in the billions?" That's nothing I can let go and fabricate my own personal cocoon around me. Just can't.

A muscle in his jaw tightens. "The risk is too great, Lee."

"I don't think so, Jamie. We have to warn the Resistance, we have to do something. We—"

He rolls on his side until I drop off, then sits up and pulls his wing out from under me. "We can't do a thing, Lee! Nothing! This is bigger than us. Bigger than the Resistance. Bigger—"

"Exactly! This is too big to do nothing! And we've got power, too! I'm the Protégée, the First, and whether I liked it so far or not, what I do matters to humans! And you, you're Luke's son! Don't you think there are Founders who'd follow you too, if your way seemed better?" Now that Jamie is clearly on our side, we can use the crucial little detail that we're pledged. Luke's son and the Protégée—*the First*—working together. Shouldn't we get people of both camps behind us that way?

"If my way seemed better?" he asks, incredulous. "Better? Do you know us Founders at all? There's no way anybody worth mentioning is backing down from this war, Lee. It has been coming for millennia. Ever since we had to leave Earth." He balls a fist and bites on it. "This war is going to come and the only question is how to survive it. Not how to avoid it."

I stare at him. Must be the difference in culture, in growing up, in perspective, but how can he say that? There's always a way, there's always hope. I shake my head so fast I get dizzy. "No. We'll find a way. We have to."

He huffs sarcastically. "Lee, they—we—have armies. All Founders will fight, Watcher or not. Humans. We've got millions of soldiers lined up. That's—"

But there you go. "Humans, Jamie! Humans! We're not all blinded by your race! I bet you there are people like Jezza, who pledged to get to the inside, or who didn't know what else to do with their lives, and they are the ones we need to reach!" If we can get them on our side, convince them war is not the way, then the

Founders won't have enough manpower and might not even start the war.

Jamie closes his eyes for an eternal second. "It's not going to work, Lee."

"But—"

"It's not going to work, you hear me? None of the humans are on your side. Not a single one of those who've been sworn in are on your side. Believe me, I know."

The way he says it brings goosebumps to my skin. "Why?" I whisper it. All of a sudden it feels cold in here.

Jamie rubs a palm over his forehead. "Because… because they can't be, Lee."

"Why?" I repeat it even though I have a pretty good idea why.

He shakes his head, skin rubbing over his palm. "You know, for years I couldn't make sense of it. Founders pledge. They flaunt their human servant like an accessory." Bitterness creeps into his voice. "And then… the human is gone."

"Gone." The goosebumps bring a shiver with them.

"Gone. The Founder is alone, his Vinculum off."

"Like… the human died?" Part of me hopes he's going to say yes, because it's still the better alternative than what I think is happening.

"No. No, unfortunately not." Heavy silence follows his last words, confirming what I feared on an instinctual level since the moment I saw robot-Frances in that shuttle.

Horror makes each and every breath raspy as I speak out loud what should be unspeakable. "You're saying, servants are turned into soldiers. That the Founders are doing *something* to them. Something that changes them into mindless robots."

Jamie rakes both hands through his hair, then drops them.

"Yes. You saw what happened at the ceremony. It's us, Lee. Us. That's what Luke told me when he took me aside today. It's our way of recruiting soldiers. They're all former servants, mind-controlled by Founders and oh so willing to die for us."

Holy cow. I work on another swallow, but can't get it down. Throat's too dry. Yes, it was obvious something was wrong during that ceremony and with those soldiers, but hearing the confirmation from Jamie...

"So typical of our race. We like our genetic games. We made you in our image. We designed your genome. It's right up our alley to modify and use you as we please." Jamie crashes a fist down into the mattress. "How sick is that? Servants become servants voluntarily, which is bad enough from my point of view, but then, as a thank you, we turn them into soldiers. You can't tell me they're willingly converting, or whatever you want to call it." He balls up some of the blanket in his hands.

I chew on the inside of my cheek. "Well, I can't say it was in my briefing of what to expect when becoming a servant."

Jamie huffs dry and without humor. "That's why Luke and the Council got so mad. *Nobody touches our servant laws. It's tradition.* Screw them—it's not tradition, it's an easy way to recruit additional soldiers!"

Click.

Of course. I pry the balled-up fabric of blanket out of his hand and weave my fingers in-between his. "So that's what you were thinking of when you tried to change the servant laws?"

A harsh breath leaves his throat. "And more. It felt wrong. Off. I tried—"

"And it got you a stigma."

A nod. "Yes. My father was... not happy with my actions."

I can imagine why. "Because it takes away a source of soldiers."

Those servants signed up of their own free will. An honor for most of them, the devout ones. But Jamie is right: they didn't sign up to be used. Discarded. Recycled.

Recycled for something they never could decide on. "I can't believe we didn't know that. I mean, it's right there, and yet…" We never picked up on it.

"I didn't know either, Lee." The sentence comes out as a hoarse whisper. "A hunch. A thought. Maybe a suspicion, once I realized Vinculums could come off."

Speaking of: "Yeah, that came out of nowhere when soldiers didn't wear theirs anymore." One short sentence said without much thought, *Vinculums are off*, yet it's loaded with implications and possibilities.

"Right? Too much of a giveaway. Turns out there is a Caeruleum-powered tool that snaps right through these things. So much for *for life*, not that I'm sad about that change in the canon. But they keep all of it quiet. From the little bit Luke said to me today, I was supposed to learn about it during my initiation. *The Founders' ways.*" His hand in mine shakes. "How can I be expected to take that path? Sometimes I can't stand I'm one of them, Lee. I can't stand I'm a Founder. I'm guilty from birth, guilty by association, guilty by passiveness, guilty, guilty, guilty. And yet I can stroll through life and take what I want when I want it. Nobody is going to punish me for it." The apple in his throat bobs once as his voice drops to barely audible. "But they should. They should."

My heart seizes and shatters with the image of that boy in front of a church who let somebody beat him up, who welcomed it. *Embraced* it. That vibe, that self-deprecating, sometimes almost depressed energy, has been there on and off for the last weeks. Easy to overlook for somebody who only sees Jamie as the Founder he is, but screaming at a deafening volume for everybody who knows him as a person: all the little tell-tales. The way he talks about his people. His father. *Luke.*

Slowly, I reach out and cup his cheek. "Jamie, don't say that. Please don't say that." I brush my thumb over his skin as Jamie's mouth opens and closes once. "No matter what they said, no matter what your laws said, you did the right thing. You stood up for the weak, who couldn't stand up for themselves. You did the right thing. Please don't think you deserved that punishment. Or any punishment, Jamie."

He presses his eyelids closed so tight, he must be seeing stars. "But I do. Maybe I did good—or at least attempted to do good— by challenging the servant laws, but then, after the Stigma…" He sucks in two harsh breaths in close succession. "I caved. I wanted to make up for what I did, for how I disappointed my father. That's why… that's why I came up with the idea of New Servitude." His voice breaks as he opens his eyes, two dark orbs shining with moisture. "That was me, trying to make my father proud of me. How disgusting is that? I threw humanity under the bus to make Daddy proud. If it wasn't for my idea, Earth would have only half as many Founders coupled to humans in high-ranking places. That was all me. All me." I can barely hear him with the last word.

A sad lump lodges in my throat. It explains so much. Luke's pride, Jamie's dark mood… "I get it, Jamie. I do." Granted, I'm missing out on ten years of having parents around, but I remember. And I can empathize. If they were still here, I bet I would want them to be proud of me. Kinda still do, although… I may not have acted that way a lot.

Jamie makes a sad huffing sound and wipes his eyes. "Then you're one step ahead of me, because I don't. It doesn't matter to my father. Nothing I do does. I knew that before, and still I didn't take the high road and accept it, no, I gave it one pitiful last try that might've been the key to keeping humanity under control. I'm disgusting."

An ache opens up in my chest. "You're not disgusting, Jamie." I crawl onto his lap and wrap my legs around his waist. His nose finds the crook between my neck and my shoulder as his arms sneak to my back and his wings curl around us.

"I am. I'm my father's son, and my father is… He is…"

"Is what, Jamie?"

He sucks a breath in and holds it. "N-never mind."

I ease my fingers through his thick hair. "You are not them." He is not. He's proven it, no matter what I might've thought a mere few hours ago. I don't want him thinking he deserved any of what Luke did to him. It was cruel and barbaric. I keep my voice gentle. "No matter what you may think. No matter what they want you to believe, you're one of the good guys. Hear me? You're on of the good ones." Welcome to my parallel universe, where I'm telling a Founder he's good, but dang it, it's Jamie, and it's true.

He gives me one short huff. "One of the good ones." I feel it more whispered against my skin than I hear it. He cuddles deeper into me and his chest expands with a large sigh.

But he doesn't say anything else.

And that silence, it makes me wonder why he wouldn't think of himself as one of the good guys.

And in the deepest corner of my mind, that scares me.

A lot.

I hold Jamie for what feels like an eternity.

Over the course of a few minutes, he relaxes against me until I feel the mood has passed. I lean back a bit and kiss him on the forehead as he lifts his head. Amazing how natural kissing Jamie can feel.

He retracts his wings closer to his shoulders. "We should probably get going. Have you thought about where you want to be? I can fly us there. We travel at night; we hide during the day—"

Okay, we're back to *that* topic. "No. No running. No hiding." We're working with the Resistance, period. Plus, I can't hide from Jamie, it appears. He found me at the pier, he found me in the hive—and the L.A. Hive is one of the biggest ones.

He groans. "But, Lee, I told you, war is unavoidable. And now we have one more risk factor." He reaches for my right arm and lifts it up. "I'm pretty sure this here, this is what eventually will get you turned into a soldier, it appears." My Vinculum reflects a bit of the ambient blue light, shining in the slightest purple hue.

With a quick twist, I free my arm, then scoot off his lap. "Maybe. Yes, maybe. But we'll be ready. And we have to try. I have to try. I won't run, Jamie. I won't hide. Not anymore. I—"

"Listen." He takes both of my hands in his. "I get it. I get where you're coming from. But I'm telling you you're throwing your life away. There's nothing you can do. It's *that* big of a deal. All I'm asking is for you to stay out of it, to come with me."

"But—"

"No but. Do you know what they're going to do to you when they scan you?" His brows turn down into a V. "With these readings, they might incinerate you on the spot. No trial, no nothing. Whichever Watcher picks up on you has all authority to kill you—not that he didn't have that anyway," he adds with a bitter undertone.

A shudder runs down my spine—the same spine I just grew when I decided to not take the easy way out. "Okay then. Well, I guess then we'll have to make sure I don't get scanned, or at least if I do, they don't pick up on it." I pull my hands out of his and cross them in front of my chest. And I know just the thing to avoid discovery.

"Yeah, right," Jamie huffs. "How are you—?"

I cock my head to the side and give him my best you're-gonna-figure-it-out-glance.

And he does, if his groan is any indication. "You want to use the maskers."

"Now you're getting with the program." I relax and lay one hand on his knee, a gesture I couldn't have dreamed of a mere six hours ago, and already it feels like we'd never been forced to keep our distance. "Yes, the maskers. We got three, but only expected one, which means two are extra. We'll use them."

"Use them for what? You can't spend your whole life wearing a masker. It's bound to fail—"

"I'm talking about short-term. Get the masker. Get the virus installed—unless you tell me you did…?"

Jamie shakes his head. "When should I have done that, Lee? While I was hidden behind a console to make sure you didn't get killed by Luke or Michael?"

I blush. "Well… You were working on that console before that."

"Not enough time."

I sigh. Okay. "Anyway. There must be a way to install it, so the resistance can see what's going on. So that we have an idea—manpower, strategies, communication—what do I know, all that stuff that's important for war." Espionage is key if we want to stand a chance.

Jamie slides his hand under mine on his knee. "And how do you plan to get the maskers? I doubt Ice is going to give them to us out of the goodness of his heart. The way it is we've lost usefulness to him. He can't *integrate us into society* as he planned to do." Not with us being marked forever. Kinda overrules everything else.

I nod. "But he doesn't know it yet, and I'm all for keeping it that way. When we return to the Resistance, we pretend nothing happened."

Jamie gives my bloody side a pointed glance.

"Or come up with a cover story, or whatever. He'll be mad we didn't get the virus installed, but we can tell him what we know about the upcoming war. He'll insist we try planting the virus again and use the video as blackmail, because our deal was we get this done, then we're out. Of course, at this point, his blackmail is an empty threat, but that's another thing he doesn't need to know. In fact, he mustn't know, because that would give him new power, wouldn't it?"

Jamie's eyes turn hard. "Yes, it would." Because one word of his, and we'd be scanned and therefore history. "I still doubt Ice is going to give us the maskers."

"I wasn't thinking of asking Ice." That would be pointless, agreed.

Jamie's brows shoot up when the puzzle pieces fall into place. "You're going to ask Jezza."

Yup. I entwine my fingers with his. "Our only chance." Jezza's the only one who's kind of on our side. On my side, at least, which by default is Jamie's side. Probably shouldn't tell him why exactly I need the maskers, considering he warned me about getting too close to Jamie, and obviously I've done the exact opposite. Not that he had any kind of say over me, but it's Jezza. My friend. My oldest and best friend.

Jamie tightens his fingers around mine. "You think he's going to go against Ice and give them to us." A statement, not a question.

"Yes, I do. And if he doesn't, we'll have to come up with something else, but I believe in Jezza. I trust him, like I trust you. And once we have the maskers, we can install the virus. We can maybe prevent this war, if we play it right, or maybe we can at least lower the casualties. I can't walk away from this. Really, I can't." Hallelujah for that revelation.

For a moment, silence hovers. Jamie pulls up his knees and lowers his head onto our entwined hands. His breath comes out in puffs against my skin. "Even with the maskers, it might still not work. None of it. It's a valiant effort, I agree, but I'm almost one hundred percent positive it's not going to work." He lifts his head, the sadness in his eyes so deep, so profound, it tugs on a heart string. "And then never mind the war. Never mind they're going to rip my wings out, then burn me. But they're going to kill *you*, Lee. Maybe so fast I won't have a chance to even try to protect you."

Guilt hits me like a punch to the stomach. I am an egoistic bitch. All I'm thinking of is my risk, my role. What about Jamie's? He's right, it's his death sentence, too. Torture first—I'd say ripping out his wings qualifies as that—then they'd burn him. How can I expect him to risk that because of something I believe in?

The answer comes easy. I can't.

It's his life. I have no power over it, and I shouldn't have.

The next sentence comes from a heavy heart. "Jamie, I… I have to do this. I will do this. But I'd understand if you didn't want any part of it. I won't hold it against you. Heck, until a few days ago, it would've been my decision too. Not anymore, but if you want out, you want to leave… It's fine. I can do this alone."

His left brow shoots up and meets his hairline. "Alone."

"Yeah."

"You've seen these, right?" He taps his Vinculum.

"Uhh—"

"And you've kind of realized that when I healed you, I did that because of my feelings for you. You were present for that, weren't you?"

I blush. "Uhh—"

"So how can you then think even for one second I'd leave you alone?"

"I thought—"

"Well, think again." A small sad smile works on the corner of one lip as he adds in a whisper, "You know, maybe getting burned doesn't sound too bad after all." He tries to give it some bravado, some sarcasm, but fails miserably.

I smack him over the head. Playfully, of course. "Shut it, Jamie." We're not talking about that whole guilt trip anymore.

Jamie braces himself against my attack. "Ow!" He turns serious. "Okay. We'll do it your way. But please keep in mind I know the Founders. I know their ways, their thinking, their cruelty. We're not the peaceful angels your Bible made us out to be. Not by a long shot. I want nothing more than to be egoistic and take you away from here, but I get it. But you have to promise me that when I tell you to, you run. Can you do that for me?" His eyes hold all the worry in the world—all for me.

"Yes," I whisper. "Yes, I can." No, *you're* tearing up. Not me. Of course, not me.

Jamie nods, the sad smile widening. He places a tiny kiss onto my hand. "Then we've got to work on a plan." He gives my hand one more kiss and stands up, pulling me with him. "Let's go downstairs. Not much time until sunrise, and we should be back before then. Although," he uses his wings to draw me closer to his chest, "I wouldn't mind this time-out to last a tad longer." He glides one wing over my back, a soft brush of feathers sending my heart into a stumble.

No, I wouldn't mind either.

But I'm happy to have Jamie in my corner for now.

I'll have him in my bed tonight then.

CHAPTER TWENTY-ONE

Lair, Repeat

Flying back with Jamie is exhilarating.

Yes, it's my second time flying with him, but the first time I'm not busy dying or partially hallucinating.

And it's breathtaking.

Before we take off, he bends slightly and lifts me by the waist, so I can wrap my legs around him. He secures my arms around his neck. "You want to hold on really well or at least tell me when you're starting to tire, okay?" He pulls me closer into his chest with both his arms. I snuggle into the hug—because yes, he holds me tight so I won't fall, but it's a hug. Jamie's hug. And I'm loving it.

Jamie coughs and laughs out once with my almost-choke around his throat. "Never mind. You're good."

And then he pushes off.

Within seconds the ground underneath us vanishes into darkness as the night sky swallows us in one big gulp. Jamie keeps us mostly upright, which makes it easier to cling to his body. I assume usually he'd lean forward a bit, as all Founders do when flying, but with me as a ballast he's keeping that to a minimum, and I appreciate it.

Wind whizzes around my head, swooshing in my ears and drowning out everything else, and that's okay. I need all those thoughts, all those worries, all the responsibility, to be shushed for a bit. And being held by Jamie, feeling his heartbeat through his chest reverberate into mine, flying with him through the skies, does just that.

I'm in awe.

His strong wings carry us high and higher, until we're out of view from the ground. Not that many people are up, curfew and all, but better safe than sorry. The last thing we need is an accidental spotting and report of a Founder carrying a human—which translates to a Founder and a human touching.

By the time we reach an altitude he considers safe, I'm an icicle. It is cold up here. The drop in temperature plus the wind from the flight… If he didn't hold me tight, I might've let go already, that's how frozen my extremities are.

Jamie flies us across the dry Simi Valley and over the mountains. Fog wafts below us, and once in a while, a low-hanging cloud brings moisture to my skin. The air is fresh and smells of rain, and together with the view… Wow. Just wow.

After about forty minutes in the air Jamie drops a kiss onto the side of my neck. "We're almost at the Hollywood Hills."

My stomach cramps up. Almost at the Old Zoo. Almost game time.

I nod into his shoulder. "You're gonna land soon?"

"Yeah. Can't risk them seeing us." Slowly, he descends until I can recognize trees and houses, despite the darkness. The closer we get to the real L.A., the brighter it becomes. Light-pollution at its best. Jamie keeps us in the shadows and the fog, but eventually we have to land. He touches down softly in a clearing somewhere in Griffith Park and folds his wings in tight.

But he still holds me in his embrace.

I loosen my legs around his waist.

He still holds on to me.

"Uhh, Jamie?"

"Huh?" he mumbles into my shoulder.

"I think you can let go now." My feet are dangling a few inches above the ground.

"I don't want to." He sighs. "Once I let go, I'll be a Founder, and you a human. A servant and her master. You'll walk behind me and not next to me. I don't want to let go."

Oh.

I give his neck a squeeze. "Me neither. But it's part of the game. We'll both know you wouldn't act like a master if it was up to you, and that's all that matters." Although I still have to swallow hard selling my part of the game.

Jamie stays quiet, then lowers me ever so slowly. "Be vigilant. Stay alert. No mistakes, Lee. No mistakes, or this goes downhill faster than we can run away from it."

"I know."

He lowers his head and touches his lips to mine. "The last one until we're safe and out of sight." His tongue brushes over my lips to part them until I feel his warmth in my mouth. He deepens the kiss until all I can think of is Jamie, and that he is doing this for me—risking his wings and his life, for me.

I'm sure even before we enter the Resistance lair down in the Old Zoo, they have eyes on us. Hud is the first to greet us from behind the old lion's den.

"Where the fuck have you guys been? You were supposed to be here hours ago. Ice has—"

Jamie holds up a hand. "Yeah. You might want to shut up

before I blast your brains out. If things had gone well, we'd been here earlier. Obviously, they didn't, and yet here we are." He points at my bloody and torn shirt.

Hud pales. "Oh. Shit," he whispers. "Are you—?"

"Lea is fine." Jamie brushes him off. "But we need to meet with Ice. He deserves an update."

I barely keep from rolling my eyes. Deserves an update—overplaying much, Jamie?

It works though. Hud accompanies us down the stairs and to the meeting room, the same room we've been practicing my servitude skills for weeks. Ice and Jezza are sitting at the table, Jezza with his head on the arms he folded on top of the table, Ice slumped down on his chair, chin on his chest. No matter the late hour and the fact that both of them obviously fell asleep waiting for us, the moment we enter Ice all but jumps off his chair, which topples back and falls down with a loud clang. He's wide awake in an instant.

"What the hell? It's like 4:00 a.m.—"

Jamie holds up a hand, and the movement, executed with the confidence and authority of a Founder, shuts Ice up. "Thank you, we've noticed, Issaac."

Ice's brows narrow. "So why—?"

Hud shoves me forward, one hand on my shoulder. "Something happened to Lea, Ice." He points at my shirt.

I fold both hands protectively over my side. "Don't touch it, or I'll punch you!"

"What?" Jezza jumps up. "What happened? Are you okay, Lea? What—?"

"She'll need some antibiotic ointment and gauze, that should take care of it. But first, you need to know what happened in the hive," Jamie says, and Ice nods.

"Meaning, you hopefully came through and took the Pledge, or—?"

"Not my main concern at this point, but yes." Jamie nods at me, and I hold up my wrist with the Vinculum. A few hours ago, it was silver, and I could swear it only showed a blush of peach, while now it shows a pretty solid rose-colored hue. I guess in terms of *how well our relationship has advanced and grown* as it was put so nicely by Frances—old, pre-programmed Frances—we are doing just fine.

Ice's shoulders droop forward. "Why don't I like the sound of that? The part where getting pledged isn't your main concern, I mean."

"Easy." Jamie pulls out a chair for me, which I appreciate. I'm not quite in top shape after the last few hours. Weak legs, headache, cold. Guess first almost dying and then flying here can do that.

Jamie sits in the one next to me. "Because we didn't get the virus installed—"

"What? The deal was—"

"I know very well what the deal was, and it hasn't changed. We will install the virus. Only, I propose a different plan."

"You do?" Ice crosses his arms in front of his chest. "Really."

"Really. And you might want to sit for that."

Of course, Ice pulls himself up straighter. What else did I expect? "Demon, the day I take orders or even suggestions, from you, is the day—"

Gosh, I'm fed up with this pissing contest. "Just shut up and sit down, Ice!" I point at the chair and to my complete and utter surprise, he sits down.

And stares at me, mouth open. "What's gotten into you, hon?"

"What's gotten into me? Easy. Super easy. I've overheard Luke and Michael, and so has Jamie. My summary would be that we don't have the luxury of fighting on the inside when we need all our strength and focus for the outside! We have Jamie, one of the good guys, so STFU and listen, dammit."

"Oo-kaay." Ice scratches over his five o'clock shadow. "Care to elaborate?"

"Sure. Like I said, Jamie and I overheard Luke and Michael. They're prepping for war. Another fleet of Founders is going to arrive in less than a week and Luke is planning on fighting them. They expect to lose ninety percent of the human troops, and who knows how many civilians. This is World War Three in the making, Ice. And if we don't get very lucky and very well prepared, we're going to lose it."

Ice stares at me open mouthed before he catches himself. He exchanges one quick glance with Jezza, then Hud. "So, it is true."

Wait—what the what? My jaw drops. "You knew?" He *knew* war was coming?

"We thought it was a distinct possibility judging by the intel we got. Which is why we wanted you to plant the virus."

My hands curl into fists. "And you're still going to get that done—"

Ice eyes harden. "Because you did such a fantastic job this time, hon?"

"I didn't have the spl—"

Click.

Because you did such a fantastic job—me. Ice means me. Ice thinks I had the splitter.

And I didn't.

I didn't, because Jamie told me Ice told him—

Oh, crap. Don't like what I'm seeing here. At all. My stomach feels weird. Hollow.

"You didn't have what, honey?"

Jamie lied to me. Ice didn't tell him to take the splitter. It was still my job. He lied. Why did he lie?

My next breath catches. "Didn't… didn't have a good opportunity." Out of the corner of my eye, I see Jamie exhale big. I was right. Oh, darn, I was so right. But… he must have had a reason. He *must.*

Ice sits up straighter and leans forward. "And the next opportunity might not come anytime soon. Or not before the war is here."

I shake off the nausea. Yeah Ice, speaking of, let's turn the blame around here. "Don't you think telling us why you wanted it installed would have helped?" Maybe that was Jamie's issue. That he couldn't see a reason. I hope.

"As if I'd tell a Founder what we know about his people's war plans so he'd could go home and warn them."

I mean, it makes sense. "But he just told you the plan—"

"Yeah, surprisingly, he did tell us what his people are up to. Didn't quite expect that." Something close to respect, or at least surprise, colors Ice's voice.

"You're welcome." Jamie's on the other hand is cool. He's recovered well from Ice's unintentional revelation. "Now, I'd appreciate if Jezza could help get Lea some medical help, and you and I, we can talk." His message is clear: in private.

What they don't hear is, *while Lea talks to Jezza.* Because that's the plan, and we're sticking to it. For now at least. No matter what Ice said, for now Jamie and I are back on schedule.

"Sure." Ice makes a dismissive hand motion at Hud, who rolls his eyes and weasels out of the room.

Jezza is next to me in a heartbeat, eyes full of worry. "Lea. Let's go. Is it bad? Do you need me to carry—?"

My dirty look stops him mid-sentence. No, I do not need to be carried, thank you very much.

"Uhh, never mind." He blushes and turns away. "Just… come with me, okay?"

I follow out of the room and down the narrow, spooky hallway, keeping my hands on top of my torn shirt. Wouldn't want anybody to notice there's nothing to see there, would we now?

Jezza brings me to one of the small rooms that used to hold food for the animals. The Resistance uses them as storage, and this specific one for their medical needs—and I'm using that expression loosely. They have a big medical bag, and that's about it. Plus a chair and a table doubling as a gurney in the middle I hop onto.

"Jezza—"

He zips the medical bag open. "What do you need? What happened? Seriously—"

"Jezza."

"Only you can come down injured from the hive of all places. How—"

"Jezza!"

He stops, one hand in the bag. "What?"

I take a deep breath that gets stuck somewhere at the level of my larynx. "Jezza, I need a favor."

His gaze darts from me to the medical bag and back. "A Band Aid?"

"No, not really." I fold my hands in my lap. There's no good way to say this, so I might as well get it over with. "I need you to get me the two spare maskers we brought from Cardoza. Please."

Jezza's head jerks back. "What? Come again?"

I swallow dry. "Well, you heard what I said. The Founders are about to go to war against their own race, and they're going to take humanity down with them. If we want to stand a chance, as little as it may be, we need to install the virus, which means, Jamie and I need to be all up in their business, and that's why we need the maskers." Or at least I'll need to be in their business… How could he take that from me? How could he take the splitter and then not use it? And I gave him a freakin' good in with my fake twisted-ankle!

In the deepest corner of my mind, a reason pops up, but it can't be. There must be something else. Jamie is on our side. No doubt about it.

As if in slow-motion Jezza takes his hand out of the bag and points his finger at me. "You're going up to the hive with Jamie again."

I nod. "Correct."

"And you need a masker."

"Actually, we need two." Because Jamie will light up just the same, and if he is scanned, so will I, and then goodbye, sweet life.

"Two maskers." Jezza tilts his head to the left.

"Yeah."

"But you were down to mustard-yellow on the scanner."

No good answer to that, because, true. I was.

Not anymore though.

I stay silent as his eyes bore into mine—questioning, pleading, begging me to give him an explanation other than the conclusion he's coming up with. "Lea? Please don't tell me you and the Demon—"

Yeah. *That.*

I drop my gaze to my hands, and Jezza jumps to the conclusion he's been warning me about.

As if he'd been punched in the gut, he exhales a long wheeze. "Fuck." He fumbles for the chair, pulls it closer and falls into it, shoving a jittery hand through his hair. "Fuck." He drags in one deep breath after another until he leans his upper body forward and supports it on his knees with his elbows.

One long inhale.

One long exhale.

One long inhale—

"I warned you to stay away from him." He speaks more to the floor than to me. "I told you he was up to no good. And now you're back, injured, and apparently marked like a flare thanks to him. What. Happened. To. Your. Common. Sense?" That's when he looks up at me, barely controlled anger rolling off of him in waves.

"Jezza, it's not what you think—"

"Really? Really, it's not? So, you come back in the middle of the night, marked up through the roof for no good reason? Stop lying to me, Lea!" His eyes flash with fire.

My insides tighten. All right, then. I throw up my arms. "Okay! Okay, Jezza! Yes, you warned me. And no, it didn't help. It… just happened." Gah. Stalled. I can't tell him about the whole healing and marked-forever-thing. Just can't.

His face turns blank. "It *just happened.*"

"Yeah." Kind of.

"You're telling me you and him screw—"

Oh, hell to the no! "I'm not giving you any details, Jezza." None of his business!

He rubs a palm over his face. "So that's why you were late."

"Yes." That, and a minor bleeding-to-death-issue.

A dry, disappointed harrumphing sound breaks from his throat, and dang it if it didn't make me feel self-conscious. Having been an orphan for over a decade, I can't really comment on what it felt like to be chewed out by your parents, but it must be similar to this. Only, Jezza isn't my dad. And he needs to realize that. "It's not as if he took advantage of me. I'm almost seventeen—"

He rams his fist into his palm with a smack. "Yeah? And he's a fuckin' Founder! What do you think he did? Of course, he played you! That's all he did! Get you pledged to him, and now you're his official play toy! Why do you think he waited until after the Pledge? Because as the Resistance thinks, eighty percent of Founders bang their servants, that's why! And you know what happens then? Do you? Do you, Lea?"

Holy cow—I've never seen Jezza so angry. Like a coiled spring, he sits at the edge of his seat, anger tightening his features. "Answer me!"

"No!" I shout back. "I don't know! And I don't care, because—"

Jezza curses under his breath. "Do you even hear yourself, Lea? You don't care? You pledged your servitude, your *life*, to a Founder. One of them. And now you have something going on with him—for whatever hard to understand reason—and if you're not careful, it's going to kill you! What the hell happened to you?" His nostrils flare, his eyes bore into me as he repeats, more in a hoarse whisper this time, "What the hell happened to you?"

What the hell happened—

Good question.

Not what, but who.

Bane happened.

Bane, a knife, and a good amount of blood loss.

I feel my anger crumbling. Jezza isn't the enemy. He cares for me, or else he wouldn't react the way he does. I trust him. We're on the same side. It's time I show my trust, because I'm losing his.

With my right hand I reach for my shirt and lift it up far enough that he can see.

Jezza sucks in a sharp gasp when his gaze falls on the blood that withstood my rudimentary cleaning. "What—?"

I shake my head. "That's not all." I twist my upper body, so that he can see my flank, where the knife stuck.

"What the fu—"

I hold the shirt up for another three seconds before I drop it again. So, I guess Jamie was right, it's an impressive scar, not that I'd seen it already. I've felt it, and the way Jamie described it makes it sound similar to the one on his back, only smaller.

Jezza swallows so hard I hear it. "What is that, Lea?"

"That's where a knife severed a couple of important things in my body."

He swallows again. "When?"

"Up in the hive. One of the Watchers. I was bleeding out. Must've been my kidney or whatever, but I was dying."

Jezza pales. "No—"

"I was. Couldn't think, couldn't breathe, and then Jamie—"

"No." This time it sounds desperate. He knows what I'm about to say.

Here comes the truth. "Jamie healed me, Jezza. Without him, I'd be dead." That sentence, it serves as a reminder I shouldn't judge Jamie without hearing him. Yes, he took the splitter for whatever reason, but he has proven he is on our side.

Maybe I shouldn't jump to conclusions.

Jezza draws in a deep, shuddering breath, and the look he gives me, full of sorrow—sorrow for me—it hollows out my chest and fills it with an ache. "No."

"Yes." I whisper it.

A blast of air escapes him and turns into a sob. "No. Tell me he didn't. Tell me—" His eyes fill with tears.

"Jezza." I'm off the table in no time, and half a second later, we're in each other's arms. He burrows his face into my neck, each breath coming out chopped, each heartbeat hard against my chest. He wraps his arms around me so tight I can barely breathe, but I let him.

He needs this.

I need this.

Pushing up on my toes, I reach higher around his neck. This used to be second nature. For one, because we were friends for so long, for another, because those months as a couple taught me the details of his body like it was my own.

His breath falls against my neck in waves. "So, the bastard healed you."

I nod into his embrace. "I would've died otherwise."

"But now you're marked. Forever."

"Comes with the deal, I guess."

Jezza huffs once. "I mean, don't get me wrong, you're standing here, alive. But I still don't know if I should thank or punch him for what he did. Know what I mean?" He sniffles and I chuckle.

"Yeah, I do. And maybe neither. We're kind of keeping it a secret, for obvious reasons." For many obvious reasons.

Slowly, he releases me, but keeps both hands on my upper arms. "Okay. Okay. I'll get you those maskers, Lea. But all I want is you away from here. Ever considered moving to the desert? Fewer Founders there."

I roll my eyes. "Wow. The day has arrived you and Jamie are on the same page. That's what he said, but I don't want to back out."

"What? Why not? You are marked—"

I give him the eye. "And I'm also the Protégée and the First, as a certain someone reminded me. I have leverage. So yeah, for once in my life, I'm going to use it."

He flinches. "Ouch. Now I wish I never said that to you."

"Not much you can do about it now. Not much either of us can do now." I shrug. The dice have fallen, period.

Jezza tightens his grip around my biceps. "Then I'll do whatever it takes to get those maskers. And I'll keep an eye on that demon, no matter how high you may think of him."

Something he said earlier comes back to mind. "Hey, Jezza? What did you mean when you said that the Resistance thinks about eighty percent of Founders are… uhh, banging their servants?" How much have I been living under a rock the last decade? How did everybody know and see, while I was oblivious? Or did I not want to see it?

Another deep sigh from Jezza, one that comes with his shoulders dropping forward. "Lea, I… I just said it out loud, it's nothing—"

"Didn't sound like nothing."

His hands increase their pressure around my biceps. "Ugh. You're going to make me spell it out?"

"Given the fact that I am pledged to a Founder, yes."

He groans. "Okay. Well, we think—the Resistance thinks—the laws are for show."

I cock my head. "What do you mean?"

"The servants. We've had people on the inside. Men and women trained by the Resistance to spy on Founders, to give us insider knowledge. They pledged, we got the intel we needed." He laughs out once, devoid of humor. "And more. More than we wanted to hear. How some of them fell for their Founders. How some of those demons made them believe they were regular people—"

Oh, hold it right there. "Maybe they were." Jamie is a person. He is not defined by being a Founder. Maybe he wasn't the only one.

"Maybe, yeah. But I'll reserve judgement, because none of those women are still here to tell us about it."

An icy shudder runs down my back. I know where this is going. "They became soldiers."

He cocks his head and raises a brow. "Yes. Yes, that's exactly what happened for each and every one of them."

Jezza lets go of my arms and falls into the chair next to the table. "They were dedicated Resistance fighters. Like, a hundred ten percent in. The Resistance watched them fall for their Founder, but they still reported back to us—until they didn't anymore. First, we thought they'd died, but then facial recognition picked up on them in a different country, in soldier garb. When Resistance members approached them, they were like completely new people. Blank slates. No recognition. None of them reacted to any signs, to any prompt."

I'm glad I'm sitting, because my knees... they're wobbly. I don't feel right. Antsy. Nauseous. Jittery. "That's because they couldn't."

Jezza's eyes widen. "What do you know that I don't?"

Too much, and yet not enough. I lick my lips. "Up in the hive, I saw one of the servants I know. They swore her in as a soldier, and by sworn in, I mean they gave her something to inhale and then… hypnotized her. Programmed her. Whatever you want to call it. But she wasn't herself. A mindless robot stuck in the shell of that girl I knew." Part of me hopes she's still in there, that she can free herself of the spell they put her under, but knowing the Founders, I'm not keeping my hopes up.

I wish I could've done more.

Jezza gasps. "You saw the demons do that?"

I nod, and Jezza rakes his fingers through his hair. "That confirms the Resistance's theory. Mind control, hypnotization, chemical dependence, who knows? Something that explains those men and women losing all sense of who they were. That's the reason—well, one of many—why I didn't want you to pledge. Resistance yes, pledging, no. It always ends for the human as a soldier, and that worries me now more than ever, because you're pledged, Lea. Who knows what the demon is going to do to you?"

"Jamie's not going to do anything to me." I shake my head. Jezza is exaggerating.

"How you can still believe that is beyond me, but because you're my oldest and best friend I am going to ignore all common sense and warning signs and support you. Like, he only agreed to this because you're the Protégée. That he's clearly using you—"

"Jezza." I roll my eyes.

"That he is clearly using you, playing you, and manipulating you. That he's making you his puppet and having you dance to his—"

"Jezza." Seriously—

"Nu-uh, you listen." He steps closer, anger shooting from his eyes. "That he is risking your life because it fits into his plans. That—"

"Oh, shut it, Jezza! Really! Jamie isn't like this, I told you that, and it's time for you to believe it! *That,* and not all servants end up as hypnotized—"

Jezza's eyes turn hard. "They do. And the harder they fall for their Founder…" His fingers form a gun, and he pulls the trigger. "The sooner it happens."

CHAPTER TWENTY-TWO

Closer

After we've cleaned the blood off my side, Jezza walks me back to Jamie's and my room. And he's not a happy camper. Tough to say what bothers him more—the fact that I almost died, that Jamie saved me, or that Jamie and I are together. Well. Yeah. *The latter.*

He stops at my door. "So…"

I lay a hand on his forearm. "It's gonna be fine, Jezza. Thanks for… getting that *thing* for us." Without him no masker, and without that… yeah, not fun to think about.

A smile flickers across his face. "Of course. I'll get back to you, okay?" He scans the area behind me. Wouldn't want anybody to overhear us.

I nod and open the door to Jamie opening it from the inside at the same time. He must've been faster with Ice than I was with Jezza. His eyes light up when he sees me—the shortest sparkle in his eyes before he has himself under control again.

Jezza, on the other hand, doesn't seem so happy. "Demon."

Jamie switches into arrogant, we-rule-the-world Founder mode. "Oaf." He can load that one word with condescension like nobody else.

I blow a raspberry. "Boys, get along. Cat's out of the bag, Jamie." I pat my right side, so he knows what I mean. "And, Jezza, you know what's at stake." I give them both my best behave-or-else glance.

Jamie takes the first step forward, figuratively at least. "Thank you for helping us. It is appreciated."

Jezza frowns. "For Lea. Not for you."

Oh, well. So much for playing it nice. In a surprisingly mature move, Jamie doesn't take the bait though. "Still. Thank you." He opens the door wider. "Lea?"

I nod, and give Jezza one more look. "Tomorrow?"

"Tomorrow." He turns to leave as I walk through the door. It must've been out of the farthest corner of his eye that he catches Jamie's featherlight brush over the small of my back as he guides me in, but it's enough.

With a roar, Jezza flies around. "Don't you dare touch—"

—and punches Jamie right in the face.

I swear, the air around us freezes.

Me—unable to process what Jezza did.

Jamie—a surprised, slightly amused look on his face, a fine trail of blood trickling down from a small cut in his lip.

Jezza—full of aggression but with wide eyes, as realization dawns of what he just did.

He hit a Founder.

It must be at the same time that Jamie realizes it too. His face hardens, and with one flick of his wrists, he lights up the Caeruleum in his palms.

Air whizzes out of my lungs like a hole was punched into them. No—

I jump in front of Jamie, forcing down on his hands with mine, never minding Jezza seeing me touch him. Because if I didn't—

"Jamie, don't."

He pushes forward, shoving me with him. "You," he growls. "Who do you think you are?" His wings pop out farther, spreading into the hallway to the left and right, curling in at the tips and trapping us—well, trapping Jezza. He can't move without doing more damage than he already did, without touching more of Jamie.

Doesn't really apply to me anymore.

"Jamie!" I put all my weight behind my arms and it barely keeps him from lifting his hands, probably because he isn't really trying. Yet.

He's more focused on Jezza, the way he's pulled up straight, and staring—no, glaring—right back at Jamie. "Me? I'm her oldest friend! It's my job to keep her safe, and all you're doing is endangering her! Watch out, Demon! I've protected her from Founders once, and I will do so again!"

Gotta give it to Jezza, he's loyal, but right now he could be a bit more humble and use less bravado.

"You don't know what you're talking about." A growl, so low I feel it more than hear it.

"I know very well what I'm talking about!" He drops his voice to a hissing whisper. "I know what you did to her, but as much as I appreciate you not letting her die, let's be honest. She wouldn't have been in this situation if it wasn't for you, so you better watch it, you devil's spawn, or I'll have them cut off your wings and—"

Wrong thing to say.

What was barely controlled anger turns into rage. Jamie barges forward at Jezza, and it's all I can do to hold him back with the full amount of my body weight.

"Jamie!" I push against him as hard as I can. He wouldn't hurt Jezza, he wouldn't—

As if I wasn't even there, Jamie rips his hands out from under me and aims them at Jezza, blue light glowing. Jezza pales to the color of the wall—

Shit.

Like in an old western movie, they stare at each other, a standoff waiting for the first person to twitch, only it's clear who's going to walk out a winner.

No, no, no. "Jamie, please!"

His chest rises sharply. In. Out. In. Out. In.

"*Please,* Jamie." I dig my fingers into the shirt, probably grabbing some of the skin on his chest as well, not that it mattered. "Jamie…"

In. Out. In—

—one quick flick of his fingers, and the Caeruleum is gone.

Jezza blows out a big puff of air, and so do I. Holy cow, that—

Jamie lowers his hands, eyes flashing at Jezza. "You owe me, oaf. Never forget that." With that, he turns on his heels and walks into our room, upping the number of times he hit Jamie and lived to tell the story to two.

As soon as the door closes behind me, I lock it. Probably a first, me locking us in. For one short moment, I lean my forehead against the door's cool wood and close my eyes. Man… that could've gone wrong. I get where they both are coming from, but we need to keep stuff like that down. If Ice, Hud, or anybody had overheard—or worse, seen—us, we'd be in a buttload of trouble.

A gasped choke comes from Jamie's bed. I cross the room within a heartbeat. "Jamie." I've said his name what feels like twenty times in the last minute, only this time it's without the urgency, and much softer.

Jamie sits on his bed, elbows propped onto his knees, face buried in his hands. His wings are open and curled in, as if they wanted to hug him. His shoulders heave up in irregular breaths.

I kneel in front of him. "Hey. Jamie?" My hands find his knees. "What's going on?"

One more harsh breath, then Jamie drops his hands and looks at me. "I almost… I… I almost lost it with him." He turns his hands over and stares at his palms. "I almost—"

I lay my hands in his. "But you didn't."

"Not because of me. Because of you." His voice breaks at the end. "He called me devil's spawn."

Oh. Didn't take that for the reason he lost it, but I guess it stings more when you consider yourself the angelic race. "He didn't mean—"

"Yeah, he did. And he's right." He turns his head away from me, the same look on his face he had after he healed me, the same self-deprecating expression. "I'm the devil's spawn."

Not again. "Jamie. Look at me. Stop this. You're not, and you didn't hurt him. Anybody could've gotten mad at Jezza. Happens to me all the time. Don't make yourself the bad guy here. You haven't done anything wrong."

Besides… One thing to clear up. I pause for a long second. "Jamie? Why did you say Ice wanted you to take the splitter?"

The next breath gets stuck in his throat.

"Jamie?"

The breath he held bursts out of him. "I'm sorry, Lee. I'm sorry. I—" He searches for words, then blows out another puff of air and looks down at our entwined hands. "I didn't want you to take the risk. If they searched you and found it…" He shakes his head. "I thought it would be easy. That I could pull it off. And… I couldn't. Maybe the step was too big, maybe I wasn't as ready as I thought I was. But when you gave me that opportunity with that twisted ankle of yours… I couldn't. I just couldn't." His voice is no more than a whisper.

"Jamie—"

"And then later, when Luke and Michael were there… obviously, my priorities had shifted. I'm so sorry."

His eyes shine with moisture, and it fixes whatever splintered when I found out he lied to me. He did it to protect me. "You should've said so."

"I know." He sweeps his thumb across my cheek. "It was wrong. Look at me. I'm screwing up left and right. I get you into impossible situations. I almost blasted the oaf into nothingness." He shakes his head once. "I don't want to be like this. I don't want to be one of *them*. Not doing what's right. Inspiring fear in people. That's not who I am, and yet it's whom I've become. My dad would be so proud."

I stand up, but keep my hands in his. It's amazing how Jamie's actions can come from such a pure place given what he had to deal with growing up. "Jamie, your dad is planning to go to war against his people and doesn't mind killing most of humanity for it. I think the scale is off a bit when it comes to his judgement." I give his hands a small pull. "You're not like him. Remember, you're one of the good guys."

A shadow crosses his face, gone as quickly as it came. He returns my soft pull with a stronger tug of his and catches me in an embrace around my waist, then snuggles his head into my stomach. "You think so? Sure? Because this good guy is not having any pure thoughts right now. Would that make me bad?" He gives me a squeeze.

Whoa. Not where I pictured the conversation going a second ago, but who am I to complain? "Not in my books." I brush one palm across his hair.

"What about this?" He sneaks one of his hands under my shirt on the back. Skin on skin. I suck in a sharp breath. Yowza. Those butterflies assaulted me out of nowhere!

Jamie smiles. "Not even this?" He rakes his fingers over the skin of my back and up and down my flank.

"Nope," I whisper. Love it, in fact.

The smile turns mischievous. "What about this?" He glides his hand toward my stomach and pushes up my shirt.

My heart decides that's a good point in time as any to skip a beat. "Mayb—" The rest of the word is forgotten as Jamie places a soft kiss onto my bare stomach, next to my bellybutton.

And another one.

A little lick.

Another kiss.

My fingers dig into his hair. "Jamie."

Jamie drops his other hand from my back to my butt, and my eyes roll back. He massages my butt, the circles of his hand getting bigger and bigger, until it slides down between my legs in one quick dip.

Holy mother of—

I can't help the way my hips push into his hands. An automatic response I wouldn't have had a chance to suppress if I had known it was coming.

Jamie smiles against my stomach. "Off," he whispers, and tugs my shirt.

No problem, sir.

The shirt is gone in no time.

Now that he has two hands available, they inch to the button of my pants.

Pop.

Button gone.

Zip.

Zipper open.

His breath is hot and fast against my skin, but I doubt my breathing is any calmer. He flattens his palms against my outer thighs and slides them down my legs, taking my pants with them. In the short moment I need both hands to lose my boots before I can step out of my pants, Jamie gets rid of his shirt.

And then he stares at me, eyes roaming over my body. Shoulders. Breasts, Stomach. Between my legs. Down my legs.

I should feel self-conscious, but I don't.

I feel empowered.

The way he looks at me, need in his eyes, adoration, maybe even the same reverence the Founders require of us humans, it makes me feel strong.

And daring.

I step between his knees and take his hands in mine, guiding them around my back and placing them on my butt. "Feel me." His words from last night, and they couldn't come at a better time. I want him to feel me. All of me. Everywhere.

Jamie exhales roughly. His touch stays light as he explores my body, every feathery brush like fireworks, every firmer grip like a whiplash of electricity, every squeeze like lightning though my heart.

One short second of hesitation—then his hand slips between my legs, and all conscious thought is gone.

My toes curl from his touch, nothing but a brush over my

most sensitive spots, but it's everything. Another brush, and I can't keep the moan in, even if I wanted to. That boy knows what he's doing, no matter he's never had a girlfriend. Must've read the user manual or something.

My back arches into his touch, until Jamie withdraws his hand and scoots back onto the bed, kicking off his boots and sliding his pants off with a quick buck of his hips, leaving him in nothing but black boxer briefs.

Tented black boxer briefs.

Somehow, I'm dizzy. Short of breath.

Jamie reaches for my hands and tugs me with him as he lowers himself down onto the mattress, wings spread under his back.

"Sit," he whispers and guides my knees to the left and right of his hips. His wings curl around my back, their light touch steering me forward, where he wants me. Jamie's gaze stays glued to mine as I straddle him and slowly sit my lower body down to meet his.

The moment we touch, our sharp inhales are simultaneous. As his wings wrap tighter around my back, his hands slide to my butt and push my pelvis forward. I'm happy to oblige, not that I needed an incentive. My body is eager to move, driven by an instinct too strong to deny. I tilt my hips and rub over the proof of how much he wants me.

Jamie gasps as he guides the rhythm, a slow, leisurely back and forth that stretches my senses to the max. At one point he lifts his right hand off my butt to release the front clasp of my bra. Don't know where it went, but it's gone not soon after, Jamie's hand brushing over the side of my breast.

"Love this," he mumbles between two harsh breaths.

My tattoo.

His hands caress the sides of my breasts, exploring, touching, inching closer to my nipples, while his hips never break rhythm.

A pressure builds inside my core, a coil tightened to the max and about to scatter my senses.

Jamie cups both of my breasts completely, pinching my nipples. He bucks his hips harder against me, harder, harder—and my world dissolves into an explosion of fireworks, of sensation, of want, of lust, of *love*. I rub myself against him like an addict, greedy for every bit of touch and pressure, until the wave subsides, leaving me breathless.

A soft, satisfied smile plays over Jamie's face. The cut Jezza gave him is almost gone. "Good," he whispers. Then, in one quick movement, he flips us around so that I'm on my back and him above me. "You're in the lead, and I intend to keep in that way." He lowers his head and kisses the corner of my lip, chin, down my throat, between my breasts. For the shortest time, he flicks his tongue out at my nipples, and I arch my back into his mouth.

"Patience," he breathes against my skin, trailing more and more kisses down my body until he reaches what's left of my underwear. One quick lick right above their hem, before his teeth graze my skin, find the thin fabric of my panties and pull them down my legs.

Oh dear Lo—

His hot breath down there brings goosebumps to my skin.

"Our time out, Lee. Our time out."

Then, his tongue touches my most sensitive parts, and the world is no more.

Jamie is everything tonight—what I feel for him, and what he feels for me.

Tonight is our night.

And nobody can take it from us.

CHAPTER TWENTY-THREE

New Developments

The next morning comes too soon.

Jamie and I are tangled up in each other, two naked bodies covered by a messed-up blanket. Oh, and wings. Don't forget the wings, because wings… they make a difference. If their owner knows how to use them, that is.

And Jamie does.

The thought about last night brings heat to my cheeks. I don't think we slept much at all, we were kind of busy memorizing the details of the other one's body. And next night… I bite my lower lip. Next night, I intend to take it all the way. It's going to be special with Jamie. Very special. My cheeks crank up the heat at the thought of sleeping with him—as in sleeping-sleeping with him. A human and a F—

Nope.

A boy and a girl.

Those differences they try to make us believe in fell along the wayside a while ago.

I stretch the slightest bit. Should be tired, but thanks to all those endorphins, I feel as awake and alert as if I'd had a good night's sleep minus the headache. That one sucks, but oh well.

Jamie is cuddled into my shoulder, his left leg crossing my lower body, his left hand playing with my hand on my stomach and the Vinculum on my wrist. His wing is spread curved around us, covering us. I could stay like this forever, but forever is kind of short for us.

And it's not going to happen.

I place a tiny kiss on his hair. "We should probably get up soon." Not that I wanted to, but we have tons to discuss with Ice.

His chest moves up with a heavy sigh. "I know." He keeps on playing with the Vinculum. I lift my hand, entwine our fingers and raise them to my lips. One kiss for each knuckle before I lower them back onto my stomach, the Vinculum catching some light shining in from under the door and reflecting it in a soft red.

We got it yesterday, and already the silver is no more. Even Frances' wasn't much darker than ours, and she and Benjamin had been together for years. "Why do you think that is?"

"Huh?"

I wriggle the wrist with the Vinculum. "Why are we red already? Fast." Faster than I thought, not that I ever sat down to think about how I expected my Vinculum to turn color.

Jamie's hand stills. "Don't know." I feel him swallow hard.

"But you have a theory."

"Yeah," he whispers hoarsely. "And not a good one."

Of course not. Nothing is good when it comes to Founders, nothing but Jamie that is. "Spill it."

"It plays into what we talked about. Servants turning soldiers. I'm pretty sure the Vinculum is what triggers it. Once it's dark red, that's when the servants are… converted. So, with the little evidence I have, I'm thinking it measures *something*, and—"

I force down a dry swallow. He might be onto something. "I'm pretty sure it does. Jezza said the more… the more the human fell for the Founder, the faster it happened." Hope he won't see my cheeks turn crimson. Way to go professing my feelings for him, by proxy, at least.

Jamie resumes his play with the bracelet. "Possible. And then, before the human becomes too attached and an obvious challenge to the Eleventh Commandment, we get rid of them. Sounds like something we'd do." He sounds bitter, and after a pause he starts again. "Hey, Lee?"

"Yes?" My fingers brush up and down his arm. I love the ease we have with each other, now that the barrier of touch is gone.

"Would you... would you consider rethinking? If I asked you, I mean?"

Huh? "Re-think what?"

"Planting the virus. Being in the middle of it. Don't get me wrong," he adds, before I can get a word in, "I just want to make sure you're safe. I can fly us away. Tonight. I'm sure I can make it up to Oregon in one night, and then Canada, maybe Alaska. We lay low, we wait, then—"

A rush of warmth shoots into my heart and lights it up, but no matter his concerns his worries, this is something I have to do. Maybe Jezza was right, maybe this is my destiny. "Jamie."

His mouth snaps shut.

"I need to do this, and I can't do it without you."

His breath stutters as it comes out. The wing covering us wraps tighter around us. "Okay. Just wanted to make sure." He kisses my shoulder. "I've got your back." One more kiss, the leg across my body tightening. "I've got your back, Lee."

Two hours later, Jezza takes me aside from our daily training drill. One should think now that I'm pledged and official, I wouldn't need to practice, but oh no. For once Jamie and Ice agree I will need to be uber-perfect before we move into the forum, if we want to avoid detection. Granted, both of them have different reasons for their carefulness. Ice doesn't want to draw attention to us to avoid discovery of the Resistance's involvement, and Jamie would prefer if nobody realized we're marked.

Ice grunts at Jezza's interruption. "Really, J? It has to be now?"

Jezza takes my arm. "I need to check her wound and apply a new dressing. If you want your Protégée healthy and ready to perform, you let me do this. Unless..." He gives a noncommittal shrug.

"Whatever." Ice waves a dismissive hand.

Score one for Jezza.

He leads me back to the medical room and locks the door behind us. I slide up on the table for the lack of space. Plus, my knees are wobbly for no good reason other than I didn't sleep much, I assume. Or it's the assault on my olfactory nerves. Smells funny in here. Faint aroma of mold, with a hint of long-gone animal. Didn't notice it last time, but today it's overpowering. Yuck.

Jezza shoves his hands into his pockets and drops his gaze to the floor. "Lea, I... I'm sorry I punched Jamie yesterday. I mean, not really. I mean, yes, but—ugh." He grunts. "What I want to say is, sorry I lost it. Not sorry I punched him."

"Jez—"

"No, let me. I'm not sorry I punched him. He deserved that and much more. I'm sorry I lost it though, but... damn, Lea. You're not just anybody to me. After you broke up with me, I..." He rakes a hand through his hair. "I was devastated. What if you didn't want to see me anymore? At all, I mean? We've been friends our whole lives..." He blows out a puff of air through pursed lips. "Then, as I got over it, I wondered what would happen when you found a new boyfriend. Would I be jealous? Would I like him or automatically hate him? I was prepared for almost anything—but not for this. Not for a Founder touching you. For a Founder playing with your life."

"He's not—"

"I know he saved you. And yet it's because of him you needed saving. If I could, I'd undo it all and keep you away from all of them—"

If only it were that easy. "But you know I would've ended up in some kind of Founder-related duty anyway, Jezza. You were the one to open my eyes to that. The Protégée was always to end that way. I had no choice, and this way… this way at least I have Jamie in my corner."

A sad smile crosses his face. "That's exactly what I'm afraid of."

The way he says it… "What's going on, Jezza?"

"Huh?"

"What are you not telling me?" I give him my best stern don't-mess-with-me-look.

"Nothing, Lea. T's all good."

"Bullshit, Jezza. I know you."

For a moment he looks at me, smacking his lips twice. "True. But things have changed."

Bullshit again. "No, they haven't—"

"Yes, they have. Do you think it doesn't make a difference you're, like, together with him? The Demon? It changes everything! Like I said, you're my best friend, but now, like this…" He crosses his arms in front of his chest and shakes his head. "You're a liability."

"What?" My eyes pop wide. A liability—me?

"You heard me," he growls. "Your loyalty isn't only with me—with us—anymore, and I can't be sure how much has already shifted over to him. What do you think, that I'd tell you everything so you can tell it to him? No way—"

"Whoa. That's what you think of me? A risk?"

Jezza nods, all serious. "At the moment? Yes. It used to be only the demon. Now the way you've connected yourself to him—and I'm talking emotionally, not physically—you're the bigger liability."

Holy cow. Can't quite process that. Jezza called me a risk. To humanity. To the Resistance. Because of Jamie. That's wrong on so many levels. My stomach cramps up. "You know what? No, actually you should know already Jamie is on our side. And so am I. Jamie's a good guy, and—"

Jezza holds up a hand. "Point proven. Right there."

I groan. "Jezza—"

The hand stays up. "A good guy. Do you actually listen to yourself? He would've not gotten you into this if he was. He would've—"

Yeah, we're not talking about that. "Jezza—"

"You know, honestly, no need to discuss it. Won't change anything. Let's move on, okay? Better for both of us." He fishes something out of his pocket, while I do my best to rein in the curse words about to burst out in response to his nearsightedness.

"I got those two. Snatched them from the vault. Doubt Ice is going to realize they're gone in the next couple of days, and when or if he does…" His shoulders lift and drop. "Then we'll have to think of something."

He hands me two small, quarter-sized flat disks. "You'll know they work because they vibrate when functioning. Just a bit, but you'll feel it. The Resistance usually carries them in their arm pit, or the females under their breasts. Safest to avoid being found out when patted down. Anyway, these are used. Don't know how long they're going to last. Not long enough that you shouldn't worry. They'll do for now. Just promise me… promise me to think about what I said. Leaving. Without *him*, if you can."

Because with *him,* I'm still a liability. I barely keep from rolling my eyes. Not going to happen. Still, I smile. Yes, this stinks, the room and Jezza's suspicions, but he is on my side. He got us the maskers—two, to be exact, although he can't stand Jamie. The only reason he's an overprotective idiot sometimes is because he's worried. "Thank you."

He nods, lips pressed into a thin line. "Anytime. Now let's go back before Ice has any reason to question what took us so long."

I pocket the two small discs and slide off the table. It's not much, but finally I feel like we might stand a chance.

When Jezza and I come back to the meeting room, the mood has changed, visibly.

Jamie's brows are narrowed, as he's tapping an irregular rhythm onto the table, not unlike Ice's. Neither of them looks too happy, and while Ice is shaking his head, Jamie is nodding. "This is non-negotiable. I can't ignore an Assembly Call," he says.

Ice shrugs. "You just got pledged. You're busy. Think of something."

"Not going to happen. I miss the Assembly, they know something is off. It's mandatory, especially for me."

Ice rolls his eyes. "Why, aren't you special?"

Jamie doesn't take the bait. "Actually, I am."

I sit in a chair next to Jamie. "What's going on?"

He keeps his gaze trained on Ice. "Assembly Call. All Founders from the California Chapter are to meet this afternoon."

Huh? "Why?" That seems short notice.

"Good question." Ice's voice is cool. "And I'd prefer to not expose you to any of that. I want to keep my ace up my sleeve. If you mess up—"

"Lea won't mess up, and I have to attend, Issaac. This is non-negotiable, as I said. We will be fine, right, Lea?" He looks at me, asking a different question: will we be fine? Do we have the maskers?

I nod and give a thumbs up to him and Ice. "We'll be fine. Nothing to worry about. We can do this." If we have to. Because we have the maskers.

Jezza falls into a chair across from me and next to Ice. "What kind of Assembly?"

Jamie shrugs. "Don't know. The last one I attended was… a tribunal." I doubt anybody but me noticed the small stumble and break. Maybe Ice, not that he cared about Jamie's feelings.

Oh, crap. "Do you think it's another one?" I give him a hard stare, because what I'm truly asking is, if they could know about us.

Jamie shakes his head. "I don't know. Don't think so. This is an urgent Assembly, or else we'd have more time. Something is going on."

Jezza, Hud, and Ice exchange glances.

"Could be it," Hud says. "We've been waiting."

"Could be. Could not be. We have enough people on the inside to find out, so you guys can stay here." Ice jerks his chin at Jamie and me.

Jamie slows his speech, like talking to a toddler. "Again, not an option. We—"

I raise my hand. "Wait, you have people on the inside? Where—"

"Oh, hon, you're so slow sometimes it's adorable. We're the Resistance. It's our job. The Assembly is at the Hollywood Bowl. Who do you think is serving the precious Founders there? Who brings their drinks? Cooks their food? Collects their trash? All our people. Well, not quite a hundred percent, but a good fifty percent of employees are either members or at least pro-Resistance. Took us years to get them all in position, but they are."

Oh.

Look at that. I keep forgetting the Resistance is more than Ice's tiny team. Must have been one of those guys who filmed Jamie's Stigma, then.

Ice leans forward. "So, if it's so important you're attending, Demon, can you plant the virus? This one Lea can't do, not under observation like this."

"Where? At the Hollywood Bowl? There's no technology that will upload anything into the hive. Forget it."

Ice harrumphs. "How convenient." He's right though, we need to get that virus installed or else our options are limited.

I raise a brow at Jamie. "I'm sure we can come up with a reason to visit the hive, right? The Protégée something-something?" Or rather, Luke's son something-something.

Jamie nods. "Yes. I'm not worried about that. I am, in fact, a little bit worried about the Assembly. Not keen about running into old acquaintances." He rubs one hand over his right flank pretend-absentmindedly, but I get it.

Blood swooshes in my ears. He means Bane. We could run into Bane—

"One more reason to keep you here, Demon."

He shrugs. "If we run into problems, I'm going to handle them."

Gotta say, I feel a tad dizzy. How exactly is he going to handle Bane, a Watcher, who's out for Jamie every opportunity he gets? This is bad. Like, really bad.

Jamie shrugs. "And, like I said, we don't have a choice. It is a mandatory Assembly."

"Well, good thing then that if you must go, you're not going to be alone. J, you're with them."

Wait, wha—

"Me?" Jezza sounds as surprised as I am.

"Of course. I hear one of your colleagues called in sick, wink-wink. You're on. Make sure you get assigned the level they'll be seated in."

One of his colleagues—

And the dice fall into place.

Oh, come on! Really? "You've been lying to me? That was all for the Resistance already?" He's been jobbing at the Bowl for over a year!

Jezza cringes. "Well—"

Ice points a finger at me. "Contrary to what you may think, honey, I tend to plan ahead. Jezza's been perfect to implant, and for today, he's going to be your… let's call it backup, because I don't want you to think I don't trust you."

And still the threat is there, out in the open.

I give my red Vinculum a spin around my wrist. "Quick in and out. Attend, leave, that's it." Nothing more.

Jamie plays with his bracelet. "That's what I'm hoping for."

Goosebumps run down my spine. What he's hoping for—I

don't like that phrasing.

At all.

The time until the Assembly flies, unfortunately. Although Ice still would like us to stay, he and Jamie are on the same page when it comes to prepping me for it. Starts to annoy me a tad when they're teaming up against me, but I see their point, especially with what I know that Ice doesn't. Jamie being Luke's son, there will be more attention on us than the average newly pledged couple. Yes, I'm a New Servant, which cuts me some slack now that basic training is over and I'm official—and doesn't that feel good—but still.

I guess as somebody marked to their core, I should avoid raising suspicion or any kind of negative attention at all costs. But if they scanned me, or rather, us, we should be fine. Jamie has already attached the little round disk to an area under his left arm, the exact same spot where I'm sticking mine, in the privacy of our room.

Jezza was right, it does vibrate slightly. At first, the sensation bugs me, but after a mere ten seconds or so, I get used to it. Guess I'll see it as a reassuring reminder all is well, as long as it works.

Here's hoping we won't get scanned, and mainly, we won't run into Bane. I mean, the Bowl is huge. No way he's going to find us.

I hope.

The only reason why I'm not completely freaking out about going to the Assembly is that so far Jamie seems to have been right: He knows how Bane ticks. After all, I'm still alive. Had Bane called in my attack on him, I'm sure the hunt for the precious Protégée would have been on.

With a sigh, I lower my black shirt and straighten it. Okay. Ready. Kind of. I wish we had more time. A nap wouldn't be bad.

Had I known we'd be out at an Assembly and surrounded by freakin' Founders, I would've tried to get more sleep last night. I blush. No, I wouldn't.

Guess I gotta suck it up and ignore the hangover-like sensation making my body feel leaden and heavy.

I slap my cheeks twice to get some color into them and something close to alertness into my system and walk out the door of our room. For one second, I pick up on voices—voices that stop in the middle of a word as soon as I'm out my door: Jamie and Jezza in the middle of what looks like a heated discussion. Jezza has both arms crossed in front of his chest, while Jamie's wings are halfway extended in an intimidating stance.

Neither of them looks too friendly, but whatever they were talking about, they're wrapping it up the moment they see me.

A hurried whisper that should be too soft for me to hear: "We've got a deal, and you better stick to it," Jamie whispers in a hurry, so soft, I'm kind of proud of myself for picking up on it.

Stick to what? I walk closer. "What's going on, guys? I'm not comfortable with you striking deals instead of being at each other's throats."

Surprise flickers across Jamie's face, gone as quickly as it came. "Nothing." He shakes out his wings and pulls them in. "Just reminding the oaf he owes me one."

Jezza scowls at him. "Just telling the Demon to behave, or he's gonna get a split lip again."

Wow. Just wow. "Boys, behave. We have one hour until the Assembly, and I would like to get it done and over with. Without drama." I give them both a pointed glance.

"Exactly my plan," Jamie says, turning and walking down the hallway toward the exit. "Exactly my plan."

CHAPTER TWENTY-FOUR

Assembly

As with any Assembly Hollywood is on lock-down.

This time, I get to ride in a limousine with Jamie, not walk my way to the orphanage through chaos. Makes a difference and feels weird. People look at us as we drive by. They know a Founder is sitting behind the dark windows—a *pledged* Founder, because everybody without a wing-less human is flying to the Bowl.

We're driving.

Being driven, to be correct.

I wonder what they would think if they knew the First was also in this limousine, working on a plan to help them.

Soon.

Soon we will be able to.

I hope.

Every couple of minutes, I press my left arm against my body. Nothing more reassuring than the slow vibration of the masker. My lifeline.

The ride doesn't take too long with all the roads blocked for this event. I'm sorry, Hollywood. No fun during rush hour. We pass the big white church on Franklin and Highland. Somebody has painted graffiti on it, and thanks to the spotlights illuminating the church it pops out even more: *Hell is coming*, it says—and then, right next to it, in a different handwriting and color: *It's here already, idiot!*

Ouch.

About five minutes later, the limousine stops at the bottom of the hill leading up to the Bowl. I get out first and open Jamie's door. "Master." My bow is deep enough Ice would clap in excitement.

Jamie straightens his black shirt. "Come," he barks at me, and like a puppy, I fall into step with him. Still hate that part.

One should think after being with Jamie, obviously a Founder, and after having been at the dinner, the concert, and up in the hive, I'd gotten used to being surrounded by Founders. The short answer: nope. Not in the slightest. Their proximity still makes me nervous, even more now that I know we're under double-scrutiny, the Protégée together with Luke's son.

I do my very best to suppress my nervous check-ins to my left and right all the way up the hill past the ticket shop and entrance. The sun is on its way down, and the Bowl's lights are on, bathing everything in bright white light. It reflects off every Founder's white wings like a warning signal to me. Appreciate that, because if I ran into any of them… yeah, not good. Touching a Founder. As it is, I have enough reasons to be worried, I don't need to add being clumsy to that list. And I can handle all of this, as long as we stay as far as possible away from Bane. I'm not sharing Jamie's optimism that he won't kill me on sight.

Jamie leads me through the entrance. Nobody but me will have picked up on the short hesitation before he passes the scanners on either side of the doorway.

No beep for him.

I swallow dry. Come on, little masker, you can do it.

I press my arm down into the vibrating little disk stuck under my armpit and keep walking, walking, walking—and pass the scanner without the alarms going off.

Phew. Okay. Okay. Deep breaths. That went well. Good sign. Still, my heart hammers like crazy thanks to the extra serving of adrenaline it just received.

Even Jamie's posture is straighter, now that we've passed this test. He walks ahead into one of the first little walkways leading to the amphitheater until he stops in front of a Watcher.

"Anywhere?" asks Jamie.

Preferably in the back, please. Far away from everybody, and with a quick way out once we're done here.

The Watcher bows. "Sons of Luke, first row."

Oh. Well. Of course.

Jamie sighs. "Thank you." He leads me to the first row of seats right in front of the stage. "Guess you'll meet most of my brothers." To anybody else, this would be a normal remark, but I hear the tension in his voice. It translates into a nervous jitter for me, or maybe it's the lack of sleep.

A short little zap, a pinch under my left armpit—

"Ow." I yank a hand to my side—and drop it. Not the best idea to point out the one spot that can get me into trouble. Besides, it doesn't hurt anymore. A slight numbness, nothing else—

F-ing crap.

The masker.

Like crazy, I press my arm against my side.

Nothing.

Again.

Nothing.

Oh no. Dizziness brings my knees to a wobble. The masker is

gone. Kaput. Broken.

Jamie realizes I'm not following. "Lea." His tone is strict. Authoritative. "Don't delay me."

I force my body into a submissive bow. "I apologize, Master, but…"

Somebody snickers next to us, some idiot Founder with a traditional human servant trailing after him, his head lowered, keeping his perfect distance.

A drop of cold sweat runs down my back.

Jamie rolls his eyes. "What is it?" He manages to make it sound like I was the biggest inconvenience in the world.

How do I tell him? Founders are everywhere. Okay… I bring my hands up and cross them in front of my chest with my palms coming to rest across the sides of my breast. My right taps the area twice, then makes a short, crisp slicing motion. "N-nothing," I stutter, hiding the motion of my hand under pretend-nervousness. "I apologize for this dysfunction."

Jamie's pupils dilate. He's got it. "Inconvenient, servant. Tonight, you will practice more." A hint of worry lights up in his eyes before he has himself under control again.

"Yes, Master." Not good. I'm in the lion's den without a working masker. If—

"Jamin!"

Blood freezes in my veins. That voice—

Jamie stops dead in his tracks. "Bane."

Oh crap. My heart lurches into my throat and brings the taste of bile with it. Bane. The worst-case scenario, of course. It's Bane—Bane, whom I kicked. Bane, who knows I touched him. If he doesn't kill me right away, one scan will be enough, and I'll be damned. No Masker. Crap, crap, crap. But even with a masker, he'd know something was off, because he knows I *touched* him and I *should* light up. Pressure builds in my chest and a wheezy breath leaves my throat as I lower into the deepest bow I've ever pulled off.

Jamie said he would handle him. He better, or this is it.

"Hello, Jamin." The smile on Bane's face is as frozen as my blood. Cold. "Look at your little human pet. She looks surprisingly well, much better than when I saw her last time." Meaning, I'm not dead from the knife he threw at me.

All color drains from my face, but Jamie knows the game being played. He steps forward, right in Bane's face. "About that. You mess with my servant one more time, *anything*, and you and I are going to have a problem."

Whoa.

Bane's right eyebrow shoots up. "Are we? I thought we had one already."

"I don't. You know that." Jamie shrugs. "But I would prefer not having to have her stitched up every time we meet you. I like her in pristine condition." He eyes Bane down his nose.

His strategy is working. Bane's gaze lowers and his features tighten. But instead of scanning me or telling Jamie I kicked him, he shoots out a hand and reaches for Jamie's wrist. "I can tell. What is wrong with you?"

Jamie yanks his arm and bright-red Vinculum away from the other Founder. "None of your business."

"Oh, but I think it is," Bane growls and raises his left arm with the scanner attached to his leather cuff. "She told you what happened? Because she—curse the crappy reception!" He shakes the wrist with the scanner on it and angles it, a smug smile on his face. "Oh well, who cares, I can transmit later. As long as I can show Luke—"

Jamie takes another step closer. If he punches him, if he does anything that—

He doesn't.

Jamie lays a gentle palm on Bane's chest. "Stop it, Bane." All aggression is gone from his voice. He's calm. Soothing.

Bane freezes in mid-motion. Inch by inch, his head lowers down to Jamie's hand on his sternum, then up to Jamie's face. *Disbelief.*

I see the apple in Bane's throat move up and down.

But he doesn't push Jamie's hand away.

And he doesn't continue to scan me.

For one long moment, he's locked into Jamie's eyes, muscle in his temple twitching, eyes wide—

Then he turns on his heels and stomps off into the masses.

Without killing me. Obviously.

I blow out a long puff of air. That… that was close. Too close. He didn't even mention I kicked him. Nothing. He didn't get there, thanks to Jamie antagonizing him.

Jamie looks after Bane, a pensive expression on his face. "What is he planning?" He shakes his head slowly once. Two Founders pass us by, both with black in their wings, both giving us curious glances.

"Jamin."

"Kedar. Salathiel." Jamie lowers his head as two of his brothers pass by. These two are much older, if they were human, I'd peg them to be in their fifties. In Founder years, that could be anything. Once they have passed, Jamie leads us to the middle of the first row. About twenty other Founders are seated already, all with black in their wings, some more, some less, all of different ages, but nobody as young as Jamie. He nods at a couple of them and ignores others.

Apparently, growing up with a family is not always an advantage. Said the orphan.

We take a seat and Jamie relaxes. Or at least pretends to. His fingers shake as he folds them together in his lap. The seats to our left and right are not taken yet, and as soon as Jamie takes a glass of something sparkly from one of the human servers, he holds it in front of his mouth and whispers at me. "Is it working again?"

My masker.

As slightly as possible I shake my head, hardly visible in this semi-darkness.

Jamie curses under his breath. "As soon as this is over, we leave. Exit to the right, stay close. I want to avoid running into Bane again."

No kidding. I give a short, almost imperceptible nod that brings the headache raging behind my forehead to another high. Ow. Although I guess feeling pain is good—means I'm not dead yet.

Over the next ten minutes, the Hollywood Bowl fills up, and with it my anxiety. Ninety percent of attendees are Founders, the remaining ten percent humans—human servants. I crane my neck to see if I can make out Jezza, but he's nowhere to be found. Thousands of Founders, a few humans far and in-between, a TV-camera farther up the hill aimed at the stage, and that's about it. Tough to see with the sun down and only the bright spotlights uphill blinding me. But just from my cursory glance, I'd say there are a good three hundred human waiters distributed all through the ranks, if I had to guess. Makes me feel a bit less alone knowing many of them are Resistance, but does nothing to make me feel safer.

Eventually, the lights dim. "Fellow Founders." A voice comes from the left side of the stage. Can't see the Founder, and am glad we're in the first row. Human ears would not do well with un-amplified speech from farther up the hill. "Please welcome your beloved leader, Luke."

The audience falls into an easy applause as Luke takes the stage. They installed a podium in the middle, and together with the Bowl's armadillo-style ridges illuminated in bright white, it brings contrast to Luke's all-black wings. It makes him look regal. Guess that's what he planned.

He lifts both hands and the applause dies down. "Thank you, my fellow Founders. I appreciate you all coming on such a short notice, but I'm afraid I do have news that requires our action. The fleet is on the way to Earth. They will arrive in what we estimate to be about one week—"

Loud murmurs and whispers come from the audience around us. Luke holds up a hand. "Quiet, please. I know this is sooner than we anticipated, but it doesn't matter. We've had over a decade of preparation. We know Earth and its people, and we have our chess pieces in place. In fact, I'm calling checkmate already. Today. They might come to take Earth away from us, but they will not succeed."

He pauses and lets his gaze drift across the audience.

"We have seven days to be ready for battle, and the fleet has seven days to enjoy the rest of their lives, because once they are here, we will annihilate them. We will fight to keep Earth ours, no matter the losses." He punches one fist up in the air, and the audience breaks out in loud cheers and applause.

All but Jamie, me, and the few humans present who

understood what Luke just said.

We will fight.

And humanity will lose, either way.

Holy cow.

My palms are sweaty and itchy no matter how many times I swipe them over my thighs. War. War is coming. It's official: we were right. Can't say it feels good.

Luke raises both palms. "Silence! Time is of the essence. Michael and I have a plan in place. Our human forces are large enough to be a substantial threat to any attacking group of Founders. Yes, the losses will be in the tens of millions, but we will prevail."

I close my eyes. It doesn't get better hearing that number a second time.

"You will be assigned to your leaders depending on region. As always, the clan of Luke shall provide the commanders for the battle. Please step forward. Northern Europe—Kedar. Southern Europe—Salathiel. Middle East—Kohath. Arabia—" One by one, Founders from the first row get up and climb the stage, taking position next to Luke.

"North Africa—Abdi. South Africa—Baalath. India—Ophel. China—"

Jamie's brothers stand tall next to their father, wings halfway extended and held high, an impressive lineup of black against the white backdrop, the occasional human servant behind them.

"South America—Uthai. And lastly, North America…" He pauses. "Jamin." His gaze falls onto Jamie in the first row. "Come on up, my son."

Wait, Jamie—

For a second, I think he's going to refuse, to stay seated, to say there's no way he's going be a part of this war—but then he gets up.

Which means I'm getting up.

Jamie walks up the few stairs to the stage like in a trance, me right behind him, heart hammering, every breath as wheezy as the one before. How do we get out of this? How—

Luke comes down the podium and shakes the hand of each of his sons. The audience goes crazy with every single one of them, as if they were rock stars, not the Founders about to lead them into war, and maybe death. But then, how could I forget: it's going to be mostly the humans doing the dying.

Luke shakes the hand of the Founder next to Jamie. "Uthai. The time has come."

"Yes, Father." Uthai bows slightly.

"And you, Jamin." Luke lays a hand on Jamie's shoulder. "My youngest. I have to admit, I wasn't sure if I should give you a command." Ouch. At least I hope nobody besides his brothers is picking up on Luke's soft words.

Jamie's wings flutter. "Why, Father?"

Oh, we know why. We heard it crystal clear.

Luke's fingers squeeze into Jamie's shoulder. "I didn't think I could trust you enough. Not after that ridiculous idea regarding the servant laws. But I must say, you have redeemed yourself. New Servitude is working well for us, and with you pledging the Protégée, I think you're ready." Jamie gets a smile full of pride, and holy hell, he eats it up.

"Yes, Father." His eyes are wide, his voice breaks at the end. "Thank you, Father." He bows, like his brothers did.

"I know you will not disappoint me, Jamin."

Jamie stands up straighter. "I won't, Father. I won't. I…

appreciate you trusting me with a command. I will bring honor to the clan of Luke." The way he says it… is that pride in his voice?

Luke smiles. "You have helped us tremendously. Thanks to you, we have hundreds of New Servants, and all of them in high positions. This will benefit us during the war. You truly are my son."

Jamie's face lights up in the most pure and happy way. "Thank you, Father. I knew it would pay off in the end."

Ouch, even if it was played. Because it was. Right?

They both hug, and even though they were probably missing what passed between those two, the audience goes crazy while I force a dry swallow down my throat. Jamie's good. Too good. Scarily good. So good, it looked like he didn't need to act at—

A Watcher flies down onto the stage and nods at Luke. He bends forward and whispers something into Luke's ear. Luke stiffens.

Nods.

Nods again.

"Anybody else?" His eyes brush over Jamie, and they have lost the warmth from a moment ago.

The Watcher shakes his head.

"Okay then." Luke raises both palms, and the chants begin to die down. "Dear fellow Founders, I ask for your patience for a short moment." The chants turn into confused murmurs. I take it usually proceedings are swift during these things.

He takes the Watcher by the elbow and directs him to Jamie. "Do it again." Gone is the joyful leader who announced going to war like it was a fun pastime. This Luke is cold, as he stares at his son. Serious. Dead serious.

The Watcher lifts his left wrist at me—and my heart stops.

No—

"Positive, sir. Red zone. As high as we can read. That's what Bane implied."

My knees turn into Jell-O. Oh, crap, oh—

A muscle in Luke's jaw ticks. "So, the question becomes why is she this deep red, and what is Jamin's involvement in it. If what Bane says is true and she is *healed*…" He spits that word out like poison. "Then Jamin is marked as well. Deep scan." Pause. "*Both.*"

Jamie stiffens, and so do I. Can't breathe, can't—

Another swipe of the scanner—over me, over Jamie—and the Watcher whistles through his teeth. "Interesting, sir."

"What?"

"As Bane says, she has an injury in her back, and it's healed."

Every breath I take comes into my lungs empty, devoid of oxygen. Bane, that snitch. Bane told them. Of course, he would. He knew how badly he hurt me, and then I'm all fine when he sees me again—

Which means, Luke's going to find out Jamie healed me, and then we're both dead. That's Bane's plan. What do we do? Do we run, do I—

Luke's eyes harden as they fall on Jamie. "Are you telling me Jamin broke the ultimate law and healed a human?" His voice stays low, level, and it makes him sound even more dangerous.

"Actually, I don't think so, sir." The Watcher turns the scanner sideways for Luke to see. "He's clear. Would show up if he did."

Relief floods my system. That part of the plan at least worked. Of course, Jamie's clear, he has the masker, while mine broke.

The Watcher continues. "Only she is marked, but it exceeds the range of our scanners. Way beyond what can be tolerated during training. Or at any time. And… look at her Vinculum."

There goes that short-lived relief. I close my eyes. Damn it. *Way beyond…*

Luke's gaze on Jamie stays cold. Evaluating. "So, Jamin broke the Eleventh Commandment." A statement, not a question, and that statement it reminds me my fate is not the only one hanging by a thread. It's going to cost Jamie his wings. Slap on the wrist for others. Punishment for the boy with one Stigma burned into his back.

And he knows it. The pulse in his neck speeds up, and so does his breathing. "Father—"

My body acts before my brain has decided how it wants to play this. I step forward, knees wobbly, heart hammering, every cell aware of the danger I'm in. But then, I'm in that danger no matter what. "Founder, I apologize. It was all me."

The line of Founders on stage—and probably every Founder present in the amphitheater who could get a glimpse of what just happened—gasps in surprise. Yes, a human just addressed a Founder without being spoken to. But as it is, I'm a dead woman walking. It's not as if this small disobedience mattered anymore. Or me taking the blame.

I lift my head and look at the man who killed my family, and who most likely will kill me. He has destroyed my life, and now he might destroy me, but I won't let him take the one thing that means the world to me—the one person who means the world to me. I won't let him take Jamie. I won't let him hurt him. Plus, keeping Jamie off their radar leaves me one ace in the sleeve. "It was all me, Founder. Clumsy. No talent. Clearly, I am not servant material. Jamin had nothing to do—"

Jamie whirls around, eyes wide and mouth agape. "Lea!"

Once more, with emphasis. "It was all my fault, Founder."

Luke looks from me to Jamie and back.

Again.

The Watcher raises his arm and taps his scanner for Luke to look at. Both men exchange a glance—and Luke steps closer to Jamie and me. "I highly doubt that he had nothing to do with it. Jamin. You took her virginity."

My jaw drops. He—what? What the hell did that thing scan for? And no, he didn't—

Luke's wings unfurl to the max, like a shield separating us and our conversation from the audience. "You took her virginity."

I suck in a sharp breath. Luke discussing my virginity—or the lack thereof—in front of the whole stage and first row audience like it was public knowledge doesn't even register. It's the implication that comes with it that makes me breathless. Jamie's mouth opens and closes. Luke has him on the hook for something illegal he didn't do, for something I can't talk him out of, because to Luke the equation is clear: all servants are virgins, the New Scripture forbids sex before marriage, yet I've clearly lost my virginity and I am marked.

One and one equals two, so no matter if unofficially *Founders bang their servants*, we're not unofficial, but very much official and on the spot. A freakishly detached part of me wonders if this is even an issue for male servants, not that it mattered.

Luke scratches his chin. "Jamin, I've got to say, I keep underestimating you."

Jamie's brows scrunch together. "Father?"

"For a moment, I was worried. I was worried you broke our laws and healed her, but obviously I was wrong. You're not marked. I apologize for thinking so low of you." He lowers his head closer to Jamie. "But you took her virginity."

I lift my hand. "No. No, he—"

Jamie steps half in front of me and cuts me off. "Yes. Yes, I admit it, Father." He lets his head hang. "I broke the law. I couldn't control myself—"

What the hell is he doing? Denial is his only chance. If I get to explain—

Luke raises his hand. That motion combined with years of PTSD… I can't help the small gasp escaping me, the adrenaline spiking and begging my body to give into the flight-reflex. I'm waiting for the blue that's sure to come, the blue that's—

Luke lifts his hand higher—and claps Jamie on the shoulder.

And chuckles.

He *chuckles.*

Wha—

"Nicely done, my son."

Nicely—

Luke's wings arch higher, like a barrier. "Clearly, you are my flesh and blood. Using the human for your own entertainment— and marking her up so quickly, so high…" He shakes his head, a smile on his face. "You've proven yourself worthy despite the lack of the black in your wings."

Jamie's eyes must be as wide as mine, but I doubt anybody but me would see the shake of his hands as they're folded behind his back. "I have… proven worthy?"

"Jamin." Another one of those chuckles that bring bile up my throat. "You shouldn't have postponed your initiation, and I'm sorry I couldn't go into more detail the other day. There are things you need to know, and this is one of them. Humans… humans are filled with sin, seduction is in their genes. We weren't made to resist, so giving in is an error, but understandable. I expected it to happen. It always does. Which is why we have the Vinculums."

"But… The Eleventh Commandment—"

"*You shalt not touch those descended from the Heavens?* Does it say anything about Founders touching humans in there, Jamin?" Luke winks at him. "But look at you, you figured it out even without my input. Humans are ours to take, as we please. That's what me made them for. Servitude—in every way possible, if you catch my drift." He winks at him, then sobers up. "Unfortunately, I have bad news. Since she is marked so high and it has become public, we can't let it slide. You understand, don't you?"

Can't let it slide?

Jamie nods once, slowly, deliberately. "Of course I do, Father."

His shoulder gets a squeeze. "Usually I would have to insist on your punishment as well to keep the façade, but as it is in this case, I'm sure we can make an exception and forego disciplining you. The public will understand. After all, this is war and you're going to be a commander in it. We need you. And…" His eyes take on an unusual soft quality. "And I'm proud of you, my son." A moment passes between them, full of unspoken words, of sorrow—and then Jamie lays his hand on top of his father's on his shoulder.

Uhh—

"Thank you, Father." His eyes shine with tears. What the hell—

Luke makes a flicking motion with his other wrist. "Grab her."

Before I can conclude he means me, two Watchers land behind me, their black boxes activated, and try to grab me.

Oh, hell to the no! I jump back like tasered. "Stay off me!"

Even though much of me is hidden from view by Luke, an outcry goes through the audience. Enough people sit at an angle that they can see the little human defying the leader of the Founders.

The Watchers charge, and I turn on my heels and run. If I can get off the stage—

A short breeze, a draft of air—and Jamie lands in front of me. Finally!

I throw myself around his neck, legs around his waist as high as I can reach. "Go! Go! Lift off, Jamie! Go—"

Strong hands wrap around my arms from behind, their fingers digging into my skin. I yelp out as they tear on me. "Jamie—"

But he doesn't whisk me away, doesn't lift off, doesn't even freakin' move.

He only stands still, hands out wide, like he was afraid to touch me. Which is ridiculous, because—

"Lord! She is—"

"Out in the open. I can't believe—"

"Touching, like this! It's—"

Luke's voice booms through the Hollywood Bowl: "Menachim, video transmit, all Earth!"

The red light on the camera farther up the hill in the middle of the audience springs to life as the two Watchers yank me off of Jamie like a piece of meat. "Jamie!" I yell. "Jamie!" I kick, I thrash, I fight—but it's useless. A third Watcher appears and smacks his Raptor like a metal neck clip around my throat. Wherever he forces me, I have to go. "Jamie," I gurgle. *Jamie.*

But Jamie only stands still, looking at me like… like a Founder looks at a human.

Luke motions him to come over. He lays one arm around

Jamie's shoulders and keeps him close. Behind Jamie's back, Luke's wings extend to their max, every black feather shining in the spotlight directed onto him. He raises his voice and this time it transmits through the speakers and most likely to every hive and screen on Earth, together with the video. "Fellow Founders, dear Humans. *The word of the Lord is gospel, and also command. It shall not be disregarded by anybody, and if it is, punishment will follow swiftly. New Scripture, New Book of Luke 23:13.*"

He pauses as he looks into the audience, left to right, and back. "Today, I stand before you to help you remember that defying the Lord is the wrong path to choose. Today, I stand before you to remind you those laws were made by Him, for all of us to live by. Failure to do so will result in punishment."

Another pause, underlined by chaotic murmurs from the audience.

"Lea Akiyama. Step forward."

The Watchers yank me forward so hard it's all I can do to not stumble and fall. "Jamie," I gurgle through the tight metal band constricting my throat.

But Jamie only stands next to his father, his shoulders straight, an air of superiority to him.

Like a freakin' Founder.

Luke's cold eyes watch every move I make. "Lea Akiyama. The Protégée. Protected and cared for by our race, despite her parents' shortcomings. I am very much disappointed in you." He jerks his chin at the Watcher. "Show them."

"Yes, sir." The Watcher raises his left wrist at me, presses a button on the scanner and then turns the wrist over for everybody to see: red. Bright, glowing red.

"Let this be a lesson to everybody," Luke calls out into the audience. "Nobody disregards the law, no matter your standing in society. Lea Akiyama was the Protégée, but she has violated the Eleventh Commandment. She has seduced a heavenly being. Disgraced the Eleventh Commandment. Made a sinner out of one of the Lord's creatures. Lea Akiyama will pay the price for her sins. She will be publicly executed. Let this"—he points at me, anger distorting his features—"let this remind you all that while the Lord has mercy, he punishes disobedience hard and swiftly. *For the Lord trusts in his Founders to uphold His law, and no human shall willingly break or disregard it.*"

One more scathing look at me, an accusing finger pointed at my chest. "Take her away."

The Watchers yank on me. "No! No! Jamie! I— Jamie!" The Raptor closes tighter around my throat, cutting off all air with a wheeze.

Luke lets go of Jamie, and only because his voice doesn't come via speakers do I know the transmission is over. "Ridiculous how much this human considers you hers." It comes with a load of disgust in his voice, but that's not what makes my heart seize and freeze in my chest.

It's Jamie's dismissive sneer and reply. "Not my fault. I warned her not to fall for me. Considered it fair. Obviously, she didn't heed my advice."

They both share a laugh that burrows itself into my soul and drains it of everything good I ever kept in there.

Jamie's tone changes to something almost worshipping. "I'm glad you understand, Father. It was a risky double game, but worth every potential punishment if it means you believe in me again."

Luke keeps his voice low. "I'm proud of you, Son. You did

well with her. A public execution will instill fear. When you chose the Protégée, you showed exceptional potential for leadership. Binding her to you made me realize how much of me runs through your veins. The perfect set-up, either way. A useful puppet while compliant, an even better example when she has outlived her usefulness. You got us the right push to show humanity breaking the law doesn't pay. It will keep them in line from now on. You might've just won us the war, Jamin. This is the push we needed. Well played. Well played."

But no—it can't have been played! Can't! Too much has happened between us, too much—

Jamie chuckles once, his warm, deep chuckle that I love so much—and for one split-second I feel hope rise against all odds. Yes, he played the game, but on my side. This is Jamie, *my Jamie*, not a Founder. Any time now he's going to choose me, he's—

Jamie turns to his father and embraces him, and this hug, it speaks volumes.

Something inside of me breaks and shatters into a million pieces.

"My son," Luke whispers into Jamie's shoulder so soft I'd be impressed I'm picking up on it if I wasn't busy dying on the inside.

Jamie pulls out of the hug, face alight and eyes shining with tears. "Whatever I can do for the success of our race, Father. Once we have time, I have even more information for you. On the Resistance."

No.

Desperation clouds my senses. No. He wouldn't do that. Jamie wouldn't—

Jamie lays one hand on his father's forearm and nods his chin at me. "Now that I know how it works, we can continue that angle with the next female. Maybe the president's daughter. Highly influential. And this time… I'll take my sweet time." He winks at his father, and both laugh out, but the moment his eyes fall on me they turn cold. "And now take her away. We're done here."

It can't be real, he can't mean what he says, yet every word hits like an arrow, every word kills a part of my soul.

The Watchers yank on my neck harder and I follow.

There's nothing else to do.

CHAPTER TWENTY-FIVE

Dark Place, Bright Light

I'm being dragged from the stage, past Jamie's brothers, down the stairs, through the audience, and past faces that either show amusement or shock. Humans, Founders, humans, Founders, Founders, Founders—Founders everywhere. Jezza's face, somewhere, horrified. Others, jeering.

I fight, I struggle, I thrash, but it's no use. Once or twice, I almost get them to let go of me, but once they work together, I don't stand a chance. They tug and tow me farther up the hill toward a little building with iron bars in front of the window. Former store, now makeshift prison.

My foot catches against an uneven step and I stumble, only to be brutally yanked up by my neck. A strangulated coughing fit breaks from my throat, yet the Watchers show no mercy. No regret.

Instead, they laugh.

"Look at her. Thought she could break the Eleventh Commandment out in the open and get away with it."

"Stupid bitch. Thinking he'd keep her, or what? He's the son of Luke, he can have every human he wants to."

"And he's quite the stud, it appears. Bane said something about it."

They snicker. "Must be. Check out that Vinculum." One of them yanks on my right arm until it comes up, bright red in the artificial light.

All three Watchers snicker again. "And they just pledged a day or two ago. They were busy."

"He must've spent all day on top of her."

Wha—?

They open the door to a grey and empty room. All three release me at the same time. "Would make a good soldier though. Much stronger than I thought she was. And having the former Protégée—"

"They won't turn her into a soldier anymore. She's the example—"

They shut the door with a bang, cutting off whatever else they were about to say.

Silence.

My legs are too wobbly to support my weight and buckle under me. Stronger than they thought? All strength is gone. I fall onto my knees, then on all fours. What happened? Those last five minutes, they *can't* have happened. They're impossible.

And yet they did happen.

The rules I thought I could live by have been rewritten. Turned upside down. Twisted. *Thou Shalt Not Touch Those Descended From The Heavens.* I mean, it's pretty clear. And I didn't plan to touch one of *those descended from the heavens.* But then Jamie happened, and it felt right, although it was wrong. So very wrong. And then turns out everybody does it, and everybody knows, and Founders don't get punished for it. Only humans do.

To be fair, Jamie warned me. Twice. Even if he didn't know officially, he had a hunch. *Breaking the Eleventh Commandment with our servants is a notch in our belts. Nothing more. You on the other hand will get punished. Easily, and without mercy.* And he warned me to not fall for him. Can't say he didn't.

And now he is praised for using me, and I will be executed. Publicly.

I huff once. Always knew the Founders would use their precious Protégée for some kind of publicity stunt. Never imagined it to be this though.

And still, in the grand scheme of things, me being locked away for breaking the Eleventh Commandment is not the most surprising of all developments.

Us really going to war is.

Jamie accepting command is.

Jamie… Jamie gobbling up his father's praise is.

Or, maybe not. The more I think about it, the more it's clear the signs were there all along. The longing for his father's attention. The fact he only agreed to Ice's plan after he heard I was the Protégée. The way he manipulated me, feeding me just the right amount of sob-story and details for me to fall for him.

A ragged breath leaves my throat. More and more little oddities come to mind. The secrets he kept, like being Luke's son. The way he downplayed what he heard about impending war. That he was the one who came up with New Servitude. That he didn't place the splitter.

All planned.

I want to doubt it. Maybe he didn't plan it—but it makes too much sense. That whole disaster about installing the virus up in the hive, his lies to take the splitter, his failure to install it—not because he wanted to protect me. No. Because he wanted to protect his people. And in the end, he chose his father over me. He chose the man who gave him the Stigma over the girl who lo—

No.

I don't.

He's not worth it.

I should've known.

I should've believed Jezza.

Should've.

But I didn't.

The first tears fall silently onto the dirty concrete.

How ironic. Whenever they get around to killing me, my family will have been completely obliterated by Jamie's.

I don't know how long I lie on the cold concrete floor.

Can't have been too long, but it could have been a lifetime.

How stupid I was.

How right everybody else was.

I hear Luke drone on and on about war and the dominance of Founders, his soft un-amplified voice ringing louder than a jet plane. The crowd cheers and applauds several times, for what, I don't know. Probably the destruction of humankind.

At one point, I look out through the bars of the only window. No guards. Because, why would they? The little human is doomed, no matter what. If I ran, I'd light up every scanner. If I hid, someone sooner or later would recognize the Protégée—or whatever they'll call me now that their protection has waned.

I lean against the wall and slide down.

My headache, the ache in every single bone, it doesn't register. It's not even a blip on the radar of pain. Doesn't hold a candle against the agony raging through my soul.

What have I done? To myself, to others?

Jezza. His face, when they dragged me past him. My oldest

friend. My dearest friend. The only one whom I could always trust.

I pull my legs in and lean my forehead onto my knees.

I wish they'd gotten it over with already.

I—

Soft, fast steps come up the hill, a scratching sound at the door, a slight squeak as it opens.

"Lea!"

Oh, hell to the no, it's not—

Jamie tiptoes into the room, and I scoot back against the wall. "Get out!"

He throws a hectic glance over his shoulder, then back at me. "Lee, come on, we've got to get going! Now!"

I shake my head. "I don't trust you." I did once, I don't anymore. Whatever he's playing at—

Jamie curses under his breath. "What did you expect me to do? That was only for show. Please. Please believe me. I came here as soon as I could, Father is starting to have the leaders pledge, I either have to be back in five, or be gone. Come on."

As if to prove his point, Luke's voice echoes over the speakers, *"Commanding the Middle East—Kohath!"*

Doesn't change a damn thing. "Nu-uh." I push harder into the wall.

With three quick strides, Jamie is through the room and kneels down next to me. "Believe me, Lee. I'm on your side, whatever happens. Look." He reaches under his shirt. A short plopping sound and his hand comes back with a small round disk in it—a disk he breaks in two. "I'm on your side. Whatever happens."

The masker. He just broke... he broke his masker and made

himself vulnerable. My heart stumbles over its own feet, but it's not ready to run with him.

Jamie's face turns soft. "Please." One hand touches my leg, and that small touch… No Founder touches a human unless he must.

Unless this is real.

This is real.

Jamie is real.

Relief as heavy as a truck falls off my shoulders. Only one way to go—and even if he still played me, because I'm dead already. Following him won't make me deader. "Okay," I whisper hoarsely. "Okay. Let's go." No time for tears, no time for anything but getting out of here.

Jamie jumps up to stand and pulls me up with him, but instead of running, his arms go around me. I stiffen. "Lee, I'm sorry. I didn't have any other choice. There are thousands of Founders here, we have to—"

"There, there." The condescending voice coming from the door has both of us jerking apart.

Bane.

Bane, standing in the doorway, arms crossed in front of his chest, wings out and blocking the way. "Ouch, Jamin. Really, ouch." His pointed glance falls onto our entwined hands—but Jamie doesn't let go.

His fingers wrap tighter around mine. "Bane—"

What is he going to say that could save us at this point? Bane caught us hugging. *After* I came back bright red on the scanner. He sees us touching. No matter all the crap going on with the Eleventh Commandment and Founders bending the rules for their own pleasure, if I've learned one thing over the last hours, it's that touch is better kept private. Never mind the small, but crucial detail Jamie was breaking me free.

Bane shakes his head and types something into his leather cuff. "Not surprised, really. Well, maybe about the depth of your involvement, *Jamin*, but to my utter disappointment, even after this infraction, you might get away with losing your command. Tied wings. Must feel good to be the son of Luke. Anybody else would get their second Stigma for freeing a prisoner and their wings cut off. Unless…" He moves his arm over Jamie, eyes glued to the reader.

A frown passes his face, followed by another swipe over Jamie.

Another one.

And another one.

I hear Jamie swallow.

So does Bane.

He types something into the scanner—the scanner that's for sure picking up our sky-high readings and transmitting them to the hive. Our secret is out. Out-out.

"*Commanding Arabia—Uriah!*"

Bane scans again. Scans me. Scans Jamie.

His eyes widen as his face loses all color. Inch by inch his arm lowers. "This… it can't…" He exhales roughly.

There's no gleeful outburst he was right, no lighting his Caeruleum, no releasing his Raptor and keeping us in check. Only a speechless panic that crosses his face.

His hands shake. "Jamie…" For one second his eyelids flutter shut. Again: "Jamie?" It's nothing but a soft whisper, but with a near-panic edge to them. "No. No, no, no. Please tell me you didn't do this. Tell me the readings are wrong. Tell me you didn't. You didn't heal her." He rakes a jittery hand through his hair and re-checks his readings. "No." This one is barely audible. Bane takes his gaze off the cuff and locks it with Jamie's.

I look left and right, from Jamie to Bane and back, but no matter how often I look, how often I blink, how often I think it can't be there—it is.

Like a fourth entity, something passes between them, something that runs deep, that has always been there, only I was too blind and maybe too prejudiced to see.

Jamie bites his lower lip. "I can't tell you that, Bane. I did it. I broke the taboo. And you know that, since you called the Watchers onto her."

A pained choke breaks from Bane's throat. "No. An exaggeration to get them to disturb Luke on stage and you in trouble. Had I known you really healed—" He sucks in a choppy breath. "Never."

Jamie flinches. "I guess that's good to hear. But I don't regret what I did. I would do it again." His voice cracks at the end.

A million emotions skate across Bane's face, mostly though sadness. Devastation. Hopelessness.

This isn't the Bane I know. The tough, bad-ass Watcher. This… is another Bane. One whom Jamie is more familiar with.

A muscle twitches in Bane's jaw as he swallows hard. "I see," he whispers hoarscly. "I scc."

Jamie's grip is all but breaking my fingers. "I'm sorry." It comes out just as hoarsely, with a single tear down his cheek.

Bane rakes that same jittery hand through his hair again. A heavy puff of air comes through pursed lips—

"Fuck!" he yells. One of his legs lashes out and kicks an imaginary object in front of him. "Fuck, Jamie. I gave you the one chance to prove yourself when I threw that knife at her, the one chance—" He bites down hard on his lip, then shakes his head. "What do you expect me to do now? I—" His hands ball to fists as he shakes them.

"*Commanding South Africa—Baalath!*"

Regret radiates from Jamie's body. "Nothing. I accept the consequences—"

Bane makes an angry slicing hand motion. "Oh, shut up," he hisses, glaring at Jamie, the Watcher's dark brown eyes boring into Jamie's clear blue ones, chest heaving up and down heavily. A sigh full of sorrow leaves his throat. He swallows once. "Are you sure, Jamester? Are you sure this is what you want—what you always wanted, if we're honest? And worth it?"

Jamie nods. "Yes. She's worth it. I'm sorry, Bane." It's the third or fourth time he's saying that.

"She isn't just revenge."

"No. She isn't. She is everything."

A slow nod. "Then so be it." Bane keeps his gaze locked into Jamie's as his right hand feels for the Black Box attached to his belt. His fingers find the connection, hook behind it—and rip it off his belt. "Look at that. No reception here. Pity I can't transmit my data to the hive."

With a quick flick of his wrist, he throws it to Jamie.

What—?

Jamie's jaw drops. "Bane—"

A small sigh, so heavy it could tear down the world. "Shut up, Jamester. You'll need it." One more sad look at Jamie. "I was never here." With that, he turns on his heels and strides out of my cell without another look back—and without killing us.

CHAPTER TWENTY-SIX

Balance of Power

Jamie stares after Bane, every breath forcing its way in and out through a tight windpipe.

"Bane…" he whispers, and it carries a story. A story we don't have the time for right now—if we want to stay alive, that is.

I give his hand in mine a squeeze. "Jamie? We should run. We—"

Jamie blinks hard, then shakes his head. "Yes. Right. We should." One more shake of his head, then he snaps into action and darts toward the door, dragging me with him. "Okay, listen. Getting away from the Bowl is critical. Leaving L.A. as well, but not as tough. Once we're out in the desert, I'll fly us—"

"*Commanding North America—Jamin!*"

Jamie freezes.

The audience claps and cheers—and turns into more of a hushed whisper within seconds, presumably when nobody turns up.

"*Commanding North America—Jamin!*" This time it sounds more urgent. Annoyed.

Jamie pales, then takes me by the shoulders. "Lee, listen. I have to go. If I don't show up, they know something is wrong. I cannot outfly this many Watchers with you holding onto me. We—" His gaze darts around, looking for something, anything, that could help us. "Okay. Here's the deal." He picks me up and races us down the hill to one of the food stands. "You stay hidden. I play the game. I find you. We leave. Easy-peasy." He ignores the stares of the few human waiters out and about, as their eyes pick up on something that should be impossible: a Founder carrying a human.

"But Jamie—"

"*Jamin, son of Luke!*"

He shakes his head. "No time." He sprints to the kitchen area. "Oaf!"

Jezza pops up out of nowhere. His eyes are red. "Lea! Is she—"

"Fine." He all but shoves me into Jezza's arms. "Plan B." He turns on his heels, crouches, ready to jump off—

—then pauses for a moment, turns around and kisses me on the lips, no matter that I'm in Jezza's arms and we have about ten human witnesses. "I'll be back. Stick to the oaf."

"Jamie—" I reach for him, but he is gone. In one big jump, he has taken flight and is flying into the amphitheater.

"Damn that demon." Jezza looks after Jamie about as flabbergasted as me. "He's going for Plan B. Seriously."

"Plan B? You kidding me? Who comes up with that?" I struggle to get out of Jezza's arms.

He sets me down. "Him. He actually had Plan C and D as well."

Oh. Okay. Jamie was ahead of the game and I was slow to the uptake. I grab Jezza by the sleeve. "Get me in there, Jezza." I need to be in there. Whatever happens. I'm not hiding.

Jezza blinks. "You crazy?"

I roll my eyes. "You should know that much by now."

Jezza curses under his breath. "Just because you're officially on their kill list, doesn't mean I want you to get killed." But still he takes a cart and lifts up the tablecloth covering it. "Slide in," he growls. "You're lucky Plan B works for you."

I throw my arms around his neck and squeeze once. "Thank you."

He harrumphs a response as I crawl under the table and pull in my legs.

"Hold on," Jezza pushes the cart out the kiosk. "Guys! Plan B!" he yells and keeps up a fast pace down the hill toward the audience. I can tell exactly when he reaches the amphitheater, and that's only partly because I can hear the voices louder, not that I'd have to strain. It's mostly because he is stopping to serve Founders on the way. My heart hammers all the way up to my throat, which, let's be honest, is not very far, scrunched together as I am down here.

"Jamin, step forward to accept the honor of commanding the Founders' troops in North America."

I part the cloth at the corner of the table and take a careful peek. Jezza has taken us a little higher up through the ranks with a good overview of the stage below, close to where the TV camera is installed. Jamie's brothers all have gotten a sword they've tied around their waists in a sheath. Jamie is the last one without a weapon. What's presumably his is still in Luke's hand, waiting for its new owner.

Jamie steps forward, hands held out. With a proud smile, Luke lays the sword into Jamie's hands. Jamie bows—and in one smooth move, draws the sword and points it at his father.

An outcry goes through the audience, swallowing the gasp leaving my throat. Like hundreds of lightsabers had just been lit blue pops up all through the audience—heck, everywhere on the stage. Every single one of Jamie's brothers has their Caeruleum lit and palms aimed at Jamie.

Luke on the other hand is calm. "What is this nonsense?" He folds his hands behind his back, keeping his wings spread out.

"Easy, Father."

I'm sure every Founder in the audience hears his words—heck, I hear them up here like he was standing next to me.

"This is about shifting the balance of power."

A confused whisper goes through the audience—but nobody fires. I can barely get a breath in. What is Jamie playing at?

Luke laughs. "The balance of power?"

"Correct, *Luke*." The way he emphasizes his name— "It's time to give humanity something worth fighting for."

"Really." Luke's comeback is bone dry. "Is it."

"It is." Jamie keeps the sword aimed at Luke's throat. Why aren't they firing—

Oh.

Smart.

One, using Caeruleum against a Founder is a sin. Nobody wants to risk that, especially—and that's point two—with the way Jamie keeps himself positioned: none of the others can fire without risking hitting another Founder. So, if they hit Jamie they might get away with using their Caeruleum, but if they miss… they sin, by the laws of the Lord. Bye-bye, wings.

Jamie's in a good position, literally and proverbially. I don't think it specifically calls using a sword against a Founder a sin. Plus, if his brothers fire, they'll risk the audience and vice versa. Not even from the sides is Jamie clear, thanks to the stage's shape.

Jamie extends his wings, pulling even with his father—no, surpassing Luke's wingspan.

I hiss-whisper. "Jezza, what does he—?" But Jezza isn't there.

I part the cloth wider—and there he is, together with three other humans, manning the cameras. Like lightning, it shoots through me. They're televising it! Whatever Jamie is going for, it's being broadcasted.

Down on the stage Jamie takes a deep breath. His attention stays laser-focused on Luke. "Execute Plan B."

Luke's eyebrows pull down into a V, but before he can ask, the screen behind Jamie's brothers springs into life—and the image of an old man pops up on it. Dark skin, white hair, long, bushy beard.

A shocked, collective gasp comes from at least one third of the attending Founders.

"You," the old man growls. "You dare using Earth against me? You dare using *humanity* against me?"

Luke takes one stumbling step back, surprise written clearly in his features—but only for a split second. Then he has himself back under control. He bows mockingly, keeping his wings up. "Greetings, Lord Commander."

Whoa—that… This is…? My eyes pop wide. In the name of all that's holy, it's *Him*! The Lord. God. Whatever you want to call him. The Lord Commander. The man who seeded life on Earth. He looks ancient compared to Luke, and Luke is ancient already.

All throughout the audience, Founders sink to their knees. Some are roughly grabbed and yanked back to their feet by their seat neighbors, others joined.

None of Luke's sons kneel. Neither does Luke.

The Lord Commander narrows his eyes. "You haven't learned from your past mistakes. Why am I not surprised?"

Luke raises an arrogant eyebrow. "Oh, make no mistake. I

have learned. A lot. And I thought it considerate to inform you that we do not intend to leave Earth this time, old man."

Wait, what—

The Lord Commander sucks in a sharp breath. "What have you done?"

Luke shrugs. "Nothing you weren't planning on doing anyway. I was just a step ahead of you—and I will continue to be a step ahead of you," he adds in a growl. "Consider this your one and only warning. Turn the fleet around, or suffer the consequences."

No way. No. No, no, no. *These* are the Founders whom we're about to go to war against? The Founders are using us to fight the *Lord? God?* I don't realize I've crawled out from the table to get a better view of the screen and stage up front. This is huge. Life-changing. For all of humanity.

The Lord Commander huffs. "You are willing to risk Earth?"

"It is not a risk from where I'm coming from. We have millions of soldiers, all ready, ready at our command." He extends a hand, pointing at his sons assembled on stage, none of them looking too friendly at the Lord Commander.

Pause.

The Lord Commander nods. "Very well then. As we did millennia ago, we will fight over Earth once more." His features tighten. "We will meet. We will fight. And this time, it will be your end, Lucifer."

Lucif—?

And with that, he cuts the connection.

Blood swooshes through my ears. I can't have heard that right. Lucifer? This is *Luke*—

With a *click,* the pieces fall into place. Jamie, reading New

Scripture, finding out *the truth about his family history*. His reaction to being called the devil's spawn. The weird way he intoned Luke's name.

That's what he must've figured out. Luke is Lucifer. *Jamie's father* is Lucifer.

Jezza exchanges hushed words with the other humans, their faces as pale as I imagine mine to be.

For the last decade Earth has been living under the devil himself.

And now we're going to die for him.

Holy crap.

I can't process what I heard.

Not angels—demons.

But there's no time to digest any of that. The screen retracts and Luke—*Lucifer*—turns on the spot and glowers at Jamie. "You," he snarls through clenched teeth, "this was your last mistake, and you shall pay for it."

His wings shoot out straight to their full length, feathers bristled, an impressive figure in black against the blinding white. "Watchers. Restrict Jamin and bring me the Protégée. They both die. Here and now."

Absolute chaos breaks out.

The same moment Jamie's brothers dart forward to obey their father's command, hundreds and hundreds of Founders jump up from their seats, obstructing my view of the stage. I have about three seconds before the first one has realized the Protégée is right in front of their noses.

But he's not getting to me.

For one, he's hesitant to touch me. Rightfully so. Grabbing me—touching me—is still forbidden and could cost him dearly.

For another, it takes less than the blink of an eye, and I'm standing shoulder to shoulder with Jezza and some other human in a waiter-outfit, both with guns aimed at the masses around us.

Won't kill them, but it will hurt like hell.

"Lea, fast!" Jezza grabs me by the arm and yanks me down the walkway toward the exit. I stumble with my first steps. We're not going to make it out of here—Founders everywhere. All they need to do is contain us—

BangBangBang!

Gunshots!

Screams!

More shots, fired in rapid succession, coming from different directions of the Bowl. More screams, more chaos, more Founders running or taking flight.

"It has started," Jezza yells over the chaos. "Go!"

I sprint forward together with him and the other guy, Founders jumping aside out of the way whenever we come near, parting for us like the sea did for Moses.

A blond Founder points at us. "There they are! Watchers! Watchers! The Protégée, she's—" Jezza fires once, and the voice squeaks once, then is gone.

Holy cow, this—

I drag in a ragged breath. This is chaos. Wings everywhere, like we invaded a cave of bats. A growl and grunt are transmitted via the speakers, a pained yelp, a mindless roar—

"Jamie!" That's Jamie—and I can't see. "Jamie!" I yell again, no I scream. Where is he? What is Luke doing? "Somebody help Jamie!" I jump up in the middle of my run, but all I can see is part of the screen. *Somebody* must still be manning the camera, because we do have a transmission. Jamie, fighting off his brothers, kicking, ducking, punching—and then finally jumping off and taking flight, followed by none other than his father.

"Jamie!" I turn on my heels and try to run back to the center of the amphitheater. I'm not leaving him behind.

"Lea!" Jezza curses. "Wait!" A Watcher lands in front of him, and he curses again.

"Catching up with your friend?" The Watcher grins and picks up Jezza like he was a toy, the force field from his Black Box sizzling once on contact. "Let me help." And with one big push he takes flight, Jezza dangling from his grip.

Jezza screams and flails—until he realizes he's too high up. Then he tries to hold on to the Watcher.

"Jezza!" I yell and reach up, as if I could pull him out of the Watcher's grasp.

Something lights up in the Watcher's face, something evil.

And he drops—no, he *throws* Jezza down toward the ground, right at me.

I have a split-second to react. I panic, realizing he's coming right at me—

And *boom*—his body slams into mine with the force of a steam train. My hands fly up out of reflex, a scream tears from my throat—

And I catch Jezza.

One small stumble-step backwards, but I caught him.

I caught Jezza.

Out of mid-fall.

For that short moment, neither of us breathes as we both realize what an impossible catch that just was. It should've broken half the bones in my body and slammed me into the ground—but it didn't. I'm standing, Jezza in my arms.

"What the fuck?" Jezza whispers. "How'd you do that?" He scrambles out of my grasp. "How'd you—"

I shake my head. "Dunno. Just did." And it doesn't matter. "Come on, we're—" A kick to my midsection doubles me over and brings me to a fall.

Somebody yells out victoriously. "I got her! I—"

BangBangBang!

The Founder who didn't mind touching a human if it meant taking her down doubles over and shuts up.

Damn it, I—

Jezza grabs my arm at the biceps. "Hate it when the regulars think touching us is worth the risk. Hope he hurts a long time." He yanks me up. "Come on. The others are doing their best, but we only have so much time." Because we're only a couple of hundred Resistance fighters versus a couple of thousand Founders. Enough for chaos and confusion, enough for cover, but nowhere near enough to win.

I stumble up to standing. "Jamie! Jezza, we've gotta get him, we—"

A blue flash of light sizzles past me—and somebody screams behind me. "Careful, idiot! It almost got—"

What the—

Another blast, another protesting scream. That's when the Founders who weren't trained as Watchers finally catch on. There are too many Founders, and the risk of hurting themselves is too great. Our advantage.

"Careful with the Caeruleum!"

"Don't shoot—constrain them!"

I see no way we can make it out of here. The sea of Founders is too deep, too thick—

Three Watchers land in front of us, their Raptor claws ready. "Submit yourselves or—"

A freakish scream pierces the chaos, demanding attention and drawing all eyes up to the sky: Luke. Jamie.

Father and son, battling for superiority, and neither of them will take a loss if they can avoid it.

At first, they're in the middle of Founders taking flight, but as soon as the others realize who is fighting amongst them, the air above the Bowl clears. Within seconds, it's only Luke and Jamie, only father and son, attacking and defending, ducking and weaving.

And Jamie is good.

Younger by a couple of millennia, he's the faster fighter, the more flexible one, and maybe even at this point the better trained one. He lands two hits for every one Luke can get in, and it shows. Luke's face is swollen, his movements more sluggish—but he's Luke. *Lucifer.*

The moment the skies clear of the obstructing crowd of Founders, his eyes light up—and so do his palms. Blue lights springs to life and illuminates his twisted and contorted features in the most spooky and surreal way. A deep gasp comes from every being under them—because Luke is doing the unthinkable: he's aiming his Caeruleum at one of their own.

At his *son.*

Jamie has no time to evade the blast. I cry out, but it's too late. Two blue bolts fly right at his chest, and—

With a soft *pop,* a shield springs to life around his body, deflecting the Caeruleum.

What—

Jamie's face shows the same relief mine does as he taps the

Black Box Bane threw him. "We don't fire on our own, Father. Or have you forgotten that?" He pulls his wings in and dives down into Luke, both of them turning into a tumbling heap of extremities and wings, falling and rising, dipping lower and coming back up.

Luke lands an elbow to Jamie's face that loosens his grip on the older man. "You might be protected, but she is not!" He twists around, breaking Jamie's hold completely. His gaze darts across the masses—until it lands on me.

My heart stops. Literally, it stops, then stutters out another beat.

Luke's focus zones in on me as he raises his palms. "Goodbye, Lea Akiyama."

Then, he fires.

CHAPTER TWENTY-SEVEN

Till Death Do Us Part

The one split second that changes everything stretches into eternity right in front of my eyes.

The distorted grimace of hate on Luke's face.

The horror in Jamie's eyes.

The blue bolt of lightning zipping right at me.

My whole world narrows down to two images: Jamie and the Caeruleum.

Until something distorts it from the right.

Bane.

Dodging down from somewhere he zooms closer, right into the path of Luke's blue lightning.

As if in slow-mo, I see him stretch to intercept the energy discharge, see Jamie's eyes widen as he realizes what Bane registers a split second too late when his hand feels for the Black Box that isn't there: no shield.

A hint of panic flies over Bane's face less than a heartbeat before the Caeruleum hits him right in the chest.

I scream out—and so does Jamie, a blood-curdling, horrified scream.

Bane freezes in mid-air, body enveloped in blue for a split second—while Luke roars, furious his target wasn't hit, and fires again, this time directly onto Bane, who dared to intercept his weapon.

The second discharge hits, and for another moment, it looks like Bane got lucky and absorbed or deflected the Caeruleum despite the fact he didn't have a shield.

But only for another moment.

The next second, his eyes roll back as all tension leaves his body and he spirals down, arms, legs, wings flailing useless through the air, doing nothing to brace his fall.

Jamie's scream is the loudest of them all.

Bane hits the ground a mere five meters away from me, and that sound, the sound of a limp body hitting concrete… it hurts.

And it does something to the Founders.

As if they suddenly understood what was happening here, an outcry breaks out. A flock rises into the air at lightning speed, attacking Luke—attacking the man who was their leader until a mere few minutes ago. The leader, who willingly shot one of their own—one of their own who was defending a *human*, of all people.

The masses begin to move, to fly, to fight. There's screaming, yelling, shoving, punching, fighting—and amidst the chaos, Bane, lying still on the ground.

I don't think. I dart through the Founders and fall onto my knees in front of Bane. "Bane," I pant. "Bane!" He saved me. Despite everything, he saved me. My hands fly over his chest, feeling for a sign of life. Hurried hisses around me—screw them, this is life or death, who cares if I'm touching—

Bane coughs, a sound so weak and pitiful it hurts my soul.

But he's alive.

"Bane!" I try to lift him up. "What can I do—?"

The slightest shake of his head. "N-nothing," he chokes out barely audible over the noise of fighting and panic. "S'rry 'bout that knife."

"Hell, never mind, tell me what to do—"

A small shake of his head. "Here." His hand finds mine and pushes something into it. "Watch out for Jamie, will ya?"

I look at the small data disk in my palm. "Wha—?"

"Bane!" Jamie touches down hard a few steps away from us, sprints over, and kneels next to Bane. Don't know from where, but all of a sudden six Watchers are around us, seriously looking and—

And forming a protective circle around Bane, Jamie, and me on the ground.

Times, they are a-changing indeed.

"Bane." Jamie's voice is soft, almost tender. He pulls Bane into his lap. I'm waiting for him to lay his hands on Bane's chest, but then I remember: *Caeruleum kills us. No chance to heal it.*

Shit.

A scattered breath breaks from Bane's throat. "Jamester." It comes with a faint smile.

"Bane, you idiot," Jamie whispers. His voice breaks with the last syllable. "You gave me your box. You shouldn't have."

The slightest shrug. "'T… sav'd you, din't it?", he mumbles.

Jamie entwines his fingers with Bane's. "It did. It did. Thank you. And thank you for saving Lea." He lowers his head and… kisses Bane's knuckles. "You're still an idiot though."

A short laugh that ends in a grimace. "'T's why you love me."

Whoa.

Whoa. I was right. Bane and Jamie—

Like it was the most natural thing in the world, Jamie lowers his head until his lips press gently against Bane's.

It's not a kiss full of passion, not a lover's kiss—yet it's full of love. Full of emotion, of words never spoken. Of thankfulness.

Support.

A faint smile spreads over Bane's face. "Knew it," he murmurs.

One more harsh, chopped breath, a short twitch of his body—

And his eyes lose focus and his face relaxes. Whatever tone was left in his body, is gone.

And so is Bane.

The Watchers around us lower their heads. "May he rest in peace," one of them whispers.

An agonized, strangulated breath breaks from Jamie's throat. Another one.

Somebody gets shoved into our circle of protective Watchers, almost breaking through and into us. Screaming, noise, fighting, crying—

And in the middle of it, Bane. Jamie. Me.

Jamie lifts his gaze off Bane. Tears shine in his eyes, yet they don't fall.

I swallow hard. "Jamie—"

"It's complicated," he whispers.

I believe that without any further details. My fingers squeeze around Bane's hand once more before I let go and reach for Jamie's still holding on to Bane's, and cover them both. "I understand." Maybe not all of it, but what matters most, that these two didn't hate each other as I thought. No, at one point they loved each other, and maybe they still do. Did. "And I'm sorry, Jamie."

One big exhale. "Thank you." He closes his eyes for a second, and when they fly open again, they shine with determination. "And now it's time we use the advantage Bane gave us." He gently lowers the dead Watcher to the ground. One more look at him, and his eyes harden. "Ichabod, Zimri, Dilean—I need your help."

The Watchers surrounding us get closer. "What is it, Jamin?"

Jamie reaches for my hand, fingers close over mine, shaking the slightest. "We're going to send a signal to the world. Follow my lead." He brings my hand to his mouth and touches his lips to my knuckles. One of the five Watchers, Zimri maybe, who knows, takes a second longer to contain his shock at this casual display of touch.

But they don't attack us.

I consider that a major plus.

Jamie gives my hand another squeeze, then drops it. "Lee, I want you to stay with Nicholas. Nick, she's your responsibility."

The Watcher he addressed nods. "Got it."

Wait—what…? "Jamie, what are you—?"

He cups my face in his palms. "Doing the right thing. Somebody told me I should convince them my way is better. This is me trying." A small smile plays around his lips. "Stick to Nicholas, okay?" Then he points at Jezza, back behind the camera, trying to capture the majority of chaos and confusion. Three Watchers and two non-Watcher Founders have taken position behind him, keeping him from getting overrun by Founders who are clearly on Luke's side. "Oh, and also, one of you please make sure the oaf makes it out alive."

"Will do," one of them confirms.

One curt nod from Jamie, and he pushes off and takes flight, the three other Watchers following.

"Jamie—" I call, but he doesn't look back.

Nicholas checks his Black Box, then takes me by the arm. Guess seeing Jamie touch me or doing it himself are two different things. "Come on, Lea." He tries to steer me away from the chaos, but I won't have it.

I rip my arm out of his grip. "Wait!" My gaze is glued to Jamie, circling above the Bowl. Two of his three Watcher friends cross pass in front of him at any time, switching positions in midair. They all keep circling around him like moths around a light, making it impossible for somebody to get good aim at him.

"Lucifer!" Jamie calls out. As if he was the teacher calling the class to attention, the wounded screams, the noise settles down below us. Guess the son of Luke does carry some authority, no matter what—and Luke listens. His head whips around, and the four Watchers protecting him raise their hands, as if they'd expect Jamie to fire at his father.

Jamie lifts his hands—but not to fire, more in a calming, I-come-in-peace-gesture. "Lucifer," he repeats. "You have tried to use humanity to your own advantage, regardless the consequences for the people of Earth. I'm telling you, this will not work anymore. With your decision, it is to be war between us, but this time, Lucifer, the disaster will be yours."

Jamie takes a deep breath. "To the people of Earth. Not all of us are your enemies. Many of us will fight with you and the Lord Commander to bring Earth the peace it deserves. You have the son of Lucifer and the First on your side, who will do everything in their power to protect humanity."

He flies down lower, hovering ten meters above the ground, looking at me, the camera following his every move. Maybe it's the adrenaline, because I see everything with this hyper-realistic touch to it, like in HD: every spark in Jamie's eyes, every little dimple in his smile, every single hair blown out of place by the wind.

I see it all, and I memorize it for eternity.

Jamie smiles down at me, one of those rare, wild, open smiles.

One of those that make me feel special, and for once he looks… free. As if a weight had dropped off his shoulders.

Like I was attuned to only him, I hear the small intake of breath before he raises his voice. It carries easily over the masses below him.

"Lea Akiyama, I hereby swear myself to you. I swear to serve you until the end of my days to my best knowledge and abilities. I swear to honor and hold you, for better for worse, for richer for poorer, in sickness and in health, to love and to cherish, until death do us part. I will first live unto the Lord, and then unto you. I pledge to you, *the First*, my life as an obedient servant."

Silence.

Absolute, all-encompassing silence.

Everybody is staring at either Jamie up in the air, wings beating calmly to keep him up, or me, eyes wide and not quite clear my brain processed that right. Founders. Humans. A TV-camera. All of them are staring at the Founder who just pledged himself to a human.

Repeat: staring at the Founder, who has *pledged himself to a human*. To the First.

His voice didn't waver, his hand didn't shake. Jamie delivered his pledge in front of thousands of Founders like he had practiced it a million times. To *the First*.

It's time to accept my responsibility. I step forward and raise my voice. "And I, Lea Akiyama, the First, formerly known as the Protégée, swear to stay at your side from now until the end." Funny how easy the words come. Funny how right they feel this time around. One more, for good measure. I look at Jamie, then into the camera, and pull on all the New Scripture I have in me. "Together we can change the world, for these three remain: faith, hope, and love. And the greatest of these is love." I hold the camera's eye for another second before I look back at Jamie.

"Jamie," I whisper, although there's no way he can hear me. Still, his smile widens. Jamie—my Jamie. Tears burn my eyes. This pledge, it means so much, and yet it's going to cost him. *Us.*

Go, he mouths. *Run.*

I shake my head. No. Not without him.

Luke growls and rises to Jamie's level. "You're pledging yourself to a human, son?"

"With pleasure, Lucifer. Yes."

Luke laughs out once, cold, cruel. With one commanding nod of his chin he sends at least ten Watchers up into the sky. "It won't do you good. You—"

Jamie flies backward, keeping his distance to the incoming Watchers and his eyes on his father. "It might not do me good, but it will show the people what is possible. It will show them not all Founders are brutal. Cruel. Egoistic. It will give somebody somewhere the hope they can rise against you and bring peace and freedom to humanity." He stops to a hover. "And it will be your downfall." Jamie forms two fingers to a V and taps them over his heart, twice. "May peace be victorious."

Then, he flies straight into the approaching Watchers.

CHAPTER TWENTY-EIGHT

Landing Bay

I wrap my fingers around the little disk Bane gave me.

Let's be honest, it's been the only thing penetrating the fog of hurt and pain over the last couple of days. The only thing that kept me sane. The only thing that helped me keep up hope.

Coincidentally, it's also the only thing that may lead humanity to victory, but the jury is still out on the details.

I swallow hard and look around. Nobody's up the street from here, nobody down the street. Wouldn't expect it, but Lucifer's Founders are everywhere and not even this sleepy little town in the middle of California is an exception.

It's a risk to come here, but it's also the only viable option, and we ran out of those real fast.

After they tore Jamie out of the sky and dragged him away, they beat every human, every Founder who dared to rise against into submission, or to death. Only a few escaped, human or Founder. Lucifer showed no mercy to either people, and the death toll was... high.

Too high.

And if it hadn't been for Nicholas, Jezza and I would be dead now too. Nick got us out, and then Jezza got us into another secret Resistance Lair—another one that now knows a Founder living there, although I'd prefer Jamie over Nick. No offense.

One step at a time, and first things first, because not only in the Bowl did people rise against a decade of oppression, but everywhere around the world, thanks to the televised shift in the *balance of power.*

A short and futile effort.

Like they did when they arrived, the Founders crushed the human efforts.

But they didn't crush our spirits.

Quite the opposite. If anything, we realized brute force won't win us this war. Scheming, planning, and organizing may. And we're on it.

For the last few days, the Resistance has been busier than ever. Splinter groups all over the world have reported an increase in new members—and not just a handful, no. Over twenty percent of humanity are now members of one or the other Resistance group. Twenty percent of us don't want to sit and watch anymore. Twenty percent of us will fight for their freedom, for their rights.

It makes me darn proud to be one of them.

I blink, or else the tears will come, and then they will fall. Been there, done that. Watching Jamie sacrificing himself… I still can't sleep. Can't think of anything else. Can't function.

And yet I must, or else his sacrifice was for naught.

My fingers curl into a fist. As long as he is alive, there is still hope. And as long as there is hope, I will fight for him as he fought for us.

All right then. I suck in a big breath and open the door to a small hotel in the middle of nowhere. The moment I step in, the receptionist greets me with a smile. "Hello, and welcome to the Landing Bay."

"Thank you." It comes out wrong. Fake. I stuff my hand with the disk deep into my pocket. "I'm looking for something for a short stay?" Can't help my voice trail up at the end. Again, fake.

"Of course." The lady's smile widens. She must be in her forties, black hair, pulled up to a bun, soft makeup. "That shouldn't be a problem. Specific amenities? Smoker, non-smoker, with a view…?"

The disk cuts into my skin, that's how hard I hold on to it, but it does nothing to distract me from the nausea raging inside my stomach. "Actually, I'm fine with whatever you have. I'd need your help though, I—"

"I got you." The lady winks at me. "You're the First. I know why you're here."

My stomach dips as always when somebody says *the First* out loud. She must be very sure she isn't under surveillance, but I guess she better be, or else this place was useless.

"Awesome," I reply lamely. Being the famous *First* is a whole new ballgame compared to being the precious Protégée. Different alliteration, different responsibility.

Something warm runs down from my nose. *Gah.* Again.

I'm about to swipe the drop of blood from my nose, but the lady's faster. "Here. A tissue. It has started already, hasn't it?"

For one long second, I stare at her. *She knows.* But then, that's why I'm here. I take the tissue. "Thank you. Yes, it has." Now I know how Frances felt with her headaches and nosebleeds.

She lays a small plastic card onto the counter. "You'll feel better soon. Take the elevator. This card will do the rest."

I take it. "Thank you. Again." Now all I can do is hope I'm right—that Bane was right—and the Landing Bay is the solution to my problems.

As soon as I'm in the elevator, I swipe the card in front of the reader. The doors close—and the elevator whisks me away to the basement, not the top floors.

Okay, that's a good start since the basement is not listed as an option to go. A secret basement. If I didn't have such a raging headache, I'd find it amusing.

The trip down takes longer than I expected. Wonder how deep we are. Deep enough to discourage any Watchers to come looking or successfully scan for us, that much is for sure.

After what must have been a trip down at least five or six stories, the cabin stops and its doors open to two young women, early twenties, both with an open smile on their face.

I take a big breath. Okay. This is it. "Hi, I—"

One of them, the brunette, waves. "We know, Lea. Hi, I'm Addison, this is Mila."

Mila, with shorter and darker hair, waves back. "Nice to meet you. We've been expecting you."

Mr. Bond, I add silently. Loud out I say, "Thank you, I appreciate that. Should we—"

"Of course." They both lead the way down a hallway that I'm sure matches the layout of the floors above us. The doors going off to either side are labelled, and have a first name written onto them. I read Addison, Mila, Jasmine, Arina, Aayden, Hailey, Tiara, Dhruv, and about a dozen other names.

Bane was right: this is big.

Addison and Mila lead me into a small, windowless room with at least ten different monitors mounted to the right wall and a huge cork board filled with dozens and dozens of Post-its on the other. In an office chair close to the panel that must control the monitors sits another female, this one a bit older, maybe closer to thirty. When her eyes fall on me, she smiles and gets up.

"Lea Akiyama. An honor to meet the First—and the first

human, a Founder has pledged himself to." She holds out her hand and gives mine a strong shake. "My name is Arina, I'm the leader of this group—"

"I know." I hold up Bane's disk. "I have intel on you."

Her eyes widen. "Is that… a Founder data disk? What—"

I throw it into the air, catch and pocket it again. "Yes. But don't worry, you're safe. It's the only copy, and as far as I know, nobody else has added one and one together." Although some came close. The Founders pledged to all these former servants must've known, or else they wouldn't be here.

Arina swipes a strand of blonde hair behind her ear. "Good. Our success and survival depends on it. Why don't you have a seat?"

As I sit down, she takes out a small, rectangular device, maybe the size of a Watcher Black Box and aims it at me. She taps something and—

"What the…?" She taps some more.

Looks at the screen.

Looks at me.

At the screen.

At me.

"Can I see your Vinculum, please?"

I hold up my right arm with the Vinculum shining in the deepest, fullest red possible.

Arina gapes. "I guess that would explain it. How long did it take for it to turn red?"

"Less than a day."

She blinks twice. "Which would make you the fastest Adjuster we've seen so far. But then, it's Lucifer's son and the First. We're kind of expecting something special." She winks at me and drops the scanner, then nods at my data disk. "Does it explain what's been going on with you?"

"The headaches? The feeling crappy? The body aches?" All the little aches and pains I've had since… well, technically speaking since a short while after I got *contaminated* with Jamie's blood at the church. Seems like a lifetime ago.

"Yeah, those."

"Humor me." My heart hammers like crazy, although I'm pretending I'm cool. Super cool.

Arina smiles. "Very well. What we have found out over the last decade is the true reason why the Founders implemented the Eleventh Commandment, and it's not because of whatever divine law the Lord may have come up with. No, the truth is far simpler. We are descendants of the Founders. They genetically engineered and seeded us on Earth in their image—minus a couple of important features, as we know, like wings, longevity, healing powers, strength, enhanced senses, etc., but still. The problem is, that they must've butchered or overlooked something in their alterations, because our DNA reacts to them."

That's the part I didn't get from Bane's records either. "What does that mean?"

"Simplified?"

"Yes, please."

"It means that whenever their DNA is close to ours, it induces changes in our double-helix. It reverts it to the natural state it wants to be in—and that would be Founder DNA. The closer a Founder is to a human, or the more physical contact there is, the faster it goes. We're still working on the exact mechanism why their DNA is affecting ours, it seems to be similar to how radiation would alter your DNA, although Founder DNA alters ours in a much better way."

My shoulders tense. "About that—"

A sparkle lights up in her eyes. "You've noticed something? Already?"

Already… I didn't notice anything until I looked through the data on Bane's disk. Then the pieces fell into place and made sense. Before that? Not so much.

"Little things," I say. "Better hearing. Vision improved. Maybe strength, but I feel like crap most of the time." But still I caught Jezza out of mid-air.

She smiles. "That's an annoying side effect, but keep in mind, your transition is faster than anybody else's I've ever seen. I'd be curious why that is."

I blush. I guess I have the scar on my back to prove it. Who could have known what Jamie's healing would do to me.

Neither of us did, and it wouldn't have changed a thing.

Arina swipes the same stubborn lock of hair out of her face. "The longer we are in contact with our Founders, the more we change. The Vinculum measures it—"

"Which proves they know about it." I clench my teeth. The higher-ups. They knew.

"Correct. Of course, the high-ranking Founders know, Lea. Luke. *Lucifer.* Michael. Some others. They know what happens to us after a certain amount of exposure, and they needed a way to prevent that. Or, to make it work in their favor."

"Hence the Eleventh Commandment for the general population and servitude for the special ones—with supervision." I tug on my Vinculum.

"Exactly. By romanticizing the Vinculum, they had our cooperation, and then, once we hit a threshold, they consider a turning point…"

"They wipe our minds and use us as soldiers."

"Win-win." She gives me a sad smile. "Especially because of our strength once the changes to our DNA kick in. First, we're useful to them as servants, and then, once we lose our value for servitude, they still use us, in our altered form, as soldiers."

Acid rises in my throat. Had humanity known exposure to the Founders evens the playing field for us, I doubt the demons could've kept us under control for the last ten years. Hell. "So, when they came up with that little one-liner about the Vinculum turning color the better the human connects to and serves her Founder, they were kind of saying the truth." For once. "What about the others? The pledged Founders. Did they know?" Because Jamie didn't. He might have been suspicious about the Vinculum's role, but I bet he didn't know about the mutation, or else he would've known why my hearing was so good all of a sudden.

"Yes and no. They do get a little hint during their initiation that if they felt the urge, they wouldn't be punished if they kept touching their human in private. My Founder was told the whole story once the Vinculum turned a certain tone. Depending on exposure, it can take a while, but it will happen, even if there's nothing going on between human and Founder. Jasmine, for example, never had physical contact with her Founder, and her Vinculum turned dark after about four years. It's the duration of the exposure and proximity then. So far all humans have been altered eventually."

"So, I'm repeating it for emphasis: they know about it." Eventually. Benjamin would've known. Frances' Vinculum was almost as red as mine. They would've told him. And yet he did nothing. He accepted her love and servitude, and threw her to the wolves later.

"Well, yes. At one point they do. But to play devil's advocate here, many Founders are loyal to the core—to their race, to Luke… To many of them, it's about obeying the law. Me and everybody else here got lucky our Founders cared enough."

"And hid you."

"If you mean they faked our deaths, then yes. And in their defense, it does come as a surprise. It's one of their best-kept secrets to keep humanity compliant. To my Founder, the news was devastating. Aayden's Founder left him with enough money in untraceable accounts to support all of us for a year. Not all of them are bad, as you know."

I nod. Still have difficulties admitting that for anybody else but Jamie, but she's right. "So, what now?"

"Now, we wait for your DNA to stabilize and your powers to set in. And when that has happened…" A determined grin spreads over her face. "When that has happened, the Founders won't know what hit them, Lea. Because we're strong. Stronger than them. And we have more to lose. They won't know what hit them."

She holds out her hand for a high five and I hit it.

She's right. They won't know what hit them.

And they won't stand a chance keeping Jamie.

Because I will get him out. I pledged my loyalty to him, and I don't intend to break that vow.

Hold out, Jamie.

I've got you, even if I have to raise hell to find and pry you out of the devil's claws.

I've got you.

* * *

ABOUT THE AUTHOR

Micky O'Brady is a pediatrician-turned-writer living in beautiful, dry Southern California with her husband and two critters (one son, one dog). Micky loves to write YA thrillers with a romantic twist, mainly because she wishes her life had been such an awesome mix of action and cute guys when she was a teen.

When she isn't up at around 3 a.m. (with a cup of tea, Earl Grey, hot) drafting stories she can't get out of her head, she can be found at a martial arts dojo, though maybe not at 3 a.m. She holds a 2nd degree black belt in Judo and a brown belt in Krav Maga, and is convinced every girl should know how to kick some butt.

Micky also is a firm believer in the healing powers of Nutella eaten straight from the glass and in the magic that can happen on a rainy day, as long as there are fuzzy socks and a cup of hot tea involved.

Her previous publications include a doctoral thesis and several medical articles as well as a medical book about emergency communication. None of them are as fun to read as her YA novels though. Her first YA-novel, THE PRESIDENT'S DAUGHTER, and its sequel TRIAL BY ICE, are published by Curiosity Quills and available through all major retailers, such as Amazon, B&N, Kobo, and Smashwords.

Through Snowy Wings Publishing Micky is the author of YA-sci-fi romance BETWEEN WORLDS and PLAYING WITH #FIRE. She is happy to announce more novels will be coming your way.